The
MX Book
of
New
Sherlock
Holmes
Stories

Part XII – Some Untold Cases
(1894-1902)

THE MX BOOK OF NEW SHERLOCK HOLMES STORIES

PART XII:
SOME UNTOLD CASES
(1894-1902)

SOUTHAMPTON
STREET

359

EDITED
By
David
Marcum

OFFICES

TRADITIONAL HOLMES
ADVENTURES
COMPILED FOR THE
BENEFIT OF THE
RESTORATION OF
UNDERSHAW

ISBN Hardback 978-1-78705-376-2
ISBN Paperback 978-1-78705-377-9
AUK ePub ISBN 978-1-78705-378-6
AUK PDF ISBN 978-1-78705-380-9

Published in the UK by
MX Publishing
335 Princess Park Manor, Royal Drive,
London, N11 3GX
www.mxpublishing.co.uk

David Marcum can be reached at:
thepapersofsherlockholmes@gmail.com

Cover design by Brian Belanger
www.belangerbooks.com and *www.redbubble.com/people/zhahadun*

CONTENTS

Forewords

Adventures

(Continued on the next page . . . .)

These additional adventures are contained in
The MX Book of New Sherlock Holmes Stories
Part XI: Some Untold Cases
(1880-1891)

These additional Sherlock Holmes adventures
can be found in the previous volumes of
The MX Book of New Sherlock Holmes Stories

(Continued on the next page . . . .)

(Continued on the next page . . . .)

PART V – Christmas Adventures

(Continued on the next page . . . .)

PART VI – 2017 Annual

(Continued on the next page . . . .)

(Continued on the next page . . . .)

Part IX – 2018 Annual (1879-1895)

(Continued on the next page . . . .)

COPYRIGHT INFORMATION

The following contributions appear
in the companion volume:
The MX Book of New Sherlock Holmes Stories
Part XI – Some Untold Cases (1880-1891)

"Some Untold Cases", *Parts XI and XII of*
The MX Book of New Sherlock Holmes Stories,
are dedicated to

Philip K. Jones

Phil passed away in June 2018.
As well as being a wonderful and very supportive
Holmesian collector and reviewer,
he was devoted to Sherlockian Pastiche
and an expert in the area of Untold Cases.
The theme for this collection grew from his suggestion,
and he will be missed.

Editor's Introduction:
Only Sixty?
By David Marcum

There are certain numbers that are triggers to deeply passionate Sherlockians. One of these is *221*. I've discussed this with other people of like mind. If you're one of us, you know that feeling – when you're going through your day and look up to see that it's *2:21* – hopefully in the afternoon, because you should be asleep for the other one. Seeing that it's 2:21 o'clock is a little thrill.

One can encounter *221* all over. Sometimes a lucky Sherlockian will be assigned 221 as a hotel room. (In her retirement home, my mother-in-law lived next door to someone in room 221, and I couldn't walk by that door without noticing it.) Maybe you have an office numbered *221*, or at least you might have an appointment in one. If you're very lucky, your house number is *221* – and I wonder how many non-London Baker Streets are there scattered throughout the world that have a 221 address?

I often notice when I reach page *221* in a book, and I know from asking that other Sherlockians do the same. (I was tickled a couple of years ago, while reading Lyndsay Faye's excellent collection of Holmes adventures, *The Whole Art of Detection*, to see that the story she'd written for the first MX collection, "The Adventure of the Willow Basket", began on page 221.)

Any American interstate that's long enough will have a marker for Mile *221*, and just east of Nashville, Tennessee, where I'm sometimes able to attend meetings of The Nashville Scholars of the Three Pipe Problem – a scion of which I'm a proudly invested member – there's a big sign for *Exit 221B* on the eastern side of Interstate-40. (My deerstalker and I have several photos in front of it.)

221 is a number that makes a Sherlockian look twice, but there's another – *1895*.

1895 is a year that falls squarely within Holmes's Baker Street practice – and I specify that location, because he had a Montague Street practice and unofficially a retirement-era Sussex practice as well, where he carried out the occasional investigation, while also spending a great amount of time first trying to prevent, and then trying to prepare for, the Great War of 1914-1918. But he was in Baker Street from 1881 to 1891 (when he was presumed to have died at the Reichenbach Falls,) and then again from 1894 (when he returned to London in April of that year) until autumn 1903, when his "retirement" began.

1895 isn't especially known as Holmes's busiest or most famous year. Make no mistake, there were some interesting cases then: "Wisteria Lodge", "The Three Students", "The Solitary Cyclist", "Black Peter", and "The Bruce-Partington Plans". But 1894 is when Watson specifically mentions, in "The Golden Pince-Nez", the three massive manuscript volumes which contain his and Holmes's work. And it was the 1880's, before The Great Hiatus, where all of those beloved adventures recorded in *The Adventures* and *The Memoirs* occurred. "The Speckled Band", possibly one of the most famous of them all, took place in 1883. All four of the long published adventures, *A Study in Scarlet*, *The Sign of Four*, *The Valley of Fear*, and perhaps the most famous of tales, *The Hound of the Baskervilles*, occur chronologically before 1895.

And yet, 1895 is still the representative year most mentioned by Sherlockians – "*where it is always 1895*" said Vincent Starrett at the conclusion of his famous poem *221B*, written in 1942, and so it is subsequently referenced in essays and gatherings and toasts as *the* year.

Written in the early days of U.S. involvement in World War II – but several years after much of the rest of the world had already tipped into the conflagration – the closing couplet of Starrett's poem reflects his likely despair at the terrible conflict:

> *Here, though the world explode, these two survive,*
> *And it is always eighteen ninety-five.*

I'm not a Starrett scholar, but I suspect that he was looking back to a more innocent time – or so it seemed when compared to the terrible war-torn world of 1942. (For many of the people actually in 1895, the world was a relatively terrible place for them too, for all kinds of different reasons.) But did Starrett simply mean to invoke the whole Holmesian era, a bygone past, or did he specifically want to focus on 1895? It's likely that the former is true, and that he simply used 1895 because *five* rhymes with *survive*. It could have just as easily have been a different number – although with less effect:

> *Here, though the world explode, these two are fine,*
> *And it is always eighteen ninety-nine.*

Imagine – but for a different word choice, we could have been finding ourselves misty-eyed when referring to *1899*. Or Starrett could have used *1885* and still made the original rhyme work. Still, it's *1895* that we have, and so that's what we'll be going on with as the year that we associate with Mr. Holmes and Dr. Watson – although I'm quick to point out that it's 1895, *along with several decades on either side of it.*

Sixty Stories

Having explored 221 and 1895, there's another Sherlockian number that might not immediately spring to mind, but that doesn't diminish it, because it holds a great deal of power for some Sherlockians. That number is *60* – as in, *sixty stories* in the original Sherlockian Canon. For some die-hard types out there, this is it. No more, forever, period, *The End*. There can only be sixty Holmes stories and anything beyond that is fraudulent abomination. (Except, of course, for those one or two stories on their lists that get a free pass because they're written by a friend, or a celebrity worthy of desperate cultivation, or by some deceased literary person.) It's amusing for me to read various scholarly works, such as Martin Dakin's *A Sherlock Holmes Commentary* (1972), that don't even really like all of the original sixty Canonical adventures, let alone anything post-Canonical, picking apart the originals and speculating that this or that later Canonical narrative is a forgery.

I don't buy into that philosophy. Early on, I ran out of Canonical stories to read and wanted more. And I found them – some admittedly of lesser quality, but some better than the originals. Even at a young age, I understood that some of the original tales weren't quite as good as others, but those first sixty stories, presented by the First Literary Agent and of whatever varying levels of quality, were about the *true* Sherlock Holmes, and they let me visit in his world, and I wanted more. Thankfully, before I'd even read all of The Canon, I'd discovered those post-Canonical adventures designated as *pastiches*, so even as I re-read the original adventures countless times, I also read and re-read all of those others that told of new cases, or filled in the spaces between the originals.

Luckily, even Watson never acted as if Holmes only solved sixty cases and that was it. No matter how intriguing a personality is Sherlock Holmes, or how vivid his adventures are that they make a visit to Baker Street sometimes more real than tedious daily life, how could we truly argue that he's the world's greatest detective based on a mere and pitifully few sixty stories?

In "The Problem of Thor Bridge", Watson tells us that:

> *Somewhere in the vaults of the bank of Cox and Co., at Charing Cross, there is a travel-worn and battered tin*

3

dispatch box with my name, John H. Watson, M.D., Late Indian Army, painted upon the lid. It is crammed with papers, nearly all of which are records of cases to illustrate the curious problems which Mr. Sherlock Holmes had at various times to examine. Some, and not the least interesting, were complete failures, and as such will hardly bear narrating, since no final explanation is forthcoming. A problem without a solution may interest the student, but can hardly fail to annoy the casual reader . . . Apart from these unfathomed cases, there are some which involve the secrets of private families to an extent which would mean consternation in many exalted quarters if it were thought possible that they might find their way into print. I need not say that such a breach of confidence is unthinkable, and that these records will be separated and destroyed now that my friend has time to turn his energies to the matter. There remain a considerable residue of cases of greater or less interest which I might have edited before had I not feared to give the public a surfeit which might react upon the reputation of the man whom above all others I revere. In some I was myself concerned and can speak as an eye-witness, while in others I was either not present or played so small a part that they could only be told as by a third person.

Thank goodness this incredible tin dispatch box has been accessed throughout the years by so many later Literary Agents to bring us all these other wonderful Holmes adventures. Many that have been revealed have been complete surprises, but sometimes we've discovered details about a special group of extra-Canonical adventures, those that fire the imagination to an even greater level: *The Untold Cases.*

Of course, they aren't called that in The Canon. The earliest references to *The Untold Cases* that I've heard of so far (with thanks to Beth Gallegos) are by Anthony Boucher in 1955, and by William S. Baring-Gould in his amazing *The Chronological Sherlock Holmes* (1955). Additionally, Charles Campbell located a reference to "stories yet untold" by Vincent Starrett in "In Praise of Sherlock Holmes" (in *Reedy's Mirror*, February 22, 1918). The *Untold Cases* are those intriguing references to Holmes's other cases that – for various reasons – were not chosen for publication. There were a lot of them – by some counts over one-hundred-and-forty – and in the years since Watson's passing in 1929, many of these narratives have been discovered and published.

For example, The Giant Rat of Sumatra . . . .

Since the mid-1990's, I've been chronologicizing both Canon and Pastiche, and as part of that, I note in my annotations when a particular narrative is an Untold Case. Glancing through my notes, I see that there are far too many narratives of The Untold Cases to list here. For example, just a quick glance through my own collection and Chronology reveals, in no particular order, these versions of perhaps the greatest and most intriguing Untold Case of them all, *The Giant Rat of Sumatra:*

- **The Giant Rat of Sumatra** – Rick Boyer (1976) *(Possibly the greatest pastiche of all time)*
- "*Matilda Briggs* and the Giant Rat of Sumatra", **The Elementary Cases of Sherlock Holmes** – Ian Charnock (1999)
- **Mrs Hudson and the Spirit's Curse** – Martin Davies (2004)
- **Sherlock Holmes' Lost Adventure: The True Story of the Giant Rats of Sumatra** – Laurel Steinhauer (2004)
- **The Giant Rat of Sumatra** – Paul D. Gilbert (2010)
- "The Giant Rat of Sumatra", **The Lost Stories of Sherlock Holmes** – Tony Reynolds (2010)
- **The Giant Rat of Sumatra** – Jake and Luke Thoene (1995)
- "The Adventure of the Giant Rat of Sumatra", **Mary Higgins Clark Mystery Magazine** – John Lescroart, (December 1988)
- "The Case of the Sumatran Rat", **The Secret Chronicles of Sherlock Holmes** – June Thomson (1992)
- "Sherlock Holmes and the Giant Rat of Sumatra", **More From the Deed Box of John H. Watson MD** – Hugh Ashton (2012)
- "The Case of the Giant Rat of Sumatra", **The Secret Notebooks of Sherlock Holmes** – Liz Hedgecock (2016)
- "The World is Now Prepared" – "slogging ruffian" (Fan Fiction) (Date unverified)
- "The Giant Rat of Sumatra", **Sherlock Holmes: The Lost Cases** – Alvin F. Rymsha (2006)
- "The Giant Rat of Sumatra", **The Oriental Casebook of Sherlock Holmes** – Ted Riccardi (2003)
- **Sherlock Holmes and the Limehouse Horror** – Phillip Pullman (1992, 2001)
- "No Rats Need Apply", **The Unexpected Adventures of Sherlock Holmes** – Amanda Knight (2004)
- **The Shadow of the Rat** – David Stuart Davies (1999)
- **The Giant Rat of Sumatra** – Daniel Gracely (2001)

5

- "The Giant Rat of Sumatra", **Resurrected Holmes** – Paula Volsky (1996)
- "The Mysterious Case of the Giant Rat of Sumatra", **The Mark of the Gunn** – Brian Gibson (2000)
- **Sherlock Holmes and the Giant Rat of Sumatra** – Alan Vanneman (2002)
- "The Giant Rat of Sumatra" – Paul Boler (2000)
- "The Case of the Missing Energy", **The Einstein Paradox** – Colin Bruce (1994)
- "All This and the Giant Rat of Sumatra", **Sherlock Holmes and The Baker Street Dozen** – Val Andrews (1997)

In addition to these that are available, there's also one that isn't – possibly the earliest telling of "The Giant Rat", the intriguing radio version by Edith Meiser, which was broadcast multiple times: With Richard Gordon as Holmes on April 20th (although some sources say June 9th), 1932, and again on July 18th, 1936; and then on March 1st, 1942 (with Basil Rathbone as Holmes). Sadly, these versions are apparently lost, although I'd dearly love to hear – and read – them!

Although Rathbone and Bruce performed Edith Meiser's version of "The Giant Rat" in 1942, they weren't limited to just that version. A completely different version, this time by Bruce Taylor (Leslie Charteris) and Denis Green, was broadcast on July 31st, 1944. Amazingly, Charteris's scripts have been located by Ian Dickerson, who is in the process of publishing them for modern audiences who would otherwise have never had the chance to enjoy these lost cases. And even more amazing, Mr. Dickerson has allowed the 1944 version of "The Giant Rat" to premiere here in these concurrent Untold Cases volumes.

What makes this twice as much fun is that also appearing in these books is Nick Cardillo's new 2018 version of "The Giant Rat", showing that there can be more than one version of an Untold Case without any of them being the definitive version.

More than one version . . . .

The list shown above is by no means a complete representation of all the Giant Rat narratives. These are simply the ones that I found when making a pass along the shelves of my Holmes Collection, and what jumped out during a quick search through my Chronology. The thing to remember is that *in spite of every one of these stories being about a Giant Rat, none of them contradict one another or cancel each other out to become the only true Giant Rat adventure.*

Something that I learned very early, far before I created my Chronology back in the mid-1990's, is that there are lots of sequels to the original Canonical tales, and there are also lots of different versions of the Untold Tales. Some readers, of course, don't like and will never accept any of them, since they didn't cross the First Literary Agent's desk. Others, however, only wish to seek out the sole and single account that satisfies them the most, therefore dismissing the others as *"fiction"* – a word that I find quite distasteful when directed toward Mr. Sherlock Holmes

My approach is that if the different versions of either sequels or Untold Cases are Canonical, and don't violate any of the same rules that define what types of tales appear in these anthologies – no parodies, no anachronisms, no actual supernatural encounters, no murderous sociopathic Holmes portrayals – then they are legitimate.

Perhaps it seems too unlikely for some that there were so many Giant Rats in London during Holmes's active years. Not at all. Each Giant Rat adventure mentioned above is very different, and in any case, Watson was a master at obfuscation. He changed names and dates to satisfy all sorts of needs. For instance, he often made it appear at times as if Holmes went for weeks in fits of settee-bound depression between cases, when in fact he was involved constantly in thousands upon thousands of cases, each intertwined like incredibly complex threads in The Great Holmes Tapestry.

Although not represented in this volume, there have been many stories about Holmes and Watson's encounter with Huret, the Boulevard Assassin, in 1894. Contradictory? Not at all. Holmes simply rooted out an entire nest of *Al Qaeda*-like assassins during that deadly summer. There are a lot of tales out there relating the peculiar persecution of John Vincent Harden in 1895. No problem – there were simply a lot of tobacco millionaires in London during that time, all peculiarly persecuted – but in very different ways – and Watson lumped them in his notes under the catch-all name of *John Vincent Harden.* Later Literary Agents, not quite knowing how to conquer Watson's personal codes and reverse-engineer who the real client was in these cases, simply left the name as written.

What Counts as an Untold Case?

As mentioned, there have been over one-hundred identified Untold Cases, although some arguments are made one way or another as to whether some should be included. Do Holmes's various stops during The Great Hiatus – such as Persia and Mecca and Khartoum – each count as

7

an Untold Case? (To me they do.) What about certain entries in Holmes's good old index, like *"Viggo, the Hammersmith Wonder"* or *"Vittoria, the Circus Belle"*? Possibly they were just clippings about odd people from the newspaper, but I – and many other later Literary Agents – prefer to think of these as Holmes's past cases. Then there are the cases that involve someone else's triumph – or do they? – like Lestrade's "Molesley Mystery" (mentioned in "The Empty House", where the most well-known Scotland Yard inspector competently handled an investigation during Holmes's Hiatus absence), or "The Long Island Cave Mystery", as solved by Leverton of the Pinkertons, and referenced in "The Red Circle". (And as an aside, I have to castigate Owen Dudley Edwards, the editor of the Oxford annotated edition of The Canon [1993], who decided to change *the Long Island Cave* to *Cove* simply because *"there are no caves in Long Island, N.Y."* (p. 206) – thus derailing a long-standing point of Canonical speculation. Pfui!)

And then there's the matter of the Oxford Comma, sometimes known as the "Serial" or "Terminal" Comma. A quick search of the internet found this example of *incorrect* usage: *This book is dedicated to my parents, Ayn Rand and God.* Clearly this author either had some interesting parents, or more likely he or she needed to use a comma after *Rand* to differentiate that series of parents, Ayn, and Deity.

And that relates to Untold Cases in this way: There are two Untold Cases that might actually be four, depending on one's use (or not) of the Oxford Comma. In "The Adventure of the Golden Pince-Nez", Watson tells of some of the cases that occurred in 1894. As he states:

> *As I turn over the pages I see my notes upon the repulsive story of the red leech and the terrible death of Crosby the banker. Here also I find an account of the Addleton tragedy and the singular contents of the ancient British barrow.*

I have many adventures in my collection that present these as *two* cases: (1) *The repulsive story of the red leech and the terrible death of Crosby the banker* and (2) *The Addleton tragedy and the singular contents of the ancient British barrow.* All are very satisfying. But I also have others that split them up into *four* cases: (1) *The repulsive story of the red leech* and (2) *the terrible death of Crosby the banker* and (3) *the Addleton tragedy* and (4) *the singular contents of the ancient British barrow.* For this collection, Nik Morton and Thomas Fortenberry have chosen to assume that the comma was intentionally omitted, and that there are two cases here, and not four, to be related.

As an amateur editor, I honor the Oxford Comma. I've been aware of it for years, ever since reading – somewhere – that editor *extraordinaire* Frederic Dannay (of Ellery Queen-fame and founder and the founding editor of *Ellery Queen's Mystery Magazine* from 1941-1982,) was a strong supporter of it. When writing this foreword, I couldn't remember where I'd read that, so I asked his son, Richard Dannay, who replied:

> *I can say with certainty that my father believed in the serial, or Oxford, or terminal (pick your poison) comma. I have no doubt. But sitting here, I'm not sure where he said that in print. I'll need to think about that. But I will send you a secondary source, absolutely unimpeachable in accuracy, where his preference is described.*

And then he sent me a PDF excerpt from Eleanor Sullivan's *Whodunit: A Biblio-Bio-Anecdotal Memoir of Frederic Dannay* (Targ Editions, NY, 1984, pp. 17-18). Ms. Sullivan was Dannay's chief editorial assistant for *EQMM* for many years, and after he died, she became the *EQMM* editor as his successor for about ten years before her premature death. (As Richard pointed out, the current editor is Janet Hutchings, only the third *EQMM* editor in its now over seventy-five-year history.)

Ms. Sullivan wrote:

> *Fred's style in editing* EQMM *could be considered eccentric, but I soon became used to it because there was his special logic behind everything he did. I didn't know he was exasperated by my non-use of the terminal comma (that is, a comma between the second-to-last word in a series of words and the "and") until one day when we were discussing some copy I'd sent him, he sighed dramatically and said, "I wish you could learn to use the terminal comma." I've been scrupulous about using it ever since.*

Recalling Frederic Dannay's passion for the Oxford Comma, I try to notice and then to add one in every place that needs it in these books. Having hubristically stated that, I'm absolutely certain that sure you will find places where I've missed it, along with many other unfortunate typos. These books live and grow as a single ever-expanding Word document on my computer – I have no publishing software – until such time as I send the final version to amazing publisher Steve Emecz, and they aren't seen by anyone else before their publication. There are no other proof-readers or editors who have a crack at them, and I'm flying without a net here. (My incredible wife of thirty-plus years has a Bachelor's Degree in Journalism, and two Master's Degrees in English Literature and Library Science, and her first job years ago was as a copy editor, but these books are neither her passion nor her problem, so I can't ask her to proofread them.) I've had several offers from volunteers to proofread, but due to the fast turn-around involved in this new publishing paradigm, that simply isn't possible. Thus, the errors that you find that throw you out of the story are on my head. Mortifying things sometimes slip through, and I apologize. But I do try to catch and fix every Oxford Comma situation that I can.

Other Untold Cases

While editing and assembling this particular set of books, I was concurrently working on *Sherlock Holmes: Adventures Beyond the Canon* (2018) for Belanger books, a three-volume set of twenty-nine new adventures that are sequels to The Canon. (It was amazing fun reading and editing all of these stories – over fifty of them between these five books – fresh from the Tin Dispatch Box, while keeping straight which went with which book.) Like the Untold Cases, these sequels don't contradict any of the sequels that have come before. One can't have too many traditional tales about the true Sherlock Holmes, and thankfully there are many more still out there. (I'm already receiving stories for next year's *Part XIII: 2019 Annual* from MX, and sequels for the next Belanger collection.)

As mentioned, there are far too many Untold Cases to list or recommend. The first encounter that I recall with attempts to reveal the Untold Cases was in *The Exploits of Sherlock Holmes* (1954) by a son of the First Literary Agent, Adrian Conan Doyle, and famed locked-room author John Dickson Carr. At the end of each of those twelve stories, a quote from The Canon revealed which Untold Case that it was – since it wasn't always clear from the story's title – and how it was originally mentioned. I liked that, and have followed the same convention with this book.

Many later stories have related Untold Cases, such as some included in collections like *The Mammoth Book of New Sherlock Holmes Stories* (1997) and *The Further Adventures of Sherlock Holmes* (1985). Others have appeared in the new *Strand Magazine* edited by Andrew Gulli, Bert

Coules' amazing *The Further Adventures of Sherlock Holmes*, or on Jim French's famed *Imagination Theatre*, broadcast on radio for decades across the U.S.

Interestingly, Untold Cases have been presented in Holmes radio shows since the 1930's, but they are much more rare in television episodes and movies. Sadly, except for some Russian efforts and a few stand-alone films, there have been no Sherlock Holmes television shows whatsoever since the Jeremy Brett films from Granada in the 1980's and 1990's. Hopefully, a set of film scripts by Bert Coules featuring an age-appropriate Holmes and Watson, set in the early 1880's, will find a home soon. I've been wanting to see (or read) these for years, and I'm curious as to whether any other Untold Cases feature in them – especially since Bert covered some of them so well in his radio scripts.

Some authors have specialized in finding the Untold Cases, like June Thomson, and more recently Hugh Ashton. For the record, I tried to recruit June twice to these books, and she wrote me some nice letters declining due to age. From the beginning of this anthology series, Hugh has been extremely supportive, and I'm very glad that he's a part of these books.

Philip K. Jones and the Untold Cases

I first became aware of Phil Jones back in the mid-when I ran across his amazing and massive online Pastiche Database. I've been collecting pastiches since I first found Holmes at age ten, in 1975, and have thousands of them on my shelves. I've scoured libraries and copied them from magazines and journals – a dime a page at old Xerox machines – and I've printed and archived them from the internet. I've bought Holmes books and asked for books – with traditional pastiches having first priority – as birthday and Christmas presents. I think that I've acquired one of the best pastiche collections ever. But finding Phil's database made me realize that it was only a drop in the bucket – and it also gave me new directions in which to hunt.

Phil was born in Missouri in 1938 and raised in Michigan. He worked in Information Technology for many years, and upon retirement turned his attention to Sherlock Holmes Literature.

In 2011, I published my first Holmes story collection, *The Papers of Sherlock Holmes* (later reprinted by MX in 2013). I desperately wanted it to be included in Phil's database, because to me that felt like I was actually (and finally) a part of this amazing World of Holmes. Phil and I began emailing, and I learned that he also wrote very respected

Holmesian reviews. I was very thrilled when he took the time to review my book.

Later, when the first of the MX anthologies appeared, he was one of the most supportive fans. I still treasure his comment about the first volume, where he said: *This first volume, on its own, is the finest anthology of Sherlockian fiction I have ever read."* That means a lot coming from a man who has read so many Sherlockian adventures.

Over the years we continued to communicate. He sent me copies of his scholarly articles, and I learned that, not only did he list in his database when a story was an Untold Case, but he had also done a lot of research into defining all of them, as well as devising his own story-title code, rather like what Jay Finley Christ did for The Canonical stories. Back in November 2011, we traded emails where he lamented that that he had found a story for every one of the Untold Cases except for "The St. Pancras Case" (as mentioned in "Shoscombe Old Place"), where a cap was found beside the dead policeman, and Merivale of the Yard asked Holmes to look into it. I was able to point him toward a fan-fiction called "Merivale of the Yard" by the uniquely named "AdidasandPie", and he was able to cross it of his list.

Also in 2011, Phil wrote a book with Sherlockian Bob Burr, *The Punishment of Sherlock Holmes* (MX Publishing), demonstrating his great love of puns. A couple of times he offered to write a pun-filled story for the MX anthologies, but I had to turn him down, as the scope of the books was absolutely Canonical. Conversely, I never stopped trying to get him to write a traditional adventure, because I thought that he, who had done so much to support post-Canonical adventures, should be a part of these books. He didn't feel that he had one in him.

On January 31st, 2017, Phil wrote to Steve Emecz and me with an idea for a future anthology volume. He stated:

> *[M]y suggestion is that you produce an anthology in this series devoted to The Untold Tales . . . . One of the good features of this project is that authors would discover that there are more than the two- or three-dozen commonly told Untold tales, some quite obscure, but intriguing. Another is that authors could fit almost any story idea into the one-hundred-and-thirty available subjects.*

As you can see, Phil's idea stuck in my head, and on February 19th, 2017, I issued the first invitations for submissions to what became the volume that you hold in your hands.

I wanted Phil to write a foreword to this book, and on July 19th, 2018, I sent an email to follow up on that. Three days later, I received a reply from Phil's wife, Phyllis Jones, indicating that Phil had passed away in June 13th, 2018.

I was stunned, and when I related the information online to various Sherlockian groups, there was shock, as well as a great outpouring of what a great guy Phil was, and what a loss this was to the community.

Therefore, as you'll see, these two concurrent volumes, *Parts XI* and *XII: Some Untold Cases*, are dedicated to Phil Jones. He was the Untold Cases Scholar, and the theme for these books was his idea. If he wasn't able to write a foreword, at least he can be honored in this way.

"Of course, I could only stammer out my thanks."
– The unhappy John Hector McFarlane, "The Norwood Builder"

These last few years have been an amazing. I've been able to meet some incredible people, both in person and in the modern electronic way, and also I've been able to read several hundred new Holmes adventures, all to the benefit of the Stepping Stones School at Undershaw, one of Sir Arthur Conan Doyle's homes. The contributors to these MX anthologies donate their royalties to the school, and so far we've raised over $30,000.

First and foremost, as with every one of these projects that I attempt, I want to thank my amazing and incredibly wonderful wife (of thirty-plus years!) Rebecca, and our truly awesome son and my friend, Dan. I love you both, and you are everything to me!

I have all the gratitude in the world for the contributors who have used their time to create this project. I'm so glad to have gotten to know all of you through this process. It's an undeniable fact that Sherlock Holmes authors are the *best* people!

Next, I'd like to thank those who offer support, encouragement, and friendship, sometimes patiently waiting on me to reply as my time is directed in many other directions. Many many thanks to (in alphabetical order): Bob Byrne, Mark Mower, Denis Smith, Tom Turley, Dan Victor, and Marcia Wilson.

Additionally, I'd also like to especially thank:

- Steve Emecz – Always supportive of every idea that I pitch – and there are some forthcoming projects that aren't common knowledge yet. It's been my great good fortune to cross your path – it changed my life, and let me play in this Sherlockian Sandbox in a way that

13

would have never happened otherwise. Thank you for every opportunity!

- Lyndsay Faye: I remember first reading her wonderful Holmes-versus-The Ripper novel *Dust and Shadow* (2009) while in a motel room in Asheville, NC, where my son and I had taken a weekend trip. (I see from the note on the front page where I wrote my name that it was a gift from my wife and son for my birthday that year.) By then, I'd been keeping my Holmes Chronology for over ten years, so I read it while making notes as to how it would fit into the Autumn of Terror, 1888 – since that's a very complex period, and certainly Holmes's finest hour.

  I recall seeing in several interviews that this book – her first – was written during a period of unemployment. Since it was published in 2009, possibly she was unemployed in 2008 – a year when I was also jobless, laid off from an engineering company at the start of The Great Recession and using my time to pull some stories from Watson's tin dispatch box.

  I continued to read her stories as they appeared in *The Strand* magazine, beginning with "The Case of the Beggar's Feast" – an Untold Case! – in issue No. 29, (October 2009). She clearly had hit a hot wire running into the Great Watsonian Oversoul.

  In January 2015, I had the idea for these anthologies and started writing to a few Sherlockian authors that I really admired, hoping that they might be convinced to join the party. On January 25th, 2015, 11:16 am, I wrote to Lyndsay, explaining the project, and hoping against hope that she would be interested. At 4:54 pm – the engineer in me had to go and check – she wrote back with: *Hi David, I'd be happy to – when do you need it by?*

  Later, when it became obvious that this would be a series instead of a one-time thing, I contacted everyone who had previously participated, including Lyndsay. However, her many commitments as a professional author prevented additional contributions – until now. On March 27th, 2018, I wrote to see if she would write a foreword. The next day, she replied, *Hey David, I would be absolutely delighted to write a foreword!*

Lyndsay is a true Sherlockian, and I'm very jealous that she's up there at Ground Zero of the U.S. Holmesian world, with Otto Penzler's Mysterious Bookshop and various Baker Street Irregular activities, while I'm looking on from out here the Delta Quadrant. Sometimes when I've pestered her too much for a story, or when she thinks that I've been too public with my views about certain television shows, she's made the effort to write and tell me how I've vexed her – and I'm glad to have her thoughts on these matters, even if she hasn't changed my mind. I'm very grateful for her time and the support that she's given to these books – and also personally to this Tennessee Sherlockian!

- Roger Johnson – From the first time I reached out to Roger, upon the occasion of my first published book, he has been amazingly supportive, and I'm glad that he's my friend. He and his wife Jean were incredible hosts when I stayed with them as part of Holmes Pilgrimage No. II in 2015, and I'll never forget the times that he has showed me Chelmsford, Colchester, and parts of London. He led me to the market where I purchased my black deerstalker – because even though I have two-dozen other deerstalkers, I absolutely needed a formal black one. And I'll also never forget when our late afternoon train to leave Colchester was delayed, and we were walking briskly through the crowds, back-and-forth, from one platform to another, trying to get the next train. I was having fun – after all, I was in England, and I was wearing my deerstalker on a British railway platform racing for a train. I told Roger that we were having an adventure, and he said indignantly, "*I don't have adventures!*"

    Roger has supported these and other books from the beginning, and I am incredibly thankful.

- Derrick Belanger –Even as I was putting these books together, I was editing stories for a three-volume set of stories from Belanger Books, *Sherlock Holmes: Adventures Beyond the Canon*, featuring twenty-nine

15

sequels to the original tales. This is just one of many past and future projects that Derrick, his brother Brian, and I have going. But additionally, I've enjoyed getting to know Derrick over the last few years, ever since our first enthusiastic emails sharing all sorts of Sherlockian thoughts. Derrick: Thanks very much for your friendship, as well as the Sherlockian opportunities.

- Brian Belanger – Brian is incredibly talented graphic artist who grows from success to success. Additionally, he's a positive and gifted person. Brian: Thank you so much for all that you do – it's appreciated by many people besides me!

- Richard Dannay – I'm very grateful that I can write Richard every few months with a question, or just wanting to discuss some aspect of Ellery Queen, and he quickly replies with exactly what I need. It's a thrill being able to correspond with him.

- Ian Dickerson – In the previous MX anthology volume, *Part IX (1879-1895),* Ian explained how he came to be responsible for a number of long-lost scripts from the 1944 season of the Holmes radio show, starring Basil Rathbone and Nigel Bruce, and written by Denis Green and Leslie Charteris (under the name Bruce Taylor). When I was writing this foreword and researching various versions of "The Giant Rat", I came across mention of the Basil Rathbone version. It was simply going to be mentioned in passing, and then I thought to ask Ian about it.

  He's published one set of the scripts – *Sherlock Holmes: The Lost Radio Scripts* (2017), and more recently another set – *Sherlock Holmes: More Lost Radio Scripts* (2018). I either wanted to mention the Rathbone "Giant Rat" if it's going to be in the current volume, or possibly use it if it won't be published until a later collection. Ian informed me that "The Giant Rat" isn't in the current book, and that I could have it if I wished for this collection. Of course I wanted it.

  Ian then worked like a crazy man, transcribing the original script into a new Word document, and within a very few days of my request, I had it in hand, and ready for editing. It was an incredible effort.

I'm very grateful to Ian for allowing this one to appear in these volumes before it's reprinted in one of the other upcoming volumes. When I first discovered Holmes, I quickly found a number of Rathbone and Bruce broadcasts on records at the public library, and that was where I first "heard" Holmes. I can't express the thrill of getting to read these rediscovered lost treasures, having been tantalized by their titles for so long. Many thanks to Ian for making these available.

- Andrew Gulli – For resurrecting *The Strand* magazine, and then for (usually) including a Holmes story, I'm very thankful. Additionally, your support, especially in publishing some of my own Holmes adventures in *The Strand* – truly a bucket list item fulfilled! – and also for your kind words about me during your interview on *I Hear of Sherlock Everywhere* are very much appreciated.

- Joel Senter – While these volumes were being prepared, Sherlockian Joel Senter passed away. I'll write more about him in the next MX volumes (in Spring 2019), but I'm grateful for everything that he did to support me personally over the years, and also how he helped these books in so many ways, including writing (with his wife Carolyn) the final story in the original three-volume set, *Parts I*, *II*, and *III*. He will be missed.

- Melissa Grigsby – Thank you for the incredible work that you do at the Stepping Stones School in at Undershaw Hindhead. I was both amazed and thrilled to visit the school on opening day in 2016, and I hope to get back there again some time. You are doing amazing things, and it's my honor, as well that of all the contributors to this project, to be able to help.

In addition those mentioned above – Bob Byrne, Derrick Belanger, Roger Johnson, Mark Mower, Denis Smith, Tom Turley, Dan Victor, and Marcy Wilson – I'd also like to especially thank, in alphabetical order: Larry Albert, Hugh Ashton, Deanna Baran, Jayantika Ganguly,

17

Paul Gilbert, Dick Gillman, Arthur Hall, Mike Hogan, Craig Janacek, Tracy Revels, Roger Riccard, Geri Schear, and Tim Symonds. From the very beginning, these special contributors have stepped up and supported this and other projects over and over again with their contributions. They are the best and I can't explain how valued they are.

Finally, last but certainly *not* least, **Sir Arthur Conan Doyle**: Author, doctor, adventurer, and the Founder of the Sherlockian Feast. Present in spirit, and honored by all of us here.

As always, this collection, like those before it, has been a labor of love by both the participants and myself. As I've explained before, once again everyone did their sincerest best to produce an anthology that truly represents why Holmes and Watson have been so popular for so long. These are just more tiny threads woven into the ongoing Great Holmes Tapestry, continuing to grow and grow, for there can *never* be enough stories about the man whom Watson described as *"the best and wisest . . . whom I have ever known."*

David Marcum
August 7th, 2018
The 166th Birthday of Dr. John H. Watson

Questions, comments, and story submissions
may be addressed to David Marcum at
thepapersofsherlockholmes@gmail.com

18

Lose Yourself in New Pastiches
by Lyndsay Faye

When kindly folks ask me to write about Sherlock Holmes, my answer ought to be carved into a woodblock so I can stamp it on every occasion: I would love to. Yes, absolutely! But I do this for a living, weirdly – the writing, storytelling, etc. And it takes me about three weeks to craft a good short story, so I am careful about my *pro bono* projects. I always say, if you're not good enough for poetry, write short stories. And if you're not good enough for short stories, write novels.

I write mostly novels, by the way.

I can recall the exact moment when David asked me to contribute a Holmes pastiche for the first volume to benefit Undershaw. I remember it because I immediately said absolutely yes, turned it in, saw it in print, and then was relentlessly hounded for more pastiches until the point when I said (pretty much) never ever ask me this again.

So he asked me to write a forward.

I'm not telling this story in a negative light, in case anyone was wondering. In fact, David is responsible for a huge amount of new stories existing. He badgers, he cajoles, he solicits, he wheedles, and he cadges. It works. I value very few things more than I value new Sherlock Holmes stories, so I applaud these results.

Let this be a proclamation: David Marcum, and the authors featured herein, have brought more Sherlock Holmes stories into the world. The tales are fantastic. They are traditional, which is tricky. They are labors of love. And David Marcum loves Sherlock Holmes the way I do, never quite forgetting about him as we walk around grocery shopping or vegetable chopping or bar hopping.

Lose yourself in new pastiches. Nitpick them. Love them. Analyze them.

Whatever you do with them, I'm simply glad they exist in the world.

Lyndsay Faye
BSI, ASH
July 2018

Known Unknowns
by Roger Johnson

To borrow a phrase from a very different discipline, the cases that Dr. Watson mentions but doesn't actually relate are *known unknowns*. [1] We know that Sherlock Holmes did investigate the singular affair of the aluminium crutch, the Smith-Mortimer succession case, and the adventure of the old Russian woman, but the details are not recorded in the sixty Canonical accounts, and therefore remain unknown.

A recent meeting of *The Sherlock Holmes Society of London* was devoted to some of these unreported exploits. Eleven members were each invited to select the story that best deserved to be published and, within five minutes, to explain why. We were encouraged to avoid the likes of the giant rat of Sumatra and the whole story concerning the politician, the lighthouse, and the trained cormorant, but there were more than eighty others more to choose from.

I commended the case of the Second Stain.

"The Adventure of the Yellow Face" opens thus: "*In publishing these short sketches based upon the numerous cases in which my companion's singular gifts have made us the listeners to, and eventually the actors in, some strange drama, it is only natural that I should dwell rather upon his successes than upon his failures. And this not so much for the sake of his reputation – for, indeed, it was when he was at his wits' end that his energy and his versatility were most admirable – but because where he failed it happened too often that no one else succeeded, and that the tale was left forever without a conclusion. Now and again, however, it chanced that even when he erred, the truth was still discovered. I have noted of some half-dozen cases of the kind; the affair of the second stain and that which I am about to recount are the two which present the strongest features of interest.*" [2]

Fascinating! But in "The Adventure of the Naval Treaty", we're told that the case of the Second Stain occurred in "*the July which immediately succeeded [Watson's] marriage*" and that it "*deals with interest of such importance and implicates so many of the first families in the kingdom that for many years it will be impossible to make it public. No case, however, in which Holmes was engaged has ever illustrated the value of his analytical methods so clearly or has impressed those who were associated with him so deeply. I still retain an almost verbatim report of the interview in which he demonstrated the true facts of the case to*

Monsieur Dubuque of the Paris police, and Fritz von Waldbaum, the well-known specialist of Dantzig, both of whom had wasted their energies upon what proved to be side-issues."

Clearly we have two different cases, each dependent upon a second stain! Even more extraordinary is that neither of them is the investigation eventually chronicled in *The Return of Sherlock Holmes*.

Having heard the outcome of each speaker's scholarly speculation – or inventive fiction – or outrageous parody – our listeners voted for the case that best merited actual publication. My preference was firmly for the case of the two Coptic Patriarchs, advocated by the Revd. Simon Smyth, who is himself a priest of the Coptic Orthodox Church. It was exciting to learn that there actually *were* two Coptic Patriarchs at the time, and their followers were not on friendly terms. (Imagine those tense years in Western Europe when there were rival Popes). However, the winner by several lengths was the Dundas Separation Case, of which Holmes said, *"as it happens, I was engaged in clearing up some small points in connection with it. The husband was a teetotaller, there was no other woman, and the conduct complained of was that he had drifted into the habit of winding up every meal by taking out his false teeth and hurling them at his wife . . . ."* According to Peter Horrocks, who claimed that an account of this investigation, more than any of the others, deserved to be published, the *"separation"* was not between husband and wife, but between Mr. Dundas and his dentures!

Fortunately – perhaps – you won't find anything of the sort in this book. David Marcum has ensured that the contributions are firmly in the tradition established by Sir Arthur Conan Doyle, and followed to their great credit by Adrian Conan Doyle and John Dickson Carr, William E. Dudley, Martin Edwards, M.J. Elliott, James C. Iraldi, Barrie Roberts, Denis O. Smith, Edgar W. Smith, June Thomson, Alan Wilson – and others who have written first-rate accounts of exploits that were merely hinted at by Dr. Watson. [3]

Enjoy!

Roger Johnson
BSI, ASH
July, 2018

NOTES

1. In 2002, speaking of the evidence, or lack of evidence, linking the Iraqi government to the supply of weapons to terrorist groups, Donald Rumsfeld used the expressions *"known knowns"*, *"known*

unknowns", and "*unknown unknowns*". This is not meaningless jargon: The terms are precise and entirely relevant.

2. At least, that's how it runs in the standard British text. The American text follows *The Strand Magazine* in classing "The Musgrave Ritual" as a case in which Holmes failed to discover the truth. Which is patently untrue.

3. I'll also recommend the adventures of Solar Pons, "The Sherlock Holmes of Praed Street", created by August Derleth and active between the wars. His cases included "The Adventure of Ricoletti of the Club Foot", "The Adventure of the Remarkable Worm", "The Adventure of the Grice-Paterson Curse", "The Adventure of the Trained Cormorant", and "The Adventure of the Aluminium Crutch". His authorised chronicler is now the amazingly industrious David Marcum.

An Ongoing Legacy
for Sherlock Holmes
by Steve Emecz

Undershaw
Circa 1900

It is three years since the first volumes of this series, and it's wonderful that we've reached Volumes XI and XII. We have raised over $30,000 for Stepping Stones School – the majority of which from the generous donation of the royalties from all the authors, but also from some interesting licensing deals in Japan and India. With this money, the school has been able to fund projects that would be very difficult to organise otherwise – especially those to preserve the legacy of Sir Arthur Conan Doyle at Undershaw.

There are now over two-hundred-and-fifty stories and well over a hundred authors taking part. We have new writers, unknown authors, established names, and even a few *New York Times* bestselling authors (like Lee Child) taking part. With more stories on the way under the careful eye of our wonderful editor David Marcum, the collection goes from strength to strength.

The critics agree that not only is it the largest, but *The MX Book of New Sherlock Holmes Stories* is the highest quality collection of new Holmes stories ever compiled. The last five volumes have all had glowing reviews from Publishers Weekly – Here are a few sample quotes:

> *"The traditional pastiche is alive and well, as shown by the 35 Sherlock Holmes stories in Marcum's excellent sixth all-original anthology"*

> *"This is a must-have for all Sherlockians."*

> *"Marcum continues to impress with the quality of his selections, many from little-known authors, in his seventh anthology of traditional pastiches"*

> *"Sherlockians eager for faithful-to-the-canon plots and characters will be delighted."*

> *"The imagination of the contributors in coming up with variations on the volume's theme is matched by their ingenious resolutions."*

> *"Sherlockians will rejoice that more volumes are on the way."*

MX Publishing is a social enterprise – all the staff, including me, are volunteers with day jobs. In addition to Stepping Stones School, our main program that we support is the Happy Life Children's Home in Kenya. My wife Sharon and I have spent the last five Christmases at the baby rescue centre in Nairobi. We have written a book called *The Happy Life Story* which explains how this incredible project has saved the lives of over five-hundred abandoned babies in its first fifteen years, with many being adopted. During the time that we have been involved, we've seen the project expand to include a school and now an incredible hospital which is saving lives every week.

Our support of both of these projects is possible through the publishing of Sherlock Holmes books, which we have now been doing for a decade. Our very first book was called *Eliminate The Impossible*, and we now have over three-hundred titles in print.

You can find out more information about the Stepping Stones School at *www.steppingstones.org.uk*, and Happy Life at *www.happylifechildrenshomes.com*. You can obtain more books from MX, both fiction and non-fiction, at *www.sherlockholmesbooks.com*. If you would like to become involved with these projects or help out in any way, please reach out to me via LinkedIn.

Steve Emecz
July, 2018
Twitter: *@steveemecz*
LinkedIn: *https://www.linkedin.com/in/emecz/*

The Doyle Room at Stepping Stones, Undershaw
Partially funded through royalties from
The MX Book of New Sherlock Holmes Stories

A Word From the
Head Teacher of Stepping Stones
by Melissa Grigsby

Undershaw
September 9, 2016
Grand Opening of the Stepping Stones School
(Photograph courtesy of Roger Johnson)

As Stepping Stones School sails into its third year at Undershaw, we reflect on the unfinished and unknown tales that Sir Arthur Conan Doyle never drew to a close or was unable to complete.

One such story was that of "The Giant Rat of Sumatra", a story that distorted one's imagination beyond the concepts of the days he sat to unfold and write his stories. Within his writings, Doyle has Sherlock Holmes declare, as an aside, to Dr. Watson:

> "Matilda Briggs *was not the name of a young woman, Watson . . . It was a ship which is associated with the giant rat of Sumatra, a story for which the world is not yet prepared.*"

The young people that have their educational journey hosted under the roof of Undershaw can at times be seen and labelled as the unknown, special, and – in our eyes – gifted with exotic rareness. People from the outside can be scared and unsure as they perceive that these young people do not fit the social norms of society. However, within the walls of Undershaw and under Doyle's watch, and with his wishes in mind, these young people participate in layered therapeutic interventions and differentiated education with the same outcomes as many young people of their age.

Like *Matilda Briggs*, they are the vessels of social mobility and changed mindset, preparing the world for the day that they dock and take their place in society.

Thank you for all your support and companionship on this voyage with the young people of Stepping Stones School.

Melissa Grigsby

Executive Head Teacher, *Stepping Stones,* Undershaw

July, 2018

Sherlock Holmes (1854-1957) was born in Yorkshire, England, on 6 January, 1854. In the mid-1870's, he moved to 24 Montague Street, London, where he established himself as the world's first Consulting Detective. After meeting Dr. John H. Watson in early 1881, he and Watson moved to rooms at 221b Baker Street, where his reputation as the world's greatest detective grew for several decades. He was presumed to have died battling noted criminal Professor James Moriarty on 4 May, 1891, but he returned to London on 5 April, 1894, resuming his consulting practice in Baker Street. Retiring to the Sussex coast near Beachy Head in October 1903, he continued to be associated in various private and government investigations while giving the impression of being a reclusive apiarist. He was very involved in the events encompassing World War I, and to a lesser degree those of World War II. He passed away peacefully upon the cliffs above his Sussex home on his 103rd birthday, 6 January, 1957.

Dr. John Hamish Watson (1852-1929) was born in Stranraer, Scotland on 7 August, 1852. In 1878, he took his Doctor of Medicine Degree from the University of London, and later joined the army as a surgeon. Wounded at the Battle of Maiwand in Afghanistan (27 July, 1880), he returned to London late that same year. On New Year's Day, 1881, he was introduced to Sherlock Holmes in the chemical laboratory at Barts. Agreeing to share rooms with Holmes in Baker Street, Watson became invaluable to Holmes's consulting detective practice. Watson was married and widowed three times, and from the late 1880's onward, in addition to his participation in Holmes's investigations and his medical practice, he chronicled Holmes's adventures, with the assistance of his literary agent, Sir Arthur Conan Doyle, in a series of popular narratives, most of which were first published in *The Strand* magazine. Watson's later years were spent preparing a vast number of his notes of Holmes's cases for future publication. Following a final important investigation with Holmes, Watson contracted pneumonia and passed away on 24 July, 1929.

Photos of Sherlock Holmes and Dr. John H. Watson courtesy of Roger Johnson

The MX Book
Of
New Sherlock Holmes Stories
Part XII:
Some Untold Cases
(1894-1902)

It's Always Time
by "Anon."

When Sherlock Holmes needs to find a fact,
he has resources – of those there is no lack.
He steps across the sitting room to look
and pulls out a wonderful commonplace book.
Many a time was a cutting so there placed,
and with it, to a solution, Holmes has raced.
Or perhaps the help he needs instead has feet,
and he sends for The Irregulars of Baker Street,
with instructions to spread and scatter on the run –
to go everywhere, see everything, and overhear everyone.
While Watson has access to these resources, too,
there's something else he knows that *he* can do.
When tasked to learn more of Baron Gruner's hobby,
he traveled round to that quiet and solemn lobby
of the London Library there in St. James' Square
to seek a friend of his that functioned there.
In the stacks was that most useful Victorian,
Good old Watson's friend, Lomax the Sub-Librarian.
But all of these resources cannot aid
when a certain aspect of The Game is closely played.
One could ask for help from all these places,
but none will get you facts about the Unknown Cases.
For that you must seek a thing with clever locks,
known as Doctor Watson's *Tin Dispatch Box*.
It's full of adventures for which the world was not prepared,
but for those who've found it, these can now be shared.
So settle back – no matter how far one roams,
it's *always* time for more about Sherlock Holmes.

The Shanghaied Surgeon
by C. H. Dye

The fourth of May, 1894, is not a day which I remember gladly. It was the third anniversary of when my friend Sherlock Holmes had disappeared at the Reichenbach Falls, and the few weeks which had passed since our dramatic encounter with Colonel Sebastian Moran had not yet convinced my sleeping brain that I hadn't dreamt up his return out of loneliness.

My morning began all too early, when I was roused from a dream of waterfalls by a call to the side of one of my elderly patients. The weather was vile, the fog thick and poisonous, and I had no sooner managed to return than I was called out upon another visit. My neighbor, Dr. Anstruther, who had so often obliged when I was called away, was equally busy, and when I returned to my Kensington practice for my surgery hours I found myself dealing with his patients as well as my own.

Mrs. O'Brien, the elderly cook whose skills I had begun sharing with Anstruther after my wife's death, stumbled as she travelled between the houses, throwing out her back, and dropping the tureen in which she was bringing my luncheon soup. Once I'd settled her into her bed next door, I sent over my maid to attend her, as the poor child's asthmatic wheezing was disconcerting to anyone desperate enough to brave the fog. After a hasty meal of bread and jam, I began my afternoon rounds. I was crossing Campden Hill Road when my horse threw a shoe, which meant leaving both horse and carriage in an unfamiliar stable while I completed my duties via hansom cabs when I could find one, and the Underground when I could not. Eventually, I arrived home to a dark house and a cold hearth. I stopped inside the door to collect the letters that had fallen through the slot and took them to my study, where I could sit whilst I ascertained whether there was any urgent message.

When I discovered the telegram from Holmes inviting me to come and have my supper at Baker Street among the rest, I thought for a moment that I was dreaming again. But no, there on the shelf was the row of books which Holmes had carried for his disguise as an old bookseller only a few weeks before. *British Birds*, *Catullus*, *The Holy War* – all as real under my hand as my stethoscope. Again I felt the burst of joy which had overwhelmed me when I first saw Holmes alive in that same room, and I confess I had to pause for a moment to compose myself. A glance at my watch showed me that it was just past seven in the evening. Early enough that Holmes might not yet have given me up, and not so late that Mrs. Hudson wouldn't find me a bite of something whether her capricious lodger had dined already or not. With a much lighter heart, I gathered up my coat and hat and set out for Baker Street.

The first cabstand I reached was empty, and so was the next, and by then I was far enough past the Underground station that it seemed only reasonable to keep walking. I was not Sherlock Holmes, but I knew my own part of London well enough to feel confident that I would not go astray. I was a few yards from Hyde Park when I heard a vigorous knocking off to my left. The rattle of a sash followed, and a voice coming down through the fog crying, "It's no good you pounding the door. The doctor's gone to Camden, and he won't be back for hours yet."

It had been a long day, and I was as invisible to the people I could hear as they were to me. But I found myself turning toward them all the same. "Do you need a doctor?" I called. A few more steps brought me into view of a lanky young man wearing the wide-bottomed trousers and pea-coat of a sailor who was just coming down the steps of a small portico to meet me. The red surgery lamp behind him combined with the fog to give him a devilish halo, I noted in passing, but he was already reaching out to take my hand.

"You're a doctor?"

"I am. John Watson at your service." I accepted his handshake and he began to lead me toward a waiting carriage.

"Jack Smith. You haven't got no bag with you," he noticed, a frown wrinkling his face.

"It's back at my surgery," I assured him. "Not a ten-minute walk."

"Best ride there anyway, or I'll never find you again in the fog. Oy, Bill, I've got us a doctor!"

Bill was a burly older man with a black beard, dressed like a tradesman with a canvas coat and a plaid cap. He appeared from the far side of the carriage as we approached, his hands jammed into his pockets as if he were cold. "Don't look much like a doctor to me," he grumbled, eyeing me with suspicion. "More like Army."

"I was a surgeon with the Fifth Northumberland Fusiliers once upon a time," I said, finding one of my cards to hand him.

He brightened at my words and took the card. "Army doc, eh? Bet you've set a bone or two in your time. All right, Jack, you take the top and I'll ride inside with the doc. And don't waste time, you hear me?"

"Right-o!" Jack leapt up to the driver's seat, whilst Bill and I clambered inside the carriage. It was a very nice carriage, I noticed. Not the sort of thing you'd expect a pair of Cockneys dressed like my companions to be driving. I studied the accoutrements as we started off. Velvet curtains drawn against the fog, an isinglass window at the back, and brightly polished brass fittings.

"You're working for a rich man," I deduced, pleased with myself for applying Holmes's precepts.

"Something like that," Bill said, and drew a revolver out of his pocket. He tossed a sack at me. "Now, put that over your head and sit quiet and you just might make it home alive."

I was far too flabbergasted to protest, and Bill was handling his gun with far too much familiarity for me to think he was neither unwilling nor incapable of using it. I swallowed my annoyance and put the bag over my head. They'd kidnapped the wrong man, I consoled myself. Sherlock Holmes would notice I was missing and come find me. All I had to do was wait.

Three days later, I was still waiting.

It did occur to me that Holmes would have precious little to go on. I wracked my brain, trying to think whether or not I had heard the window close above our heads whilst I was meeting Jack and Bill. I tried to remember whom I had spoken to as I walked, and could only summon up a nod to the newspaper vendor a few feet from my front door. I had passed one or two other pedestrians in the fog, exchanging nods in the way of strangers caught by the same unpleasant circumstance, but I hadn't looked at their faces and I very much doubted they had looked at mine. And even if Holmes did find that I had been taken away by carriage, how on earth was he to trace that carriage to the docks, or me across the water to the battered steam freighter where my patients were waiting?

Jack and Bill, it turned out, were working for a mysterious figure they called only "Himself", whom they feared as much as trusted by the way they spoke of him. I didn't dare ask for a name. It was bad enough that I had already turned over my card to Bill without advertising my connection to Sherlock Holmes. If it was Colonel Moriarty taking up the reins of his brother's criminal empire, or worse yet, the Professor himself somehow back from the dead, then my life would not be worth tuppence. Not that being taken at random for my medical expertise was much better. It meant, if I were not mistaken, that Holmes would have even less chance of finding me.

My services had been required to repair the damage from an altercation between two rival dockyard gangs, both of which "Himself" wished to recruit for his purposes. That five of my patients were traditionally rivals to the rest complicated matters, despite Bill's insistence that the fight had ended in a temporary truce. I quite had to engage in a demonstration of my own skill at fisticuffs to ensure that the ship's hold which served as a makeshift hospital didn't become the scene of a new battle.

My authority established, I proceeded to work myself into a state of exhaustion, chipping away at the difficulties: Stitching wounds here, binding broken limbs there, and attempting to convince eighteen filthy ruffians that their health would be better served by soap and water than the gin they guzzled endlessly. The honest citizens of London might have preferred me to do less than my best, but my medical instincts had come to the fore. I contented myself with memorizing names and descriptions, and the hope that the men whose injuries were mending would mention my name somewhere that Holmes might hear it as I released them from my care.

I was down to nine patients when it became clear that in at least one instance, my attempt at antisepsis – despite my situation – had failed to prevent the worst. I placed new bandages over the gangrenous wound, patted the patient – an older man named Willis with a singular collection of rude verses to popular songs – on the shoulder, and went to find Bill in his cubby at the end of the hold.

"I'm going to need my surgical instruments," I told him. They had been fairly good about providing me with the basic necessities, but Willis had gone beyond the point where needle and thread, bandages and hope would be enough. "My *personal* instruments." I rubbed at the shoulder wound which had cost me my army career. "I've got to take that leg off, and my own instruments have been made to compensate for the damage which was done to my arm at Maiwand."

"What damage?" he scoffed, looking me up and down. "You seem healthy enough to me."

I bristled, not being accustomed to having my word disregarded. It seemed as if the only way to convince him would be to show him the scar, and I had no intention of parading it around. I was about to say so, when a small voice in the back of my head observed that whether or not Sherlock Holmes could trace a man who had disappeared from a foggy street, he had a much better chance than most at tracing a surgical kit that had been stolen in the night. The burglars would leave clues behind, and I'd be rescued.

"This damage," I said, trying to keep the triumph from my voice, and began to unbutton my collar.

It was the next morning – at least, I assume it was morning – and I was attempting to drain the pus from my patient's wound for the fifth

40

time since supper, when the hatch at the far end of the hold opened and Sherlock Holmes dropped through, clutching my surgical kit. He was a mess. His hair was standing on end and his face was white with cold, where it wasn't dark with bruises. He was also wearing a battered suit of bright blue and yellow checks and an air of untrustworthy *naïveté*, which meant that he was playing a role of some kind, so I bit my tongue instead of calling out his name. He looked about like a man in an unfamiliar shop until his eyes lighted upon me. His smile bloomed. "Doctor!" he cried, coming hurriedly to my side. "There you are! Those fellows said you wanted your surgical kit, but there weren't no note, and I said they couldn't have it. Said they weren't going to fool Stanley Hopkins, I did, and that if they wanted it they'd have to take me, too, so I could put it into your hands me own self."

"So I see," I said, hoping that my moustache would hide the twitch of my own lips. Stanley Hopkins, was it? Well, at least the initials were the same. Aware that Bill had popped out of his cubby to see what was happening, and that I had an audience amongst those of my patients who were well enough to take an interest, I steered Holmes into the chair at the corner of my makeshift ward so I could examine his injuries. His left eye was swollen half-shut, and he had a bruise on his chin, but his teeth all seemed to be in place, and there was no damage to his ears. He hadn't shaved, I realized – not for at least two days. And his pallor wasn't only from the cold. "Have you been eating or sleeping?" I asked softly, although I knew the answer. I had seen Holmes drive himself into this state before, far too often. "Did Lestrade bring you a case?"

"I've been looking for you," Holmes grumbled indignantly. "Everywhere." And in that moment, I could see how much my disappearance had disturbed him. He is not a sentimental sort of fellow, not in the usual way of things. His mind spends so much time among the clouds that I sometimes believe people are often quite unreal to him. Death and murder are often only the source of grist for the extraordinary mills of his mind. But I am a doctor, and have witnessed too many times the fear of loss as war or disease seek to rob a man of the ones he loves. I knew the look in the grey eyes which were searching my countenance for signs of damage as avidly as mine had done his.

"And now you've found me," I said gently, dropping a hand to his shoulder for a moment to convey my gratitude. I smiled and reached for the kit he'd brought me. "And you can make yourself useful, as my assistant. We've got an amputation to be done."

The operation went as well as I could hope for. Holmes hadn't eaten enough to be sick, and Willis was too weak and I suspect rather too

41

drunk to fight the ether before the scalpel bit into his flesh. We got the leg off in good time, and I made a decent job of the stump, pouring antiseptic everywhere I could, and injecting morphine now that I had access to a trustworthy supply. Within the hour my patient's fever was coming down, and I felt able to relax my vigilance.

Holmes offered to take on the task of sterilising my surgical instruments in case they might be needed again. He somehow persuaded Jack to escort him to the boiler room of the ship, where he could blast them with steam from a valve. He brought back a bucket of clean, hot, water for our own use as well, and the news that the ship's crew appeared to be preparing for a long sea voyage.

"That's torn it, then," I told Holmes, as we washed up before retreating to the cot which I had claimed for my own use. "Not much chance of Lestrade finding us if we're not in London to be found."

Holmes wrinkled his nose at my mention of the Scotland Yard detective. "Lestrade hadn't much chance of finding us in the first place," he whispered back. "But don't worry. I have a plan."

"A plan?" I repeated, feeling my eyebrows rising. "And did your plan, by any chance, begin with letting yourself get kidnapped too?"

"Well, it was the fastest way to find you," Holmes admitted. "We just have to wait for our captors to lock us away somewhere that they can't observe us."

"Holmes," I said with weary dismay. "I have spent the last several days here, in this hold, under constant observation."

"*Hopkins*," Holmes reminded me, and then shrugged, undaunted. "Any plan is subject to change, isn't it?"

I closed my eyes, suddenly overcome with exhaustion, and rubbed my face in my hands. We were about to vanish from the face of England, and quite possibly the face of the earth entirely, and I didn't have optimism enough to sustain myself without some sleep. "You think about it, 'Hopkins'," I told him. "And let me know when you've thought of something clever."

He patted me on the shoulder before pulling a short clay pipe and his tobacco pouch from his pocket. "I will, old chap," he said. "I will."

It was the most restful sleep I'd had since I was kidnapped, but I woke when the ship shuddered and the ominous rattle of gigantic chains announced the raising of the anchor. I had been covered with a blanket as I slept, by Holmes no doubt, who was stretched out belly-down on another blanket on the floor beside me, his head pillowed on his jacket. He lifted it, at the clang of a hatch somewhere out of view, looking for all the world like some wild creature scenting danger on the wind. I glanced to see how my patients were reacting to the deepening beat of the engines and realized that four of them had gone while I dozed. I was down to just Willis and the men from the smaller gang.

"Where do you suppose we're going?" I asked Holmes.

"The dock, first, to take on a load of freight," Holmes said. "And from there, who knows?"

Jack, who was just coming up with the bread and beans that would constitute our luncheon, laughed. "You're right clever," he told my friend. "Clever enough to make yourself useful as the doc, do you think?"

"I'm bright as a lark," Holmes said cheekily, sitting up and leaning his back against the cot before accepting the tin plate Jack offered. "Will we be going as far as India, do you know?" he asked, all enthusiasm, but with glance at me as a clear reminder of his charade. "The doctor's been there, but I never have. Or China! Now there's a place to see!"

"Hopkins!" I exclaimed, sitting up to take my own plate. "Don't tell me you're looking forward to being dragged halfway round the world!"

"Well, it will be an adventure, won't it?" Holmes appeared perfectly happy at the prospect. "Think on it, Doctor. Just imagine the possibilities!"

"I have been," I said drily. "And I can't say I'm pleased." I turned to Jack. "Come now. You said that once I'd taken care of medical matters, you'd let me go home."

"Well, that was before," Jack said, blithely.

"Before? Before what?" I blustered, waving a hand at my other patients. "I've done my best, and they'll all be on their feet in a week or so, barring Willis, who'd be better off in a proper hospital."

"And so he will be," Jack said. "Once you get him ready to be moved. His hands are worth something, yet, but there's no one what's got need of a one-legged sailor. But the Captain's been trying to get a decent doc aboard for years, and now that he's paid Himself two-hundred pounds for a finder's fee, he's bound and determined to get his money's worth."

"Two-hundred pounds?" Holmes whistled. "For Doctor Watson?"

"How do you mean?" I said, growing quite angry. "I'm not a prize to be bought and sold!" I shared my glare between Jack and Holmes. "This is intolerable!"

"If you'd've been incompetent," Jack pointed out in an infuriatingly familiar manner, "we'd've let you go."

"If he'd been incompetent," said a new voice with a thick Dutch accent, "we'd have dropped him over the side." A tall, heavyset blond man wearing the uniform of a ship's officer had come up behind me, and now he put a heavy, possessive hand on my shoulder. "You should be grateful," he told Holmes. "The doctor's competence will keep you alive too."

First Mate Duykens made it clear that Captain Clavart had little patience with complaints – mine, or my patients, who were not happy to discover that they too (with the exception of Willis) were about to become seafarers. In fact, Duykens wanted them to begin work straight away, and had come down to the hold with the ship's book, where we were expected to sign on as members of the crew. Holmes was the only one who did so with aplomb, the scrawl he put on the page being nothing like his usual signature. I signed with a gun literally at my friend's head, and a similar incentive was used on my patients.

I did have to insist that Duykens leave all but the two who had recovered the most to continue to rest in my care. "Either I am competent, and I know that these men cannot be set to lifting heavy objects without setting back their recovery by weeks, or I am incompetent and your captain has made a bad bargain," I expounded. "Which would you rather tell him?"

"How long until they can work?" Duykens asked, looking at the other men as if he were calculating whether or not it would be simpler to just dispose of them.

"A week, two at the most. And they'd recover faster with foods that would build up their blood." I'd asked for that already, but iron wines are expensive and I did not expect a concession now.

"I can work," Holmes piped up. "I'm much stronger than I look."

Duykens studied him suspiciously. "Very well," he said at last. "But if you try to escape, the doctor will pay for it. He does not have to die to suffer the consequences."

"I wouldn't dream of getting the doctor into trouble," Holmes said, very much on his dignity.

I snorted, remembering the many times in which Holmes had endangered me. Although to be fair, he generally endangered the both of us. "You think this is all some grand adventure, don't you, Hopkins?" I said.

"Of course," he replied easily. "It will be something to write home about. Speaking of which," he turned to Duykens, "is there any chance I can send a wire? I'd best let Mrs. H know to put my things in the shed in the yard if I'm to be away a while, so's she can let the room to some other bloke."

Duykens frowned. "You are married?"

"No, no. She's my landlady is all. She gets a bit fussed when I don't come in for supper."

Duykens frowned at Holmes, and then at the ship's book with our names in it. "I will ask the Captain," he said at last. "Perhaps he will let you post your message when we reach Leyden. Now finish your meal and then report to the bosun." He scowled at the newest members of his crew. "You have much to do to earn your keep."

It wasn't until Bill and Holmes were busy removing my remaining patients to a small crew cabin on one of the lower decks that I discovered Holmes's message in my pocket. It was written in the curious shorthand he sometimes used to communicate with his Irregulars, which I thought placed far too much confidence in my memory, but with a little though I got the gist of it. Lestrade was watching the hospitals, and I should take any chance I could find to send a message to him. Accordingly, I fetched out my notebook and wrote two messages, one for the doctor who would take on Willis, recommending that he replace the bandaging as soon as possible, and another to the Inspector, which I managed to tuck inside the top layer of the bandage on Willis's leg while Jack was checking through my surgical kit for the supply of ferrum tartaratum I kept there. Willis complained about the taste when I mixed a bit of the stuff into his gin, but I made no never mind, as I felt quite pleased with myself for having managed the business with the note under the bandage. I dosed him once again with morphine for the trip to the nearest hospital ashore, and hoped it would keep him from interfering with whichever doctor chanced to read my note.

Once Willis was gone, I was escorted out of the cargo hold, and Holmes was hustled off to be of use in loading the ship. The cabin which held my patients had no room for me, and so after a consultation with First Mate Duykens, I was locked into a neighboring compartment to keep me from causing trouble until the ship was safely out to sea. My new prison cell was carved out of the curve of the hull near the prow, an awkward shape with no more space than an ambitious broom cupboard, and was already half-filled with the crew's cold weather gear. There were no portholes to the outside world. The only light came from a small round window set into the middle of the door. Frustratingly, it was set too high to be of use. Even had I been able to break the glass, my arm would never have stretched far enough to release the lock. I tried peering along the passage for a while, but there was precious little to see.

Apparently this was the first area where supplies had been stowed away for our journey, and no one needed to come this way. The shouts and thumps from above decks as the cargo was loaded were muffled and the beat of the engines so rhythmic that I was hard-pressed to stay awake. I soon found it necessary to abandon my vigil and curl up on a pile of duffle bags in lieu of being able to lie down properly. I may have daydreamed a bit. I certainly found myself wishing that I'd insisted that Jack hand over my surgical kit before I was confined. Imagining what I might do with a morphine-loaded syringe in my hand was a far pleasanter occupation than wondering when and whether I might be allowed to go ashore once the ship had reached the far side of the world.

A tapping at the door brought me back to myself. With a start, I realized that by the motion beneath me the ship had sailed. The tapping came again and I disentangled myself to go see who it was.

It was Holmes. He grinned at me from a face that would have done a chimney sweep discredit and held up a hand with a filthy rag tied round it. "I have need of your medical skills, Watson," he shouted through the glass.

I sighed. "Naturally," I said, and then shouted back. "You'll have to get someone to let me out!"

"Oh!" Holmes said as if the thought had just occurred to him. "Right!" His face ceased to block my view, and I watched as he trotted up the passage. He was nursing the bandaged hand a bit, but he didn't seem badly hurt. And he had clearly already ingratiated himself with the crew. Jack, coming back with Holmes chattering after him, didn't even bother to adjust the pistol in his belt as a threat.

There was no sign of Bill, or any other guard. Perhaps now that we were on our way our captors felt safe in lowering their vigilance. I bit down a smile. They'd soon learn otherwise.

Jack unlocked the door and swung it open. "Come along, Doc," he said. "It's time you checked on your charges."

"More than time," I growled. "Why, we must be halfway to France by now."

"Not quite,' Holmes said. "I believe we are just passing Tilbury Fort."

Now that was news I could use! There was little point in obtaining control of the gun if we were too far to swim for land, but with the shore of the river so close, we had a chance of escape. Besides, I owed Jack a few bruises from my kidnapping. I waited until he had turned his head to answer one of Holmes's questions about the port of Calcutta, and then spun on my heel and delivered an uppercut that felled him like a rotted tree.

Holmes looked down at me as I bent to fetch the revolver, his eyebrows high. "That wasn't necessary, Watson," he said, as if he resented having the answer to his question go unfinished.

46

"It most certainly was," I replied, checking to see how many bullets I had now at my command. Only three, unfortunately. "We're getting off this ship while it's still in England."

"Of course we are," Holmes said, lending me a hand as I hauled Jack back into the compartment where I had been stranded. "I'm just saying that you didn't need to hit him. I've already arranged for us to go."

For a man whose bruises were only obscured by the filthy condition of his person, Holmes seemed unreasonably certain of himself. "Don't tell me you've bargained with this scoundrel," I protested, indicating Jack. "He's not to be trusted, Holmes."

"Oh, nothing like that," said Holmes. "I've sabotaged the coal store. It should catch fire any minute now."

"You *what*?"

Well, obviously, we couldn't lock Jack into a compartment if it meant he might be trapped aboard a burning ship. Nor could I, in good conscience, leave my patients to flounder ashore unaided when they were in no condition to go for a swim. A single pistol was no good against an entire crew of men, either. We debated the difficulties whilst finding rope to tie Jack – a much more difficult proposition aboard a steamship than it would have been on the sailing ships of our youth. Holmes was uncertain of his timing. The glass flask of sulfuric acid which was the core of the exothermic reaction that he had rigged needed only to tip, rather than break, but in either case the process needed to be triggered by the settling of the coal in the bin as the stokers did their work. Then there was the need to find my surgical kit, and to clean out the gash Holmes had deliberately given himself so as to be allowed to find me. And all the while, the ship continued to make its steady way farther and farther away from London.

Fortunately, my patients were willing to cooperate with us. Unfortunately, my kit wasn't with them – Duykens had taken it away, along with the gin – and the poor fellows were in a good bit of pain. That, and the necessity of hauling a gagged Jack along with us, impeded our decision to acquire one of the ship's boats by stealth. Nevertheless, we crept our way through passageways and up gangways until we reached the upper deck, and only had to take one additional hostage on our way. I've never been so glad to see Southend in my life. We were close enough to make out the workmen, just finishing construction on the great pier, and I wondered whether they could have heard a shout for help, or paid attention to it if they did.

Holmes waved me back into the shelter of the passageway. "You keep an eye on things, Watson," he said. "I'll scout ahead."

"Good plan," I said. And it might have been, if at that moment Duykens and two of the crew hadn't come around the corner and seen us. Duykens immediately drew a gun from his pocket, so I potted him one in the arm to keep him from using it. The gunshot *did* attract attention from shore, so I can't say that it was any great surprise that the battle which followed was interrupted. Eventually.

By that time, of course, Holmes and I were losing. We'd done our best to defend our position, but we were badly outnumbered. Duykens cared little about Jack or the other sailor we'd taken hostage, and he knew exactly how many bullets I had left. He threatened us with charges of mutiny, pointing out that we'd signed the ship's papers, and we countered with charges of kidnapping. And then he sent men around to attack us from the rear and the fistfight began.

All of which led to a grand brouhaha spilling out onto the main deck. I rather enjoyed that part, having wanted to hit someone for days. But even with the other shanghaied men joining in our side it couldn't last, and first Holmes, and then I went down under a pile of sailors. Duykens was hauling me to my feet by my collar when the thump of a shot from a boatgun and the sight of a small cannonball striking the quarterdeck startled us all into silence.

"Steamship *Friesland*!" came a shout through a bullhorn off to our side. "This is the police! Return to port, or face the consequences!" Duykens didn't let go of me as he went to the side to see who had shouted. I looked over the side and saw an armed police launch, with Lestrade and standing midships whilst two constables reloaded the gun. "The navy has been alerted!" the good inspector continued. "Give it up! You won't get five miles from shore!" The real Stanley Hopkins was commanding a second police launch near our stern, and I could see a third official boat approaching beyond that.

"Excellent!" Holmes said, a few sailors down the rail from me. "Look, Watson, we've been rescued!"

Which was when the ship exploded.

Holmes admitted later that he had miscalculated. He meant the fire in the coal store to distract the crew, not sink the ship. Luckily, the entire ship's crew had come above decks in the fight and no one was below to be killed. Still the force of the blast was enough to hurl us all off the deck, and render our ears useless with ringing as we plunged into the water. The water was cold, and my collar bone, weakened by the old wound, could not withstand the strain. Worse, when I came the surface there was no sign of Holmes. I flailed about in search of him, one-handed, till something bumped against my leg. For some reason I thought first of sharks, and struck out with knee and hand, but when my fingers encountered hair, I swallowed my fears and pulled the owner to the surface. It was Holmes, barely conscious, and it was all I could do to keep his nose and mouth above the waves. We were both within a hair's breadth of drowning by the time Hopkins swam to us with a rope and we were pulled onto the launch.

It was some time before the rescues were complete, and Lestrade could lead his flotilla of police launches back to London. There everyone was bundled off to Charing Cross Hospital, where it was discovered that Holmes had two broken fingers, and three cracked ribs, a mild concussion, and a blackened eye to match the bruise on my knee. My own injuries, apart from the broken collarbone, were equally minor. Giddy with elation, exhaustion, and exposure, we took a cab to Baker Street, where Mrs. Hudson fussed over us as if we were errant schoolboys rather than full grown men. She forbade me to leave until I'd had a hot bath, a good dinner, and a decent night's sleep. Then she turned her batteries on Holmes, who accepted her admonishments with an uncharacteristic meekness when he discovered that she had confiscated every scrap of tobacco in the house against his good behaviour. But despite her eucalyptus steam, mustard plasters, and other old fashioned precautions, by morning we were both quite ill.

It was not until a day or so later that I felt well enough to face the prospect of returning to my practice. I had fallen all too easily into the indolent habits of the invalid, and the comforting rhythms of my old home. Holmes, once we were both able to manage staying awake for more than an hour or two, had recruited me into helping reduce the great drift of newspapers which his brother had accumulated for him over the past three years, but that occupation, however pleasant the company, was unlikely to save me from penury. Accordingly, I dressed before breakfast, meaning to make a start as soon as I had fortified myself.

When I descended to the sitting room, I found that Inspector Lestrade had joined Holmes at the table and was working his way through a plate of kippers. The little inspector's usually natty attire was rumpled and damp, and I could see at a glance that he was short of sleep. But he greeted me all the same. "Good morning, Doctor. I see you're recovering nicely."

I nodded my thanks as Holmes got up from his place to retrieve our spare chair and set it by the table for me. "Lestrade's come by to tell me that I shan't be arrested for creating a nuisance in a major shipping lane," he said, a smile tugging at the corners of his mouth. "It seems I've done the nation a service, after all."

Lestrade nodded, and put a coin on the table by my plate. "Take a look at that, doctor."

It looked like an old sovereign, one that had been minted in King George's day and passed from hand to hand through the generations until the pattern had worn down. But on the obverse someone had scratched through the gold, revealing a center of dull grey metal. "An old counterfeit?" I asked.

Lestrade shook his head. "A new one. We found that, and near five-thousand more just like it, in Captain Clavert's quarters when we salvaged the ship."

"It's a clever ploy," Holmes said. "By counterfeiting an old coin instead of a new one, any discrepancies in the electroplating of the gold outer layer can be dismissed as a result of the aging of the coin. At least in poor light. Or somewhere that most men have seen few of these coins."

"But you can imagine the problems that much false coinage would create," Lestrade said.

"Five-thousand of these?" I certainly could. But I couldn't see an ordinary counterfeiter making the effort and said as much. "Even as a thin finish, that must have taken quite a bit of gold." I passed the coin back to Lestrade.

"Clavert claims he never looked in the money chests. He was given them by a man he calls Lord Downey. Money to purchase spices and coffee in the East Indies, according to his tale. Not that there's any noble by that name and description."

"'Himself'," I said. I'd told Holmes about my misadventures, and now I explained what had happened to Lestrade. "For a time I thought Bill and Jack might be referring to Professor Moriarty, come back from the dead." I admitted with an apologetic smile to Holmes.

"You weren't the only one wondering about that," Holmes said. "The timing of your disappearance seemed significant. I thought at first that Colonel Moran might have arranged it. And yet, however unlikely it seems to us, the date was a mere coincidence. Any physician at all might have fallen afoul of the gang's need for medical assistance. I think this so called 'Lord' is either an opportunist, seeking to create a new spider's web, or, far more likely, an agent of a foreign government, looking to cause grief and upset in our distant colonies."

Lestrade sighed and pushed away his now-empty plate before getting to his feet and reaching for his hat. "He made a mistake in taking you, Dr. Watson, no matter what his reason. He'll live to regret it, considering all the evidence the Yard and the Foreign Office have amassed against him during this salvage job. Which reminds me – young Hopkins found your kit." Lestrade nodded to the hearth, where I saw the familiar leather case propped against the coal scuttle, still dripping into a pile of Mrs. Hudson's rags. "Not that you'll be needing it now that you've come home to Baker Street."

I started to say that of course I would need it, and that I'd be returning to my practice quite soon, but I found myself unwilling to say the words. Instead I stammered out something about my gratitude and busied myself with plate and cup whilst Holmes saw Lestrade out. Holmes, too, had fallen into a brown study. He abandoned the table in favor of his pipe and chair, and it wasn't until I had finished my breakfast that he spoke again.

"Lestrade has always been a master of the obvious, but I think that in this instance I shall have to concede him the prize." My friend focussed a fierce glare upon me. "You *should* stay."

"My patients . . . ." I began, and Holmes waved away the objection.

"Physicians are two-a-penny in London. Sell your practice and they'll be none the worse for it."

"And how am I to live, then?" I asked. "You've made it clear you don't want me writing more about your cases." It was a sore point with me, for Holmes had stated with certainty that I was not to publish again without his permission.

Holmes made a moue of frustration. "From the two stories that you first published before my supposed death, Moriarty learned enough about my methods to begin obscuring the evidence. It's what made him so difficult to pin down. And now that there are even more examples for a clever criminal to . . . ." He stopped and shook his head. "I don't need a biographer, Watson. But I've reviewed my past cases, and it's clear that the work goes better when I have a . . . a sounding board. An amanuensis. A . . . ."

"A *friend*?" I asked, feeling a smile trying to escape. "One who takes notes and calms down elderly ladies with missing cats?" That had been my role, once, and I knew Holmes would remember the case, for he'd grumbled about it for months afterwards.

Holmes laughed, much relieved. "Yes. It might not pay as much, given that hardly any of my potential clients know that I'm alive, but I think in time it might equal the income from your medical work."

It would probably pay better. Mary's illness, and my own after her death, had reduced my list sharply, and I'd scarcely had time to rebuild it before Holmes had returned. The house in Kensington held mostly bitter memories. And whether or not Holmes let me *publish*, I could always *write* about our adventures. "I'll think about it, Holmes," I told him. "I'll think about it."

> *. . . I find, on looking over my notes, that this period includes . . . the shocking affair of the Dutch steamship* Friesland, *which so nearly cost us both our lives.*

Dr. John H. Watson – "The Adventure of the Norwood Builder"

The Trusted Advisor
by David Marcum

Sherlock Holmes sniffed. He was not ill, and he wasn't encountering an unpleasant odor, or checking the result of some test in his chemical corner. Rather, he was glancing through my notes regarding a past investigation, presented to him for his thoughts, and it was the sniff of distaste.

I knew that for the present he would let pass whatever had caused this sentiment – for that is certainly what it signified – but at some point in the future, it would be mentioned whenever we chanced to discuss my writings. In fact, there was more to discuss than before, as Holmes had only recently returned from a three-year hiatus in which he was believed to be dead, and during that time a great many of my efforts, previously contained in my private journals, had, by way of a literary agent of my acquaintance, come to the attention of the public within a relatively new monthly periodical.

I considered ignoring him – either leaving the room for other business, or focusing more intently upon the volume of sea stories which was singularly failing to hold my attention. But then he sniffed again, and physician that I am, I decided to address the symptoms in order to identify the cause of the problem before it could spread.

"To what," I asked, my voice sounding more formal than I would have wished, "do you object?"

He flipped back a page or two – carefully, I was glad to see, since he was reading from one of my personal journals. It contained the only extant copy of an unpublished case, and was not one of the easily replaced blue-backed magazines that were stacked on my nearby desk, containing the published stories.

Finding the example that he sought, he read, rather theatrically, "'*I am not sure that of all the five-hundred cases of capital importance which I have handled there is one which cuts so deep.*'"

I raised an eyebrow. He was farther into the journal than I had realized, and I had expected that he would object to the earlier passages relating the budding romance between our former client and his beautiful neighbor. She had lived across the dangerous expanse of Dartmoor, and in spite of many warnings and attempts to circumvent it, she had still served as bait in a trap. I had been prepared to defend my narrative relating to this factor of the case, as it had occurred just as reported, during a time when Holmes had not yet been there to observe it. Instead, he had focused on something that he himself had said.

I remarked on that fact, to which he replied, rather peevishly, "Surely I would not have placed the number so low."

"I am certain that you said five-hundred."

"Five *times* five-hundred, perhaps," he retorted. "Perhaps you are unaware of exactly many cases that I *have* handled."

"That *is* an accurate statement," I replied, shifting in my chair, the battle joined. "As you well know, you are the original clam in terms of keeping facts to yourself." I found that I was becoming rather heated. "I know surprisingly few of your early cases, except for those few that you've chosen to relate – the old Russian woman, and that business down at Hurlstone, and the Eye of Heka, of course." I would never again be able to smell ammonia without recalling the madman's plot that was so narrowly averted.

"I think," he replied, shutting my journal with a finger to mark his place, "that I've shared quite a few more than just those."

"Still, you cannot deny that you jealously retain facts – sometimes for no other reason than the dramatic effect that they will produce during their revelation. And – "

I stopped myself abruptly, for I had nearly crossed a line that I had drawn for myself – namely, to avoid mentioning the still-painful revelation, upon Holmes's recent return to London, that he hadn't shared with me that he had been alive during those three years when he was presumed dead.

He'd explained the reasons why I wasn't told, while his brother Mycroft had been aware, and they made sense. He was doing work for the government around the world, and Mycroft had provided him with necessary funds and transportation. The late Professor Moriarty's organization, though broken, was still in existence, and they – especially the Professor's two brothers who had attempted to revive it – had been watching me, and any indication that Holmes still lived would have caused disaster for both him and me, and those that I loved. Finally, during that time my poor wife's health had been steadily declining, which is where my attention needed to be focused. Still, I don't think that Holmes realized, until he returned, just how the loss of both my best friend – more of a brother to me than my own by blood had ever been – and my wife in the space of just a couple of years had nearly broken me.

I had filled some of my time by writing up narratives from my cases for publication in a popular periodical, knowing at the time that, if Holmes could see from beyond the veil, where I believed him to be, he would certainly be disappointed. He had been tolerant –at best – of my first writing effort in late 1887, and less so with the second in 1890. Now, he had returned to London to find that another round two-dozen of them had appeared in print while he was gone – "Like drodded mushrooms," he had muttered at one point.

Discussions about this had already occurred since his return, as might be expected. Sometimes cordial, sometimes less so, but the upshot was that Holmes wished for the cessation of publication of his cases – but only, I was happy to hear, for the present. The door wasn't entirely shut, and in a quiet conversation, he had allowed that I might keep recording events as they occurred – "for the archives", he had said – with an eye toward future publication.

But I was somewhat disappointed at the immediate embargo, as I had already completed a number of polished manuscripts that I had hoped to place – this time on my own, as my literary agent had grown quite weary of his own works being overshadowed and neglected by his association with Holmes. That morning, I had – unwisely, as it turned out – showed Holmes the write-up of our trip to Dartmoor to investigate a scheme wherein an old family legend was used to attempt the theft of an inheritance. I had thought that reading it might convince Holmes to lift his stricture on publications – but of course I was incorrect.

While I swallowed what I'd been about to say regarding Holmes's failure to tell me that he was actually alive between 1891 and 1894, he had been flipping through my journal, likely looking for some other example to bolster his argument. He seemed to find what he wanted, and was about to jab with another quote when we heard the front doorbell ring.

We fell silent as we listened to Mrs. Hudson move downstairs. The front door opened, and there was murmured conversation before her steady step climbed to the sitting room. She knocked and entered, handing a small card to my friend. As his return to London was not yet common knowledge, I believe that we were both a bit surprised that he had a visitor. He looked at it with a tightened expression of distaste and then dropped it onto the low octagonal table that stood beside his chair, placing my journal more carefully beside it. "Show the gentleman up, Mrs. Hudson."

I raised an eyebrow. I considered asking who was now climbing the stairs, but I could see that Holmes was arranging his own thoughts, his mouth in a tight line and a frown closing his eyes to slits.

The caller's identity was soon revealed when the door opened to Mr. Nathaniel McGhee Hale. A small man in expensive clothing, he was one of the more recognizable figures of the day, and had been since before Holmes's presumed death. He had a bobbing head, set on narrow shoulders, and topped with neatly combed white hair, very thin and fine. His eyes were blue, and with his pinkish skin and reddish eyelids, he almost looked albino.

He had made a substantial fortune in any number of areas after decamping from the southern United States to England in the 1870's. He seemed to have the Midas Touch, steadily multiplying his wealth, but not without controversy and negative shades upon his reputation. The year before, although not widely known, his maneuverings had left the military low on cordite. At that time, cordite was a still relatively new munition, and mistakes had been made when estimating how much was available when re-outfitting the army, particularly for the .303 rifle.

This was the public account. Holmes and I had privately learned, during a recent visit with his brother Mycroft at the Diogenes Club regarding an unrelated matter, that the situation was much more serious than the public had realized, and that the man now facing us had been more heavily involved than followers of the daily press knew. And he had augmented his already substantial fortune because of it. More recently, his name had been associated with a number of mine disasters throughout Britain.

Holmes and I had stood as the man entered, and my friend directed Hale to the basket chair between us. Hale seemed as if he would offer his hand to the detective, but perceiving that it might not be readily accepted, he instead settled himself and began to speak.

"I'm here, Mr. Holmes, at the advice of Lord Evers," he said, his accent – Alabaman, I believe – even stronger than I had been led to understand from the news accounts. "He seems to think quite a bit of you, although he wouldn't say why."

"Then far be it from me to provide more information than he would," said Holmes. "I'm sure that you can expect the same sort of discretion, should I decide to accept your case."

"But you must!" countered Hale. "Why wouldn't you?"

"I'm not a public servant," replied Holmes. "I am a private consulting detective, and as such, I may pick and choose such work that interests me . . . and also the clients with whom I wish to associate. You arrived with no appointment, and I have a few minutes to spare to hear your story, but it remains to be determined whether I will be able to help you, or whether your case will be of interest."

Holmes clearly didn't like the man, and made no effort to hide it. Hale's face rotated through a series of expressions as Holmes spoke, clearly unaccustomed to this disdain in person. His countenance tightened and released while he considered his response. Finally he chose to simply present his story and hope for the best.

"I'm sure that both of you are aware of the events of recent months. I don't deny my involvement – I'm a businessman, and I took advantage of opportunities. I won't apologize. I could have just as easily lost everything."

Holmes glanced at me. I knew what he was silently asking, as it was likely that he did *not* know of all of the recent events, as he had only returned to London a month or so earlier, and since that time, he had been steadily involved in a number of cases, not the least of which was dealing with the matter of Professor Moriarty's nefarious brothers, both fighting each other to take over the criminal enterprise left by their late sibling, but managing to arrange a temporary truce to attack their common enemy, Mr. Sherlock Holmes.

I cleared my throat and mentioned the cordite affair, which Holmes knew about. Hale's mouth tightened, but he didn't speak. Then I continued, laying out the details, as I recalled them, of the more recent mining disasters. "The Dwfn Mine in Gwent, and more recently, the Albion in Yorkshire. Explosions. Several dozen men were killed, due to poor safety practices, likely caused," I concluded, glancing at Hale, "by the niggardly attitudes of the owners."

Holmes nodded and looked back at Hale. "I am not an engineer. I cannot advise you on mine explosions, except to say that you should open your pocket-book and make these hellish places somewhat more survivable for those who have to labor there."

"Those disasters," said Hale tightly, "are not why I'm here, Mr. Holmes. They are only the events that set me in motion to consult you. If I may continue?"

Holmes waved a hand.

"The doctor is correct. It was due to my stinginess – my own, and my partners – that safety in the mines was in such a poor state. But I have a widespread range of affairs, and I can't keep my eye upon every small detail. I assure you that I didn't know how bad that it was. I bought the controlling interest in those mines five years ago, and they were just as bad then, although I didn't know it. I had never actually visited them, you see. One allows oneself a certain comfortable ignorance. But I've since traveled to each of them, not just the ones where the explosions occurred, and I've taken steps to remedy the situation – both improving conditions in the mines, as well as providing compensation to survivors. I'm not a monster, despite what you might read.

"But a couple of months ago, when the worst of all of this was happening, and one disaster seemed to occur right after another, I made a mistake. I was lamenting my affairs to a fellow at my club, and he suggested that I visit that consulting fellow Lamont, of No. 12 Burleigh Street."

I knew the site well, since it was the office where *The Strand* had initially been located, before it quickly outgrew its digs and shifted to nearby No. 8 Southampton Street. I hadn't been in Burleigh Street in several years, despite passing its entrance on the Strand countless times.

I glanced at Holmes, to see if he had observed my reminiscences. He might not realize the significance of that address, as the magazine, which had published a substantial number of the accounts of his cases, had only established itself a few months before his supposed death at the Reichenbach Falls in early 1891, preceding my association.

He spoke, surprising me, as I had expected him to query about the significance of the address. Instead, he posed a different question.

"Lamont?" he said. "You mention him as if I should recognize the name."

Hale raised an eyebrow. "The consultant," he said, describing Lamont in the same manner as before. "The fellow who advertises himself as 'The Sherlock Holmes of Business Consulting', or some such. His motto is to make him your 'Trusted Advisor'."

Holmes looked at me, true puzzlement showing on his features. "Do you know of this man, Watson?"

I nodded. "He set himself up sometime last year as a type of problem-solver. From all accounts, he has made a fast rise." I turned toward Hale. "Although you may not have been aware, Holmes has been out of the country for an extended period. He hasn't yet had a chance to catch up on some of what has occurred in the capitol during his absence."

I rose from my chair and stepped over to Holmes's desk, where a tall pile of newspapers threatened to tip and avalanche to the floor. These had accumulated just since his return in early April, saved for when he had a spare rainy morning and could clip those articles of interest which would then find their way into his voluminous scrapbooks.

Pulling a recent edition from the top of the stack, I opened it to an inner page, turning past two or three sheets until I found the advertisement that I sought. Folding back the pages, I handed it to Holmes.

> *Difficulties? Complications? Disasters?*
> *Consult Dunmar Lamont*
> *"Your Trusted Advisor"*
> *Problems Solved – None Too Large or Small*
> *"The Sherlock Holmes of the Business World"*
> *12 Burleigh Street, London*

Holmes laid the paper aside. He glanced toward his scrapbooks, but I interjected, "It's unlikely you'll find anything about him there. He's quite new on the scene."

Holmes nodded and spoke to Hale. "Continue."

The little man cleared his throat. "When the various . . . difficulties were occurring – the continued problems associated with the cordite affair, and then the mine disasters – I had a period of a week or two where I felt exceptionally despondent. In a moment of weakness, I discussed it with a chap at my club, Edward Woodhouse. I shouldn't have spoken of it all all, but I was in a low spot, and Woodhouse asked me at just such a time that I'd be likely to reply. He suggested that I consult this Lamont fellow. 'He helped me to get on my feet again,' said he.

"I knew that Woodhouse had had a rough patch a few years ago – he had been a partner at Coxon and Woodhouse's, until they were nearly sunk in the spring of '89 through that disastrous Venezuelan loan. Woodhouse went on to explain that Lamont had given him advice a few months ago, and since then he'd been in such better shape that he was now a convert, steering people in that direction whenever he could.

"Well, the short of it is, I didn't see what it could hurt, although I wasn't clear on what exactly this Lamont fellow could accomplish. If nothing else, I'd learned that he was an American, like myself, so I thought that we might have some common ground. It took a couple of weeks to obtain an appointment, but finally Woodhouse took me along to the office in Burleigh Street. It's a little building on the corner, nothing special, and inside Lamont seemed to only make use of a couple of ground floor rooms – an empty reception area, with tall windows looking out upon the street, and an inner office – his sanctum, he called it.

"He only had a few comfortable chairs spread around on an expensive-looking rug. There was no desk, although there was something like a drafting table along one wall with papers spread across it. While Woodhouse waited outside in the reception area, Lamont and I found our seats, and I explained that I didn't know what he could do to help me, but that I was a bit stretched at the moment, dealing with various business issues. He asked a few pointed questions, and I ended up telling him more than I ought, but I'd researched him since Woodhouse had suggested a consultation, and it seemed as if he would be a good resource – a 'trusted advisor', as he puts it.

"After Lamont's questions were answered, we stood, and he said I should hear some good news soon. Woodhouse and I left, and when we were outside, I found that I was uncertain as to what to expect, or whether I had been a fool."

"Was there any discussion of compensation?" asked Holmes.

"I'd asked that question, and was told that it would be discussed when my problems were settled."

"Rather an open-ended arrangement for someone as reputedly canny as yourself to enter, sir,"

Hale nodded. "I agree. I can only say that I was at a low spot, and open to manipulation."

"And were your problems solved?"

"Let's just say I exchanged them for a different set of problems. Within a few days, Lloyd Addington, a rival and a very effective critic who was pressing me about the mining problems, was found dead, apparently of heart failure. Then, just a week or so ago, Lord Graeme, who has been quite the vocal antagonist over the last few months, fell in front of a speeding cab, dying instantly."

Holmes raised an eyebrow. "I recall reading about that. There was some question as to whether he was pushed from behind. Additionally, his own driver, supposed to meet him on another street, was puzzled as to why Lord Graeme was nearly two blocks away when he was killed."

Hale nodded. "Exactly. I thought nothing of these events – except, I will admit, to believe that they were fortuitous occurrences from my perspective – until I received a visit from Lamont a couple of days later.

"He presented himself at my home, asking if I found that my affairs had become less complicated of late. He had a smirk, which only grew as he perceived my puzzlement. Then he said, 'Surely you will find your way easier going forward without Mr. Addington or Lord Graeme to vex you?' His implication, of course, was that he was taking credit for their removal.

"I'll admit that I was shocked. If what he implied was true, then he was a murderer – and apparently proud of it, too. Why would he be admitting as much to me, unless he was somehow trying to implicate me in the matter?

"Leaping ahead, and understanding that he might try to make me complicit in the deaths, I replied, 'There is no way that you shall involve me in this matter, nor shall you press me for any payment! My consultation with you in no way connects me with any crime you have since committed on your own.'

"He laughed, and then said that it was beyond that. 'You think that I simply want money?' he asked. 'I shall have much more than that before we're done." He leaned forward. 'You fool. You didn't know just how much you revealed during our conversation. I was able to take what you told me, and use it to know exactly where to look for more of your secrets. By now, I know more about your affairs than you do. And certainly more than the authorities, who would dearly love to hear some of what you've been up to. Perhaps you'd be surprised to learn that I know about the – '"

Here, Hale broke off and swallowed. "Well, perhaps that's not something I want to discuss here, even with you, Mr. Holmes. Suffice it to say, Lamont had a pretty good idea of my business, including parts that I'd nearly forgotten myself. I can't say that I'm proud of it, but I did what had to be done. And now this man knows all of it, and wants to somehow use the leverage against me."

Holmes uncrossed his legs and leaned forward, as if preparing to stand. "You will have to take your medicine, Mr. Hale," he said. "There is nothing worse than a blackmailer, and normally my sympathies lie with the victims. But in your case, it rather sounds as if the two of you will cancel each other out. You really have only two options – pay him, as I assume he wants compensation, or kill him. I will be quite curious to see how it plays out, but I must intervene, at least peripherally, by letting the police know that Lamont should be evaluated in light of Lord Graeme's death. I thank you for that bit of information."

He rose, as if terminating the interview. Hale raised his hands in a placating way, indicating that he was not yet done. "Wait, Mr. Holmes! Hear me out. There is another factor to consider."

Holmes frowned and then reseated himself. He made a gesture to continue with his fingers. "I have a daughter. Christina is twenty years old, and I have raised her by myself. She's a beautiful girl, inside and out. Her mother died when she was but a child, during those years when we were living in America. Since coming to this country, I haven't devoted the time that I should have to being a proper father. Perhaps that's a good thing, because she has turned out to truly be an angel – which might not have happened if I'd had more influence over her.

"In any case, this can't continue. For her sake. I've done much to be ashamed of, and the burden is getting too heavy to sustain itself. I'm calling Lamont's bluff. I'm going to go to the police myself, and 'take my medicine', as you say. But I want you to find out more about Lamont before I do so. Sew him up, Mr. Holmes, so my own downfall won't be in vain."

Holmes sat quietly, contemplating his steepled fingers inches before his eyes. Finally, he said, "I will look into it, Mr. Hale. But have a care! If you are playing a game with me, you will lose. And I should prefer to know more about your affairs, and your true involvement, such as it may be. If Mr. Addington and Lord Graeme were murdered, the truth will come out. In any case, it seems unavoidable that the rest of your secrets will be exposed."

"I understand that," said Hale. "Anything to put an end to this and preserve my daughter."

Holmes stood, indicating that the interview was at an end. "I will gather information, and determine the best way to proceed. You'll hear from me soon."

Hale looked puzzled at this abrupt dismissal, and then pulled himself to his feet. "Mr. Holmes, I was serious. I'll do anything to save my daughter. I . . . I'll tell you the information that Lamont has discovered and is using to blackmail me."

"I intend to make myself aware of your history later today," replied Holmes. "I have no doubt that within a few hours, I will know as much or more about you than even Mr. Lamont does – and quite frankly, I suspect that what I determine will be unbiased, for I would suspect that what you might tell me would be presented in such a way that, even unintentionally, the truth would be obfuscated to show yourself in a favorable light."

Hale opened his mouth to reply, and then gave a small shrug, as if he had no choice in the matter – which indeed, he did not. Sherlock Holmes had agreed to look into his problem, and that meant there would be no secrets.

Hale once again seemed to consider and then reject the idea of offering his hand. Instead, he turned and departed. Even before we heard the street door open and close, Holmes was stepping toward his bedroom. I had seen this reaction many times before. "Going out?" I asked rather vacuously.

"Indeed," he called. "I must learn more of this Dunmar Lamont. Have you met him?

"I know nothing except the little that I've heard mentioned at my club – some think he is a miracle worker, and others a fraud, but in a harmless way."

"Then, if you and he aren't personally aware of one another, perhaps you would care to accompany me?"

I affirmed that I would, and then proceeded to disguise my appearance slightly – but never with the skill of Sherlock Holmes. He returned from his bedroom and stepped to the door, pausing only to grab his weighted stick. I could see that he had altered his appearance, combing his hair forward, and adding an ascot 'round his neck and a set of *pince-nez* to the bridge of his nose. He appeared to have gained two stone in an instant, even as he had lost six inches in height. I would not have recognized him.

Five minutes later, we had obtained a cab and were traveling toward Burleigh Street.

Along the way, Holmes chose not to discuss the case. Instead, he looked around at the passing streets, his eyes full of joy at seeing London, which he had missed for so long. Changes that I had taken for granted were new to him, and he plied me with questions. I answered on a superficial level, while thinking about the questionable prospect of working to assist Nathaniel McGhee Hale.

We arrived in Burleigh Street, quiet after the bustle of the nearby Strand. The doorway of No. 12 was curiously angled at the corner of the building, directly across from the back northwest corner the Lyceum Theatre. Looking along narrow Exeter Street toward Bow Street to the east, I could see the stage door, with various crew members leaning around it, smoking and gossiping.

Holmes, dressed as an older man, adjusted his very countenance as he collapsed into a crabbiness that implied money and bad luck. "I am Mr. Asenath Bridges," he explained, his voice rather shrill and unpleasant. "It is a fictional identity that has been established by Mycroft for use when needed. The man's background is pedigreed. 'Mr. Bridges' has carried out Mycroft's tasks around the Empire for years, and my borrowing him for a day or so won't inconvenience anyone, should Mr. Lamont need to check the man's assets and affairs."

With that, he led me up a short series of steps and into the Burleigh Street office.

It had changed greatly since 1891, when I first visited there with my literary agent to see about publishing those short sketches relating some of Holmes's adventures. Then, the magazine had been quite new, only a few months old in fact, and the energy here had been electric. Now, after shutting the door to the muted sounds of the street outside, the silence was overwhelming.

But not quite. I became aware of muted conversation through the closed door between the reception area where we stood and a room beyond – Lamont's sanctum, according to Hale. We had been inside for barely a minute, with Holmes looking sharply to the left and right, when a woman's voice raised suddenly, and then the door flew open.

A young lady in her early twenties came out suddenly, her face tearful and angry. Even in her haste and in such an emotional state, I could see that she was beautiful. She passed us without a glance and threw open the door to the street. It closed behind her, and when I turned back, I saw Dunmar Lamont standing in front of us, looking smugly toward the departed girl.

He was of average height, with dull brown hair trimmed rather Caesar-like across his high and somewhat hydro-encephalitic forehead, making his face seem heavier than it was, widening toward his neck like a hanging fruit. There were unhealthy bags under his eyes, and something thin and smudged that he probably thought was a beard staining the lower half of his face, emphasizing the weak chin and throat, bulging beneath like a sack. The beard was shot through with white threads, making him look older than he probably was. He probably felt that it gave him an air of *gravitas*, when in fact it simply made him look rather seedy. I couldn't imagine how anyone would believe this man to be a "trusted advisor", but I knew that there were countless people wandering the earth who were foolish enough to seek advice and comfort from charlatans such as this.

"I only consult by appointment," he said in a thin voice, turning his attention our way. His American accent was flat but noticeable.

"But I insist!" said Holmes, his own voice querulous. He shook his stick toward Lamont. "My business is urgent!"

"Perhaps if you leave your name, I might be able to fit you into my schedule in a few weeks."

"That is not satisfactory! By then, matters will have progressed to the point where I might very well be in personal jeopardy!"

"Possibly, then, if things are that serious, I might be able to do something a bit sooner, but certainly not today. Your name, sir?"

"Asenath Bridges. Formerly of the Foreign Office, and now an investor." He felt around his waistcoat. "I thought that I had a card . . . ." he muttered. Then he gave up and continued. "I have been lured into some questionable financial arrangements, and I – "

"That is enough for now, Mr. Bridges. Your address?"

Holmes responded with a house in Mayfair. I recognized it from a previous investigation as one maintained surreptitiously by Mycroft Holmes's department.

"Very good. I shall be in touch as to when I can see you. Good day, sir."

"But . . . but . . . ." Holmes sputtered, and then seemed to realize that this would be the entire substance of this consultation. With a cold nod, he turned to the door. I followed, having never been required to utter a single word.

Outside, we walked in silence down the hill to the Strand. Only there did Holmes give a short barking laugh.

"Did that accomplish anything?" I asked, wondering what had been the purpose, for a mere moment of conversation.

"It never hurts to get a look at the enemy," came the reply. "I will alert Mycroft to be aware if inquiries into Mr. Bridges' affairs begin to become apparent. No doubt, Lamont will use the time between now and when he schedules the appointment to find out all that he can about Mr. Bridges' affairs, with a mind of using it to his own advantage."

We stopped walking, and Holmes said, "This is where we part ways, Watson. I need to conduct similar research into Lamont's background, and I can move faster alone. I will see you this afternoon in Baker Street." And with that, he turned and, still moving in the character of Asenath Bridges, lost himself in the crowded street.

I returned home in time to find that Mrs. Hudson was preparing lunch. Letting her know that Holmes would be out, I went upstairs and considered.

I had only recently moved back to Baker Street, and in truth I was not entirely settled yet. While he had been away for three years, Mrs. Hudson – at Mycroft Holmes's request – had maintained Holmes's rooms, unknowingly in preparation for his eventual return. I had been aware of this peculiar arrangement at the time, and while thinking it unusual, I suppose that I had accepted it at some level, as had Mrs. Hudson, believing that Mycroft wished to preserve them as some sort of memorial museum. That had seemed less likely than thinking that he was in any way sentimental about his brother's supposed death. It had certainly never occurred to either Mrs. Hudson or myself that one day Sherlock Holmes would once again resume his tenure at 221 Baker Street.

After Holmes's return to London, and his invitation to me to return to Baker Street, I had moved my own possessions from my former home in Kensington. Now I only had to find a place to put them. When Holmes and I had first agreed to share these rooms in January 1881, we had spent a day or two busily employed in unpacking and laying out our property to the best advantage. However, over the years, Holmes's own possessions began to crowd mine out, bit by bit. At the time of my first marriage, I had moved out, leaving some things behind in Baker Street. Upon my first wife's death in late '87, God rest her soul, the return wasn't too confusing, as I had only been gone for a little over a year. When I had married again, Mary and I had set up a home and practice in Paddington, and it seemed more certain this time that I had truly moved away, so Holmes had steadily expanded to fill the space. This was how it was left when he was believed dead in May 1891.

Three years later, I was tasked with once again fitting my possessions, admittedly less voluminous than my friend's, into a very carefully organized puzzle. While I had earlier waited for Holmes to complete his disguise before our expedition to Burleigh Street, I had looked around the sitting room, and the task seemed hopeless. Now, looking again, I was tempted to throw up my hands and abandon the field.

Instead, I walked across the room, retrieved my journal from Holmes's side table, and placed it with the others, ready to make my case again at some later date to plead for its publication. A moment later, Mrs. Hudson came upstairs with my lunch and once more expressed her happiness that I had returned to the fold, so to speak. I marveled yet again at our fortunate luck in initially finding such a treasure of a landlady. Through my association with Holmes, I'd encountered men and women from every walk of life, the highest and the lowest, and all sorts in between. In England and elsewhere, we had interviewed, interrogated, and pursued a vast variety of humankind, and that had included countless examples of the *genus landladius* – often suspicious, surly, and definitely inclined toward distrust.

Our Mrs. Hudson was none of those. From the start, she had helped to nurse me back to health following my military misadventures, and she had also, in her own way, nurtured Holmes's profession as a consulting detective, regularly falling into the spirit of his investigations, helping where required, and tempering her frustration at some of his more outrageous habits with an almost motherly affection. When one considered how, only weeks before, she had risked injury or even death to crawl across our sitting room floor to rotate a bust of Holmes so that it could be shot by an air rifle, there was really no doubt that she was truly indispensable.

It was late afternoon when Holmes returned, this time as himself, his disguise abandoned at some point during his travels. He dropped into his chair and filled his pipe.

"Our Mr. Lamont is quite a piece of work, as the Americans say. He's been rather too careless at constructing his shell, leaving a great many thin places that were easily scraped away. For instance, his name is not Dunmar Lamont, although there is a fellow by that name in the United States who has a sterling reputation. Rather, our new acquaintance is, in truth, Dick Brooks, who fled from America last year under quite the cloud. They are still looking for him for a series of unanswered crimes ranging from forgery and fraud to a possible murder."

"Indeed. And how did you discover this so quickly?"

"Criminals settle into the same habits, the *modus operandi*, and a few wires to some Americans of my acquaintance quickly pointed me in the right direction. A subsequent check of the passenger logs at the approximate time he came to London confirmed everything. I spoke with Landau at *The Times* – you know that he keeps files on things like this – and he was able to fill me in on a number of Brooks' schemes since setting up shop here.

"There are whispers – no more – of a number of wealthy men held in his thrall. It has become known in certain circles that Brooks – identified of course to his victims as Lamont – gains control, although specifics are not known. It's unfortunate for Mr. Hale that he isn't friends with more of these other men. They might have warned him. Yet, it's fortunate for society as a whole, as it led to our becoming aware of the circumstances in time to put a stop to him."

"And this Woodhouse, formerly of Coxon and Woodhouse? Is he in on it as well?"

"Doubtless. Let me check my index, for *he* is certainly in it."

He rose and found his way to the shelves where his scrapbooks reposed. Choosing one of them – and I knew that, with his peculiar filing system, it didn't necessarily have to be the volume labeled '*W*' – he read for a moment and then closed it with a satisfied snap.

"My books are far out of date," said with a wistful look at stacked newspapers here and there around the room, "but even before my departure, I noted that Mr. Woodhouse was on a wrong road. You will recall that our young client from a few years ago, Hall Pycroft, had worked for him. When Coxon and Woodhouse went under, old Coxon wrote letters of recommendation, while Woodhouse made himself scarce from the whole business. I later satisfied myself that the entire Venezuelan loan debacle was engineered by Woodhouse, and unsurprisingly he came out of it quite flush. Since then, however, he's apparently fallen in with a thief of similar ilk."

He was about to resume his seat when the front doorbell peeled with urgency. We looked at one another, and then waited as quick footsteps rose from below, approaching our sitting room door.

I don't know who was more surprised, Holmes or me, to find that our visitor was the same beautiful girl whom we had met only hours ago, as she angrily left Lamont's – that is to say – *Brooks'* office. Then as now, she was upset, but in a different way. Her expression, looking from one to the other of us, was now frightened.

Unerringly, she spoke to my friend. "Mr. Holmes, I am Christina Hale. I must beg you to drop the matter that you discussed with my father. Really you must! It can only lead to disaster!"

Holmes stepped toward her with a welcoming smile. "Come in, Miss Hale. Please have a seat and tell us about it."

She wavered, and then seemed to realize that she needed to explain further in order to convince us. Holmes led her to the basket chair, where she sat, perched toward the front, and leaning forward with urgency.

Lowering himself into his own armchair, Holmes said, "Really, Miss Hale, I'm not certain what you mean."

"Oh, Mr. Holmes. There is no need to be evasive. I know what my father came here for. I've known for quite a while about his reputation and his activities. I've hoped to be something of a good influence on him over the years, and I think that I've succeeded to a small degree. But now he is under the power of Dunmar Lamont, and any attempt to shake him loose will only lead to his total downfall."

"And how did you learn of this, Miss Hale? Did your father share it with you?"

"Certainly not! Not at first. I . . . I . . . ." She couldn't bring herself to tell the rest. Holmes supplied the answer for her.

"Did Mr. Lamont tell you himself? During your visit to his office earlier today?"

She seemed shocked that he knew of it, but then she glanced at me. "You were there," she said with narrowed eyes. "When I left. With another man."

"Actually," said Holmes, "that other man was me, although my appearance was altered. However, we didn't know who *you* were at the time. Was that when you learned of your father's dilemma?"

"It was."

"And how did you come to be there at all?"

"He . . . Mr. Lamont sent me a note. He said that we had items to discuss that would benefit my father."

"And so you went."

"I did. He told me in great detail some aspects of my father's business – more than I had ever realized. And he . . . and he . . . ."

"Come, come, Miss Hale. Time to be frank with us."

She took a breath. "He said that he knew enough to have my father imprisoned. But that he . . . he would keep it all a secret if I would agree to marry him!"

I sat up in shock. This was intolerable! Such a beautiful girl could not – must not! – align herself with so corrupt a soul.

Holmes smiled at her. "Do not worry, my dear girl. The situation is not as grim as you imagine. Your father has already approached us to help him. Although he doesn't know it yet, Mr. Lamont has no power over him any longer, and more importantly, none over you as well."

His brows narrowed, and he leaned forward abruptly. Reaching to take her wrist, he said, "May I?" Then, drawing her arm upward, he pushed back her sleeve, showing a cruel spacing of fresh bruises, obviously fingermarks, on her otherwise pristine flesh.

"From Mr. Lamont?" Holmes asked.

She nodded, unable to speak further.

Holmes's tone lowered, and I, who knew him so well, recognized his cold outrage. "I repeat, he no longer has any power over you."

I was tempted to rise then and there to race across town and thrash the brute, but I knew that a planned and reasoned campaign would be much more effective in the long run. I forced myself to breathe deeply and relax into my seat. However, the girl's next statement made me realize that I wouldn't be relaxed for very long.

"But Mr. Holmes, it's too late! I returned home today, and my father wished to know why I was upset. I couldn't help it. I told him. I threw it in his face about his own crimes, and that I was now bound horribly to Mr. Lamont because of them. He . . . he was aghast. That's when he told me that he had consulted you, although I didn't realize to what extent. Then he raced out. I'm sure that he was going to Mr. Lamont's office. I didn't know what else to do, so I came here, hoping that if you made it known that you would no longer be involved, events might play out along their necessary, if distasteful, path, and my father will no longer be in danger."

It was an innocent but naïve statement, and I realized as well as Holmes what had been set into motion. Without a word, we both stood, and Holmes took the girl's hand to lead her with us to the door.

Downstairs, a four-wheeler fortunately waited for Miss Hale, and we bundled her inside. I followed, and Holmes was about to join us when he noticed a constable just up the street. Holmes called him over, and the man lumbered to us, where his stolid expression suddenly turned to surprise.

"Why, Mr. Holmes!" he said. "I'd heard that you were back, but I almost didn't believe it! Why, I said the other day – "

"No time, Oakes!" said Holmes. "Get a message to the Yard – Lestrade or Gregson or Bradstreet, or any of them. Have them join us at No. 12 Burleigh Street immediately. It might be a matter of murder!" And with that, he bounded into our carriage and we were away.

We rode silently across the city, each absorbed in our own thoughts. Miss Hale chewed her lip, no doubt wondering what we would find upon our arrival. Holmes caught my eye and nodded toward my pocket. I nodded. On our way out, I had retrieved my service revolver.

Turning north off the Strand and so into Burleigh Street, Holmes bade the cabbie to stop before reaching our destination. He and I left the cab, urging Miss Hale to remain within until she was summoned. She started to protest, but at that moment, a hansom arrived in haste and stopped behind us. Inspector Lestrade, having travelled the short distance from the Yard, leapt to the ground.

"I received Oakes' telephone call, Mr. Holmes. Murder, you say?"

"Possibly. But perhaps we're in time to prevent it. This is Miss Hale. Her father is being blackmailed by Dunmar Lamont, and – "

"Dunmar Lamont?" growled the inspector. "We've had our eye on him. The 'Sherlock Holmes of the Business World', he says."

Holmes snorted. "Not likely. Listen, Lestrade. Lamont, whose real name is Brooks, also attempted to force a betrothal between himself and Miss Hale. When her father heard, he rushed here. We may be in time to prevent violence. Let Watson and me go in first, and see what we shall see. After a moment, you slip in silently. Possibly we can get him to make a confession if he's thrown off balance."

"Hurry!" cried Miss Hale. "While you talk and talk, he might be killing my father!"

Holmes nodded, and we made our way up the street to the corner office.

The sun was going down, and already the narrow lane was in shadows. Down Exeter Street to the east, leading to Bow Street and the front of the Lyceum, I could see the bright lights of the theatre's marquee, along with the jumbled mess of carriages starting to drop off their passengers. Yet all was quiet where we stood.

Holmes reached forward and gently opened the door, fortunately unlocked. Closing but not latching the door behind us, we stood and listened, but heard no arguments, no blows, and no violence. Holmes frowned, and we stepped inside. I had my gun in hand.

The front room was dark, lit only by the fading daylight through the tall windows. The door to the back room was ajar, with gaslight spreading a wedge across the floor toward us. We stepped that way, and then Holmes pushed it open.

Brooks was standing by the fireplace, lost in thought, and a frown upon his face. He didn't see us at first. Then, coming to himself with a start, he glanced up to where we both stood. His eyes immediately fastened upon my gun.

The smug expression we had seen earlier in the day slid over his face like a hood. "I'm sorry, gents, but I never see anyone without an appointment."

Holmes stepped forward into the light. "I think that you'll see me, Mr. Brooks."

The man seemed to rock from a double shock – both the use of his correct name, and also the fact that he recognized the man standing

70

before him as Sherlock Holmes, still believed by many to have died three years previously.

Before he could recover, Holmes demanded, "Where is Mr. Hale?"

Brooks' eyes narrowed. He could certainly put together enough of what was going on to respond. "Hale? I don't know what you're talking about."

"Listen to me, Brooks. Your game is finished. We know about what you tried to pull with Hale, and since then I've already found out about your previous activities in America. Does the name 'Morriston' ring a bell?"

The man seemed to growl, and started to take a step forward before looking again toward my gun. Behind me, I heard the outer door opening softly. I knew that Lestrade was entering. To distract Brooks, I stepped further into the room, away from Holmes to cover the man from a different angle.

"Look around," said Brooks. "There is no Mr. Hale here. I don't really know what you're implying, but I'll see you in court for assault."

"It won't do, Brooks. We know he was coming here. A man that angry wouldn't be diverted."

And yet, I could see that the room was empty. As previously described to us, it consisted of a couple of chairs and some sort of tall table against a side wall.

"Perhaps there's another part of the building," I offered, "in addition to these two rooms that he uses for his office."

"You're more right than you know, Watson," said Holmes. "I didn't have time to tell you, but during my researches this afternoon, I checked into Brooks' rental of this property. It turns out that he leased the adjacent space as well, and that he fixed up a hidden doorway between the two. I believe that, with a bit of searching, based on information that I received from the very carpenter who constructed the door, I can find it!"

Brooks' puffy eyes narrowed as Holmes moved around the room. I watched him while my friend searched. He then stepped purposefully toward the tall drafting table, pulling it away from the wall in one great sweep. Papers tumbled to the floor, but Holmes ignored them, dropping and examining the baseboard and running his fingers along the wall.

As Holmes moved, I watched the supposed trusted advisor. At one point, following Holmes's shift along the wall, the man seemed to relax.

"Holmes," I said. "Back up. He was relieved that you passed by that last section."

This was too much for Brooks. Seemingly forgetting my weapon trained upon him, he made as if to leap upon Holmes's back. It was too much for me as well. While not enough cause to shoot the man, it was certainly enough to incapacitate him otherwise. Calling out, "Holmes!" and thrusting my gun into my coat pocket, I took two steps forward, grabbing Brooks' shoulder with my left hand before he could reach my friend. Then, spinning him around toward me, his expression filled with sudden surprise, I pulled my right fist back. I had a sudden memory of his finger marks up and down the girl's arm as my fist drove forward, slamming into his mouth with such force that a great many of his front teeth crumbled inward. I pulled my arm back, ready to hit him again, when he lurched forward, a rain of broken teen flying to the left and right.

The man dropped to the ground, unconscious, blood and mucous already pooling beneath his ruined mouth. To this day, I still have a notable jagged scar at the junction of my metacarpophalangeal joint – undoubtedly obtained from one of his canines or incisors – that I sometimes notice with pride.

In the meantime, with only a glance over his shoulder, Holmes had managed to open the hidden door. With one look, he called, "Watson! Your man!"

I stepped past him and into a room of equivalent size to the one reached from Burleigh Street. There I found Mr. Hale, laid out upon the floor at the foot of a small table. Upon it was a bottle of wine and two half-filled glasses. Kneeling beside Hale was another fellow, later identified as the disgraced Woodhouse. He began to blather about how he never meant for things to go this far, and that Hale might still be alive. As were to learn later, he was in it nearly as deep as Brooks, and then only trying to save himself. I pushed him aside and knelt to examine the unconscious man. His breathing was faint, and his pulse thready. "Lestrade!" I called. "No time for an ambulance! Get our four-wheeler up here."

Within moments, Lestrade and I were manoeuvring the little man into the cab, while his daughter stood weeping nearby. I helped her back inside and climbed in myself. I turned to ask someone to retrieve the two glasses and the wine bottle that had been standing near the body, but Holmes was already there, carefully handing them to me.

I directed the cabbie to waste no time in getting us to Charing Cross Hospital, just to the west. There, I explained the situation, and how we surmised that Brooks had contrived for Hale to join him in a drink. A quick analysis showed that the bottle simply contained wine, but the contents of one of the glasses was thick with a known and easily treatable poison. In just a few hours, Hale was out of the woods.

But not entirely, as his affairs were now unavoidably public knowledge. Still, it was a fact that he had made an attempt to do the right thing as promised, and this, along with his recent actions toward improving safety in his mines and the simple fact that he was wealthy, went a great deal toward lessening any scandal or punishment that he might have faced after "taking his medicine". He was turned loose with a slap on the wrist and, under his daughter's future influence, he actually became something of a force for good well into the new century.

Both Brooks and Woodhouse, however, didn't quite fare so well. Further investigation revealed that a number of prominent men throughout London had been fooled into consulting Brooks, often at the behest of Woodhouse. Their appointments would be delayed until Brooks could adequately research them, and then he would either simply blackmail them based upon what they revealed during their supposedly confidential consultations, or arrange to assist their situations by removing their enemies – sometimes fatally. Then, he would make it known to his clients that they were complicit, and demand even more illicit compensation.

He had no fear of getting caught, or that one of his victims would turn on him someday, as he had operated this system before, and he trusted his animal senses to perceive when the situation was about to go wrong, thus allowing him to escape ahead of the law. He believed that the same would be true this time as well.

But he hadn't counted on meeting Sherlock Holmes.

All of this information came from Woodhouse, who anxiously provided as many facts as he could in order to save himself. It worked in his case, to a degree, as he received only a life sentence. Brooks was not so fortunate.

At first, many of the men whom he had been blackmailed kept silent, out of shame, or possibly to avoid exposure of their own activities – illegal and otherwise. But one by one, when confronted with information provided by Woodhouse, and also obtained through Brooks' own records – many of which were found in the secret room – the story was pieced together.

Additionally, Holmes's associates in America provided additional information about the scoundrel's background, further sealing his fate.

Throughout the rest of 1894, and most of the next year as well, Brooks carried out legal dodges and appeals, while finding ways to pass threatening messages to Holmes, stupidly ignoring the fact that such behavior only prejudiced opinion against him even further. Occasionally we even received word that he was attempting to hire someone to carry out an attack on Holmes, although no one apparently ever took him up on his offers.

Finally, in early 1896, he was led to the gallows. I understand from someone who was there that he cried at the end, and that, after it was over and the leather hood was removed, he had chewed the inside fiercely with his toothless gums as he crossed to his more eternal punishment.

As Holmes later said when recording this epilogue in his scrapbook, "Five times five-hundred . . . *plus one*." Then, closing the book, he added, "No great loss, Watson."

I had to agree.

> *"Suppose that I were Brooks or Woodhouse, or any of the fifty men who have good reason for taking my life, how long could I survive against my own pursuit? A summons, a bogus appointment, and all would be over."*

Sherlock Holmes – "The Bruce-Partington Plans"

A Shame Harder Than Death
by Thomas Fortenberry

I

It is rare that any of the cases Sherlock Holmes and I encounter border on the macabre, or move into the realm of the supernatural, but this one did. It began as a ghost story and ended in one of the darkest tragedies we ever recorded together. There are certain times in life when you feel yourself crossing the borderland between the living and the dead, when you step off the sure safety of the shoreline and feel the boat shift beneath your weight, hear the creak of the oars, and find yourself actually being ferried across the River Styx by that horrifying guide Charon. I had felt that moment of transition years before, being shot in Afghanistan. I felt it again in this case.

It was a quite singular affair that began in the ancient past and moved forward into the future. But there was more to it than this. This was during the spring of 1894. It was fitting that ghost stories be foremost in my mind during this time period for a number of reasons. It was only weeks before when a deformed, old bibliophile had bumped into me on the street in London with an arm full of tree and bird lore, like some wisened Druid of ancient times, and then followed me home, only to melt away before my eyes into none other than the missing and presumed deceased Sherlock Holmes.

Oh, how I had fainted at that moment of dreadful shock!

But, perhaps due to that first shock, every day thereafter was somewhat like living in a state of shock. My mental faculties often failed me and I was either overwhelmed with emotion at his return to the world of the living, or would sit utterly drained, emotionless, and just observe this apparition that was Holmes moving through the Baker Street rooms. During this season of his return, it was almost like having a ghost haunting the place. Thought dead for three years, it was still almost unbelievable that Holmes was back, rambling about, disorganizing once more the rooms which had been so carefully, albeit sadly, cleaned during his presumed death. He was once more displacing books and papers which had been organized and shelved, and filling the air with clouds of tobacco smoke and malodorous vapors from his interminable chemical experiments.

That particular morning, Holmes had stretched out upon the floor, his robes a spray of color about him, staring up at the ceiling. Occasionally I would hear varied strains of tunes arise from him, hummed verses or perhaps lilting memories, which would arise hauntingly to fill the room and then just as eerily fade away to leave a silence hovering in the air. I didn't break his reverie, and had no idea what he was actually considering in that amazing brain of his, but I fancied that he was lying yet upon the soft green moss of the ledge in the cliff above Reichenbach Fall where he had hidden "unseen in the most perfect comfort" while we had searched frantically for his body below in the maelstrom of water upon the broken stones. He waited while I had agonized over one of the greatest losses that death had dealt me.

In these early days of our re-acquaintance, there was an awkwardness with each other – at least on my part. Having grown used to his absence, it was now startlingly familiar to have him back in his old routine, with him acting as if nothing had happened and it were the day after. But, as his drawn, somewhat-whitened visage attested, we knew better. It had been hard times on us all.

I attempted many times to engage him and gain insights into his activities during the three years that he was missing, but he would only supply bits and pieces, a brief scenario here or there, or the details of a stranger's unique garb or idiosyncratic way of speech that he had encountered. The memory of a meal, or the view of a prosaic landscape such as during his time climbing the rugged Himalayas into Tibet. Fascinating architectural details of a building in a city he had passed in his travels, before drifting off or just dismissing it all as "the boring past". So often we sat in silence and simply shared the rooms together once more.

Sometimes I prayed for distractions from these long hours of quietude, but the surprise of a knock at the door that morning proved to be the most profound distraction. Mrs. Hudson came to the sitting room and presented the card of a gentleman caller.

He was a young man, not yet thirty – tall and vigorous, a dark-haired lad with ginger highlights in his scant beard. His eyes were bright and intelligent, and he eagerly launched into his discourse. He rushed forward with outstretched hand to greet my friend.

"Mr. Holmes! It is such an honor. My name is – "

"Martyn Brennard, or so says your card. An archaeologist, no less. But, here in England. Not abroad."

"Why, yes."

"Your pallor reveals the dig sites. I have worked historic sites in Egypt and Persia, suffering that bronzing heat, and knew you were not a victim of the harsh Middle Eastern sun."

The young man smiled. "Too true. Under the auspices of the British Museum and in conjunction with the Lord Pitt Rivers, our first Inspector of Ancient Monuments – "

"Ah, Mr. Augustus Lane-Fox, the famed ethnologist! He has fascinating theories on cultural evolution. He possesses a great, methodical mind. That museum of his is always worth a visit. But yes, since the Cranborne Chase inheritance, I suppose we must defer to his newly acquired Pitt Rivers name these days."

"Y-yes. Quite so. I studied under him at Oxford University, he and Professor Jonathan Darke as well. They are both great mentors to me. Which is actually how you came to be recommended to me for this current problem. Not just my professional honor is at stake, but the sacrifice of a child."

The name of Dr. Darke aroused interest in me. We had, on occasion, sought his rather unique counsel concerning past cases. He was something of a celebrity in certain circles.

Holmes steepled his hands. "Truly? How so?"

Mr. Brennard reached inside his coat and produced a folded letter. "I'm sorry. I almost forgot to present this. Professor Darke sent me with this letter as way of introduction and explanation."

As Holmes perused the document he said, "Yes, this is his handwriting. He refers you to me with a case of a missing body. Professor Darke is a very interesting man. I have known him for years. His philosophical and spiritual studies run to the esoteric."

"Yes! He is quite fascinating! Out of all my professors, he was always the most engaging and the most . . . strange."

Holmes chuckled. "Indeed. It seems, then, his lectures have lost none of their fire."

"None! And the amazing anecdotes and backstories he tells to illustrate his points. The time spent with Aborigines and Indians. With shamans and witch doctors. With those lost Stone Age tribes in the Amazon and those pygmy tribes in the Congo. I could listen to his tales for hours! He has seen and done so much. He will travel anywhere in pursuit of answers – which is exactly why I went to see him at first with this problem. You might remember his interest in supernatural mysteries, as well."

"Yes. He has a quite analytical mind, despite his obsession with the supernatural. Speaking of which, you are aware this event reads like a ghost story?"

I cocked an eyebrow at Holmes and he passed the letter over to me. "Dr. John Watson, my associate."

Brennard and I shook hands and I read the letter from Dr. Darke as the conversation continued. I will not reproduce it here, since it also contains personal asides of no relevance to this case, though it is filed with the rest of our notes on this case. Apparently, late one evening the young archaeologist had discovered a body in a barrow that was more recent than the other barrow contents. However, he had been frightened by shadows and ghostly sounds and fled. When he returned the next morning with the local police, the body was gone and he was ridiculed for having an overactive imagination and for frightening himself.

Some of the local constabulary even thought he was a liar, out for fame and attention, while a few more superstitious people believed him, thinking he had actually seen a ghost. Dr. Darke concluded that he didn't believe the latter supernatural aspects in this case, but that there was enough of interest to warrant Holmes's attention. In fact, he ended with this observation which made me smile: "*I had heard of your return to the land of the living, and was quite pleased. The world would be the lesser with you gone. Being that you have just returned from the Realm of the Dead, I find the timing of this case of a ghost quite wonderful. Nevertheless, I know of your tendency towards idleness, which is a habit that leads to unwarranted disappearances and that general malaise which will eventually afflict you negatively if you are not careful. Idle hands in the Devil's workshop, as the old proverb warns. Thus, I urge you to seize this opportunity. I believe that this case is a perfect thing upon which to whet your keen mind.*"

"You see," our guest continued, "I am working my way through the Midlands, out Worcestershire way. You may be aware that both Dor Barrow and Avebury are being excavated this year. There are simply dozens of fantastic sites around Salisbury, such as Rockbourne Down, Harnham Hill, or Swallowcliffe Down. I have been tasked with exploring many of the hundreds of lesser barrows, stone rings, and hill forts from Stonehenge, all the way to Caer Caradoc. I have been making my way through the Malvern Hills of late, which is how I came to be inside this particular barrow on the Addleton estate."

"The family has given their permission to excavate their barrow?"

"Well, in a sense. All the families in the region were notified last fall by the Malvern Conservators that specialists such as myself would be working in the area, documenting ancient sites and contents therein."

"So there was a general awareness of the project, but no specific deal with the Addleton family, or other families in the region."

"Yes, sir. We just move through town to town, hill to woods, and try to disrupt as little as possible. These are just general surveys we are making to create an extensive record of the ancient sites in this region, so we can return at a later date and excavate the premium locations."

"Continue. But let us skip the generalities of the project and move directly to the barrow in question. Explain what you saw, both the body and within the barrow. Please be thorough." With this, Sherlock Holmes leaned back in repose and closed his eyes, seeming to drift into a slumbering state.

To his credit, Martyn Brennard gave a very thorough accounting of the appearance and design of the barrow and his actions inside it that day. The body in question turned out to be that of a very young female child – not freshly dead, but not ancient either.

Eventually Holmes aroused and offered, "Barring child ghosts floating through barrow walls, I think we have a singularly interesting mystery as to a disappearing body. You do not strike me as a madman or some youth who is easily confused and terrified by stormy nights out in nature. Thus, if not frightened by the ghostly prospects, would you accompany us back to the Addleton estate? I should wish to examine the barrow in question."

"Pshaw, I certainly am not afraid of ghosts. In fact I don't believe in such superstitions. I have devoted my life to rehabilitating the lives of those long past, in fact, and returning their stories to life. Of course I will accompany you. This is the outcome for which I hoped!"

Holmes clapped his hands. "It is settled then. We leave immediately. However, sir, I warn you, before this is done you may reappraise your fears. Professor Darke may come to regret not taking up this case as well. He knows far better than I the realms of the supernatural. However, this is a fascinating case, and I will wager there is more than meets the eye interred in that tomb. Sometimes ghosts are malevolent indeed!"

II

We left London and made our way out into the western Midlands, past Worcester and into the Malverns, that long, low range of rather beautiful mountains beyond the Severn River Valley.

As we moved across the valley and into the hills to the west, Holmes gave an impressive review of the similarities and differences in the flora and fauna of the two river valleys, contrasting the longer Severn to the Thames, especially in the species of birds. Being that we were usually only around the Thames flowing sluggishly through London, I

79

was very pleased to find this river much less tainted by the sewage and refuse which our metropolis generated. The smell was pleasant, and everywhere one looked, the beauty of nature abounded.

Along the way, I was treated to Holmes being rather effusive, as he is around certain types of people. He and Brennard discussed the history of the region for the most part, from the ancient ruins of Stonehenge to the legend of King Arthur and the iron age hillforts that dot the region. As we were riding in part through the lands of the old Kingdom of Mercia, for one long episode they discussed the relative merits of taxation and the tale of Lady Godiva. They even treated me to a rousing rendition of a few medieval songs, sung with verve. It was nice to see Holmes in good spirits again, the best I had seen him in since his return from the grave.

Brennard returned the favor to Holmes, relating some folktales indigenous to the Malverns, which he had learned from the famed antiquarian of the region, Jabez Allies. Allies, he noted, had claimed the etymology of the ancient Welsh term "Malvern" meant not just "Bald Hills", but actually was far older and stood for "Seat of Judgment". He believed the Malverns had been the center of the most ancient Celtic kingdoms of ancient Britain. From King Arthur to the Druids with their great stone calendar, this mountainous region had stood supreme in judgment over all.

I could see the appeal of living out here in these quiet, gentle mountains, with their deep history and clear streams. But there is a restlessness in me, one which I share with Holmes, and even though I could imagine the peace this region might bring, I had actually had my fill of mountains whilst marching through the much more rugged Afghan peaks. There was a reason I preferred the hustle and bustle of city life.

The barrow itself was somewhat hidden. An ancient and foreboding-looking tripodal rock dolmen dominated a barren, rocky hill before it, with a strange jagged line of standing stones marching away from it across the ridge, giving the hill the outline of a jawbone. But the barrow itself was in the wooded vale below the hill. It could easily have been mistaken from afar as any number of other slight rises in the woods that covered the valley. In fact, as Brennard pointed out, it was truly only seen during the winter months. During the summer, amidst the profusion leafy foliage, it would be fully invisible.

"This is one of the reasons we are conducting surveys during the early spring," Brennard explained. "Across the countryside, ancient sites like this lie buried, hidden, and forgotten. Often families use them for their own family crypts, or simply for storage or as a root cellar. They clear them out, damaging or discarding all the artefacts. Sometimes farmers plow over them. Occasionally, these landowners build over the existing site and incorporate the barrow like a cellar into their house – or simply dismantle it and use the stones to build a new manor. You wouldn't believe the amount of damage done throughout the ages!"

"A pity," Holmes commented. "This particular barrow survives, I see. Was it intact when you found it?"

"For the most part. The Addleton family has known of it for a few generations, and they or others have accessed it time and again in the past. There is some damage, and probably many missing artefacts, but for the most part it's survived. Surprising that they haven't used it more, but I think the remoteness of it from the house on the other side of the hill, and that it lies deep in this uncut wood, keeps it undisturbed, unlike most of the barrows on neighboring properties. Sadly, a lot of those are manor houses have been turned into tourist destinations, or dens for those historic parties that are all the trend nowadays. You know, everyone claims to be descended from a Knight of the Round Table, if not from Arthur himself!"

The entrance to the barrow appeared to be an overgrown cave or overly large rabbit hole burrowed into a hillock. We entered down a sloping ramp. It was small, perhaps the size of a room or two, and constructed out of an oval-shaped ring of massive stones that had been either placed in the ground or covered over with soil. Naturally, it was dark inside and we had to use torches. They threw all sorts of strange shadows, weaving and twisting upon the rocky protuberances of the walls.

Holmes waved his hands and created a weird, writhing show. "This effect is perhaps why the police dismissed your report of a shadow moving?"

"Yes, exactly. They outright laughed at me. One said I had scared myself and implied I had to change my pants before reporting the body at the station."

"Ah, the jocularity of the constabulary. Where was the body?"

"Over here." He showed us to a niche with a flat stone that protruded slightly, as if a table was shoved into an alcove. There were several of these stone niches at various spots around the end of the barrow. All had a few urns or clay bowls resting upon them, with many more on the floor. Those these were mainly broken into shards and scattered. "These are where the ancient Celts would have lain the bodies of those they interred. The urns and beakers contained either foods stuffs, wines, and grave goods for the departed, or embalming oils and herbs, and some may have contained the organs removed from the bodies at burial. None of the original bodies are left inside this particular barrow as they are inside some, but there would have been nothing left but bones, or at best, heavily mummified corpses."

"But you insist that there *was* a body."

"Yes, which is why I say it was not remains from some Celtic tribe or Druidic ritual. I've studied those for years. These remains were modern. Very recent, perhaps, though not within the past year or so. But the body wasn't ancient. A child. It was wrapped in blankets and resting right here. There was even a little pillow beneath the head."

Holmes made a detailed search of the shelf and the surrounding areas. Scraping the stone with his nails, he recovered wax and stated that candles had been lit here. He even picked up every ceramic vessel throughout the tomb, examining it thoroughly, and many of the broken pieces upon the floor. Occasionally he would murmur something to himself, but only once did he exclaim, "Ah-ha!" It was while bent over in the niche, and he raised one finger into the air.

"We have proved a part of your story, Brennard! Here, snagged by a jagged piece of rock in the crevice, are threads from a blanket. Look at the yarn – soft, colored, modern. This is no coarse, primitively woven grave shroud from the past. No, this is from a modern blanket, as one might wrap a child in order to put him or her to sleep."

"Fantastic!" Martyn Brennard exclaimed. His ruddy face lit with joy. "Thank God, something positive has turned up! I was beginning to doubt my own sanity."

"That is not all. This one vessel differs from the others in that it has a residue, a much more modern residue. Look . . . ." Holmes held it out to myself and the archaeologist. "One can see that the ring is not faded and weathered like the more ancient ones. So, my dear archaeologist, you have studied any number of these ancient clay vessels. Is this residue from the distant past or modern?"

Brennard examined the bowl for a few moments. "By Jove, you are correct! This is very modern. If rewetted, we could even determine what the liquid was. It is not desiccated beyond recovery."

"Indeed we shall!" Holmes said, taking the clay vessel back. "However, simply by coloration and consistency, we can rule out that it is blood, can we not?"

"That's right," Brennard answered.

"And you testified that the child's body, when you observed it, was not cut or otherwise injured in a way to show wounds or blood."

"Correct."

"Very good." Holmes seemed pleased. "You see, in this vessel, we have proof that it was used by the living, not the ghosts of the past."

Brennard's brow furrowed. "I thank you so much for these discoveries. Proof of the child at last! However, it does not gain us the child. Likewise, this stained beaker that contains no blood. Whatever could it mean?"

"Any number of things. But, of paramount importance is that we have placed people, and most importantly a young child, inside this barrow within the recent past. We are making progress. Now, I must ask one last favor in reconstructing the scene. Please reenact exactly your movements when you came inside the barrow that harrowing day and found the child, only to be frightened off. Place the torches as you had them and move through your motions as best you remember them. The good doctor and I shall watch from the entrance."

This was done to Holmes's satisfaction. At the end, he had Brennard reenact the fright of seeing the shadow twice, and then moved his own body into the torchlight that emanated from the torch place by the sloping entranceway. When he did this, shadow moved across the wall in such a way that Brennard leaped and exclaimed, "That's it! That's the shadow I saw!"

Holmes smiled broadly. "Thus we have solidified your ghost story! Plus, I will wager that if we sing a rousing chorus of 'Brambling at Sunset' inside this barrow, the echoing effect might in fact create an eerie enough version to scare any sane person. I believe we have explained your ghost story satisfactorily."

As we ascended out of the ground and left the past behind, Brennard asked, "I am humbled and grateful to be thusly proven correct. However, there is still the question of the missing child. She was not a ghost. She was quite real. So where is the body?"

"Quite real indeed. 'Why?' and 'To where removed?' become of paramount importance. We must answer the question: 'Who is the child?' When we do that, I believe the mystery will be solved."

I said, "Solved? But I am still wondering why? Why was the little girl here? Was she perhaps playing and became trapped? You said there is no evidence of an injury or blood. Maybe she simply starved to death, alone in the cold? Or perhaps – "

"Perhaps, nothing, dear Watson. She was murdered. Have there been reports of a missing child? Have parents been scouring the Malverns yelling her name, with hounds let loose through these very woods to sniff out the one who was lost while playing? No. Brennard was derided by the local police who said there were no missing children and that he was imagining the one he saw. No parent was there thanking our young archaeologist, crying that finally someone believed them, and that their missing child had been found. So, one must ask why?

Furthermore, when discovered, it was of utmost relevance that the body was swiftly removed. To where? If we can solve these things, we can solve it all. But let us move as swiftly as possible before the proof is lost to us forever."

"Very well. Important, if not horrifying points. So, what are we to do next?"

"We are splitting up. Please, Watson, accompany Mr. Brennard to meet the Addletons. They are the owners of this land and should, more than anyone, know of events that occur on their property. Inquire into the use of the barrow and if they know of anything concerning it."

"And you?"

"I'm going to the local police to look into missing persons cases and other events of note in the area. I believe I might have a more favorable reception than Brennard. Occasionally, even a buffoon of a local police can be of great value. Sometimes, they do not even realize it. Also," he said, holding up the ceramic vessel, "I will utilize their laboratory equipment."

III

That evening I met the rather dour Mr. Cyrus and Mrs. Adele Addleton. Brennard and I were led into a sitting room that had glass doors that offered a rather magical view of the gardens behind the house at sunset. But the beautiful view outside did not pervade the house. The couple sat, cold and austere, even as they were surrounded by a warm sea of rose red color from the setting sun.

They had no surviving children. We learned that their estranged older son, Anthony, had drowned two years earlier in a naval mishap, sailing somewhere in the Indian Ocean. They hadn't seen him before that in more than a decade. Their teenage daughter, Elizabeth, had tragically died in a local accident several years before that, while the mother was away on a long vacation in Italy. It was the first and last vacation she had ever taken, she assured me. I believed her, for the way she stared hollowly at the floor, I felt that she would never leave from this place again. Her husband was a cold, brooding man, as stolid as the mountain behind us and as empty as the barrow on it. The loss of children for a parent is one of the most brutal of psychological traumas. Other than sensing her overwhelming grief, I truly gained nothing of pertinence from the Addletons.

Likewise, they offered little of value on the history of the barrow itself. It was old, it had always been there, it was unused.

The manor home of the Addletons seemed just as gray, old, and unused as the barrow. It was part wood and part stone. The stone was bleak and gray, so common to the Malverns, and gave the house a washed-out, dreary, and exhausted appearance which the wooden portions, with their chipping paint which had once attempted gaiety, failed to remedy. The furniture was older, worn, and – much like the carpets and rest of the house that I could observe – were largely unkept. I have never met two people who were more empty – merely breathing, awaiting their final days to arrive.

Martyn Brennard and I were happy to finally excuse ourselves and leave the solemnity of that house after nearly an hour of mumbled regret and clinking cups and saucers. There was only one thing of future note that arose out of that conversation. I had inquired into who maintained their lands, since there were gardens behind the house and paths down into the woods and around the hill towards the side where the barrow lay. They maintained no real staff, having only a cook, a maid, and a gardener. The first two, a Mrs. Griffith and Miss Driscoll, had let us in and served us tea as we talked. The Addleton grounds were all maintained by one man, a Mr. Jim Evans, an odd loner who grew up in the area and knew those woods like the backs of his weathered hands.

Evans was not there, as he only worked odd days. He lived in a cottage midway around the slope of the hill. Brennard and I, with little else to do that evening, struck out for his cottage. It was momentous that we did so.

He was at home when we knocked. Perhaps out of boredom or to add a touch of excitement to his evening, Martyn Brennard followed our introduction with a pompous sounding statement that we were there to investigate the disappearance of a young girl's body from the barrow.

That got a startling response. Mr. Jim Evans said nothing, but opened his eyes very wide and seemed on the point of choking. He then slammed the door in our faces. We could hear him moving through the small cottage and, having accompanied Holmes for so many years, I moved directly around the house towards the back while Brennard pounded on the front door. I was in time to see Evans flee the cottage and race away down a path.

It wasn't the longest of chases. He knew the woods and I did not, but he fled directly, ran without looking back, and though he could have lost me easily in the woods to either side, he ran down the path straight to a little smoke house that was used for skinning and processing hunted animals. I soon caught up and, opening the door, entered the structure behind him.

He was in the process of moving a small object when I stepped inside. A cabinet stood open, most probably from where it had been concealed, and he was frantically wrapping it up. Dead animals hung from cords everywhere around the walls of the small structure.

I ordered him to stop. He turned on me, frantic, with a wild look in his eyes like a cornered animal. I was horrified to see that the object in his arms was the mouldering corpse of a child – a babe.

"Dear Lord!" I cried.

He darted forward and slammed into me. I hit the door frame behind me and, using that to hold myself upright and with my stick in my hands across my chest, I shoved back at him as fiercely as I could. He stumbled backwards and crashed into the wall, with dead rabbits and foxes swinging around his head. He reached out, clawing at a shelf. Then he lurched snarling at me, a beast, and I saw the glint of a skinning knife in his left hand.

I don't know to this day how I avoided his savage thrust, though I think his clutching the dead child to his chest with his right arm helped me. Realizing that it was the end if I failed, I pivoted and struck at his head with the metal head of my walking cane with all my might. There was a sharp thump as I hit his temple The gardener collapsed to the ground.

I heard the pounding of feet behind me and Martyn Brennard arrived in time to witness the blow and his collapse.

"Good Lord, man! Are you all right? Did he attack you?"

"Yes," I panted, wilting some as the nerves hit me. "I defended myself. But, look . . . in his arms."

Brennard gasped as he turned the gardener over and discovered the desiccated corpse of the child. "It is the child that I saw! In the same blanket! The one from the barrow!"

IV

We brought the gardener back to his cottage and tied him tightly to a chair before he regained consciousness. Since he was a younger man, fleeter of foot, and knew the region, Brennard went to fetch the police and Holmes as well, if he was indeed with them at the station.

While I paced, awaiting their return, Jim Evans awoke. After some moments of struggling and yelling, he calmed down and sat quietly. I had feared that he might break his bonds and, if he escaped now that night had fallen, he might vanish into the darkness of the forest,

A half-hour later, once I assured myself he couldn't free himself and that he had calmed down and given up on escape, I tended to the slight bleeding related to the bruise I had left on his scalp. I decided I should question him. I gave him some water and then sat in front of him. At first, I just talked about the Malvern Hills that I had seen on the way in, the tranquility of the Severn Valley, and the way the forest here was calming to me. I talked about some of my own experiences in the war, and how different these mountains felt from those. We began to talk about his gardening and his work for the Addletons.

It turned out that he had worked for years to try and ease their pain. He had labored tirelessly in their gardens, filling them with flowers and shrubs that the Missus especially found most pleasing. He had done so to help show them see the beauty of the world and lighten their suffering. After a while, I couldn't see the savagery in him at all, or that cornered animal look. He was really quite simple, and he truly cared about the Addletons. I wondered how such a seemingly kind-hearted man had come to kill a young child.

I asked him to his face.

He seemed utterly dumbfounded. "I didn't kill anyone! Especially not a child! I wouldn't ever hurt a child!"

I pondered whose child this could have been? Did Evans kidnap someone from a local family? What if there were more that were missing?

I got up and checked his bonds again. Then I walked down to the little smokehouse with one of the torches we had brought from the barrow. The swaddled body was still there, on a table, where we had left it. I shuddered as I looked at all the hanging animals, some skinned and some not, swinging their shadows. I had seen the work of deranged killers before, and often the most disturbed began by mutilating beasts.

I checked through the animals and then through the cabinets as well. After searching the entire shed from top to bottom, I was sure. There were no other human remains hidden in the smoke house.

I returned to the man's cottage. He was weeping. I could see from the red chafing on his wrists that he had tried the ropes again. "Why are you holding me here? Please, let me go! I didn't do anything to Lizzie! I would never hurt her! I was trying to protect her." He cried more and the sobs grew deeper, wracking his entire body. Clearly his reason, what there had ever been of it, was slipping away.

I sat back down in a stunned silence. He was completely broken inside. I could see his genuine remorse. But there was no sense of guilt or deceit. He meant what he said and he actually seemed incapable of killing a child. But I knew he was a trained hunter and had witnessed his trapped fury firsthand. Furthermore, he had now called the dead girl by name. He knew her. I had to find out more. Then, I had an insight.

87

"So, Jim, I . . . I am a doctor, as I said. I work with families and have treated many children. I understand completely. Sometimes you have to give your all to protect a young child, because they are so frail, so very helpless. Parents especially. They will do anything to protect their children. Is this . . . is Lizzie your child? Is she your daughter?"

He stopped crying and sniffed real loud. He looked up and me through red-rimmed eyes. "I wish'n she wore. Been better if so. But no, she ain't mine. She was Ellie's girl. I can't have children. I was gutted by a boar during a hunt when I were a teen. Fixed me up good. You might a noticed I haven't a wife."

"Ah," I said, nodding. I started to ask about Ellie, the mother, but instead said, "So, then, why were you keeping . . . Lizzie? So you could have a child of your own? Maybe you were lonely?"

"Are you sick or something? No! Why would I take a child? No, she isn't mine, but I didn't take her either."

"Did you . . . find her in the . . . tomb?"

"No. Well, in a way, I mean, that's where I was told to keep her. Now listen, I better not say nothing else. I need to talk to Mr. Addleton and the local police before you go confusing me. You act like I kidnap and kill people. You're crazy!"

"No, I'm simply trying to figure out what happened. What happened to the young child – Lizzie? Why did you have Lizzie's body in your house? I'm trying to help, to untangle things."

"You aren't! You keep saying that I killed her or something. I was protecting her, you damned fool!"

"Protecting her from whom?"

He glared at me. I tried several times more, with different approaches. That was the end of of conversation.

It was another hour before Martyn Brennard returned with Holmes, Mr. Addleton, and the police. It seemed that Mr. Addleton had insisted on coming with them, having learned that a child's body had been recovered on his property. There were fully a dozen police officers, although half of those deputized men looked as if they had never seen the inside of a courtroom – at least from a policeman's perspective. They were led by a giant of a man who was named Lieutenant Owen.

He clapped me soundly on the back and proclaimed, "Well, well! Look here, chaps! We have the man who single-handedly brought down the Monster of the Malverns!"

I looked questioning at Holmes, who frowned but offered no insight.

Martyn Brennard broke into a breathless explanation of what he had learned from the police on the way over. Apparently during the last several years, villages dotting the Malverns had suffered a number of attacks on young women, even some little girls. These horrible crimes had as yet gone unsolved. But now, with our capture of the simple-minded and mutilated gardener, in the possession of a young girl's corpse, they were assured that we had captured the "*Monster*", as the local yellow press had dubbed the attacker.

Holmes ignored the loud talk and gratuities as they tried to crowd into the little cottage and pulled me free of the press of hands trying to shake mine. Joining Brennard out front, he asked about my health. Assured that I was hale, he then turned quickly to Brennard and ordered, "Go retrieve the blanket from the child. Say nothing. Bring it to me at once. Now!"

Holmes then desired I relate all that had transpired. I knew his methods, so I did so in detail. He was most interested in the conversation I had with Evans.

During this time, most of the police, in a loud boisterous group led by the waddling Lieutenant Owen, left the cottage and went down the path to the smoke house to view the corpse.

Holmes was having me repeat exactly the words Jim Evans had told me when a scream came from inside the cottage.

We raced inside in time to see a policeman pulling Mr. Cyrus Addleton away from the tied form of Jim Evans. It was too late for Jim Evans, as a profusion of blood showed on the front of his clothes. Cyrus Addleton still clutched the knife that had been wielded to cut the throat of the gardener. A policeman wrestled the blade from his grip and then Cyrus Addleton slid down the wall.

I stepped over to examine Jim Evans, in case there was a chance things weren't as bad as they looked. There was no hope. The cut was savage and deep. Evans was no longer among the living.

Holmes stared at Addleton for several moments. He then folded his long legs and crouched beside him along the wall. "It's over now," he said softly. "You no longer have to worry."

"Yes," Addleton murmured.

"Evans was a threat to you. You did what you had to do."

"Yes."

"You got the man who hurt Ellie," Holmes whispered, his grey eyes flashing.

"Yes," Addleton said, and then his face froze. "No. What did you say?"

"Lizzie," Holmes said. "You got the man who took Lizzie."

"Y-yes," Addleton said very slowly. He pushed himself up from the floor. "I . . . I don't feel well. I need to sit down."

"You were sitting down," Holmes offered, rising to his own feet.

"I mean in my home. I want to go home. I need to rest."

It was not long before the broad Lieutenant Owen, possessor of the massive moustache instead of wits, was falling over himself to allow Addleton to return home. He even went so far as to praise him for his act of heroism.

"If you don't mind, Dr. Watson and I will accompany Mr. Addleton to his house. It's quite late and will be morning soon enough, and I would appreciate a rest before we have to get back on the road to London."

Lieutenant Owen liked the idea of fewer people at the cottage interfering with his lack of investigation and Addleton acquiesced.

Addleton didn't speak on the way back, but we found an agitated Mrs. Addleton waiting for us in the sitting room and demanding answers.

Uncharacteristically, Holmes suddenly spoke up in a bold yet warm voice, explaining what had occurred.

"We came to the Malverns, Mrs. Addleton, to investigate the discovery of a baby girl's body in the barrow on your property. It turns out that the body was not from a murder yesterday, the day before that, or even recently, but from years before. It seems the baby was poisoned. We recovered some of the poison from a dish in the barrow and analyzed it. It is a toxin local to the area and familiar to everyone from farmers and gardeners today, all the way back to the Druids of eld. Much to our horror, though, the body of the child was whisked away, in an apparent attempt to prevent investigation and identification of the child. However, we were successful is tracing it to your gardener's house – "

She blurted out, confused by what she was hearing, "At Jim's cottage? But, what – "

"Yes," Cyrus Addleton suddenly chimed in. "It turns out he was a disgusting murderer and kidnapper of little girls, Adele. He was killed while they captured him. A horrible tragedy!"

"Oh, my God!" she gasped.

"A horrible tragedy, indeed," Holmes continued. "Because, despite his best and most loyal efforts, Jim Evans didn't prevent us from learning the identity of the little girl whose body we discovered in the barrow. You see, her name was Lizzie."

Mrs. Addleton was standing as if frozen, still staring at her husband. "*Lizzie?*" she said in a weak voice.

"Yes," Holmes said. "Lizzie. A beautiful little girl. This was her blanket." He crooked a finger at Brennard, who produced the blanket and handed it to Holmes.

Holmes put the boldly patterned, knitted blanket into Mrs. Addleton's hands. "Lizzie's blanket. According to Jim Evans, Lizzie was the daughter of someone named Ellie."

Mrs. Addleton was staring down at the blanket. He face drained white and she swayed. A stark horror filled her eyes. "Ellie's," she whispered in a voice so shallow and broken, that it seemed to come from a great distance away.

I looked at Holmes and then stepped forward quickly to grab Mrs. Addleton as her knees buckled.

Mr. Addleton seems to have had the same idea and reached out to stabilize her by holding her right elbow. She hissed and jerked away as if scalded.

"Don't! Don't you dare touch me!" she shrieked and I quickly withdrew, before realizing she was only staring at her husband and moving closer to Holmes and me.

"Dear," Cyrus Addleton said, reaching out again and grabbing her arm firmly, "I can see the shock of this horrible news is overwhelming you. Let me take you upstairs – "

"Don't! You – you – !" she screamed and the words reverberated in the room.

Addleton let go of his wife's arm and stood straighter, staring at her. His eyes were cold, hard bricks of coal now. "Go upstairs, Adele. Now."

"Don't you ever tell me what to do again!" she hissed. She pointed a finger at him and said, "You told me she killed herself because of that Granger boy moving away and breaking her heart. I came back from my trip and you told me you had arranged things and buried her with some of her effects, including her baby blanket. This! This blanket!" she screamed, waving the death shroud of the little baby we had found in the barrow.

"You didn't bury it with Ellie! You buried it with her baby! She was getting sick when I left, but you and her hid the truth from me. That is why you sent me on that damned vacation to begin with. To hide the truth from me! She was pregnant!"

Mr. Addleton didn't say anything. He just stared bitterly at his wife.

"Why didn't you tell me? Why did you lie? Why didn't you let me stay here with my daughter while she was pregnant and gave birth to a child – to my granddaughter? She named her Elizabeth?" she wailed.

Addleton growled, "Yes, little Lizzie. I named her. Ellie was embarrassed. We felt it was better not to tell you about the pregnancy. She died in childbirth. I named her. We felt it was a name we all loved."

"*We* felt? *We*? Since when did she ever put any trust in you? She hated you and your loathsome affections. She used to cry all the time and

91

tell me that you would watch her, or touch her, and sometimes even come visit her at night – Oh my God!" She gasped and looked ill.

"Now, Adele. Hush yourself and get up to bed. This is all too much to take in right now. We need to get these people out of the house and – "

She pointed a trembling finger at him again. "Oh my God, it was you! It was you! It was you! That was *your* baby! I used to scold her, say that she was imagining things. Used to tell her not to make up such horrible stories. Thought it was her moodiness and rebellious streak. She was telling the truth! You *did* come to her at night and touch her!"

Cyrus Addleton grabbed his wife's hand harshly and said, "Shut up! Shut your mouth, woman! *Get . . . up . . . stairs!*"

She screamed and her other hand arced up and flew down as she drove her nails into her husband's face like daggers.

He shouted and reeled back, with four rows of blood welling down his cheek. His clenched fist rose in the air and he glared red hatred.

Holmes stepped between the two. He grabbed Cyrus Addleton by the shoulders and pushed him roughly into the adjoining room. "Calm down, sir!"

I stayed by Mrs. Addleton, who was near collapse. The shock was more than evident and I was worried that her heart might give out at any moment. She seemed to have slipped into near catatonia and her lids were half closed. With a nod to Brennard, he helped me move her over into a chair. Her entire body was trembling beneath my touch. I held her wrist and her pulse was racing wildly. If she didn't have a massive stroke sometime tonight, it would be a miracle.

Brennard was making faces at me. He waggled his eyebrows and mimed words several times, which I didn't understand. "What?" I finally asked.

"Should I go . . . ?" He nodded towards the door. "Go get the lieutenant?"

It dawned on me that perhaps he had a point. "Yes. Go get the police."

Several minutes passed and I was still by her side when Holmes rejoined me. Mrs. Addleton hadn't moved in a while. She was staring into space, barely even breathing.

Holmes pulled me into the corridor. Whispering, he said, "You must go get the police, Watson. We have unveiled the true murderer – not that loyal servant, Jim Evans. He was silenced before he could reveal the truth about the grave he attended out of sorrowful duty. However, Mr. Addleton has murdered at least twice and probably three times now, to cover his unspeakable crimes of molestation, including the murder of his own child and grandchild. We must stop him before he strikes again."

"I've already sent young Brennard."

"Excellent! Swift thinking! Now, I must return to my vigil, lest – "

Before Holmes could finish his sentence there was the loud report of a firearm.

We raced to the room of the gun's report, the room where Holmes had taken Cyrus Addleton. Adele Addleton came out the door at the same time, holding a pistol. The smell of gunpowder was strong. Holmes and I drew up short, unsure of her intentions.

Mrs. Addleton giggled, almost like a little girl. "He won't hurt anyone ever again. I ignored my own daughter. I ignored the rumors from neighbors and friends over the years that Cyrus was a lecherous brute. That he liked to . . . touch little girls. I believed him and ignored all the signs. But now I know he was a monster."

"Yes, madame," Holmes said matter-of-factly. "He truly was a monster. But you have provided a remedy. You have ended it. Your daughter can finally be at peace."

As he spoke he reached out and gingerly took the pistol from her drooping hand. He put it inside the pocket of his coat as he guided her into my arms. I walked her back into the sitting room where I had left her mere moments before.

After a few minutes of consoling her, I joined Holmes at the scene of the fresh crime. I checked the body for any signs of life, but it was apparent that Addleton was already quite dead. Mrs. Addleton had shot him through the face.

Holmes breathed, *"Chevaliers ne doit por paor de mort nule chose fair."*

My Classical education eluded me in that breathless moment. I later read the quote and those Arthurian tales from which it derived in full, which I found in the French Vulgate, but at that moment I inquired of Holmes and he explained, *"That shame must have been harder for him to bear than death."*

There was a crash from the parlour that startled me.

"Sadly, to be expected," Holmes offered as I ran past him into the other room.

Mrs. Addleton was hanging from a chandelier, her body still swaying above the overturned chair she had kicked away. One leg was bare and the silken stocking she had worn was what she had used to tie around her neck as a noose. The stocking was joined to the child's blanket which draped over two of the chandelier's canted arms. Adele Addleton's face was a blackish-purple in death and her neck had the unnatural bend that only occurs when it is snapped quickly in the violent tug of a noose. She was beyond the aid of any medical resuscitation.

At a loss, I stared at the body of the former lady of the household. She had taken her own life after leaving us in the room where she had killed her husband for his unspeakable crimes only moments before.

I finally said, "We should take down the body."

Holmes walked past me and opened the double doors to the gardens. He stared out into the pre-dawn lightening of the sky. Mists moved like ghosts across the lawn out into the barren, rocky ground that spread outwards towards the base of the Malverns.

"The police will be here within minutes. I cannot wait to leave this godforsaken place," said Holmes. "The Addleton family died years ago. This is nothing but a house of ghosts. It truly is a barrow."

"Vengeful ghosts at that," I acknowledged.

When I look at the three massive manuscript volumes which contain our work for the year 1894 I confess that it is very difficult for me, out of such a wealth of material, to select the cases which are most interesting in themselves and at the same time most conducive to a display of those peculiar powers for which my friend was famous. As I turn over the pages . . . I find an account of the Addleton tragedy and the singular contents of the ancient British barrow.

Dr. John H. Watson – "The Adventure of the Golden Pince-Nez"

The Adventure of the
Smith-Mortimer Succession
by Daniel D. Victor

No detective, not even an amateur, wants to admit that he has been the victim of thieves. And yet that was precisely the situation in which I found myself after moving back to Baker Street in late April of 1894, some two weeks after the dramatic return from the dead of my friend and colleague, Mr. Sherlock Holmes.

By now the whole world knows the astounding story of how Holmes had appeared to plunge to his death at the Reichenbach Falls in Switzerland on 4 May, 1891, how he had spent the next three years traveling incognito, and how he had finally reappeared in London to solve the murder of one Ronald Adair. Today, of course, such facts are readily available. Yet it must be remembered that for reasons never made entirely clear to me, Holmes prohibited my publishing an account of the case for some ten years following the actual events.

Adhering to Holmes's request, I waited patiently until the autumn of 1903 before he allowed me to produce the sketch I entitled "The Empty House", the narrative that detailed Holmes's so-called "hiatus". Even though he had made it quite clear that my account would not be published for a decade or more, I stood firm about recording the facts as soon as Holmes reported them to me – that is, in April of '94.

Only by noting the details while they were still fresh would I be able to fulfil the role of faithful Boswell that Holmes had attributed to me. To that end, I maintained a notebook in which I set down the salient features of the Reichenbach Affair as provided by Holmes. I kept the thin volume in a drawer of the writing desk in our sitting room, and it was the purloining of the notebook in question that placed me in the predicament to which I referred at the start of this narrative.

I discovered the theft one balmy afternoon in late May. It happened this way. Upon returning from my surgery, I encountered the perfect opportunity to write. There was no Sherlock Holmes to be found, and an hour yet remained before Mrs. Hudson would bring up our tea. No sooner had I seated myself and opened the desk-drawer, however, than I discovered that my notebook had gone missing.

I immediately summoned Billy the page. "Has anyone entered our rooms recently when Mr. Holmes and I have been out?" I asked him.

"Why, um, yeah, Doctor," said the boy, tugging self-consciously at his burgundy tunic. "Funny you should ask."

"And why is that?"

Billy shifted uneasily from foot to foot. "Some bloke, a young man 'e was and very short, came in yesterday with a bucket and sponge – said 'e was 'ere to wash the windows."

"And you," I charged in disbelief, "let him in without so much as a 'by your leave'?"

Billy blushed, unable to conceal his miscalculation. "Mrs. H. was out, Doctor, so I couldn't ask no one about the fella's story. Both you and Mr. Holmes was gone, and, strange enough, the chap sounded like an educated fellow. I reckoned no 'arm could be done, so I opened your door for 'im. You know 'ow Mrs. H. allows the police inspectors free run of the place."

"Window cleaners are not Scotland Yard detectives, Billy," said I, shaking my head in annoyance. "You should be aware, young man, that this window cleaner took an important notebook that belonged to me."

Rather than apologizing for his blunder, Billy raised a forefinger and said, "Do you know, Doctor, I thought something seemed a bit dodgy about 'im – besides 'is posh speech."

"And why is that?" I said, my voice tinged with irritation.

"Because 'e 'aint been in 'ere but five minutes, and then out 'e rushed, bucket in hand, saying 'e'd forgot 'is soap, and just like that 'e run out the front door."

Now that Billy had mentioned it, the windows looked no different from how I remembered them, dark soot sullying the glass of each pane. The strange behaviour of the window cleaner certainly seemed to confirm the intruder's guilt.

Whilst I could not let Billy leave without admonishing him for his poor judgement, I also found myself thanking him for offering so straightforward an admission. Only after the lad had gone did I stop to consider the peculiarity of the theft. Nothing else seemed missing, and I had no clue concerning what vital interest there could there be in my simple notes of Holmes's return to London. They contained no secrets. If the details of Holmes's escape from Moriarty's clutches were not already public knowledge, Holmes's reappearance in the fight against London's criminal class most certainly was. How could it not be? Elsewhere I have noted the many cases he tackled in 1894, and his presence was obviously known to all the participants in each of those investigations.

Holmes himself returned in time for tea, and I related to him the mystery involving my notes.

"Curious, Watson," said he, cocking an eyebrow. "But 'tis no great matter. Disturbing as it is to be the victim of a minor crime, no great harm can come from missing the notes of my reappearance. I shall merely repeat the details for you, and you may take them down again. More to the point, during my long absence a number of criminal acts have occurred that demand our attention. Fear not. I have no doubt that with the passage of time, your little puzzle will be solved."

Although we did not know it as we sat sampling Mrs. Hudson's tea and biscuits that afternoon, the solution to that so-called "little puzzle" was destined to appear much sooner and with greater implications than we had expected.

It was a week to the day since I had discovered the invasion of our sitting room, and I had almost succeeded in pushing the matter out of mind. Having questioned Holmes once more and recorded for a second time the facts required to complete a satisfactory account of his actions in Switzerland, I no longer had the need to dwell upon what I had come to call "The Strange Case of the Missing Notebook". That morning, however, along with the breakfast dishes and the coffee, Billy presented a letter that had been left for Holmes.

"Brought in early this morning by a footman in livery, sir," said Billy on his way out the door.

Holmes examined the envelope with its thick-stock paper, overly large monogram, and red-wax seal.

"Someone important," said he with a wry chuckle, "or at least someone who thinks he is." Holmes broke the seal and quickly scanned the letter. "Note the shaky hand in contrast to the firmest of tones," he said as he pushed the paper in my direction. It was dated that morning at Windstone Hall, Gloucestershire.

Dear Mr. Holmes [it read],

> *I shall meet with you this morning at ten a.m. in your rooms.*
> *It is of the utmost urgency, and I must insist that you cancel*
> *any other plans you might have.*

It was signed, *"Sir Lionel Smith-Mortimer, Bart"*.

"Watson," Holmes said over the rim of his coffee cup, "The *Who's Who?* if you please."

I gulped down a piece of toast and rose to fetch A.C. Black's familiar listing of influential people. It took but a moment to locate the book with its dark-blue boards and gold-lettered spine. I thumbed the pages, found the appropriate entry, and handed the open volume to Holmes.

Sipping his coffee, he read the entry quickly and summarised the salient features: "Lionel Smith-Mortimer, Baronet. Born 1822. One son named Leigh. Wife died in childbirth. In addition to an inherited title and fortune, he is the owner of Windstone Hall, a manor house in Oxfordshire. He – "

"Wait a moment, Holmes!" I cried. "I remember reading something about the man just yesterday in *The Times* – a rather tragic piece about a suicide, as I recall." I retrieved the newspaper from the small pile of spent dailies residing on a nearby table. It took me but a moment to locate the report. "Here!" said I, pointing to the story. It was indeed a melancholy announcement – *"Death of Baronet's Son"* – so sad an account that I had not gone on to read the details. Had I done so, I would certainly have called them to my friend's attention.

"Holmes," said I after quickly reviewing the piece, "it says that the young man died in the Falls of Reichenbach."

Sherlock Holmes put down his cup and stared at me with his steel-grey eyes.

"'*The coat of the deceased,'*" I read, "'*was discovered neatly folded on the path above the falls. His footprints along the path led to the edge of the precipice above the water – a drop of more than eight-hundred feet. His body has yet to be recovered.'*"

I laid down the paper and looked at my friend. If I did not know better, I could have sworn that the slightly upturned corners of Holmes's mouth displayed a hint of amusement.

"I returned from death but a month-and-a-half ago," said Holmes, "and already I seem to have created imitators." He looked at our mantel clock. "Come. It is almost ten, and unless I am very much mistaken, I hear the hooves of a pair of disciplined horses pulling a four-wheeler to the kerb. We should prepare to meet our distinguished guest."

Sherlock Holmes exchanged his mouse-coloured dressing gown for a dark jacket, and I proceeded to don my coat. It was a matter of minutes before Mrs. Hudson herself climbed the stairs to introduce our guest. No pageboys for the likes of a Baronet.

"Enter!" Sherlock Holmes commanded at her knock.

Mrs. Hudson stood at the portal and announced, "Sir Lionel Smith-Mortimer." Then, bowing her head and straightening her skirt, she backed out into the hallway and closed the door.

I must say that, whilst I knew this Baronet to be a septuagenarian, I nonetheless expected to behold someone of erect and noble bearing.

Instead, I saw before us a scowling old man with a stoop to his back and a hand curled like a great claw over the round, silver head of his walking stick. With a nod to fashion, he wore an expertly tailored suit, its dark frock coat contrasting with his yellowing white hair. Patent leather boots and kid gloves complemented his attire.

"Sir Lionel," said my friend, "I am Sherlock Holmes." He introduced me as well and gestured towards the armchair reserved for his clients.

The Baronet gave a quick frown in my direction and then, with some effort, shuffled to the proffered seat and sat down. Holmes and I took chairs opposite him.

"Let me first say, sir," announced the elderly client with a thump of his stick, "that I don't fancy being here one bit." He rapped his stick on the floor a second time to punctuate his point. "Only because of Leigh's faith in you have I come at all."

Holmes stared at the man, offering no discernible response.

"Without doubt you have seen the reports of my son's accident."

We both nodded respectfully.

"Simply put, I don't believe them. I want to know what really happened. All I do know is that he was off in Switzerland wandering about with a friend."

"A friend?" Holmes asked.

"Yes. One Reginald Bentley. A barrister by profession. Known each other for about a year. Bentley and my son travel together when the opportunity presents itself. London not good enough for them. They want to see the world."

"And where was this Bentley at the time of your son's death?" Holmes asked.

"*Alleged* death, may I remind you. He remained at the hotel near the Reichenbach Falls, don't you know."

"At the *Englischer Hof*?" I asked. Noting the similarity to our own ill-fated trip three years before, I guessed the two men might have stayed in the same hotel Holmes and I had occupied.

As if he suspected that I possessed too much arcane information, Sir Lionel knit his brow. But all he said was, "By Jove, when I hear of a mysterious death and no corpse is produced, I have my doubts. You may think I sound like some suspicious figure in one of your adventures, Holmes, but that may be in part because of the interest that Leigh expressed in reading them himself."

"I appreciate the compliment, Sir Lionel," said Holmes, "but under the circumstances, one cannot escape an uncomfortable conclusion. The apparent death of your son mirrors – however imprecisely – my own

99

rumoured demise. Given the fact that I have only just returned from that narrow escape, one has to marvel at the coincidence."

"Quite," muttered Sir Lionel.

It was all I could do not to call attention to the theft of my notes. The young man posing as a window cleaner whom Billy had observed, the one with an educated manner of speech – might he be none other than Leigh Smith-Mortimer, whose father now sat before us? Recreating the death of Sherlock Holmes, someone he admired, might have been his morbid motivation. Perhaps Leigh Smith-Mortimer had sought to end his life in dramatic fashion not unlike the storied suicide of young Romantic poet Thomas Chatterton.

"I must confess," said Holmes, "that my personal history in this situation adds impetus to my curiosity. I, too, would like to know what happened to your son, Sir Lionel. I shall take your case."

The Baronet withdrew a wallet of light-coloured leather from inside his jacket. "Name your fee, Holmes," said he.

"Later," my friend replied. "All my clients pay at the same rate, Sir Lionel. But concerning this case in particular, its proper resolution will furnish me with additional reward."

The Baronet gazed at his wallet. "I almost forgot," said he, extracting a photograph and a small card from the billfold. "My son and Bentley," he explained in reference to the photograph. "Inseparable friends. The card contains information about Bentley's chambers in Gray's Inn."

Holmes took the items, examined them briefly, and handed them to me. In the photograph, two serious-looking young men in straw boaters – the taller one with a moustache, the shorter, clean-shaven – stared back."

"Leigh is the one without the whiskers," said Sir Lionel as, using his stick as a brace, he struggled to rise. "As for Bentley, he works at Mapplethorpe and Ruggles, and I have already prepared him for a possible visit from you."

"We'll see him post-haste," said Holmes, ushering the old man to the door.

Sir Lionel stopped to address my friend. "This matter is of great importance to me, Holmes. In addition to the welfare of my son, I feel compelled to point out that he is my only issue. He arrived late in my life, and his mother died tragically during his birth. It was quite horrible really. The babe chose to appear when Lady Smith-Mortimer and I were vacationing in the mountains near Lake Windermere. It was all so sudden. We were alone in the woods, and I had to deliver the child myself as my wife lay dying.

"Horrible," I said.

Sir Lionel ignored my sympathetic response. "What's more," he added, standing up as straight as seemed possible for him, "neither can I neglect the deposition of my estate."

"It is entailed?" Holmes asked.

"Indeed. All I possess will be inherited by my closest male heir. If Leigh is truly no longer living, then Windstone Hall will be dealt off to some distant cousin in Canada. That is why it is imperative that I find out what happened to my son."

"Understood," said Holmes. "I will report to you as soon as I learn anything."

We listened as Sir Lionel made his way down the seventeen steps, his walking stick producing a distinctive thump on each one.

Holmes moved a window curtain aside so he could watch Sir Lionel enter the four-wheeler that awaited him by the kerb .

I heard the latch of the carriage door and then the rumble of the coach as it clattered down Baker Street.

"Come, Watson," said Holmes. "This investigation will begin with an interview of Leigh Smith-Mortimer's traveling companion, Mr. Reginald Bentley, Esquire, at the Inns of Court."

The chambers of Mapplethorpe and Ruggles had been established in Gray's Inn during the early years of the century. It was in the Gray's Inn Gardens that Reginald Bentley had agreed that we meet him. To that end, we flagged a hansom at our front door and were soon rattling along Oxford Street. Southampton Row brought us to High Holborn and the Inns of Court. We alighted at the wood-panelled frontage of the Cittie of Yorke public house that stands at the narrow alleyway leading to Gray's Inn. Entering the grounds through the main gate, we passed the South Square to our right and made our way under the archway leading to the green swards of the Walks, as the spacious gardens are commonly called.

Holmes had arranged our meeting for one o'clock, and under the mid-day sun we strolled along the gravel path enveloped by the iridescent colours and sweet aromas of the season. Spring seems so wrong a time to hold discussions of death – especially among the yellow daffodils and blue hyacinths and roses of pink and white and red attempting to distract us. After a few additional paces, however, we recognised the moustachioed chap from the photograph seated on a nearby bench.

Reginald Bentley was sitting in the shade of the London planes and elms that populated the Walks, and he rose upon our arrival. "Gentlemen," said he, "Thank you for agreeing to see me outside of chambers. This tragedy is no one's business but our own. Besides, I also

101

appreciate the moments I can spend away from my desk." He pointed to a low-slung block of yellow-brick offices across the lawn. "Mapplethorpe and Ruggles suffer the confinement of the Raymond Buildings over there. As you must already know, Leigh and I always enjoyed our walks through the countryside."

"Which leads us to the Falls of Reichenbach," said Holmes. "As I understand it, your friend seemed intrigued by my personal history – so much so that he literally walked in my very footsteps. How does one account for this obsessive interest?"

"Let us sit," said Bentley, gesturing towards the bench. "Justice was paramount for Leigh," he explained once we were settled. "I should imagine his concern was based upon his own sense of victimhood."

"Victimhood?" I echoed, imagining the rich surroundings of Windstone Hall in which the boy had grown up. "In what way?"

"I know what you're thinking, Dr. Watson – the money that must have smothered Leigh when he was a child. But, you see, it was that very legacy that constantly weighed him down. His father had made it clear to Leigh that he had to marry and have sons to carry on the line – you know, gentlemen, the usual upper-class prattle."

"You don't approve of the British aristocracy?" I could not refrain from asking.

"Look," he said, "my own father is a banker, and fortunately for me was able to send me to university. I have benefitted greatly from my education. After all, here I sit, installed in the legal profession and quite able to pay my own bills."

"Rather proves my point, eh?" I said.

"Within reason, Doctor. I don't believe one should be forced to live the life one's father confers upon him, however much money that involves, if that is not the life one chooses for himself."

The young man may have had a valid point for the common fellow, but one cannot allow the upper classes to make such choices. Where would we be if the heirs to the throne could choose willy-nilly whether they wanted to be king? One could scarcely imagine a royal monarch giving up the crown to marry a commoner. Of course, such dilemmas did not concern a mere medical man like myself – not that sort of money in my family, I'm afraid.

Holmes brought the conversation back to practicalities. "Tell me about this trip the two of you took to Switzerland," he said.

Bentley patted down his moustache. "When Sir Lionel notified me that you'd be coming to talk about Leigh, I assumed you would ask about that final journey." He withdrew a map from an inner pocket and, unfolding it, proceeded to lay the sheet flat on the bench between

Holmes and himself. "Leigh invited me to join him with the understanding that I would follow his instructions without questioning them. He told me he had a plan, and I agreed to go along."

Sherlock Holmes studied the chart, his eyes flashing as he noted the familiar route now coloured in red.

"I took the liberty to mark our course," said Bentley. "It was a singular excursion." As the young man spoke, he traced the progress of their trip with his forefinger. "We boarded the *Continental Express* here at Victoria. I had originally thought we would cross the Channel at Dover and sail the twenty-two miles to Calais, but Leigh had other plans. He insisted we change trains at Canterbury for the run to Newhaven, a decision that caused us to switch twice more at Ashford and Lewes. When I asked him why, he answered with your name, Mr. Holmes."

"Quite so," Holmes nodded. "Pray, continue."

"I'm sure you yourself can supply the details. At Newhaven, we sailed to Dieppe – " Here Bentley's finger on the map slid across the blue of the Channel. " – a crossing, I might add, three times the duration of the crossing at Dover. From Dieppe we travelled by train to Brussels, and then on to Strasbourg and Geneva. Following a week's walk though the Rhone Valley, we made our way to Leuk, climbed the Gemmi Pass in the Central Alps, and finally arrived just a short distance from the Reichenbach Falls in a town called Meiringen. We stayed in the *Englischer Hof*, run by – "

"Let me guess," I interrupted, "Peter Steiler the Elder."

"Correct, Dr. Watson. But from what I understand, you and Mr. Holmes stayed in the same hotel."

"Quite so," said Holmes again. Then he added vaguely, "It was all done for professional reasons."

Leigh Smith-Mortimer may have stolen my notes concerning the geographical route Holmes and I had taken to Meiringen, but obviously Holmes still wanted to conceal the details connected with the criminal activities of Professor Moriarty and his associate Colonel Moran.

"We had travelled so far a distance in so roundabout a fashion, gentlemen, that once we had reached our destination, I saw no reason to suddenly start doubting my friend's sanity. Thus, when early the next morning Leigh told me he wished to go alone to view the Reichenbach Falls, I acquiesced. It was the last time I ever saw him." Here Reginald Bentley hung his head. Had I been less sympathetic, I might have regarded it as an altogether too theatrical a pose.

"And then?" Holmes asked. "No doubt you alerted the police."

"When Leigh failed to return, I myself walked up to the Falls – ran, really."

I nodded with appreciation. Had I not made the same fateful run under the most similar of conditions?

"That," Bentley resumed, "was when I found Leigh's folded jacket and tweed cap lying at the end of the small path leading to the rushing waters. Once I saw those personal items, I suspected that something was truly wrong, and I summoned the police. We all returned to the scene, and they examined the footmarks leading to the edge and not returning. Alas, there was but one sad conclusion to draw – that Leigh had thrown himself from the precipice, his body disappearing in the churning waters below."

Holmes arched his eyebrows. "It would certainly seem so," said he. "Did you detect anything in Leigh Smith-Mortimer's nature that would lead you to imagine he could do such a thing?"

Sighing heavily, Bentley stared up into the cloudless blue sky. Perhaps he was hoping to find an answer somewhere in the heavens. "I can only tell you," he said, "that he hated the role in which his father had placed him. But I assure you, gentlemen, that I never suspected that Leigh was unhappy enough to do himself in. There's really not much else I have to say on the subject – except that I miss my friend greatly."

Holmes stood up. "Thank you, Mr. Bentley," said he. "You've been a great help to us."

The barrister collected his map and gently folded it along the creases. Replacing it in his coat pocket, he shook hands with the two of us and wished us well. We accompanied him as far as his chambers and then bade him good day.

"Do you realize, Watson," said Holmes once we reached High Holborn, "that thanks to Mr. Bentley – not to mention the dead Mr. Smith-Mortimer – we are going to have to return to the scene of some of our most unpleasant memories." When he raised his hand to flag a hansom, he bore the gravest of expressions.

Unlike our first trip to the Reichenbach Falls, we required no subterfuge on this occasion. We faced no adversary like Moriarty in his special train to fool into thinking we were going to Paris. The *Express* from Victoria took us directly to Dover. From there, a ship conveyed us to Calais. With no need to pose as carefree pedestrians touring the Valley of the Rhone or exploring the Alps of central Switzerland, we utilised the various railroads traversing the French and Swiss countrysides to deposit us at the chalet-like train station in Meiringen.

Holmes and I may not have looked like the tourists we had hoped to resemble three years before, but even on that earlier occasion we had no cause to conceal our true identities. When we reached the *Englischer*

Hof, therefore, old Peter Steiler greeted Holmes in particular like an old friend.

"*Ach*, Herr Holmes," said Steiler, his English helped by an earlier stay in London, "it is as though you come from the dead. I heard of your return and am pleased to know that you did not die in the Reichenbach waters."

"And yet someone else just did, *nicht wahr*?" Holmes asked.

"*Ja*," answered Steiler. "A young Englishman. Like you, from here he went walking on his own."

"It is his death, Herr Steiler, that I am here to investigate. How was he dressed?"

The old man thought for a moment, then smiled broadly as he remembered the details. "Heavy trousers. Heavy coat. Good boots. Flat cap."

Holmes nodded. "Nothing else?"

"But of course," said Steiler. "*Schon vergessen*. A very large rucksack he carried on his back."

"Ha!" ejaculated Holmes, slapping his hand on the counter. "Precisely as I expected. Come, Watson. We shall soon get to the bottom of this mystery."

Snow-covered mountain peaks served as backdrop when, for the second time in our adventures, Holmes and I marched up the incline towards the series of falls. From the bottom of the road one cannot see the water itself, only the winding trail leading up and past the three mighty torrents that ultimately rain down as one. It took us some ten minutes to reach the lowest of the falls, an additional fifteen to reach the central, and another thirty to get to the uppermost.

Veiled in the shadows of the numerous fir trees, we plodded upward. Holmes kept his eyes on the ground searching for any tell-tale clues. For me, however, the path served only to conjure terrible memories. During that first ascent three years before, I had been called back to the hotel on a ruse, and I shall never forget the horrible fear I experienced when I rushed back up this same mountain trail hoping against hope that my friend still lived.

Now as then, the fearsome roar of the waterfall attracted us like a magnet. Skirting the ominous rock walls that towered above, I followed after Holmes in the direction of the thunderous din. To witness the waters cascade in waves of white foam down the glistening black walls of stone and plunge into the cavernous abyss is to see unmasked the overwhelming power and beauty of Nature.

Yet once we reached the narrow path leading to the edge of the final precipice, my morbid recollections eclipsed the grandeur. A wave of nausea overcame me as soon as I encountered the very boulder against which Holmes had leaned his Alpine stock and upon which he had left his farewell note. Enveloped by the clouds of mist and spray that hovered above the roiling waters, I forced myself to halt at a safe distance from the brink. The world around me was beginning to spin. With the mountain wall on one side and the straight drop a short distance before me, I placed my palm against the wet stone and took a series of deep breaths.

Holmes, who was stooping over a handful of black soil a few steps ahead, looked back over his shoulder and saw my condition. Whether my unsettled appearance affected his judgement, I shall never know, but with a quick shake of his head, he shouted at me over the water's roar, "No need to go any farther!" Then he gave the dirt in his hand a final peremptory look and tossed the stuff to the ground. "The path is of no use to us," said he loudly, slapping his hands together to rid them of any residual muck. "It's too moist, and too many footprints have already marred the trail. I should imagine that the authorities themselves have stomped across it and obliterated whatever clues we might have hoped to find."

"Are we done here, then?" I shouted back hopefully.

In answer, Holmes looked up at the sheer mountain wall by our side. "Do you see it, Watson?" he asked, pointing to a projection some twenty feet above our heads. "The ledge that shielded me when you brought the police here to examine the scene."

So long ago, and yet the memory of my exclusion from his plan still stung. I imagine that I will always harbour some resentment towards Holmes for letting me continue to think him dead. It was only the ultimate jubilation I experienced upon his return that alleviated the pain.

"We need another point of vantage," said he and, keeping his eye on the wall to our left, he proceeded to march back in the direction from which we had come. Though each step away from the edge helped restore my strength, I suddenly feared Holmes was searching for the invisible footholds he had employed in his earlier escape in order to scale the wall once again. At the point where the wall fell away, however, he stopped and, turning to his left once more, stared at a network of overgrown brambles and ferns.

"A-ha!" he said at last and roughly pushed aside the overgrowth.

In an instant I perceived a hidden pathway ascending round the back of the mountain, and together Holmes and I scrambled up the steep terrain. Only when we reached a small plateau did I realise that we must be at the same spot where Colonel Moran had watched the struggle between Moriarty and Holmes unfold. It would have been here that

106

Moran, intent on completing the job that Moriarty had thankfully been unable to consummate, rained down upon Holmes a shower of large rocks and stones.

Today, of course, there were no such dangers. In spite of the tumble of tree branches that blocked part of the view, we could now readily discern some twenty yards beneath us the rectangular outcropping that had served as Holmes's hiding place. The ledge was several feet deep, and verdant moss, like a green wool rug, blanketed the small nooks and crannies of its stone floor.

From an inner pocket, Sherlock Holmes drew a pair of binoculars, which he trained on the area below. "Owing to the proximity of the Falls," he observed as he peered through the lenses, "the moss-bed remains continuously moist. I can assure you from experience that not only does it provide a comfortable nest, but it also retains footmarks exceedingly well."

For a few moments more he proceeded to scan the ledge. *"Eureka!"* he suddenly shouted and, handing me the glasses, commanded, "Look for yourself."

I adjusted the lenses and observed the patterns in the moss more closely. Where before I had seen only gentle folds, I now made out among the rear shadows a long indentation where someone had recently lain. I could also begin to distinguish a few scattered footprints. At one edge of the projection, I detected what appeared to be the broad marks of a man's boots. At the other edge –

"Hold on," I said to Holmes. "Are those not the footprints of a woman's shoe?"

"Precisely what I expected," said Holmes, clapping his hands together.

"But what can such footprints mean? For that matter, Holmes, what does any of it mean?"

"To London, Watson!" said he by way of answer. Motioning me to follow, he hurried along the downhill trail, his eyes focused on the path before him. Thanks to the information furnished by the binoculars, we now knew for what to look. And truth be told, clearly discernable along the way were the occasional woman's footprints mingling with all the other marks that had churned up much of the earth.

"We have learned all that we could hope for here in Switzerland," proclaimed Sherlock Holmes. "It is now time to reacquaint ourselves with Mr. Reginald Bentley."

Amberwell House, a modest building of soot-darkened stone, can be found in Southampton Row between Russell Square and Theobalds

Road. Thanks to its proximity to the Inns of Court, the establishment provides lodgings for many of the solicitors and barristers who work nearby. Two days after our return from the Continent, Reginald Bentley suggested the Amberwell in response to our request to speak with him.

"*Amberwell House at the end of my workday,*" he had wired back.

As he led us to a group of grey-leather-backed chairs in the corner of the small lobby, the moustached barrister seemed ill at ease. He continually looked round although, except for the clerk at the front desk and a man across the way hidden behind a newspaper, the lobby was deserted.

"We have just returned from the Reichenbach Falls," Holmes began. "Let us get straight to the point, shall we?"

Avoiding Holmes's gaze, Bentley fidgeted with the cuffs of his jacket. "I don't know what you mean," he mumbled.

"We believe that your friend, Mr. Leigh Smith-Mortimer, stole Dr. Watson's notes that dealt with my near-death experience three years ago. Just a few days later, you accompanied him in the re-creation of our previous trip to Switzerland. You have alleged that he left you in your room at the *Englischer Hof* in order to go walking on his own. Further, you maintain that he never returned – that he fell, or hurled himself, to the bottom of the Falls."

"As I have already said."

"Then, sir," came Holmes's blunt reply, "not to put too fine a point on it, I do not believe you."

Bentley's eyes grew wide. He was about to sputter out some retort, but Holmes kept speaking.

"Oh, I do not doubt that Smith-Mortimer went off to the Falls on his own, but I must conclude that you knew of his plans from the start – that, in fact, the two of you conspired to make it appear that Leigh Smith-Mortimer had leaped to his death never to be heard from again."

"Now, see here, Mr. Holmes," Bentley countered, "I won't have you disparage Leigh that way, not to mention myself. Do you not remember that it was I who notified the police?"

"And yet, Mr. Bentley, it was also you who failed to inform them that the presumed-dead Smith-Mortimer was in reality hiding on the ledge not twenty feet above them. You, must admit, sir, that – " But Holmes never finished the sentence.

"Enough!" came the forceful, high-pitched voice of the man whom I supposed to have been reading the newspaper. He slammed the pages to the floor and stalked over to us. "Leave Reginald alone, Mr. Holmes. *I* am the one you seek. I am Leigh Smith-Mortimer."

Holmes and I both stared up at the man – though, in truth, not very far up. From his photograph, we knew him to be shorter than his friend. But in the flesh, his entire stature appeared much slighter in spite of the well-cut, dark suit that must have come from Saville Row. His face bore delicate features, and his dark hair was cut short.

Reginald Bentley offered him his own seat while Bentley himself collected the chair that Smith-Mortimer had just been occupying.

"Well, well," Holmes said with a quick smile. "The very man we speak of. He who has dogged my footsteps to death's door at the Reichenbach Falls appears very much alive. What do you have to say for yourself, *sir*?" This last word was heavily emphasised, and at the same time there appeared in my friend's eye the same inexplicable twinkle that I had seen when he had first heard the details of the young man's disappearance.

"Reginald has told me," Leigh Smith-Mortimer replied, "that you already know how much I detest my father and his domination – all in the name of his legacy. A plague on that legacy! I tell you, Mr. Holmes, that I could take it no longer. I wanted a means of escape. I've read of your investigations, and when I heard of your so-called death and resurrection, it gave me the idea to do the same.

"Your return being so recent, I assumed that Dr. Watson would have his notes concerning the affair lying about. As you have surmised, I entered your rooms in disguise and stole his notebook. Reginald and I then followed all of your steps to be certain we didn't miss any of the planning that led to your success."

"Stealing my notes," I muttered. "Not very sporting."

"I'm sorry, Doctor, but your notebook furnished me with the kind of details I needed – like the footholds leading to the ledge above the path. As did you, Mr. Holmes, I hid there from the police during their investigation, and when they had gone, I made my way back to London. Under a pseudonym, I took a room here at the Amberwell down the hall from Reginald. Now, I suppose, you will notify my father, and he will attempt to have me return to Windstone Hall."

"Your father is my client," said Holmes. "He has contracted me to find you. And yet, should I so choose, a rejection of his money would rid me of the responsibility."

The young man's eyes suddenly blazed with hope. "You'd do that, Mr. Holmes?"

"I assure you, Mr. Smith-Mortimer, that in the name of fair play, I have committed a number of unconventional actions. I am no official police force, you understand. But I must give your situation some thought. I don't overturn my clients' requests lightly. And whilst there is

109

no law that will force you to go back to your father, the law of decency makes it imperative for me to let him know that you are alive and well. I suggest that we meet at Baker Street tomorrow afternoon. I shall send you a telegram once I have arranged the matter with Sir Lionel."

With that Holmes rose, and I followed. As we exited the Amberwell, I could not fail to notice that behind us an animated discussion was going on between the two young men.

"Well, Watson, what do you make of the situation?" Holmes asked once we had found ourselves in Southampton Row again and walking towards the Strand.

"I believe that you were quite right in reserving additional time to consider your responsibilities. Still, I must say that there seems no let-up in young Smith-Mortimer's grudge against his father. Unreasonable, I should think – in light of the rules that dictate the responsibilities of a titled son."

Sherlock Holmes stopped in his tracks. "Good old Watson – forever faithful to the traditions of our culture. And yet you miss the salient feature."

I could not see where Holmes was leading me. The antagonisms between father and son seemed quite clear.

"My dear fellow," said Holmes. "You have failed to recognise the fact that Mr. Leigh Smith-Mortimer – 'the titled son', as you call him – is in reality a woman."

Even I, the so-called man of words, was speechless. At last I spat out, "You – you can't be serious, Holmes."

"But I am, old fellow. Of course, you noted the delicate features, the short but luxuriant hair, the small frame, the lilting voice."

"Yes, all of which proves nothing."

"But when you couple those decidedly feminine characteristics with a masculine life dictated by the unforgiving laws of primogeniture, you discover a wretched soul forced to play a part counter to her nature."

"But, Holmes. Surely birth certificates, doctors' statements – all would discount your inflammatory charges."

"Remember the birth, Watson. The couple were alone wandering the woods. Who knows? Perhaps Sir Lionel had purposely arranged their isolated perambulations to coincide with the time the birth was expected. Fortunately, he managed to deliver the child, but unhappily could do nothing regarding the complications that killed Lady Smith-Mortimer. Clearly, there would be no more children. I imagine that in the confusion that followed, the doctors devoted their attention to saving the poor mother and simply taken Sir Reginald's word for the sex of the baby.

Money paid out to wet-nurses and nannies would have purchased the silence of any others who knew the truth.

Such a wild plan certainly explained Holmes's fantastic accusation.

"I suspected some sort of ruse," said he, "as soon as Sir Lionel began complaining so bitterly about his son. I thought the old man protested too much. Upon observing the young person, I am now convinced."

"But the pretend suicide, Holmes, the climb up the mountain to the ledge. Surely, no *woman* could be expected to perform such feats!"

"Ah, Watson," Holmes smiled, "how did Hamlet put it to Horatio? *'There are more things in heaven and earth than are dreamt of in your philosophy.'* I find women quite as capable as men in accomplishing whatever they put their mind to." He turned silent, and I knew he must have been thinking of the machinations set up by Irene Adler a few years before that had succeeded in thwarting him.

"But what's the point, Holmes?" I asked breaking into his thoughts. "Even if Sir Reginald had succeeded in passing the girl off as a boy, there could be no children in her future, no male heir to claim the estate."

"A crazed old man trying to hold on to what is his for as long as possible," Holmes offered. He grew silent again. In fact, the only words he uttered after we had reached Aldwych, were, "Let us continue on and dine at Simpson's. Afterwards, I shall make arrangements with Sir Lionel for tomorrow's meeting."

With the late-afternoon sun to our backs, we negotiated the Aldwych Crescent, our long shadows stretching out before us. I remember thinking at the time how well those shadows epitomised the case. Whatever had been going on in the mind of Sir Lionel Smith-Mortimer for the past twenty years must have been very murky indeed.

Mrs. Hudson had prepared tea for five people as we had requested. The stooped form of Sir Lionel arrived first, his trek up our stairs punctuated by the beat of his cane. He looked at the tea service and chocolate biscuits set out on the dining table, shook his head, and selected an armchair to sit upon that was far removed from the table.

"Tell me your news, Holmes," he demanded.

"In due time, sir. We await the others."

"What others?"

As if in answer, a sharp knock rattled our door. Holmes opened it to Reginald Bentley. The barrister entered the room, but not by himself. He was accompanied by a magnificent young woman in a dress of yellow cotton, accented in white at the neck and cuffs. Adorned with a white feather, a small yellow hat perched coquettishly upon her short black curls. It nearly took my breath away to realise that only the day before I had been conversing with this very person under the impression that I was speaking to one Leigh Smith-Mortimer, the only son of a Baronet.

"Watson," said Holmes with a gesture towards the lady, "may I re-introduce you to Leigh Smith-Mortimer. That is, *Miss* Leigh Smith-Mortimer."

"Now see here!" interrupted Sir Lionel. "I won't stand for this *charade*."

Miss Smith-Mortimer had been about to take my hand when she wheeled upon her father. "*You* won't stand for this *charade*?" she charged, cheeks reddening, nostrils flaring. "I've been play-acting in your little game for as long as I can remember. Always the boy – to preserve the line! Even though you've always known that the line would end with me. You knew I could never marry as a man. And now I have found someone who has seen through this masquerade and wants to love me as a woman should be loved. I am through with your game, Father. May Windstone Hall crumble to the earth for all I care!"

"Leigh," Sir Lionel said, holding out both hands. "After your mother died and there was no possibility for a male heir – "

"Stop, Father!" she cried. "I have heard all this before. Let the succession fall to cousins twice-removed – or *three*-times removed. It doesn't matter anymore. You robbed me of my proper childhood, and I won't allow you to rob me of my marriage." She turned to Bentley. "That is," she said, her voice now lowered, "if you'll have me."

Reginald Bentley took her in his arms. "I love you, Leigh. Your beautiful nature has always shone through your disguise. We did our best to kill off the male version of yourself, and now, thanks to Mr. Holmes, you've been able to speak the truth."

The young woman stood as tall as she could. "I am leaving you now, Father," she said simply. "As you've just heard, Reginald and I will soon be married. Good man that he is, he has convinced me to invite you to the wedding. It is your choice whether you want to gain a daughter and, God willing, grandchildren or live on in isolation. The choice will be yours."

Before leaving, the couple turned to Holmes and me. "Thank you, gentlemen," said Bentley. "At first I feared you might bring ruination upon us, but now I see that shining a light on this bizarre story has brought us salvation instead." The two of them smiled and hand in hand slowly made their way down the stairs.

With a dissatisfied grunt, Sir Lionel leaned on his cane in order to stand. He took a deep breath and, without looking at either of us, placed a one-hundred-pound note on the table as he shuffled to the door. Not a word was spoken by anyone.

Once the door closed, I walked to the table set for tea and sampled one of Mrs. Hudson's chocolate biscuits.

Reginald Bentley had relatives who lived in the hamlet of Icomb in Gloucestershire It was there in the tiny church of St. Mary the Virgin that he and Leigh Smith-Mortimer chose to marry a few short weeks after the events described. Although Holmes and I were invited to the ceremony, we decided not to attend. It was to be a small affair, and our presence would only serve to raise uncomfortable questions. Happily, there were no pressmen in attendance, and Miss Smith-Mortimer sent us an account in her own hand of all that had transpired.

True to her word, she did request her father's presence. And I am pleased to report that, difficult as it was for him both physically and emotionally, Sir Lionel travelled to Gloucestershire to give his daughter away. Villagers must have wondered about the splendid carriage and liveried footman at so simple a ceremony, but their wonder never reached the spiteful arena of London gossip – at least not then.

Three years later, however, Sir Lionel died, and the facts regarding his mistreatment of his daughter became the fodder of scandal throughout the land. Just as the Baronet had predicted, with no son to inherit the estate, the grand manor house along with the rest of the riches was passed on by virtue of entailment to a distant Canadian cousin called Randolph Carlton Smith.

It had been my desire to maintain the privacy of the newly-married couple. To that end, I included the Smith-Mortimer affair in the collection of cases from 1894 that I chose not to make public. Yet however noble in intent, the gesture turned out to be laughably feeble.

Periodicals could not print enough about the story to satisfy the public. Newspapers constantly rehashed the details; magazines furnished long-winded biographies of the principals. So widespread were the accounts of the ugly business that one can understand why I had originally referred to the entailment case as "famous". In retrospect, I believe that "infamous" would have been the more appropriate adjective.

When I look at the three massive manuscript volumes which contain our work for the year 1894 I confess that it is very difficult for me, out of such a wealth of material, to select the cases which are most interesting in themselves and at the same time most conducive to a display of those peculiar powers for which my

113

friend was famous . . . . The famous Smith-Mortimer succession case comes also within this period . . . .

Dr. John H. Watson – "The Adventure of the Golden Pince-Nez"

A Repulsive Story and a Terrible Death
by Nik Morton

It was Thursday, the twenty-eighth of June, 1894 when he stepped into our chambers. Mrs. Hudson hovered anxiously in the background. He was tall, dressed in an immaculate broadcloth suit, his rim beard neatly trimmed. He removed his bowler hat and strode forward with confidence, his hand out-stretched.

"Randall Gresham, if I am not mistaken," said Holmes, shaking his hand.

"Yes," Mr. Gresham replied, his hazel eyes wide in astonishment. "But we have not met before, Mr. Holmes . . . ."

"I keep abreast of the society periodicals. I recall your wedding was reported last month in *The Illustrated London News*. My belated congratulations."

"Thank you. You are most kind." His countenance did not reflect a life of marital bliss.

"What ails you, sir?" I ventured to enquire.

"Dr. Watson is the man for you, perhaps, Mr. Gresham. He has vast experience in the state of matrimony." There was a twinkle in my friend's eye. He was sorely aware of my dear Mary's recent demise, but his badinage over these weeks since our eventful reunion had helped me shrug off dread despond. With regard to the adage, *"Physician, heal thyself,"* I need not worry, for I had the irrepressible Sherlock Holmes to cure me of any morbidity.

"Oh, my concerns do not relate to my good wife," our prospective client revealed.

"Then it must be one of your two partners, Crosby or Dors," Holmes suggested, which left me nonplussed.

I peered at my friend and his thin lips twitched in amusement.

The light dawned on me. "The private bank triumvirate!" I exclaimed, rather pleased with myself.

"You are aware of our business dealings, I see, good sirs," responded Gresham. "That is most gratifying."

Holmes nodded. "Crosby, Gresham, and Dors, is reputed to be a reliable bank with a select clientele."

"Dors is a sleeping partner, actually," Gresham elucidated.

115

Despite being familiar with French verb conjugation, I refrained from commenting on the fitting aspect of Mr. Dors's name and role.

"Please be seated." Holmes gestured to the chair by the fireplace, and then reached for his pipe and the Persian slipper on the mantelpiece.

I took out my notepad, pencil poised.

"Mr. Crosby has gone missing . . . ." Gresham blurted out.

"Start at the beginning, if you will," Holmes instructed with characteristic firmness, tamping down the tobacco.

"Oh, well, yes, I do tend to get ahead of myself sometimes. Josiah Crosby is a far more adventurous soul than either myself or Lucien Dors. But he also has a first-rate brain with exceedingly good financial acumen."

Holmes lit his pipe. "Your bank relies on this acumen a great deal, I take it?" he observed.

"We do. Yet, since his return from an expedition with a Dutch explorer, he has begun to behave erratically."

Holmes exhaled smoke. "You refer to the Nieuwenhuis Expedition?" said he.

Gresham stared in surprise. "Yes. He was elected as treasurer for the expedition and arranged all the finances for the transport, money-changing, and so forth. Mr. Nieuwenhuis said Crosby was a boon. While it presented good publicity for our bank, Crosby's presence was sorely missed."

"The expedition," said Holmes, "is at present on its way to the Mahakam, is it not?"

"You are well informed, Mr. Holmes. Indeed, that is so. But alas, Crosby stayed behind with Dr. Büttikofer at the village of Nanga Raun until last month."

"Büttikofer, the Swiss zoologist?"

"That is him, yes. While in that village, Crosby contracted a mysterious illness and returned to England a matter of three weeks ago in the company of a Belgian, Dr. De Smet, who has acted as his physician."

I turned to Holmes. "Have you heard of Dr. De Smet? I must confess that I haven't."

Holmes nodded sombrely. "He is an adherent of Sigmund Freud's brand of medical psychopathology. His analysis regarding unconscious repression is in its infancy, but the work bears further study." Holmes turned to Gresham and raised an eyebrow. "Immediately on arrival home, Crosby began exhibiting abnormal behaviour?"

"Yes, Mr. Holmes. Precisely!"

Holmes harrumphed. "What kind of behaviour?"

116

"He is so unlike the man I knew." Gresham's hands fidgeted with the bowler in his lap. "He has evinced terribly poor attention span, and that he seemed to have great difficulty reading and writing!"

"That must be of great concern in your business," Holmes said, which I construed as a remarkable understatement.

"Precisely, Mr. Holmes!"

I leaned forward, intrigued. "Did you question him about his difficulties?"

"I was most solicitous. Crosby's eyes were sunken in their sockets, though I attributed that to his recent illness. Whenever I spoke to him, he cocked his head to one side, as if listening to something or someone else. I found his whole manner most disconcerting."

"I can well understand that, Mr. Gresham," my friend acceded. "Even so, it sounds as though you should be consulting Dr. Watson rather than me." He placed his pipe on the mantelpiece and strode over to the window and looked out, as if bored with the direction of the interview.

Gresham gave me a sidelong glance. "Perhaps. But two days ago, Crosby left his home and has not been heard from since. And shortly after discovering his absence, I learned that a number of private deposit boxes in our bank have been interfered with and items removed from them!"

Still with his back to Gresham and myself, Holmes asked, "And do you know what is missing from the boxes?"

"Not entirely, regrettably. We pride ourselves on being discreet. And we have yet to inform most of those box owners affected regarding the situation . . . ."

"But this is a matter for the police, surely?" I suggested.

Holmes swung round and gave me a nod of encouragement.

"Normally, I would agree, Dr. Watson," Gresham said. "However, the stolen box contents relate to a singular subject of considerable sensitivity . . . ."

Holmes steepled his fingers and placed the tips against his chin. "You mean with regard to the Prince of Wales?"

The mouth of Gresham gaped open and he let out a gasp. "How do you know?"

"You are known to play baccarat a number of times with the Prince."

I knew of the Prince of Wales's predilection for gambling. Two or three years ago, he had been embroiled in an illegal card game and subsequently appeared as a witness in court in a slander case. It was common knowledge that Queen Victoria's son and heir was exceedingly trying.

"Furthermore, my dear fellow," Holmes went on, "the Prince's carriage deposited you at our door. It is still outside, and presumably the Prince is within, awaiting your report on this consultation."

"Well, yes, that is so . . . But . . . ."

Holmes took two paces and stood glaring at Gresham. He pointed his finger. "Let us stop all this prevarication, shall we? Be so good as to escort the Prince here, there's a good man!"

Rather sheepishly, Gresham stood and bowed briefly. "I will try."

"If the Prince requires a solution to his dilemma of a delicate nature, it would be advisable for him to speak to me here in the privacy of this room."

I showed Gresham the door.

Once the banker had departed, I turned to Holmes. "Will the Prince come?"

"Most assuredly."

Needless to say, Holmes was proved correct yet again. After a short while, there was a hard rapping sound on our door.

"Come in, Your Royal Highness – and bring Mr. Gresham with you!" Holmes barked.

The door opened.

Despite the Homberg hat casting a shadow over his face, it was quite obvious that the newcomer was the Prince of Wales. He carried a silver-tipped cane and was followed by the rather diffident Gresham.

"Mr. Holmes," said the royal personage. He wore a smart tweed suit, the bottom button of his waistcoat unfastened doubtless due to his over-generous girth.

Holmes stepped forward and inclined his head slightly. "Your Royal Highness."

The Prince moved his rather large head to face me. "And this is your estimable biographer, Dr. Watson?"

I nodded. "Your Royal Highness."

Holmes gestured at the seat by the empty hearth. "Would you take a seat, sir?"

The Prince nodded a little and settled into the chair. "I presume Mr. Gresham has mentioned the delicate matter?"

Holmes sat opposite him. "Perhaps you would be so good as to tell me directly, sir?"

Looking askance at Gresham, the Prince sighed. "Very well," said he. "The matter concerns my late son." He paused, perhaps expecting some utterance of condolence from Holmes. There was none. Prince Albert Victor had been dead almost two-and-a-half years now. Presently, he went on. "Eddy's predilection for Gaiety Girls some time before his untimely demise has resurfaced."

It was well-known that Prince Albert's son was referred to with affection as "Eddy".

Holmes tilted his head to one side. "In what way have they surfaced, sir?"

"Apparently, there are a number of letters that purport to have been sent to certain women by Eddy. They were kept in one of the bank deposit boxes which have since been broken into."

"I must confess, sir, I am surprised that you retained the letters rather than destroying them," Holmes observed.

The Prince fingered his moustache and the pitch of his voice rose slightly. "The box is not mine, but that of a Gaiety Girl, Maude Lancey. She had been in touch with me through intermediaries and we were agreeable to a settlement of two-hundred pounds for the delivery of the letters to us. Unfortunately, before she could produce them, they went missing from the pilfered box." He glowered at Gresham. "One of several, by all accounts."

Gresham explained hastily, "Miss Lancey's discovery of the theft was the first inkling that we had that there was anything amiss. She was most vociferous in her condemnation of our system and did not hold back regarding the importance of the letters. I immediately got in touch with His Royal Highness . . . ."

"I see," Holmes responded and turned to the Prince. "Your son was well-liked and the nation was shocked by his tragic passing. I can understand that you wouldn't wish for his good name to be besmirched in a scandal."

The Prince nodded. "Gladly would I have given my life to save his. His mother even now is inconsolable."

It was indeed a tragedy. Albert Victor was due to marry Princess Mary, Duchess of Teck, in February of '92. Alas, a month before that event the twenty-eight-year-old Prince developed pneumonia at the tail-end of the influenza pandemic that had begun in '89. He subsequently succumbed. Albert's brother George shared Princess Mary's period of mourning and, over time, the pair grew close and then fell deeply in love. They had married last year.

Holmes turned his gaze upon Gresham. "Are we to presume that Mr. Crosby now has the letters?"

Gresham nodded. "I – I thought so, Mr. Holmes. That is, until I received a note in this morning's post."

He placed in Holmes's hand a single sheet of paper, which had been folded once. I peered over his shoulder. It was written in scrawling black ink: *Tell the Prince he can have the letters for £50,000. Enclosed is a sample to show they are genuine. No police.* It was signed *Maurice Bourdin.*

"The name rings a bell," I ventured.

"I suspect that is not his real name," my friend remarked.

The Prince's face clouded, reflecting confusion rather than ire. "What is in a name, sir? It is my late son's good name that I care about!"

Holmes nodded, ignoring the Prince's outburst. "Watson, you are doubtless thinking of Martial Bourdin, the French anarchist who blew himself up while ostensibly attempting to destroy the Royal Greenwich Observatory."

"Yes, that must be it!" I exclaimed. "It happened this past February . . . ." Almost two months before my friend materialised as if from the dead, some years after the dreadful incident at Reichenbach Falls.

"Had I been in the country," said Holmes with a gleam in his eye, "I would have enjoyed investigating that calamitous occurrence. I am sure it was not what it seemed."

At the time I had followed the case. Superintendent Melville, armed with two revolvers, led a posse of Special Branch officers on a raid on the Autonomie Club on Windmill Street shortly afterwards, I recalled. The club had been a hotbed of anarchists. "A number of arrests were made and some anarchists were deported," I declared.

"No one went to trial," Holmes stated, his brow ruffled. "There was no enthusiasm for creating concern among the public by holding trials and publicising anarchist propaganda."

"I comprehend your reasoning, Mr. Holmes," the Prince vouchsafed. "But why would my blackmailer use the surname of a dead anarchist?"

"It is too early to say, sir. As I understand it, the Socialist League is now dominated by anarchists, having ousted the socialists. They naturally espouse anarchy – and if all government is abolished, which is their avowed aim, then it is not a great stretch of reasoning to impute that royalty would be a prime target also. If they can create a scandal that can turn the populace against you and your family, sir, then that could well signal the fall of the monarchy."

"Good heavens!" the Prince exclaimed. "Do you think it could come to that?"

"Look to the Continent, sir. Monarchy is imperilled in several countries. The worst conspirators are most assuredly the anarchist-communists."

I marvelled at my friend's grasp of the complexities of social politics, particularly since much that he referred to occurred while he was far from these shores. It had already been plain to see that he had returned from his lengthy absence the previous April notably rejuvenated, and this exposition was additional proof.

Solemnly, the Prince nodded. "I receive Cabinet papers – unbeknown to my dear mother – courtesy of Lord Rosebery. I have been informed that Mr. Melville's Special Branch is on the alert for anarchist factions, naturally, but they haven't detected any of late." He shook his head. "I cannot fathom how Eddy's letters are connected to their violent cause."

"Not all anarchists are adherents of violence, sir," opined my friend. "They are quite content to bide their time and chip away at those freedoms we take for granted . . . ."

Holmes clicked his fingers. "Might I now be allowed to scrutinise the 'sample' letter?"

The Prince cast his gaze on Gresham. In a tone of reluctance he said, "Go on, man. Show him."

Gresham removed another sheet of paper from his jacket's inside pocket. He gave it to Holmes.

An alert light of interest figured in Holmes's deep-set eyes. He held the sheet by a corner and raised it up to the light from the window. Although I was unable to read the text, I could discern that there were four lines of hand-writing, a salutation, and a signature. "I suppose you have both fingered this?" Holmes enquired sourly.

"Yes, most certainly," replied Gresham.

"Anyone else touched it?"

"No one is aware of its existence – beyond the blackmailers."

Holmes turned to the Prince. "Do you have a sample of your late son's writing, sir?"

"It appears genuine to me. He had a neat hand . . . ."

"All the same, sir, I would like to examine both styles of writing most closely. I take it that you have not employed anyone to analyse the handwriting?"

"No, the contents are too private . . . ."

"I gathered as much, since you seemed unwilling to show me. Be assured, while I have read the contents, the actual wording and nature of the missive will not be divulged by me."

The Prince glanced at me.

"And Dr. Watson would not be so indelicate as to transcribe the text, even should he be able to read it – which he cannot from where he is standing."

121

"Thank you, Mr. Holmes. But does this mean that you might consider the letters to be forgeries?"

"It is too early for me to say. Deliver to me a sample of your son's handwriting and I will study and compare. But now, tell me, has a meeting been arranged with 'Maurice Bourdin' to exchange the seemingly indiscreet letters for money?"

"Yes, this Saturday," the Prince responded, "while I am opening the new Tower Bridge. My man is to make the delivery."

"Two days' hence." Holmes bustled into his frock coat. "Then we have much work to do, and little time to accomplish it. Come, Watson, come!" he cried.

Later that evening, an envelope was delivered by special messenger. Within was a sample of writing by the late Prince Albert Victor. Holmes sat with it and the blackmail note for over an hour. In addition, there was a brief note that had been delivered from "Maurice Bourdin", outlining how the exchange of money and letters was to take place at the bridge opening. A civilian member of the royal household was to carry a satchel containing the bank notes. He was to stand at the rear of the ceremonial group, well apart from the police presence. At the slightest indication that the police were involved, the deal would be called off and the letters would be published in England and abroad.

"Isn't the blackmailer being outrageously bold?" I enquired of Holmes. "I mean, choosing such a prominent venue?"

"Outrageous, most certainly not. Bold, yes. He is confident that the authorities will not indulge in gunplay that would injure innocent bystanders. They have safety in the numbers."

"They?"

"There are at least two of them, I am certain of that, my friend." He hunched over the sheets of hand-written paper. "Now, be a good fellow, and leave me to study these samples."

Somewhat irritated, I picked up the evening newspaper. My fingers clenched tightly. I was being a fool, of course. My friend had not changed over all the years that I had known him. Perhaps I had, and now considered his brusque manner uncomfortable. Married life had altered me, most certainly. Somehow, I managed to submerge my feelings and reviewed the news, noting that the Manchester Ship Canal was already a great success since its opening the previous month.

Finally, Holmes sat back and exclaimed, "This is an excellent forgery!" He proceeded to enlighten me on the minute discrepancies in the slant and whorls of certain letters, though I had to strain my eyes to discern any marked difference.

"Then there is no need to pay the blackmailer!" I observed.

Holmes chuckled. "If the letters are released to the general public, they will damage the reputation of the late Prince. By the time that they are established to be fake, it will be too late, and the harm will have been done, I fear. No, the 'exchange' must go ahead.

"But for now, we must repair to the home of Mr. Crosby, my friend. Bring along your revolver, though I doubt if you will need it."

We caught a crawler – an empty cab that tended to clog up the streets but proved useful for summoning at a moment's notice. The driver made haste for the Aldwych end of the Strand, where Crosby resided. On the way, we passed lines of music halls, theatres, and restaurants – the Tivoli, the Adelphi, and notably the Gaiety. I saw a flower girl with a basket of buttonholes and posies, a common enough sight. A policeman was gently moving her on.

Holmes had obtained the address of Crosby's house from Gresham. However, he did not require a key, as his picklocks proved adequate to the task of gaining access.

As it was in the middle of the day, sufficient light percolated through the windows to illumine the interior.

Unerringly, Holmes led the way up the stairs to the bedroom that overlooked the street. The bed was unmade, the sheets riven as if the recent occupant had suffered severely disturbed sleep.

Holmes knelt on the bare floorboards and examined them near the bed-side cabinet, pointing to three small dark spots. "Halloa, what have we here? Drops of blood, I warrant, Watson!"

"Not sufficient to signify a fatal wound," I hazarded.

"I agree. Mr. Crosby was incapacitated." His nose twitched. "Do you smell that?"

I nodded and moved over to a waste-basket beside the dresser. Within were several crumpled newspapers and a handkerchief. Gingerly, I removed the piece of linen and detected a faint whiff of chloroform. "You're right, Holmes. He was made unconscious."

Springing up, Holmes emptied the waste-basket. All of the newspapers were called *Freedom*. "A periodical of Peter Kropotkin!"

He then hurried into the adjacent bathroom. He pointed his cane at a jar which was empty but for a slight deposit of red slime smearing its interior walls. "Watson, take this with care to our chambers."

As I used a discarded towel to lift the jar and place it in my medical bag, Holmes added, "I must leave you, Watson, while I pursue other avenues. I will see you at Baker Street at six this evening . . . ."

Not for the first time, I champed at the bit, waiting for Holmes to return from one of his clandestine forays into the underworld. I quite understood that he couldn't take me with him. He was a master of disguise and an accomplished actor, while I was neither. Long ago I had become resigned to contenting myself with listening to his reports – when he deigned to voice them.

At about five-thirty that evening, Mrs. Hudson urgently called to me to join her downstairs. I put down the newspaper and met her at the front door.

A swarthy individual stood on the threshold and insisted that he speak to the man of the house.

Mrs. Hudson pointed to me. "He will do," she said.

Boldly, I demanded, "What is the meaning of this? You should not be bothering folk at this time of day!"

He nodded repeatedly, filthy hands washing. "My sincere apologies, sir." He spoke with an Eastern European accent, and his back was bowed. He removed his felt hat as he introduced himself. "I am a poor sailor, sir, down on my luck. Can you spare a copper or two?"

"Be off with you," Mrs. Hudson riposted, "before I call the coppers to lock you up!"

Abruptly, the fellow straightened and remarked, "Mrs. Hudson, I am surprised at your lack of Christian charity."

Mrs. Hudson chuckled. "I knew it was you, sir, straight away! You neglected to smear grime on your earlobes."

Holmes glanced at me and we both laughed. "You are to be commended, dear lady." He bowed. Then he turned to me. "Come, Watson. I must change, and we have an appointment in an hour's time!"

Superintendent William Melville was in his early forties, with a high forehead, hair receding, prominent eyebrows, and a full moustache. His eyes were alert and he was clearly intelligent, having attained the high rank at a comparatively young age. His bravery was renowned too. In April of this year, he had personally arrested the bomber Meunier after a hand-to-hand fight on the platform at Victoria Station.

"It is good of you to see us, Superintendent," Holmes said, sitting opposite the head of Special Branch. "I appreciate that you are exceedingly busy with the preparations for the ceremony on Saturday."

"True enough, to be sure, Mr. Holmes, but I thought it was time that I met you." He nodded briefly at me. "And Dr. Watson, of course." His voice displayed a faint Irish intonation, doubtless modified by years of employment in the capital. "I presume that your presence may be connected with the opening ceremony, no?"

124

"You are most perceptive, Superintendent. I am involved in an interesting case which may overlap with your department's aims," Holmes explained.

I found this exposal quite startling.

"Go on."

"When you cleaned out the anarchists from the Autonomie Club in February, were you satisfied there were no other members?"

The superintendent chuckled. "I can be certain that other ill-disposed individuals have escaped our widespread nets. The Fenians, the communists, and the anarchists are like a contagion. Why do you ask?"

"I have reason to believe that a faction of anarchists has been set up in Rathbone Place."

I gaped. "Just off Oxford Street?" I interjected.

"The same," Holmes averred and turned his cold grey eyes upon the superintendent. "Not far from Windmill Street, in fact."

"This is news to me," Superintendent Melville said.

"I gained entrance to the place in disguise, of course," Holmes revealed. He cast an amused eye at me. "I used the old standby name of Basil." I felt like echoing the superintendent's words, for I had not known of this alias.

Holmes went on, "I was cordially invited to join by an exile Peter Kropotkin."

Superintendent Melville cleared his throat. "We know of him. An anarchist-communist. He was imprisoned briefly in France, before coming to London in '92."

"I do not perceive that Kropotkin is a danger to the realm," Holmes said. "While at the meeting I counted twenty members, among them our friend George Bernard Shaw and the Belgian, Dr. De Smet."

"Good heavens!" I expostulated.

"I do not know of De Smet," the superintendent said.

"He pertains to our case, sir," Holmes said. "He had recently returned from an expedition to Borneo. De Smet is a cunning fellow. He is an advocate of suggestion."

"Suggestion?" Melville queried.

"In many ways similar to hypnosis," Holmes explained, "which he employs on some patients. He was most forthcoming on the subject, giving a brief talk at the meeting. De Smet believes that the general populace can be cajoled by persuasive suggestion – much as modern advertisements attempt."

"And what suggestions does the good doctor implant in the hapless populace?"

"Anarchy. Revolution. The defeat of capitalism."

125

"Good heavens, man, he faces an impossible task!" the superintendent exclaimed. "He could never convince enough people to overthrow the established order!"

"I am sure you are correct, Superintendent. But, sadly, De Smet believes otherwise, and will destroy a good number of lives in his attempts to prove his case."

"I've met his sort before," the superintendent revealed. "Content to use other people as their weapons of disorder, rather than dirty their own hands."

The sun shone on this auspicious Saturday, the 30th of June. Crowds had gathered on both sides of Tower Bridge. Colourful bunting was draped aloft between street lamps and there was an anticipatory hum of voices in the air. The populace seemed orderly, cordially contained by hundreds of policemen along the route to the new bridge.

Over the last few years I had viewed the bridge's construction with mixed feelings. I perceived that it had an eye-catching grandeur, contrary to the *Pall Mall Gazette* which merely saw "*a subtle quality of ungainliness, a certain variegated ugliness.*" I found the bridge imposing and that it strangely complemented the nearby Tower of London. Perhaps only time will judge the aesthetic merits of its structure.

Certain members of officialdom stood on the high walkways that stretched between the two towers. Superintendent Melville had informed us that a number of his men were there, too, observing the crowd through binoculars; a couple of sharpshooters also carried bolt-action rifles. It seemed that the superintendent was not taking any chances.

Today, the bridge certainly stood out on the skyline of the Thames. The two bascules that were presently raised to allow the access of shipping were a stupendous feat of engineering. Foolishly, I voiced once that I regarded them like the jaws of a beast, to which my friend Holmes riposted, "Inanimate objects are not beasts and never will be, dear Watson. Do try not to be too fanciful when scribing our little adventures, won't you?"

We had arrived in a growler. I had obeyed Holmes's injunction to bring my medical bag and a Webley "Bulldog" revolver. He had instructed the cabman to stay put. Agilely, Holmes swung out of the cab and mounted its rear, obtaining a raised vantage position.

I stayed inside the cab, peering up at him.

He withdrew a pair of opera glasses and methodically scanned the throng. Presently, he released a slight bark of satisfaction. "Watson, I can see the footman carrying the satchel!" His lips pursed. He said nothing more.

After a frustrating moment or two, I enquired, "What's happening now?"

Silence was the only response I received.

Impatient, I eased out of the cab and balanced my feet precariously on the wheel, hands clutching for dear life on the roof of the cab.

"Here," called the cabman, "mind how you go, that's my property!"

I ignored the good fellow.

My view over the heads of the crowd revealed the royal entourage, the Prince of Wales walking alongside his wife, Alexandra, both in their glistening finery. Fleetingly, the Prince peered over his shoulder at the footman. He must have wondered why the exchange had not taken place.

Movement caught my eye. "Holmes, what's wrong with that ungainly fellow?"

"Who, where?" Holmes swivelled round, aiming his glasses in the direction of the royal group.

"Over there! Near the Prince!"

"I see him!" Abruptly, Holmes jumped down. "Quickly, come with me. And bring your medical bag!"

I snatched the bag from inside the cab and followed my friend, the thrill of adventure in my heart – but tempered with fear, for there were several armed police in the vicinity.

"Make way there!" Holmes announced in firm tones not to be gainsaid. It was quite extraordinary how he wove through the crowd, nudging and edging his way forward. I was pleased to be in his wake, for I wouldn't have had the temerity to be so forceful.

Suddenly, we were on the edge of the crowd, a policeman facing us. To our left was the man who had piqued my interest. He was tall, yet stooped, his brown hair unruly, his complexion tanned, his eyes staring. He swayed slightly and mumbled to himself in two distinct voices.

"Crosby, don't do it!" Holmes called out.

This was Crosby? Surely not.

The demented man rushed out, past the policeman, and pulled a revolver from his jacket, aiming it at the Prince of Wales.

Yet in the same instant Holmes struck, the silver tip of his cane landing firmly on Crosby's gun-hand. The weapon discharged, the bullet hitting the ground and harmlessly ricocheting into the river.

People screamed.

Holmes punched Crosby on the chin and the fellow collapsed to the ground like a sack of potatoes.

Two policemen converged on us.

Anxious, I glanced up. The Prince of Wales continued walking with his wife towards the ceremonial tape draped across the roadway.

127

Most of the crowd followed the royal entourage, doubtless mollified by the swift presence of the police.

"Stand clear, officers!" Holmes told the two policemen.

"Do as he says!" ordered Superintendent Melville.

Pleased to see the superintendent, I knelt beside the unconscious Crosby. The entire side of his face pulsed, as if independently alive. I had never seen anything like it.

"Cut it out, doctor," Holmes urgently directed. "Clean and quick!"

I removed a scalpel from my bag and my fingers palpated the pulsing bulge on Crosby's temple. I cut, and with deft manipulation flicked out a bloody glistening bright orange-red vermiform creature, its maw still sucking at a tiny ganglion of grey matter. "Dear Lord, what is that thing?" I exclaimed.

Holmes used his magnifying glass to peer at the shape that twitched on the ground. It must have measured at least twelve inches in length. "I believe it is *mimobdella frontotemporal* – a relative of the *mimobdella buettikoferi*, the Kinabalu giant red leech discovered by Dr. Johann Büttikofer."

None the wiser, I quickly staunched the incision with gauze and bandaged Crosby's head. "But what is it doing feasting on his brain?" I demanded.

"The *buettikoferi* leech only feeds on worms. But a Kinabalu tribe is renowned for its shaman who uses the *mimobdella frontotemporal* to control the minds of his enemies."

"What has a shaman from Borneo have to do with an attempted assassination of the heir to the British throne?"

"That will be made abundantly clear when we repair to a certain address."

In the background, there were three almighty cheers. I glanced up and observed the bascules lowering the road. In a short while the people on both sides would cross the new bridge over the Thames.

I returned my attention to my patient.

"Will he live?" Holmes asked.

"It is difficult to say. I cannot vouch for his mental state. I suspect the leech has been feeding off his temporal lobe, and there is no telling what harm has been done . . . ."

Holmes turned to the superintendent. "It sounds as though the opening ceremony went without a hitch."

Superintendent Melville nodded. "It was a success, to be sure – the Prince neatly cut the tape." He grinned at me. "Not as accomplished as you at cutting, however, Doctor!"

I smiled ruefully. "What do we do with our would-be assassin?" I asked. Crosby's complexion had paled alarmingly. "I think he is in need of an ambulance."

"That will be arranged." Superintendent Melville signed to a plain-clothes man who ran off.

"What about the man from the royal household who carried the blackmailer's payment?" Holmes queried.

The superintendent shrugged his shoulders. "He's none the worse for a scuffle with the blackmailer."

Holmes said, "The attempt on the Prince of Wales's life was meant to be a distraction, while the blackmail money was stolen. If it had succeeded, two goals would have been accomplished."

"That seems to be the case," the superintendent answered. "Fortunately, two plain-clothes men were nearby and apprehended the miscreant."

"Excellent!" Holmes cried. "May I be the first to interview Mr. Dors?"

"Mr. Dors?" I queried as two medical men approached with a stretcher for Crosby.

"Oh," replied the superintendent, "I would be happy to let you have first shot at him, Mr. Holmes."

"Let him sweat for a while, Superintendent. We first have a Soho address to visit."

For many years, London's Soho has been the adopted home of foreign artists, dancers, musicians, and singers. It has also offered sanctuary to political refugees, conspirators, deserters, and unsavoury characters of all nations. By the early 1890's, there had been an influx of Germans, Italians, Swiss, Jewish refugees from Eastern Europe, and among these were – according to Superintendent Melville – anarchists and communists.

Accompanied by the superintendent and two of his men, we entered the doorway, hurried along a passage, up a flight of creaking stairs, and arrived on a landing.

"Doctor De Smet, this is the police!" barked the superintendent, grasping his revolver. "Please open the door and give yourself up! The building is surrounded."

After a lengthy pause, the door locks clicked, bolts were opened, and the door swung wide.

Finally, I saw De Smet. He was quite gross. His face was bloated. He had treble chins, and appeared to have no neck. His body was so broad that I estimated that he would have to pass through the doorway sideways. His arms and legs possessed the girth that a mature oak would be proud to own, if that was not too fanciful. I glanced at Holmes.

"Move back, please," ordered Holmes, raising his cane.

Obediently, Dr. De Smet managed to waddle backwards.

There was little furniture in the room: A table, a settee, a gas stove, and a set of shelves on which stood eight glass jars, each containing squirming orange-red vermiform things.

"Sit," instructed Holmes.

Dr. De Smet lowered himself onto the settee. It groaned in protest but survived the ordeal.

"What do you want with me? I am a doctor of note. I do not know why you are here."

"Let me enlighten you," Holmes said. "I attended your meeting and talk on suggestion at Rathbone Place."

"You?" De Smet shook his head. The flesh wobbled. "I don't remember seeing you there."

"I was in disguise. I used the name Basil. In truth, I am Sherlock Holmes."

De Smet's fleshy mouth opened and closed. He was speechless. Holmes has that effect on those who attempt to best him and fail.

"Tell me, Doctor De Smet, why you abused Mr. Crosby so horrifically."

"I will do no such thing!"

"Then let me tell you. You can interrupt to amend where necessary." Holmes began pacing back and forth, his hands behind his back. "You formed an alliance with Mr. Dors. You are both staunch anarchists. Do not attempt to deny that fact. I saw and heard you both at the meeting." That hit home. De Smet winced. "From what I overheard, Mr. Dors clearly harboured a grudge against the Royal family, which suited your purpose, is that not so?"

De Smet nodded. It was an unpleasant sight. "Your name has reached me, I admit, Mr. Holmes. You are correct. I returned from the expedition with Mr. Crosby, who was seriously ill. I had also brought with me a number of jars." He pointed to the shelves. "In my brief time in Borneo, I had learned about some of the local shaman's methods. He was not averse to using those red leeches to affect his victims' – or clients' – minds. I was curious to try a few experiments myself. As Crosby was in so parlous a state anyway, I used him as my first guinea-pig. I inserted the leech while he was unconscious and it seemed to work well. Crosby was surprisingly open to suggestion. Dors and I saw a way to use him. We hid him until he could do our bidding."

"The assassination," the superintendent said.

"Yes." His little piggy eyes stared out of mounds of flesh. "Did it work?"

"Happily, no," Superintendent Melville said. "What will happen to Crosby? Do you know?"

De Smet shrugged. "The whole process is experimental. I doubt if he will survive . . . ."

"If he does," I said, "his brain function will be seriously impaired."

De Smet licked his lips. "Don't you see? If we can use these leeches under controlled conditions, we could help the mentally afflicted!"

As we entered the gaol, a sergeant informed us that Crosby died in extreme agony on arrival at the hospital.

Grimly, we stepped into Dors's cell.

He stood up, pale blue eyes darting. "What am I going to be charged with, eh? You have no evidence!"

Superintendent Melville smiled. "Your friend Dr. De Smet has told us all we need to know."

Dors spat out an indelicate imprecation.

Holmes said, "I have researched your past. Your loved a girl Lydia – a Gaiety girl."

Dors started at mention of her name. "She committed suicide. She drank carbolic acid." He shuddered.

"You do not shudder at the thought of her suicide, but at the fact that she had broken off her engagement to you to be with Prince Albert Victor."

"So? She was unfaithful to me!"

"You killed her in a fit of jealousy and made it appear as a suicide."

He shook his head. "You won't be able to prove that."

"I suppose that Lydia had earlier told you about her friend Maude, who possessed some letters, apparently written to her by the young Prince."

"She might have . . . ."

"You blamed the Prince for the events that led to Lydia's 'suicide'. You wanted to obtain those letters and use them against the Royal family. Unfortunately for you, before you could act on that, Prince Albert Victor died. I have spoken to a couple of other anarchist members and they say you joined them in 1892. It was at their meetings that you made the acquaintance of Dr. De Smet. When your banking partner Crosby joined the expedition to Borneo, you conceived a plot.

"It was you who raided the bank clients' security boxes. Since the bank employees had rarerly seen you before, as you were a silent partner, you arranged to enter under another name. Before Crosby left on his ill-

131

fated expedition, you obtained copies of his security keys, knowing that he would be blamed.

"As it happens, Crosby returned home earlier than planned. However, he was in the company of Dr. De Smet, ostensibly his patient. Dr. De Smet was quite happy to use Crosby as a research subject – and as a pawn in your scheme for revenge . . . ."

"A pretty theory, Mr. Holmes, but it is all conjecture!"

"What have you done with the letters?" the superintendent demanded.

"Hidden away where they will not be found," Dors snapped smugly. "I will use them when your case collapses!"

"Dr. De Smet's evidence will condemn you, Mr. Dors," said Superintendent Melville.

"And," Holmes added, "I found your fingermarks on the empty leech jar left in Crosby's bathroom – the same jar that led me to discover that you were making use of an unknown giant leech. You had felt the need to handle it and examine the leech because you were so intrigued by De Smet's scheme."

I perceived a stillness that betokened defeat in Dors's eyes. He chose to reveal the whereabouts of the letters.

That interview concluded the repulsive story of the red leech and the terrible death of Crosby the banker.

> *When I look at the three massive manuscript volumes which contain our work for the year 1894 I confess that it is very difficult for me, out of such a wealth of material, to select the cases which are most interesting in themselves and at the same time most conducive to a display of those peculiar powers for which my friend was famous. As I turn over the pages I see my notes upon the repulsive story of the red leech and the terrible death of Crosby the banker.*

Dr. John H. Watson – "The Adventure of the Golden Pince-Nez"

The Adventure of the Dishonourable Discharge
by Craig Janacek

The first weeks of January 1895 found my friend, Mr. Sherlock Holmes, in fine spirits. His successful conclusion of the distinctive case of Dr. Lowe had temporarily satiated his passion for the unusual which kept burning the fires of his mental engine. He had consulted on a few trivial problems for private individuals, none of which were of a sufficiently remarkable nature to warrant more than a few lines in my notebook. However, he was also in the throes of one of those fits of energy which came upon him from time to time. He spent many hours hunched over his chemical bench working upon an ill-smelling distillation of carbolic acid, which he thought might prove to explain the strange preservation of the body pulled from the Wash near King's Lynn. The following day he spent organizing the various papers littering his desk, followed by him dusting off his old typewriter in order to peck out a monograph upon the role of microscopes and magnifying lenses in the investigation of crimes. I watched this burst of dynamism with weary amusement and one night finally turned in, despite the fact that he had not quite concluded his composition of *Variations on a Theme of Campion* for violin. [1]

On the morning in question, I awoke and had just sat down at the breakfast table to enjoy Mrs. Hudson's excellent eggs, black pudding, and oatcakes, when Holmes marched into the room with a cudgel tucked like an umbrella under his arm.

"Good morning, Holmes," said I, mildly. "I note that you have retired as a pugilist."

Holmes stopped in his tracks and looked at me with puzzlement in his eyes. "Whatever gave you that impression, Watson?"

"When a man skips breakfast three days running and returns carrying a singlestick, it is not difficult to conclude that he has re-dedicated himself to the art of *canne de combat*."

"I might be carrying it for protection rather than practice."

I shook my head. "Unlikely."

"Why?"

"For two reasons. First, you would have told me if you were on a case, especially one that might involve the threat of violence. For I hope that I do not flatter myself when I note that you still rely upon me in such

133

circumstances. Given that my service revolver is at the moment safely nestled in my desk drawer, I conclude that you are not presently in need of the singlestick for protection."

His right eyebrow rose with interest. "And the other reason?"

I pointed. "The evolving purple bruise upon your right wrist, just visible under your shirt cuffs. Clearly, your opponent is a man of considerable skill if he managed to disarm you."

Holmes smiled ruefully. "Mr. Castle is the top expert in London. I fancy that I am the equal of virtually any other man alive. However, Castle still has a few tricks to teach me. But tell me, Watson, why the reference to my boxing days?"

I shook my head. "Last month, I saw you practicing the sabre, and now it is the single-stick. However, it has been some seven years – since before the Norbury case – when I last saw you enter the ring. I therefore concluded that you have abandoned your plans to join the Fancy."

"Yes, well, there is little doubt that the pugilistic arts are an attractive study, for they require a scientific level of precision. Furthermore, a high level of proficiency with one's fists comes in handy from time to time for a man with my chosen profession. However, Watson, do you recall McMurdo?"

"Bartholomew Sholto's bodyguard? How could I forget him? What of him?"

"I ran into him at Alison's rooms a few months back. He was a pale shell of the man who once blocked our way at the entrance to Pondicherry Lodge some seven years ago."

"What was wrong with him?"

"McMurdo was always known as a man who could take a hit or two. Have you ever heard the term 'punch-drunk'?"

"Of course. It refers to the state when a man can hardly walk under his own power after repetitive blows to the head. It wears off eventually."

"But what if it doesn't?"

"Doesn't what?"

"Wear off."

I shook my head. "I have never heard of such a phenomenon. Surely such a thing – if it did exist – would be the subject of an examination in *The Journal of Psychology* or *The British Medical Journal*?"

"Perhaps not. Not if it has yet to be recognized. However, after encountering McMurdo, I have made the rounds to call upon several of my former opponents. Some are seemingly fine, but others share certain of McMurdo's features. Tremors, slow movements, confusion, and speech problems." He shook his head and a look of horror passed over

134

his face. "You can imagine, Watson, how greatly I fear the permanent loss of my mental facilities. Without them, I am no longer Sherlock Holmes. As such, I have determined to refrain, whenever possible, from engaging in further activities which actively encourage unnecessary blows to my brain."

I shrugged. "That seems a wise course, if perhaps a trifle overly cautious."

However, the look upon Holmes's face made it plain that his thoughts had moved on from this conversation regarding the best method of self-defense. "Unless I am mistaken, we are about to be consulted upon a case," said he.

I frowned in confusion, but before I could ask how he came to that conclusion, there was a brief rap upon the door and the page boy brought in a telegram for Holmes. I can only presume that Holmes's preternatural sense of hearing allowed him to note the boy's light footsteps. Holmes opened the telegram and glanced at it with a look of interest forming upon his face. He glanced over at me with a smile. "What do you say to a jaunt out of London, Watson?"

I shrugged. "I see no impediments. Where did you have in mind?"

"I have here a wire from Inspector Lestrade. It seems that he is currently in the west of Scotland in connection with the Lochaber tragedy."

"That name is unfamiliar to me, I am afraid."

"I share your ignorance, Watson, but it promises to be an interesting one if Lestrade is asking for our assistance."

I reached over for my Bradshaw's. "I see an express train leaving Euston at quarter-past-nine. It is due at Glasgow at four o'clock. From there we should be able to find a local to wherever your services are required."

Holmes glanced at his watch. "That will do nicely, though it gives us only half-an-hour to pack."

Fortunately, Holmes was even faster than I at gathering up his few and simple wants, such that twenty minutes later we were situated in a hansom cab with our valises upon our laps, rattling away to Euston Station. I was amused to find my friend had changed from his typical city attire into his long grey travelling cloak and ear-flapped travelling-cap. When we arrived at the platform, Holmes instructed me to secure some corner seats in a first-class carriage, while he vanished in order to purchase the tickets. However, upon his return, he also carried with him an immense pile of newspapers.

We had the carriage to ourselves, and Holmes spent the time rummaging about and scanning the papers, with intervals of note-taking and meditation. Once we were past Carlisle, he suddenly folded them all into a gigantic wad, and tossed them under the seat. I should note that Holmes had jealously guarded the papers and I was forced to be content with spending my time reading Mr. Stevenson's further adventures of David Balfour.

"I am most happy to have you with me, Watson. You are by now well aware of Lestrade's limits, and from my perusal of the papers, it is clear that the local aid will range somewhere between worthless and actively obstructionist. While you are not yourself brilliant, you have a remarkable ability to direct light into the dark corners of a case. Have you heard anything of the Macpherson murder?" he asked.

I ignored his unintended slight and shook my head. "Very little. The name sounds a bit familiar."

"Yes, well, it was poorly covered by the London papers, but I know a man who carries *The Glasgow Herald*, *The Scotsman*, *The Aberdeen Journal*, and most of the other Scottish dailies. Shall I summarize for you?"

"I would be much obliged, as you have rather monopolized the papers."

A sheepish look appeared on his face. "I apologize, Watson. Surely, you are accustomed to my habits by now?"

"Indeed I am, Holmes. Which is why I have not taken offense, but rather waited patiently for your explanation."

He smiled. "Lochaber is a province in the western Scottish Highlands, centered upon the town of Fort William, where we shall need travel in order to meet Lestrade. North of that town are numerous lochs, all of which are ringed by various old castles and estates. The one in question, Gleannlaithe Castle, belongs to a certain Lady Emma Abercromby. [2] Three days ago, two shots were heard by members of the household emanating from the palm house situated upon the estate. One of Lady Emma's guests, a Mr. Rufus Macpherson, was found dead. Macpherson was a local landowner who had called upon Lady Emma and had been staying at her castle for the last fortnight."

"I believe that I have heard his name before in some other context," I interjected.

"You very well may have, Watson. According to the papers, Mr. Macpherson was once a member of London society, but he had been exiled due to some scandal at the St. James's Club, the details of which have not been made public."

"Perhaps that disgrace was the reason for his death?"

Holmes waved his hand. "It is certainly worth looking into, Watson. However, it is far too early to form any theories which might distract us from an unbiased observation of the facts. It seems that Mr. Macpherson was in the habit of a vigorous morning walk around the estate, followed by taking his tea alone in the palm house. On the day in question, he appears to have followed this routine, but was fatally interrupted during the later activity."

"And do they know by whom?"

"The local police have a man in custody."

"Then what is our role?"

"That is precisely the interesting part, Watson. It seems there may be a difference of opinion between the local force and the C.I.D., or Lestrade would not have wired for my assistance."

"And what is Lestrade's opinion?"

He shook his head. "Neither the papers nor his wire relates that information. In fact, the papers are universally certain that the arrested man is guilty. Their major concern, of course, is not this particular man, but rather how Parliament plans to prevent others of his like from murdering every country gentleman at his table."

I snorted in wry amusement at such hysterics, which reliably sold bushels of papers. "How can they be so certain?"

"At Macpherson's feet was found a hand trowel. Upon questioning of the staff, this item was promptly recognized as belonging to one Donald Scott, who is employed on the estate as a gardener and laborer."

"You said that Mr. Macpherson was shot to death. Most gardeners do not go around armed with pistols."

"Very good, Watson. In fact, a gun was found at the scene and was quickly identified as Macpherson's own weapon. It had clearly been recently fired. Now we must ask why Macpherson would need to carry such a thing on his morning walk?"

"Perhaps he was afraid for his life?"

Holmes nodded. "That is an excellent hypothesis, Watson, and one into which we must hope Lestrade has thought to inquire. The local police believe that Scott came upon Macpherson from behind, seized the murdered man's gun, and fired a shot into him when he turned around."

"For what reason?"

"Ah, there indeed lies our problem. The papers have concluded that robbery does not appear to be the motive, for some French coins were found in Macpherson's pocket."

I raised my eyebrows. "Why would a man residing in the west of Scotland be carrying about French coins?"

Holmes smiled happily. "You are scintillating this afternoon, Watson! I asked myself the very same question. It is an anomaly which I

137

am willing to wager has escaped the attention of Lestrade and the local authorities."

"And if robbery was not Scott's motive, what was?"

Holmes smiled. "The police are at a loss. However, the papers are certain that it was a fit of homicidal madness."

"And what does Scott have to say about the matter?"

"Unfortunately, Scott was born a deaf-mute, and is rather simple. He communicates with the estate's keepers through a crude sign language, and is plainly not up to the task of answering the interrogations of the police."

I shook my head. "If such a man is innocent, his advocate will have a hard time proving it without the actual guilty party being conclusively identified."

"That thought had occurred to me, Watson," said Holmes with an immodest smile. "It is thus a good thing that I will soon be on the scene."

At Glasgow we changed trains, and soon passed over the remarkable new viaduct – constructed only eight years prior – on our way to Fort William. The twenty-one arches spanned a hundred feet over the valley floor, blessing us with a fantastic view. Even Holmes, typically immune to such things, seemed stimulated by the scenery. I was moved to break out in song:

> *Oh, you'll take the high road, and I'll take the low road,*
> *And I'll be in Scotland afore you;*
> *But me and my true love will never meet again,*
> *On the bonnie, bonnie banks o' Loch Lomond.*

Holmes glanced over at me with surprise. "Wrong lake, Watson."

I shook my head at my friend's lack of poetry – save only his singular gifts upon the violin. "It's a metaphor, Holmes. The 'low road' is the fairy-folk's route back to Scotland. When a true Scotsman dies, the *daoine sith* will transport his soul back to his home."

"Fascinating," said Holmes, dryly. "I will endeavor to forget that fanciful belief, Watson, rather than allow it to unnecessarily clutter my little brain attic. I can state with reasonable confidence that such knowledge will not advance us during this case."

It was nearly seven o'clock when we at last found ourselves at the highlands town of Fort William. Inspector Lestrade was waiting for us upon the platform, a shoulder bag clutched to his chest. He had thrown off his typical city clothes in favor of the light brown dust-coat and leather leggings which he wore whenever he ventured to more rustic surroundings. With him, we drove northeast some thirteen miles to the crofting hamlet of Gairlochy. A room had been engaged for us at the White Rose. We brought our valises into the common room and Lestrade motioned to a table and chairs.

"I apologize, Mr. Holmes," said Lestrade. "For the hour is rather late, and the way is dark. I know well your dynamic nature, but I fear that we must postpone our visit to the scene of the crime until tomorrow morning."

I could detect a strain upon Holmes's face at this pronouncement. However, he quickly shrugged it off and slumped into one of the chairs. "Macpherson has been dead three days now. Any evidence that existed at the scene has surely been thoroughly trampled by this late juncture. I suppose a few hours more will matter little."

"If you ask me, the case is as clear as crystal," Lestrade continued. "Still one cannot refuse a lady. Lady Emma is distraught at the thought that Donald Scott is guilty. She has heard of you, Mr. Holmes, and insisted that you be consulted. I told her it was a waste of your time and her money, but she would not be put off." He spread out his hands in a supplicating fashion. "Though to be fair, I suppose I once said the same at the Boscombe Pool and was ultimately proven wrong. I would hate for there to be a miscarriage of justice, especially when the poor fool can hardly defend himself."

Holmes nodded. "Your concern is well-warranted, Lestrade. Someone who cannot speak or write is the perfect scapegoat for a crime committed by another."

Lestrade shrugged. "Yes, well, there aren't many others for you to question, Mr. Holmes."

"Who else was present at Gleannlaithe Castle during Mr. Macpherson's demise?"

"The castle maintains a staff of butlers, footmen, maidservants, and the usual servants. I suppose that any of them could have shot Macpherson, though why they would want to is beyond me. And there are the estate groundskeepers and stable staff, of course, but it has been verified that none of them were in the vicinity of the house on the morning in question, save only Donald Scott. There is Lady Emma, of course. But she may be discarded as a potential suspect."

"Why is that?"

"She was having her hair combed by her confidential maid at the time the gunshots were heard."

Holmes shrugged, as if he did not consider such an alibi to be air-tight. "And is there a Lord Abercromby?"

Lestrade shook his head. "Not for many years now. The lady was widowed when her husband died in the Soudan. There is also Lady Honoria Murray, who is visiting from Broughton. She is Lady Emma's spinster sister."

"And where was Lady Honoria at the time of the murder?"

"Reading in the library."

"Any witnesses who might confirm her location?" Holmes inquired.

"None," said Lestrade with a frown. "But what reason would Lady Honoria have for murdering Macpherson?"

Holmes held up a hand. "It is far too early to begin to assign motives, Lestrade. We must seek the facts and then fit theories to them rather than your widdershins approach. Who else?"

"There is also Mr. Carruthers. He is a Scotsman visiting Lady Emma from Dumfries."

"For what purpose?"

"A social call, I presume," said Lestrade, offhandedly.

"To the Scottish Highlands in January? An odd time of year, don't you think, Lestrade?"

The inspector shrugged. "I hadn't really thought about it."

"Of course not," replied Holmes, acerbically.

"Mr. Carruthers has been most helpful," said Lestrade, his tone bristling.

"In what way?"

"It was his evidence which sealed Donald Scott's fate. He saw the man enter the palm house around the time of the murder."

"Oh?" said Holmes, his eyebrows rising with interest. "He volunteered that, did he?"

"Not at all. In fact, it took a great deal of skillful questioning to bring it out. Mr. Carruthers did not wish to unfairly implicate Mr. Scott. It was only with a great deal of pressure did he reluctantly admit to seeing Scott lurking in the garden that morning. It's all in his deposition."

"Do you have an account of the inquest?" asked Holmes.

"Of course," replied Lestrade, reaching into his bag in order to extract a pile of papers. "Is there something particular you are interested in?"

"The surgeon's deposition."

"Page seven, I believe," said Lestrade, handing over the file.

Holmes turned to the aforementioned page and read through it carefully. In several parts, his eyebrows rose suggestively. Finally, he handed it back to the inspector with a smile upon his face. "Most instructive."

140

"In what way?" asked Lestrade, suspiciously.

"Well, we will need to examine the scene in order to put everything into its proper context. What about the coins found in Macpherson's pocket?"

"What of them?"

"The newspaper account reported that they were French in origin."

Lestrade shrugged. "Yes, we believe that is why Donald Scott didn't take them. He must have realized that they were not British coins and therefore held no value to him."

"May I see them?"

"They are with Macpherson's effects at the local constabulary. But there is a drawing of one of them at the end of the report."

Holmes flipped ahead until he found the page in question. "This is a Louis d'Or," said Holmes, with some surprise. He passed the sketch to me, which I reproduce here:

Lestrade shrugged. "Yes?"

"These haven't been minted since before the days of the first Napoleon."

"So the man collected old coins. What of it?"

"Perhaps nothing, but it is rather curious. We shall make note of it."

"Is there anything else, Mr. Holmes," asked Lestrade, the irritation apparent in his voice.

"No, nothing else," said Holmes, mildly. "Though, pray see to it that Mr. Macpherson's effects – including the coins and his gun – are all brought round to the castle so that we may reconstruct the scene."

Lestrade nodded. "Well, then, the trap will bring us around to Gleannlaithe at eight o'clock tomorrow." He took his leave of us, and I stood up in order to inspect my room for the night. I paused when it became apparent that Holmes was not stirring.

"Go on, Watson," said Holmes, with a wave of his hand. "I will see you in the morning."

I was surprised that he planned to remain awake, as there seemed little to accomplish at the moment. "It's a little premature for a ratiocination session, don't you think, Holmes? Certainly you are not yet in possession of all of the facts."

"I concur, Watson. I do not propose to seek the solace of my old black pipe, but rather the company of men. We passed a country public house on the way into the village, if I am not mistaken. I think a glass or two of beer is in order."

I stared at Holmes in amazement, for he was much preferential to a fine Beaune or Montrachet when he was in a gregarious mood – which was rarely. I had not seen him order a beer since we paid a call upon Mr. Windigate at the Alpha Inn some years prior. "Do you require my assistance?"

"No, no, Watson. Off to the Land of Nod with you. I promise to share with you in the morning any local gossip which I manage to acquire."

Finally comprehending Holmes's sudden and atypical interest in socialization, I turned in for the night. However, shortly after I turned out the light, a heavy wind arose, bringing with it a wild beating of rain. I was much used to enduring such tempests while comfortably surrounded by ten miles of man's handiwork upon every side of me. But out here in the countryside, under leaking eaves which had likely been laid before the days of the Usurper, the elemental forces of Nature seemed most awesome in their power. [3] I never felt more conscious of my insignificance, and sleep was long in coming.

By the following morning, the storm had passed and the sun was bright in the sky. It was as fine a January day as the Highlands ever witnessed, and despite a briskness to the air, I felt reinvigorated and confident that the day would prove to be a fruitful one in the search for Mr. Macpherson's true killer.

When I repaired downstairs, I found that both Holmes and Lestrade were waiting for me. I quickly partook of some toast and coffee, and then we were off. I wished to know what Holmes had learned in the public house, but knew that – with his reticent nature – he would only share his news when he gauged the moment proper. Fortunately, he was in a garrulous mood this morning.

"Did you know, Lestrade, that Loch Arkaig is the home of a water-horse?" said Holmes, suddenly, as we rode along in the trap.

"Excuse me?" said the inspector, plainly startled by this strange pronouncement.

"Also known a *kelpie,* it is a shape-shifting water spirit known to devour unwary folks who linger at the water's edge. According to some of the local men, the Loch's water-horse was even witnessed by one of our foreign ministers, the Earl of Malmesbury, less than four decades ago."

"Whatever could a *kelpie* possibly have to do with the death of Mr. Macpherson?" Lestrade spluttered.

Holmes smiled and shrugged. "One never knows."

The ride from the White Rose was a short one. All around us we were surmounted by rugged hills, and as we approached Gleannlaithe, which lies rather low, I noted that it was surrounded by some very fine trees. Dappled by sunlight, the tangled woods could even be termed luxuriant, though I suspected they took on a more sinister nature under a moonless sky. The grey-stone castle, no longer fortified against invasion from the south, was now better described as a manor house. Its windows were no longer barred, and its turrets were now more whimsical than menacing.

"Straight on to the palm house, if you would, Lestrade," commanded Holmes.

"You don't wish to talk to Lady Emma?" asked the inspector, with some surprise at Holmes's flouting of societal niceties.

"No, no, that can wait," said Holmes. "Enough time has passed that I fear most of the clues have been long ground to dust, but we live in hope."

"Very well. I had the room sealed," Lestrade noted as he led the way around the back of the castle.

"Capital!" cried Holmes, beaming. "You have outdone yourself, Lestrade."

The palm house proved to be a fine greenhouse of white-painted metal and glass grafted onto the rear of the ancient castle. A series of walled gardens extended beyond it. Lestrade unlocked the door with a key and we stepped inside, though Holmes bade us pause at the entrance. The interior was considerably warmer than the outside temperature, and I thought about removing my coat, but did not wish to set it down atop some critical piece of evidence. Holmes stepped along the cobblestone paths, taking care to not disturb the dirt areas around the palms and other tropical plants. Each of these locales he inspected for signs of footprints, though I saw him shake his head with disappointment and heard him muttering "elephants" under his breath. When he reached the far edge of the room, he stopped at a small white-painted wrought-iron table and

143

chair. Situated upon the table was a small tea service for one, collecting both dust and a smattering of insects in the days since Macpherson's death.

After studying this tableau for a moment, Holmes straightened up. "And now I think we are in a position to undertake a thorough examination of the room. First, did you bring Mr. Macpherson's gun, as I asked, Lestrade?"

The inspector nodded and reached into his bag. He brought forth a revolver and handed it to Holmes. Holmes carefully stepped over to the table and glanced about. "The gun was found here, I presume?" He pointed to where a small yellow flag rose from the ground.

"That is correct," confirmed Lestrade.

"Capital!" said Holmes, placing the gun upon the ground. He then proceeded to stand in various spots about the room and stared at the windows and trees around where the man's body had been found. I noted that he paid especially close attention to the man's teacup, even going so far as to lift it up and sniff it.

Lestrade snorted in disbelief at the apparent absurdity of this action. "Earl Grey or Prince of Wales?" he called out with some derision.

Holmes shook his head. "Neither. A simple English breakfast blend."

"And does Macpherson's choice of morning tea tell us who killed him?" asked Lestrade.

Homes turned to him with a smile. "Not immediately. Though it has no small bearing upon the case, I assure you. As does the peculiar matter of the broken glass."

Lestrade frowned. "But there is no broken glass."

"That is what is so peculiar. Now, then, Lestrade, I believe I read in the papers that there were two shots fired?"

"Yes," said Lestrade. "Every member of the household confirmed that detail."

"Then why did the surgeon's report note that there was only one bullet hole in Mr. Macpherson?"

The inspector shrugged. "Obviously Donald Scott is hardly an expert shot. I expect the first one sailed wide."

Holmes nodded. "That is a reasonable hypothesis, Lestrade. Let us attempt to verify it." He walked about the table until he stopped in front of the chair. "According to the report, Macpherson was shot directly in the heart. Therefore we may presume that his assailant fired from directly in front of him, on or about where I am presenting standing. Do you agree?" When Lestrade and I concurred, Holmes continued. "Now, if I raise my finger at a man sitting in the chair, you may see the potential

144

avenues the bullet may have flown. In fact, it is rather remarkable that the wayward bullet did not shatter any of the panes of glass in front of me." He waved his hand at the spot he indicated. "So, now, where then is the second bullet?"

Lestrade frowned as his gaze followed the direction indicated by Holmes. "Perhaps it is buried in the ground?"

"It is not," Holmes declared.

"How can you be so certain?" the inspector protested.

"Because it is right there," said Holmes, as he performed an about-face and pointed towards one of the palm trees behind him.

"What?" exclaimed Lestrade. He strode forward to verify Holmes's claim for himself. Once he had done so, he stepped back from the tree with a confused look upon his face. "However did you think to look there, Mr. Holmes?"

"I looked because I expected to find it there." He pointed to the gun on the ground. "That is an Adams Mark III. It fires a .450 caliber bullet. However, the surgeon was most clear in his report that the bullet he pulled from the chest of Mr. Macpherson was a .476 caliber, such as used by the Enfield Mark I. Therefore, Macpherson's gun did not fire the fatal shot, yet fire it did, for it was found in a recently discharged state. I presume he fired it in turn upon the man who shot him."

"This changes the complexion of the whole crime," said Lestrade with a hint of wonderment in his voice.

"That is but the first item you overlooked, Lestrade," said Holmes, calmly. "The second is of far greater importance."

"Which is?" asked the inspector, crossly.

"Only that Mr. Macpherson's tea was poisoned."

Holmes strode out of the palm house, leaving a bewildered Lestrade in his wake. I hurried after him as he rounded the house, heading towards the front entrance. "Holmes!" I exclaimed. "You cannot be serious."

He shook his head. "I never jest, Watson. There was something added to Macpherson's tea, of that I am certain. I would, of course, need access to my chemical bench in order to identify the exact substance."

"But who would do such a thing?" I cried. "To shoot a man after having just poisoned him? It's disgraceful!"

"I am not certain, Watson. However, I believe that this finding may be the key to the whole thing."

Holmes reached the door, where he pulled upon a massive knocker. When the butler opened the door, Holmes presented his card. The man glanced at it, and said, "You are expected, Mr. Holmes. If you would please follow me, sir."

We trailed the man through a series of old stone corridors and halls. In one of them, we encountered a short man passing the other direction, walking with some degree of a limp. He was some fifty years of age, with lion-like hair and beard. He had a stiff spine, and his lined face carried an air of authority. He wore a hunting outfit with baggy pants and carried a Penang lawyer in his left hand. The man met us with a respectful smile, though did not remove his bonnet.

"Ah, you must be Mr. Holmes," said the man. "I heard rumors of your arrival. Alistair Carruthers at your service."

"Well, Carruthers, you've served in the army," said Holmes, suddenly.

"Aye, sir," the man replied, a wary look entering his eyes.

"Not long discharged?"

"Aye, sir."

"A Highland regiment?"

"Aye, sir."

"An officer?"

"Aye, sir. I was a colonel in the Lennox Highlanders." [4]

"Stationed at Barbados?"

"Aye, sir. If I may ask, how could you know all of that?"

"I noted that your pants are rather baggy, and your loosely-laced boots far larger than typical for a man of your height," said Holmes, motioning to the man's feet. "I concluded that your lower extremities are afflicted by swelling. Since you have none of the plethoric nature of a man with cardiac dropsy, tropical elephantiasis seemed likely. [5] That condition is commonly acquired only in the West Indies, such as Barbados."

"That is most perceptive, sir. I was invalided out of the army because of it."

"Simplicity itself," said Holmes with a dismissive wave. "May I inquire as to the reason for your visit to Gleannlaithe Castle, Colonel Carruthers?"

The man frowned. "As you have already divined the nature of my illness, I suppose it little matters if I reveal all. I have grown frustrated with the failures of the fools at Teviot Place. [6] They had me repeatedly swallowing an everlasting Antimony pill, but that achieved nothing save purging my bowels. [7] Then I heard from a friend that some of the herbs growing in Lady Emma's garden have had success in treating elephantiasis. I knew the lady slightly, having once served with her husband. I wrote to her and was invited to call upon her for a consultation. I must say that I have been glad with the effects. Over the last week, the swelling has diminished by at least half."

146

"Very good, Colonel. I am most pleased for you," said Holmes, amiably. "Perhaps Dr. Watson here has a thing or two to learn from our hostess, who we are on our way to meet."

"I daresay he might," said the man with a laugh. "I won't detain you any longer."

We set off again after the butler, who had waited unobtrusively for the three of us to conclude our conversation.

"Well, Watson," said Holmes. "What do you make of Colonel Carruthers?"

"He seemed a typical Scottish soldier, though I am uncertain how you knew him to be an officer? I don't recall Lestrade mentioning that fact."

"He didn't. As to Carruthers being an officer, it was most obvious. He had a strong air of authority and the bearing of a military man. For instance, he had a handkerchief in his sleeve, something no pure-bred civilian would contemplate. He was obviously Scottish and thus likely from a Highland Regiment. The man was respectful, but he did not remove his hat. They do not remove hats in the army, but he would have re-learned civilian ways had he been long discharged. However, it is most unusual that he does not utilize his rank for his honorific, but instead prefers to go by plain old Mr. Carruthers."

"What do you mean?"

"I wonder if it was a condition of his discharge?"

I frowned in confusion. "To be stripped of his title, he would have to be dismissed with disgrace."

"Indeed. And that is a most rare thing. Even Colonel Sebastian Moran, who once made all of India too hot to hold him, never invoked a scandal sufficiently grave to warrant such a fate."

Anything more Holmes was going to say upon the subject was cut short by our arrival at the drawing room, where we were presented to the lady of the house and her sister. The two women were most alike in form and face, though Lady Emma had a graceful figure and presence, while Lady Honoria's expression was more pinched and haggard. Both women had the luxurious dark waves of hair common to the Highlands, and I guessed the former was still a half-decade shy of fifty, while the other was some seven or eight years her elder. Lady Emma wore a loose riding outfit over which was thrown a fine tartan shawl, and her head was bare. Her sister wore a high-buttoned gown with a sequined neckline and a rather unfashionable mob cap.

"I am most glad that you have come, Mr. Holmes," said Lady Emma, waiving us to chairs opposite them. "I am sorely troubled to think that poor Donald Scott could be involved in this terrible matter. I have known him since he was a wee lad. He was the son of our head gamekeeper."

"Was he always so afflicted?"

"Oh, no. He was once a bright little boy. When he was four years old, he developed high fevers and inflammation of the brain. His life was much feared for, and when he finally recovered, his facilities had fled. [8] After that, there was little to be done for him in terms of education, but I saw to it that he was gainfully employed."

"To think that he repaid your generosity so poorly," interjected Lady Honoria.

Holmes shook his head. "I think it rather premature to judge him, Lady Honoria. In fact, from what I have seen thus far, I think it highly likely that he is innocent."

"Really?" Lady Emma exclaimed. "That is wonderful! But if Donald is not to blame, then who shot Mr. Macpherson?"

"It might have been anyone," said Lady Honoria with some rancor.

Holmes turned to her with interest. "You did not care for Mr. Macpherson?"

Lady Honoria sniffed in disdain. "Rufus Macpherson was a Black Saxpence in human form."

Holmes cocked his head. "I am afraid that I am unfamiliar with that term."

"A Black Saxpence is a Scottish term for a silver sixpence which has tarnished to such a degree that it turns black in color," I explained. "It is received from the devil as a pledge of a person's body and soul. For the person who keeps it constantly in his pocket, however much he spends, he will always find another sixpence beside it."

"And you think Mr. Macpherson sold his soul to the devil, Lady Honoria?" asked Holmes.

"He didn't need to. He was the devil incarnate."

"If he was so awful, then why open your home to him, Lady Emma?"

"My sister is prone to exaggerations, Mr. Holmes," said she, magnanimously. "Certainly, Mr. Macpherson was unpopular in the neighborhood. He had sold much of his family's ancestral lands to various mining concerns. The locals are rather conservative and do not appreciate such rash changes."

"I am less concerned about the opinion of the locals than I am about your thoughts, Lady Emma," said Holmes. "Unless you think some local nursed a sufficient hatred to warrant shooting him?"

"Yes, well, I suppose such a thing is possible," Lady Emma conceded. "He was a charming sort of rake, but he was also insolvent and owed money to virtually everyone. He had racked up such massive gambling debts in London that he was recently forced to retire from society. This is why I permitted him to call upon me. I rarely get down to London and wished to hear the news which he still received from some of his old friends. He had a most vivacious way of recounting the scandals and foibles of the first families of the kingdom."

"He also wished to steal all of your wealth," interjected Lady Honoria.

Holmes's eyebrows rose with interest. "In what way?"

"Rufus Macpherson was courting my sister," she explained. "He was playing upon her isolation and loneliness, in hopes of acquiring control over Gleannlaithe. As soon as I heard he was paying a call, I came around in order to defend her."

Lady Emma smiled wanly. "Though my sister had little to fear, of course. Not only is the estate entailed upon my son, Malcolm, who is currently in Edinburgh studying law, but I am hardly as naïve as she fears. I was in no danger from the glamor of Mr. Macpherson." She turned and waved to the butler. "I think it is time for elevenses, Campbell."

The butler wheeled around a silver tray containing a tea pot with cosy, cups with saucers, and some biscuits. Our hostess performed the ritual of adding the loose leaves from the wooden caddy to the boiled water, placing strainers over our cups, and then pouring the tea. She handed a cup to both Holmes and I, and then offered us both fresh milk and white sugar.

I took the cup gratefully, but then reacted with surprise. "Green tea?" I exclaimed.

Lady Emma arched her eyebrow at me. "Surely you don't be believe those tales, Dr. Watson? Visions of evil monkey spirits?" [9]

I cleared my throat. "There is a well-documented case in *The Lancet* . . . ." [10]

"Adulterations, Doctor. Unscrupulous merchants who add preservatives and dyes in order to bulk up the volume and color the tea green for those credulous fools who believe the pale leaves look wrong. I assure you that it will not cause you harm."

"You are quite well-versed in your toxicology, Lady Emma," remarked Holmes with a smile.

"Of course, Mr. Holmes. Although the University of Edinburgh has opened its door to women, it is still an uncommon profession for one such as myself. However, I have long been fascinated with the curative properties of plants. Have you not yet visited the gardens?"

Holmes shook his head and reported that he had not partaken of that pleasure.

"Well, you may find it of interest."

"And why is that?" he asked.

She smiled coyly. "I hate to spoil the surprise."

We took our leave of the ladies, and Holmes decided to defer the next step of his investigation in favor of taking Lady Emma's advice. We made our way to the rear of the castle, near the palm house, where we found a curious old-world walled garden. Rows of ancient wych elm trees, some carved with strange designs, encircled the walls like a hedge. Inside, a profusion of flowering shrubs and small trees nestled between gravel paths. The whole effect was rather soothing and restful.

We pushed open the gate, and as we walked about, I watched with some degree of satisfaction as a look of amazement crept onto Holmes's face. It was a rare enough sight that I thought it worth savoring, even if I was myself uncertain of its etiology. Finally, I could not stand the suspense any longer. "What is it, Holmes?"

He shook his head. "Do you know what this is, Watson?"

"It looks very much like a garden."

"Indeed, but it unlike any other garden upon which I have ever set eyes. I read about such a park surviving in Padua, but to find one tucked into the glens of Scotland is quite a surprise indeed."

"And what makes this particular garden so remarkable?"

"Perhaps if I identified these particular plants, you would share my interest. This one here is *Conium maculatum*, better known as Socrates' Bane."

"Hemlock?" I cried, with some alarm.

"Certainly. Here is foxglove or *Digitalis purpurea*, which has significant effects on the beating of the human heart. And next to that you can see a prickly shrub. It is Dr. Purcell's favorite, *Atropa belladonna*." [11]

"Deadly nightshade!"

"And here we have the Laburnum, or Golden Chain tree. All parts of it are deadly to all beings save the *Lepidoptera*. Next to it, I spot the *Ricinus communis*, the castor-bean plant. And here is the Javanese mulberry tree, from which the fabled *uvas* poison derives. Then there is this little tree, known in some parts by the quaint name of Quaker Buttons. Its Latin name is *Strychnos nux-vomica*. From it is produced that substance which I have heard you counsel your patients carries great dangers when taken in excess of two drops."

"Everything in this garden is poisonous!" I exclaimed.

"Indeed," said Holmes, with a smile of pleasure which made me think he found it all rather wonderful. "It is unique in my experience. Few people are brave enough to have so many deadly substances growing within close vicinity to their vegetables."

"Brave or foolhardy?"

"That may be more accurate than you know, Watson. Do you see this?" he motioned to a small tree, with large, pendulous, fragrant orange flowers. "This is the angel's trumpet."

"That sounds benign enough."

Holmes shook his head. "Unfortunately, I know of ladies who enjoy putting a little of its pollen into their tea. A small amount is known to produce the most pleasurable visions. However, it is a rather fine line, since if you consume too much you may hear the angel's trumpet your entrance into the undiscovered country."

"Do you think that Macpherson was poisoned from something obtained here?"

"It seems a reasonable hypothesis, Watson, given the ease of access. However, the question remains . . . who slipped the fatal dose into his tea?"

His brow furrowed in concentration and he clasped his hands behind his back. He began to stroll about, and I knew better than to disturb the train of his thoughts. I followed him silently as he passed through a gate and wandered into a neglected area of the garden. This un-walled part was considerably wilder, with its shrubs growing unchecked into the pathways. A pillar – which once supported an old sundial – lay toppled over, and a stone bench sat crumbling off to one side. There were some signs of attention, however, with evidence of freshly turned dirt in one corner, along with an attempt to prune back some of the bushes.

"Now this is an odd item," said Holmes, suddenly.

I followed the line of his gaze, and noted an old, gnarled, English Oak. Dozens of coins had been hammered into its bark.

It looked familiar. "Unless I miss my guess, I would say that it's a Wish Tree."

"Pray tell, Watson. What is a Wish Tree?"

"It is an ancient tradition, Holmes. People festoon special trees with coins in order to have one's wishes granted. It is connected with the origins of tree worship, a topic with which I thought you would be well-acquainted," said I, with some feeling.

He turned his head and peered at me for a moment. "I see. Are they commonplace?"

"Not really. They typically occur only in special locations. There is a Wish Tree at Loch Maree which was famously visited by our Queen nearly two decades ago. If I recall correctly, it was situated near a sacred healing well."

"And what is so unusual about the site of this particular tree?" he inquired.

"Nothing that I can see."

"No?" said he, with an arch of his eyebrow. "Perhaps not. However, you will note this abrasion here." He pointed to a linear notch where the bark had been freshly rubbed. "What do you make of that?"

I considered it for a moment. "It appears as if a rope was tied around it."

"Indeed, and recently too. And do you see that the earth around the base has newly been dug up?"

"Certainly, but there has been much work of late in the gardens," said I, waving my hand about to illustrate my point.

Anything further he was going to say upon the matter was interrupted by the appearance of Inspector Lestrade.

"There you are, Mr. Holmes," the policeman exclaimed. "Now, what are you going on about with this poison nonsense? Who in their right mind discharges his pistol into a man whom is already dying? It's nefarious."

Holmes smiled at the inspector. "An excellent point, Lestrade. And one upon which I mean to meditate, as soon as a few other items are checked off my list."

"Such as?" Lestrade inquired.

"First, I plan to avail myself of Lady Emma's fine library. After that, since I am a firm believer in the *genius loci*, I shall stroll down to the Loch and see if the atmosphere of the woods begets inspiration."

With little left to do while Holmes was engaged in his act of meditation, I decided to interview the members of the household staff, in hopes that one of them might have noticed something which they were reluctant to mention to Lestrade and the official force. This task, however, proved in vain. They were all prepared to swear that – at the time the shots rang out – the two women were inside the house while Mr. Carruthers in the garden. Only Donald Scott was sufficiently near to the palm house to be capable of carrying out the murder of Mr. Macpherson.

When Holmes finally reappeared several hours later, he was resting his weight upon a rough Scottish walking stick with a hooked head, similar to an Irish shillelagh. His breath was rapid, as if he had just run or hiked some great distance, and he leaned heavily upon the *kebbie*. He asked Lestrade to gather Lady Emma and her sister, Mr. Carruthers, and the butler, Campbell, in the palm house.

Once this group was assembled, Holmes smiled. "Ladies and gentlemen, if you will spare me a few moments of your time, I would like to demonstrate how and why Mr. Rufus Macpherson was killed."

The five of them, even Lestrade and the unflappable Campbell, simultaneously burst into a series of questions. However, I knew – from long experience – better than to interject. Like a master dramatist, Holmes would reveal the *dénouement* at his own pace.

"First, let us consider the possible suspects," he continued. "There is Lady Emma. She has a most unusual interest in poisonous plants, and I have established that Mr. Macpherson was poisoned before he was shot."

"My garden is for healing, not for killing, Mr. Holmes!" Lady Emma interjected. "Ask Dr. Watson! He will tell you that most so-called poisons may be beneficial in small doses!"

"Pray hold your protests until the end, Lady Emma," said Holmes, holding up his hand to forestall the woman's angry retort. "Thanks to your maid, you have a rather ironclad alibi, though certainly maids have been known to lie before in order to protect their mistresses." He turned back to Lestrade. "However, Lady Emma also has little motive. And then there is Lady Honoria. Her means and motive are both greater than those of her sister. She has no direct alibi, save only her word that she was in the library. I inspected the library not two hours ago and can confirm that – thanks to a loose sequin from her dress – she visited it at some point in the last few days. Of course, I am unable to corroborate a precise time for her visit. And she plainly hated Macpherson, whom she considered a dangerous ne'er-do-well."

"Not enough to kill him!" exclaimed Lady Honoria.

Holmes smiled and shook his head. "Perhaps not. And then there is the quiet Mr. Campbell. Like Lady Emma's maid and sister, he would be quick to come to her defense if he thought she and the estate were imperiled by an unscrupulous man. I note that your whereabouts during the murder are unaccounted for, Campbell."

The man stoically shook his head. "I was in the pantry, sir."

"Alone, we may presume?"

"Yes, sir," replied Campbell.

"Pity," said Holmes. "Nevertheless, we also have to consider the case of Colonel Carruthers. Did he have any cause to dispatch Rufus Macpherson?"

"None, sir!" the man protested. "I just met him a few days ago!"

"So you are not a member of the St. James's Club? You are not one of those myriad London gentlemen to whom Macpherson owed a considerable debt?"

"No, sir."

"I believe you, Colonel," said Holmes with a smile. "And you were in the garden at the time of the gunshots, were you not?"

"That is correct."

"Where you saw Donald Scott exit the palm house?"

"No, sir. I was too far away for that. But I did see him enter it some amount of time before. However, I don't wish to claim that Scott was definitely involved. I cannot claim to be an eyewitness."

"Your reticence is admirable, Colonel," said Holmes. "But who else could it have been?"

The man shrugged. "As you say, sir. Though that's up to a coroner's jury to decide."

"Indeed. Now, let us turn our attention to one other matter." Holmes reached into his waistcoat pocket and pulled out a small tumbler containing a substance with a deep indigo color. "This, gentlemen, contains a most potent drug derived from one of the woad plants in Lady Emma's charming garden. It is extremely bitter to the taste and most offensive to the sense of smell, though not poisonous in small quantities. However, I wish for you – ladies excluded, of course – to test it by smell and taste, for it is pertinent to the case at hand." Opening the vial, he stirred the liquid with his finger. "As I don't ask anything of you which I wouldn't do alone with myself, I will therefore taste it before passing it around." He licked his finger and grimaced at the unpleasant taste.

The tumbler was then passed round and with a wry and sour expression, I watched as Lestrade followed Holmes's lead. One after another, Campbell, Carruthers, and I all tasted the liquid, and varied and amusing were the grimaces that were manifested upon our faces. The tumbler, having gone round, was returned to Holmes.

"Gentlemen, I am deeply grieved to find that not one of you has developed his power of perception, the faculty of observations of which I speak so much. For if you had truly observed me, you would have seen that while I placed my middle finger in the awful brew, it was my index finger which actually found its way into my mouth."

Lestrade threw up his hands in protest. "What the blazes was the point of that little exercise, Mr. Holmes? Are you mad?"

Holmes chuckled. "Not at all. I am merely pointing out the dangers of visual evidence. Had you been placed on the witness stand, Lestrade, you would have sworn under oath that I had tasted the tincture of woad. And you would have been factually incorrect, though you believed it wholeheartedly."

"I ask again, Mr. Holmes," said Lestrade, testily. "What is your point?"

154

Holmes turned to the butler. "Mr. Campbell, you saw Lady Honoria arrive upon the scene of the crime from the direction of the library, did you not?" The man nodded his silent affirmation. "And Mr. Carruthers from director of the garden, correct?" he asked, and was answered with another nod.

"And yet, what is there to prove that either individual was actually at those sites at the time of the gunshots? Either one could have discharged the gun into Macpherson, raced partway back to their supposed locale, and then turned back around, as if summoned by the noise."

Lestrade's anger began to fade. "Yes, I suppose that is true."

"Now we come to the most interesting part of the case. First, if you will all follow me into the garden." Holmes led the group out of the palm house, through the poison garden, and to the old Wish Tree. He then turned to Lestrade. "Inspector, now if you would be so kind as to display the coins the police found in Macpherson's pocket?"

Lestrade brought out the French coins as requested. I watched everyone's face as they were displayed, and all appeared only mildly curious, save Lady Emma. For a brief moment, I could have sworn a look of amazed recognition swept across her now placid features. "Here you go, Mr. Holmes."

"Hold onto them for a moment longer, Lestrade. Now then, in Lady Emma's library I found a long, but clear and fascinating, account of the Jacobite uprisings as written by one Archibald Cameron." Here Holmes drew an old volume from his jacket pocket. "It incalculably enriches the piquancy of an investigation, my dear Lestrade, when one is in a state of mindful understanding with the historical ambiance of one's environs. I will refrain from reading it verbatim, but permit me to summarize for you. As you may recall from your school-days, the English Oak is a tree with great symbolism to the Jacobite cause. For it was in the boughs of the Royal Oak at Boscobel Woods that the future Charles II hid from Parliamentarian soldiers on Oak Apple Day in 1651."

Lestrade was speechless at this apparent tangent. I frowned in confusion. "Whatever do the Jacobites have to do with this matter, Holmes? I thought their line had died out many years ago."

"You are correct, Watson. After the Young Pretender died without legitimate issue in 1788, his brother Henry, a Cardinal of the Roman Church, was the final Jacobite heir to publically claim the throne of England. However, unlike his father and brother, Henry never made a serious effort to seize the throne. He died childless and the claim passed to a lesser branch. As far as I am able to determine, the Princess of

Bavaria is the closest successor, though at this late date she is rather unlikely to ever press her claim."

"And how is this pertinent?"

"You have some Scottish roots, Watson. What was often performed during the Loyal Toast?"

I considered this for a moment. "A Jacobite sympathizer would pass their drink over a glass of water upon the table, to symbolize their concealed loyalty to the King over the Water."

"Correct. Here we have an oak, the symbol of the Jacobite King. And here, at our feet, we have the water."

I glanced down at the patch of earth. "What do you mean, Holmes?"

"I suggest that this disturbed earth covers a forgotten well. And if we were to have it dug up, it would reveal a surprise or two."

Lestrade finally grew impatient with Holmes's leisurely revealing of the truth. "Come now, Mr. Holmes, we don't need to be digging up old wells in order to figure out who killed Macpherson!"

Holmes smiled. "But if you do, Lestrade, you may find yourself the recipient of a medal from a certain gracious Lady at the southern end of the Mall."

I had before seen Lestrade completely astonished by some words or actions of my friend, but the look on his face at this moment was beyond compare.

"Here is how I see it," Holmes continued. "Mr. Macpherson and Colonel Carruthers were having a morning walk in the gardens when they came upon Donald Scott digging in the South Garden. By sheer happenstance, Scott had unearthed an old well, and he was likely considering what to do about it when he was joined by the two gentlemen. Macpherson and Carruthers were both true Scotsmen and knew the legends attached to Loch Arkaig. They immediately made the connection of the well to the oak tree, and Macpherson hurried off to fetch a rope. Being the more nimble of the pair, I presume it was Macpherson who climbed down into the well. When he was finally hauled back up, he was several hundred-thousand pounds richer. Presuming, that is, that he could remove the contents of the well without arousing the suspicion of Lady Emma, who would have been certain to alert the authorities."

"What is in the well?" Lestrade demanded, hotly.

"The Loch Arkaig Treasure, of course," said Holmes, mildly.

I rocked back upon my heels at the mention of this legendary treasure. But Lestrade was clearly unfamiliar with the name.

"What in the blazes are you talking about, Mr. Holmes?" he spluttered.

156

"As I learned today from my researches, in 1745, Bonnie Prince Charlie was raising troops in Scotland with the goal of overthrowing the Elector of Hanover, George II, from the throne of Great Britain. The Spanish, the French, and Pope Benedict XIV all contributed money to the cause, and a large fortune in French *livres* was sailed to Scotland and unloaded near here at Loch nan Uamh. However, by the time the gold arrived aboard the ships *Mars* and *Bellona*, the Battle of Culloden was already lost, with the Prince in hiding and his army scattered. There was no immediate use for the money, so it was sent to be hidden away by his trusty lieutenants. Its precise location has been lost to the history books for a hundred-and-fifty years . . . until now."

Lestrade took in all of this information with increasing incredulity apparent upon his face. "And you believe it to be buried under our feet?" he spluttered.

"I am certain of it," said Holmes. "After instructing Donald Scott to rebury the well, Macpherson and Carruthers met in the palm house to discuss their plans over tea. Plainly, neither of them wished to turn over the treasure to the Crown. [12] But it is equally clear that the two men quickly decided not to share between themselves. I believe that Carruthers surreptitiously slipped some ground-up angel's trumpet into Macpherson's tea. However, once Macpherson began to feel its effects, he must have realized what Carruthers had done. Macpherson pulled out his pistol and shot at Carruthers, but missed in his befuddled state. Naturally, Carruthers returned the favor."

"That is why Macpherson was shot even though he was already poisoned!" I exclaimed.

"Precisely, Watson. And why the bullet found in Macpherson did not match his gun. Instead, it came from the revolver of Colonel Carruthers."

"You will never prove that," sneered the colonel.

Holmes smiled and shook his head. "Did you know that you have a most distinctive gait, Colonel? With the marks made by your Penang lawyer, it was child's play to track your steps, even after a heavy rain. I followed them along the dark path of interwoven trees down to the Loch. There I paid some local fishermen to retrieve your gun from the spot where you flung it." He reached into his pocket and pulled out a pistol wrapped in a handkerchief, which he displayed for our viewing. "Unfortunately for you, there has been insufficient time for any rust to obscure the markings which will identify its owner. I am certain we shall have no trouble matching it to the service revolver once issued to you."

157

All color drained from the man's face as he realized that the noose had just been drawn about his neck. "It was self-defense! You said so yourself. Macpherson shot first."

"Of that I have no doubt. Sadly for you, Colonel, the little matter of the poisoned tea conveys the lie to that particular defense strategy. Nor do I think the jury shall look kindly upon your subsequent action. For not only did you flee the scene, but when you returned, you intended to ensure another man would hang in your place."

"The trowel!" I exclaimed.

"Precisely, Watson. Knowing that the sounds of the gunshots would raise the members of the household, Colonel Carruthers hurriedly exited the palm house into the gardens. There he came upon the gardener's trowel. He slid it into his pocket and dashed back into the palm house, pretending to have been summoned by the noise. While everyone else was distracted by the sight of Macpherson's body, Carruthers surreptitiously placed the trowel where it would be easily found."

As we considered this act of perfidy, Carruthers suddenly sprang into action. First, he swung his Penang lawyer into the head of the butler, Campbell, who collapsed to the ground. As Lestrade reached into his pocket for his revolver, Carruthers changed the direction of his stick and brought it crashing down upon the inspector's arm. I was too far away to stop him, so Carruthers turned to flee. However, before he could make it more than a few steps, Holmes glided forward and raised his *kebbie*. Carruthers turned to ward off the blow with his own stick, but Holmes's initial swing proved to be a feint. With a quick reversal, Holmes swept the man from his feet. Carruthers collapsed heavily to the ground, and Holmes kicked away the man's weapon.

Holmes turned and faced Lestrade, who had recovered his revolver and by now had it trained upon the horizontal form of Carruthers. "Now, then, Lestrade, Watson and I shall stay at the village inn again tonight before our return to London in the morning. You will, of course, lock up Colonel Carruthers and ensure that you enlist some trustworthy men to stand guard over this well until it is properly excavated. It would be most terrible if the gold vanished before it could be properly placed into the hands of the Queen's agents." [13]

Late that evening, as we sat together smoking our pipes in the village inn, Holmes gave me a chance to ask any questions which remained.

"So what did the water-horse have to do with the crime, Holmes?"

Hu chuckled. "Very little, Watson. But it was most instructive to learn about the local legends. It was those loquacious gentlemen at

Gairlochy's public house who first whispered to me about the treasure. I was merely demonstrating to Lestrade the importance of seeking out all potential information about one's locale."

I shook my head. "I worry that message was lost on the inspector. So when did you begin to suspect Colonel Carruthers?"

"Since the moment we met him, my dear Watson. Other than former members of the Royal Army Medical Corps, such as yourself – who instead utilize the salutation of 'Doctor' – I have never met an ex-officer who did not retain the use of his rank. As I noted at the time, if Carruthers had a reason for doing so, it would have been a grave one. In fact, as Lestrade has learned from a quick wire down to London, Carruthers was drummed out of the army for his role in the questionable death of a native porter. Nothing was categorically proven, but there was a sufficient stain upon his name such that he was unable to obtain an honorable discharge."

"So Carruthers and Macpherson did not know each other?"

"No," said Holmes, shaking his head. "The fact that two such dangerous rogues happened to be present when Donald Scott unearthed the lost Jacobite well is but one of those strange coincidences which conspire to ensure that life does not remain commonplace and dull."

"So, Scott will be released?"

"Oh, yes. Carruthers sealed his fate, and cleared Scott's name, when he struck at Lestrade with his Penang lawyer."

"Who would have thought that Macpherson was both poisoned and shot over possession of a hundred-year-old treasure?"

Holmes smiled. "Certainly audacity and romance have not passed from the criminal world, Watson. But if there is one worldly lesson to be learned from this case, it is that there is no honor among thieves."

"My dear Watson, you know how bored I have been since we locked up Colonel Carruthers."

Sherlock Holmes – "The Adventure of Wisteria Lodge"

NOTES

1 – Thomas Campion (1567-1620) was an Elizabethan composer. Holmes's *Variations* have sadly never been recovered.
2 – There is no "Gleannlaithe Castle" near Loch Arkaig. The name appears to be a contraction of the Scottish Gaelic words for Valley and Fowl.
3 – Presumably a reference to William III of Orange, who along with his wife, Mary, usurped the throne of England from James II in 1688 during

the so-called Glorious Revolution. He was not popular amongst the Scottish.

4 – There is no such regiment listed in the British Army.

5 – *Elephantiasis tropica*, now known as lymphatic filariasis, is caused by parasitic worms spread by the bites of infected mosquitos. In the era before the development of anti-parasitics it could be a very debilitating affliction.

6 – A reference to the Medical School at Teviot Place, part of the University of Edinburgh, from where Watson's first literary editor, Sir Arthur Conan Doyle, obtained his MD in 1885.

7 – An Antimony pill is made from the metal antimony. It was designed to be swallowed, passed through the intestines, and then recovered for reuse, thereby giving rise to the name of the "everlasting pill". It was thought to have purgative effects, as well as having some anti-protozoal effects on infections such as *leishmaniasis*. Unfortunately, filarial worms are not protozoa. Such were the perils of 19th century medicine!

8 – Bacterial meningitis has a terrifyingly high mortality rate in the pre-antibiotic era, and for those fortunate few who did recover, hearing loss, cognitive impairment, and epilepsy were common *sequelae*.

9 – Sheridan Le Fanu (1814-1873) was an Irish writer of Gothic tales, including the story "Green Tea", from the collection *In a Glass Darkly* (1872), wherein such visions were recounted.

10 – In 1839, Dr. George Sigmond published a lecture regarding the "Effects, Medicinal and Moral" of green tea. This describes the risk of becoming "hysterical" after drinking green tea on an empty stomach, with possible "fluttering of the heart".

11 – As described in the non-Canonical tale "The Adventure of the Fateful Malady" by Craig Janacek (published in *The MX Book of New Sherlock Holmes Stories – Part I: 1881-1889* [2015] and also *Light In The Darkness: The Further Adventures of Sherlock Holmes* [2017].

12 – Treasure Trove laws in Scotland are clear that: "*bona vacantia quod nullius est fit domini regis*" ("vacant goods [objects which are lost, forgotten, or abandoned] that which belongs to nobody becomes our Lord the Queen's").

13 – Lestrade must have seen that the treasure was recovered with great secrecy, for it officially remains unfound to this day.

The Adventure of the
Admirable Patriot
by S. Subramanian

A Preliminary Note for the Reader . . . .

The case recorded here by Dr. Watson occurred in the year 1895. It was discovered amongst a collection of his papers which came to light after his death, and is published in what follows (with the permission of his Estate) for the first time. Internal evidence strongly suggests that the piece was written in 1897, shortly after Watson made a record of those events, which happened in 1896, that he described under the heading of "The Veiled Lodger" *– an account that was, however, published only in 1926 as a part of the compendium titled* The Casebook of Sherlock Holmes. *When Watson, in* "The Veiled Lodger", *speaks of an attempt made* "lately" *to get after his papers, he is forgetfully and mechanically reproducing what he wrote in 1896, omitting to realize that the reader would be left with the mistaken impression that the attempt in question was probably made not much before 1926, when* "The Veiled Lodger" *made its substantially delayed appearance in print. – S.S.*

On going through my notes I find that it was on a cold March morning in the late winter of '95, about a year following my friend's dramatic return to London in the aftermath of his fateful encounter with Professor Moriarty at the Reichenbach Falls, that Holmes requested me to make a point of getting back by six that evening to our lodgings at Baker Street. "I am," he said, "expecting a client this evening, and I would greatly appreciate your being present during his visit. I might tell you, briefly, that these humble quarters are to be honoured by the presence of an important personage from the world of scholarship – a Professor Augustus Bradshaw, linguist and philologist, who heads the Faculty of Languages at a London college. The case, I understand, has to do with some missing papers of a confidential nature, and the College, naturally, is anxious to apprehend the culprit at the earliest and dismiss him from service, even if it is unable to avert the impending scandal of a disclosure of the papers' contents." I assured Holmes that I would be honoured to lend him what assistance I could, and took off on my rounds.

161

Promptly at six that evening I returned to Baker Street, and was surprised to find that a coach was already parked on the street by our lodgings. After ascending the stairs, I was greeted at the door by Holmes.

"Ah, Watson, welcome! You have arrived not a moment too soon. Please meet our client, Professor Bradshaw, who has preceded you by just a couple of minutes. The Professor, as I believe I have already informed you, is the head of the Faculty of Languages at one of our London colleges. Dr. Watson here is my trusted friend and colleague. Professor Bradshaw, Dr. Watson."

Introductions over, and with all three of us seated comfortably around the fire, Holmes invited our visitor to present his problem.

The professor displayed an amiable, if distinctly absent-minded, personality. He was a tall, stringy individual, with a good-natured if vague and vacant face. His head was quite bald, a pince-nez was perched somewhat hazardously on the bridge of a long nose, and his face had an abundance of unkempt fuzz which betokened not so much a well-groomed beard and moustaches as a prolonged neglect of the activity of shaving. He had the typical scholar's myopic, peering eyes and rounded shoulders that come from hours of reading fine print while hunched over a desk. Abruptly jerky and ill-coordinated movements of the arms and legs completed the picture of an altogether eccentric personality.

"I am here on the strong recommendation of my counterpart at Oxford, Professor Drummond-Smith, who advises me that you were once of signal help to him in a most delicate matter."

"Ah, a trivial affair, as I remember it."

"It is in a state bordering on nervous prostration, Mr. Holmes," said Professor Bradshaw in a high-pitched voice, "that I approach you for your assistance in averting, if that should at all prove possible, what threatens to be a major scandal, should the matter of the missing papers come to the attention of the public, as all too often happens in such cases. Mine is a small but very well-respected department, one which I have nurtured over the years, and it breaks my heart to think that its high standards of scholarly competence and academic integrity should be threatened by this dreadful event."

"Rest assured, Professor Bradshaw," said Holmes in a soothing voice, "that Dr. Watson and I will do all that is in our power to get to the bottom of this affair. But for that to be a possibility, one must have a complete and coherent account of the events that have led up to the present crisis. Pray compose yourself, collect your thoughts, and let me have as clear a statement as you are capable of. Perhaps you can begin with a description of the members of your faculty which, I believe, is a small one."

162

"Very well, Mr. Holmes," said the professor. "Forgive me for my earlier inchoate presentation, which was brought on by my ill-controlled state of agitation. Let me do the best I can. You must know, to begin with, that my faculty is indeed a small one, and when one considers the set of persons who had any knowledge of the papers in question, or had anything to do with the matter, one's count dwindles to a group of just three individuals, all of whom occupy senior positions in the department. The first is Dr. Richard Titmuss, a specialist in Mediaeval German. The second is Dr. Martin Arne, an expert in the Scandinavian Languages. And the third is Dr. Navrozbhai Cursetji, who teaches the Indian language of Gujarati. He is a Parsee of Indian origin, and I suppose it is most unlikely that you would have any acquaintance with members of his community."

"To the contrary," said Holmes. "As it happens, I am very well acquainted with the Banaji, *père et fils*, Parsees from Staffordshire who have been most unjustly accused, for reasons arising from shameful racialist prejudices against them, of being involved in the writing of obscene anonymous letters. Upon my coming to know of this sorry state of affairs, I initiated my own enquiries into the matter, and despite coming up with clinching evidence that the Banajis could not possibly have been implicated in the crime of which they were accused, I was unsuccessful in preventing the wrongful conviction of the son, Victor Banaji. But this is a digression. Pray forgive me for diverting you from your narrative, which I will be happy for you to resume."

"The problem with which I am confronted," said Professor Bradshaw, "is barely twenty-four hours old. It has to do with the confidential performance reports of the members of my faculty, which are prepared in March of every year, and forwarded to the University's Chancellor, for appropriate action in the matter of confirmations or promotions or terminations, as the case may be. A preliminary draft of these assessments is written by me, on the basis of my judgement of the teaching and research undertaken by my staff in the course of the academic year under review. It is my custom to put together these draft evaluations and pass them on, for approval, to the three senior-most members of my Faculty – Professors Titmuss, Arne, and Cursetji.

"The normal procedure is for me to invite them to an extended meeting, at which I read aloud each report to my colleagues and request them to vet the assessments in sequence, to ensure that they are fair, that they emerge from a proper evaluation of the syllabus that has been taught to the students and of the students' success in their examinations, and that due weight is given to the original research undertaken by the members of the Faculty, which is expected to adequately represent the

163

standards of scholarship on which the College's reputation is built. Corrections and amendments suggested by my colleagues or myself are effected by me on the manuscript containing the entire roster of reports.

"This master document, with all the prescribed emendations incorporated in it, is then typed out by me, personally, and each of the ten reports (which constitutes the strength of the rest of the Department), running together to ten typewritten sheets, is then signed by myself and each of my three senior colleagues. These final typed evaluations are then inserted in a cover, sealed and addressed, and despatched to the Chancellor's Office via a courier from my subordinate support staff. We pride ourselves, in the College, on attending with care and conscientiousness to the execution of this vital and delicate task.

"In line with earlier practice, the four of us – Titmuss, Arne, Cursetji, and I – met yesterday morning (the first of March, as it happens) at ten in the morning. The vetting of the preliminary reports prepared by me is, as you will have gathered, a long and elaborate process, and it has been our experience that the meeting could go on for up to eight hours, that is to say till about six in the evening, before concluding with the production of the final version of the Faculty Evaluations. Naturally, we break at intervals for refreshments and nourishment, which are sent for and brought into my study by the office staff. Mine is a large study. My colleagues and I perform our academic work sitting around my large desk, and we repair to the far corner of the room, which is furnished with a table and chairs, to partake of refreshments. At these meetings we usually break once for lunch at around one o'clock, for tea at around four o'clock, and for a glass of sherry at six o'clock when the labours of the day have been completed. The study is equipped with an *en suite* facility, and it has never proved necessary for any of us to leave during our report-vetting sessions.

"We had a fruitful meeting yesterday, at the conclusion of which the finalised Evaluation Reports were duly signed by the four of us, enclosed in a cover, and pasted and sealed before they were carried by Jenkins the porter to the Chancellor's Office, where an acknowledgement of receipt of the parcel was issued. I left the amended draft of my preliminary consolidated evaluation in a buff-coloured cover on my desk – right next to my pen-holder, as I happen to remember, and sticking out a little under three other heavy books. We then ambled over to the refreshments stocked in the far corner of the room, and – saving Cursetji who is a teetotaller – helped ourselves to a glass of sherry each.

"After that, we left the study, my colleagues preceding me on our way out. A customary precaution which the three senior Faculty members have always voluntarily submitted themselves to, is for each of them to check the pockets of their two colleagues' vestements, to ensure that no document is carried out of the study. This ritual verification was performed last evening too on our way out of the study. Just before leaving, I distinctly remember seeing the buff-coloured cover containing the amended evaluation reports exactly where I had left it, upon the conclusion of the meeting, next to the pen-holder and under those three other books. I locked my study-door behind me, as I usually do when I wind up for the day.

"This morning, Mr. Holmes, when I returned to my study and made to put away the buff-coloured cover in my desk-drawer – and I found it exactly where I had left it last evening – I was shocked to discover that the cover was empty! The amended confidential reports had vanished clean away. I conducted as thorough a search of the room as I possibly could, to allow for the possibility that I might – contrary to my memory and my impression – have put the collection of reports away elsewhere in the room, in a fit of absent-mindedness such as I am told I am prey to from time to time, but all to no avail.

"What is worse is that in the late forenoon of this morning, I received in my pigeon-hole a cover containing the missing amended draft of evaluations, presumably as proof that the document had indeed been spirited out of my study. The document was accompanied by a strange and menacing anonymous message. Clearly, the thief has made a copy of the evaluation reports from the amended draft, so that – in effect – he is in custody of the confidential Faculty assessments now in the Chancellor's possession, which one imagines he is free to circulate amongst the Faculty. This is a dreadfully embarrassing and delicate state of affairs in which to be, Mr. Holmes, and as you may well imagine, I am a sorely tried man. I have, I may add, brought the Chancellor and my three senior Faculty colleagues up-to-date with developments, and informed them of my decision to consult you in the matter."

Holmes, who had been leaning back in his armchair and listening to this account with his eyes closed and his fingers steepled, now sat up and addressed the Professor.

"That," he said, "was an admirably lucid presentation. Before I examine the communication you found in your pigeon-hole this morning, I have one or two questions for you. To begin with, when the four of you repaired for refreshments at the end of the day's meeting, did you do so together or separately?"

The don knitted his brows in concentration, before replying, "It hardly occurred to me, Mr. Holmes, to register the detail which you seek. As far as I can recall, our visits to the refreshment corner were not necessarily simultaneous, and at the conclusion of the meeting, as on other occasions, it might have been two or three minutes from the time of our adjournment before all four of us were gathered together at the far corner of my study. I am, of course, in absolutely no position to remember the order or the combinations, if any, in which we assembled."

"No, of course not. Now tell me, did you yourself carry any papers out with you at the end of your meeting last evening?"

"No, I did not – but wait a minute, please, my absent-mindedness does me an ill service! As it happens, Arne, who for some time has been seeking an opinion on a paper of his on the provenance of the Norse legend of Fenrir the Wolf, gave me a copy to take with me and read at home."

"Pray be precise as to details."

"Well, there isn't much to report. As we were finishing our sherry, Arne handed me a pale-blue cover containing his article, with a request that I read it and tell him what I thought of it, and I put it away in the breast pocket of my coat."

"And did you have an occasion to read it later at home?"

"Why, yes. I must say though that the thesis in the paper is somewhat needlessly provocative and disputatious. You will readily appreciate my point of view when I tell you that the fortifying of Agard during the Ragnarök is scarcely compatible with Arne's attribution of the time of the Yggdrasil's shaking to – "

"Quite so, Professor, quite so," said Holmes hastily. "Now, can you tell me how you gentlemen disposed of yourselves after the meeting?"

"Cursetji and the rest of the three of us parted company as soon as we emerged from my study. He took the right staircase leading down to the building's exit, while Titmuss, Arne and I took the left staircase leading down to the Senior Common Room, where we thought we might indulge in some sherry and a bit of socialisation with a few other senior colleagues, as we often did of an evening before returning to our respective homes. I was there, in the Common Room, for about a half-hour. Titmuss, if I recall right, was the first to leave, after about fifteen minutes, followed by Arne ten minutes later."

"Excellent. Are there any means of ingress to your study, apart from the front door?"

"There is a set of four large windows at the far end of the study which look out upon the College lawns, but they are all securely latched from the inside, and furthermore, the windows are barred with iron grills."

"Your study is on the first floor?"

"Yes."

"Is there any means by which a determined individual might climb up to the windows of your study?"

"Now that you ask me, yes. There is a sturdy drainpipe fixed to the wall of the building, which runs all the way down from the third floor, and passes alongside one of the windows of my study. Nevertheless, I imagine the individual in question would have to be substantially determined, and athletic, in order to shimmy up the drainpipe, which I suppose he could do without danger of being observed and only if he did it under cover of darkness."

"Is there a ledge beneath the windows?"

"Yes, there is one, projecting out from the base of the windows."

"So, in principle, it should be possible for someone to climb up to the ledge and, should one of the windows be open, to remove objects from your desk by means of a hook or similar appurtenance attached to the end of a sufficiently long pole?"

"In principle, yes, though I would think it is unlikely in fact. Besides, the windows showed no signs of having been tampered with when I entered my study this morning, and they were still securely latched on the inside."

"No doubt. And now, Professor Bradshaw, may I trouble you to show me the communication you found in your pigeon-hole this morning?"

"Here it is, Mr. Holmes." Opening his briefcase, the Professor withdrew a square of slightly dirty white paper on which some words, composed of unevenly-sized letters presumably cut out from elsewhere, appeared to have been pasted.

"Has anyone but you handled this sheet of paper since you received it?" enquired Holmes.

"No, sir."

"I would suggest that you leave this with me. It is valuable evidence, which carries with it every prospect of bearing clues as to the perpetrator of the crime. It deserves to be handled with the utmost care. Watson, may I trouble you for a pair of your surgical gloves? Thank you. What have we here?"

Holmes laid out the sheet of paper on the table in front of him. As I have said, it was a smudged and less-than-clean sheet of paper, on which had been pasted, in an irregular and jagged line, a series of words, mysterious as to origin, and ominous as to import:

he will smite the most oppressive of the oppressors of men

"A message," said Holmes, "that combines aspects of both warning and retribution, addressed to those that are perceived to be tyrants. Are you aware of any matter on which your Department could be held to ransom?"

"It may or may not be fair for me to speculate on the question, but since you ask, I cannot rule out the possibility of an attempt to force the Department's hand in the matter of a forthcoming appointment to the post of a Lecturer in Comparative Grammar."

"Specifically?"

The Professor shuffled his feet uncomfortably, before responding, "As it happens, a young Indian called Krishna Prasad has been strongly recommended to the position by Navroz Cursetji. My own judgement is that the young man, though promising, presently lacks the experience and scholarship needed for the appointment. A denial of his application could lend itself to interpretation, by a colonised subject of the Empire, as a decision motivated by racialist bias."

"On a different plane: Is there a spare key to your study, and if so, who is in possession of it?"

There was a stricken look upon Bradshaw's face, as at the sudden recollection of a forgotten and unpleasant fact. "Oh my goodness, Mr. Holmes!" he cried, clapping his palm to his brow, "Oh my goodness! On at least three occasions in the past I have arrived at the College to discover that I had left behind at home the key to the study, and its spare. It is my cursed absent-mindedness. On the day following the last occasion on which this occurred, in the middle of the previous Michaelmas term, I called a brief meeting of my three senior colleagues, and handed the spare key over to the one person who struck me as being the most completely responsible and organized individual in our lot. At the time, it seemed to me to be an effective insurance against further episodes of being locked out of my own room. I vastly fear, Mr. Holmes, that I have trusted my colleagues not wisely, but too well!"

"And to which one of them did you entrust the guardianship of your study?"

"To Navrozbhai Cursetji, who has frequently come to my rescue on various occasions when I have been potentially threatened by the consequences of my absent-mindedness."

"Well, well. Things do indeed look black against Dr. Cursetji! As for the anonymous message you have received, pray leave it with me. I should like to subject it to further forensic examination. For the time being, I would urge you most strenuously not to breathe a word to anyone on our meeting or the content of our conversation. Meanwhile, I shall pursue my own line of investigation, and if you could kindly

168

arrange it, I should like to meet and confer with your three senior colleagues at the College. Tomorrow, at, say, two in the afternoon? Very well then, sir. Let us hope that the mists of mystery which have till now shrouded the case will soon be dispersed." And with that, Holmes led our client out of our sitting room.

"What now, Holmes?" I enquired.

"Now, Watson, we turn to two of the profoundest repositories of knowledge that any seeker of the truth can hope to benefit from. The first is the Good Old Index. If you will be so kind as to stretch out your arm in the cause of Volume Z – thank you! Hmm. Zanos the strangler. Zen Budhism. *Zend Avesta* – Ha! What have we here? A nugget, if ever there was one, although there are those that might be inclined to entertain the peculiar notion that the Index is a clutter of insensible information. An excerpt from the Zoroastrian religious text *Avesta* – listen to this, Watson: '*He exclaimed, did Angra Mainyu: Woe is me! Here is the god Asha-Vahishta, who will . . . smite the most fiendish of all fiends, . . . who will smite the most oppressive of the oppressors of men, he will afflict the most oppressive of the oppressors of men . . . .*'"

"The text of the anonymous message received by Bradshaw! Is not Zoroastrianism the religion of the Parsees? This seems to implicate the man Cursetji rather squarely in the scandal, Holmes, especially when you consider that he has for long been campaigning against what he calls 'Un-British Rule in India', a charge which he has strenuously expanded upon in his capacity of the first and only British Member of Parliament of Indian origin – elected in the '92 General Election, if I am not mistaken, as a Liberal Party candidate from Finsbury Central."

"I am afraid so, Watson. And for more than just the reason you have mentioned. A criminologist of any competence must have a thorough knowledge of, and ability to distinguish between, the type-faces of different newspapers. It is an elementary matter, really – although, as I believe I once confided in you, as a very raw hand I made the mistake of confusing the *Leeds Mercury* with the *Western Morning News*. But there can be no mistaking the source of the words pasted on Bradshaw's anonymous message. They bear the unmistakeable stamp of the cheap half-penny eveninger *The Finsbury Gazetteer*. (And if you are wondering about words like 'oppressive' and 'oppressor', it is not unusual to describe the weather in terms of the first word, or to find the second on a newspaper's Entertainments page carrying reviews of books and plays.) Taking everything together, it does seem – on top of the Zoroastrian scriptural quotation and the plausible motive and opportunity advanced by Bradshaw – to make the case against Cursetji conclusive. And now,

Watson, I am famished. Will you be a good fellow and ask Mrs. Hudson for our supper?"

"I am happy to be a good, as well as a hungry – and therefore self-interested – fellow. By the way, Holmes, a while ago you mentioned two profound repositories of knowledge. What did you have in mind for the other one?"

"Ah, Watson, tomorrow I shall consult the supreme oracle on the private lives and criminal propensities of the denizens of this great city. I refer to Mr. Shinwell 'Porky' Johnson, a man with a distinctly shady past, who now, however, swears to treading the straight and narrow path. This, fortunately, is no impediment to his continuing to be a veritable encyclopaedia when it comes to the sorts of information I frequently have need of in my enquiries. Speaking of which, my dear fellow, let us take our minds off the present investigation, in favour of one into the ineffable delights of Mrs. Hudson's roast."

The following morning proved to be a busy one for Holmes, who left shortly after breakfast to consult with his friend Shinwell Johnson. My day was a dull one, and with no appointments having been made for the afternoon, I decided to wind up early, leaving the clinic to the charge of Hetheridge, an accommodative young fellow. Also, I was keen to take Holmes up on his invitation to accompany him on his visit to the college where he had made arrangements for meeting the three senior dons of the Faculty of Languages. When I returned at about one o'clock to our lodgings, it was to find Holmes putting away the anonymous message which he had, I gathered, been examining minutely with a microscope. He gave every indication of having spent a productive morning with Shinwell, and it was in the company of an eager and energetic detective that I arrived, at two of the afternoon, at the college.

Our first meeting was with Dr. Martin Arne, who came across as a pleasant, well-mannered individual kindly disposed toward those around him. This included a grey cat that responded (when it chose to) to the name of Baldur. It appeared to have the run of Arne's study, and when we entered his room, we found the cat lying stretched out languorously on the desk in front of its owner, on whom it conveyed the privilege of tickling it under its chin whenever it demanded that treatment. Arne was bent over a page with black-and-white squares on it, and when asked what he was working on, he smiled and said that, having just corrected a pile of exam scrips, he was endeavouring to relax his mind by devising what he called an exercise in "acrostics", or a "crossword puzzle", which he apparently contributed from time to time to the *Evening Standard*.

Arne seemed to be delighted to learn that Holmes was acquainted with the Rev. Charles Dodgson, a mathematician and logician at Oxford

University, who was also an expert in devising word-games, including crossword puzzles. (For the benefit of any reader who may not be aware of the fact, Dodgson wrote under the pen-name of Lewis Carroll.) Arne asked Holmes if he would care to come up with a two-word solution to a crossword clue. The first word, he said, had eight letters, and the second, eleven, and the clue was embodied in these words: '*Flit on, cheering angel*'. Holmes thought for a minute, and then said with a smile, "That is a clever clue, Dr. Arne. It is an anagram. By reordering the letters in that sentence, one obtains the solution, '*Florence Nightingale*', who was indeed a *cheering angel* that *flitted on!*"

On matters relating to the case, Arne proved to be taciturn and reserved. He volunteered little information, and had nothing to say on the anonymous message when Holmes showed him the communication that Professor Bradshaw had received. However, he confirmed, readily enough, all that the Professor had conveyed to us. On being pressed for an opinion on what might have happened, Arne finally said, "Mr. Holmes, I must be a complete fool if I cannot see that the case looks black against a particular colleague of mine. But I try to go through life without judging my fellows too harshly, and least of all in the absence of clinching evidence. Professor Bradshaw has requested you to get to the bottom of the affair, and for the sake of the Department's good name, I wish you all the best in your efforts. But pray do not press me for a speculative opinion that may accomplish nothing more than advance the prejudices of race and colour from which few of us are exempt."

Our next interviewee was Dr. Richard Titmuss, who proved to be quite a contrast to Dr. Arne – a blunt, even brusque and frank-spoken individual – large, untidy, unshaven, and endowed with a full head of shocking red hair atop beetling red eyebrows, from beneath which a pair of piercing blue eyes looked out with disconcerting directness. "I fail to see what all the fuss is about, Mr. Holmes," said he. "What need have we for the services of a professional consultant? Isn't it as clear as daylight and plain as a pikestaff who the culprit is? From what I know of the case, it is an open-and-shut affair. Cursetji must be every sort of damned idiot to believe we have forgotten that he is in charge of the old man's spare key to his study! And that anonymous message is no great mystery to penetrate. I was in correspondence for many years with the German philologist Friedrich Nietzsche when he was teaching at the University of Basle, and after the publication of his book *Also Sprach Zarathustra*, I took the trouble of making a thorough study of the *Avesta*, so it is both silly and arrogant for Cursetji to believe that the scriptures of his religion are available to him alone. Not, mind you, that I have anything against Cursetji, poor fool. It's just that I think it would be an hypocritical

171

affectation to make special concessions to members of a different colour or race, for that would amount to a perverse acknowledgement of differences amongst humans based on these criteria. Also, and in the end, I have a pretty dim view of the human race. It is uniformly constituted, in my view, by a bunch of blighters, though I suppose it would be fair to suggest that some blighters are more blighting than other blighters!"

"That was nothing if not refreshingly frank," murmured Holmes, as we made our way to the room of the last scholar on our list. We were greeted with courtesy by a dapper little man with close-cropped white hair and a white beard and moustache, dressed in a traditional Parsee coat and trousers. He spoke fluent English, characterised by great refinement and gentleness of expression. He must have sensed our own awkward embarrassment in initiating a dialogue with him; so it came almost as a relief to us when he himself opened the conversation, with what struck me as a quaint mixture of amusement and sadness.

"Mr. Holmes, Dr. Watson," said he, "It is obvious, is it not, that I am the villain of the piece? Only, I would urge you to consider the possibility that it is altogether *too* obvious. After all, it is public knowledge that Professor Bradshaw entrusted me with his spare key. And surely, it would be absurd on my part, in the company of a distinguished set of learned fellow-scholars, to expect not to reveal myself by quoting from the *Zend Avesta*. Of course, it is possible that I might be securing indemnity for myself precisely through the excessive obviousness of my stratagem. But please, gentlemen, consider this: Given the vulnerability of the office I occupy as a Member of Parliament, and the gravity of the cause that I have campaigned for all my adult existence – my country's gradual emergence into independence from imperial rule – is it conceivable that I would gamble my reputation and my life's struggle on the slender probability of getting away with a dangerously foolish double-bluff? And in what cause would I do this? You may credit me with the necessary wickedness, but surely such an order of wickedness would be incompatible with the level of sheer idiocy it also seems to entail?"

"That, among other reasons, Dr. Cursetji," said Holmes, "is why it never occurred to me to suspect you of complicity in the matter. Of course you are completely innocent of any wrong-doing."

"What a relief it is to hear you say that, Mr. Holmes!" cried the old Parsee gentleman. "Will you advise Professor Bradshaw accordingly? And if you know I am not guilty, is there reason to believe that you also know who *is* guilty? Would it be too much to ask you how you have come by your conclusions?"

"All in good time, Dr. Cursetji. I happen to know that you are due to make a public address at five this evening, at the Lighthouse Methodist Church in Walthamstow. It is already three o'clock now, and there is no reason for me to detain you further here. Dr. Watson and I hope to be in the audience at your lecture later this evening. We shall find our way to Walthamstow just as soon as we have transacted some urgent business that awaits us now."

"Why, it would be a pleasure and a privilege to have you in the audience, gentlemen. I only hope you will not consider your time to have been wasted in listening to this old man lecturing to you on un-British rule in India!' The Professor of Gujarati had a twinkle in his eye, as we shook hands and took our leave.

Stopping briefly at Professor Bradshaw's study, Holmes told the scholar, "If you should drop in at 221b Baker Street by seven o'clock this evening, I should be in a position to clear up this mystery for you." Leaving behind a stunned don with his mouth slightly agape, we made our way out of the gates of the college. "Now, Watson," said Holmes, "we need to have a word with friend Lestrade. I shall endeavour to explain as we go along. Cabbie! Scotland Yard – and drive like the devil! Tell me, Watson, what did you make of The Three Wise Men?"

As an old campaigner who had taken a Jezail bullet in the cause of Queen and country, I felt obliged, albeit with doubtful vehemence, to speak up on behalf of the Empire. "Well," said I, "I have to admit, Holmes, that I am not favourably impressed by the fellow Cursetji. He *is* a thorn in the Empire's flesh."

"No doubt, and that is his avowed intention. But is it the sign of an English patriot to be intolerant of such as Cursetji? Your own somewhat perfunctory and half-hearted criticism of the man does you credit, and shows where you really stand on the matter. For what use, in the end, does one have for a patriotism which Dr. Johnson described as the scoundrel's last refuge? Love of country is not undiscriminating endorsement of its government's policies. No Englishman of conscience should, for instance, countenance the record of repeated famine which the Empire's administration has visited upon hundreds of thousands of its hapless Indian subjects. Rather, I hope I am right in thinking – with Cursetji! – that it would be un-British to do so. As un-British as it would be to deny that that great anti-monarchical patriot Tom Paine was a product of these Isles. Speaking of which, what did you make of the two home-grown specimens?"

"It occurred to me that Titmuss is a rough and unfriendly fellow, rather too eager to nail Cursetji, and probably driven by that same suspicion and intolerance of the foreigner which you deplore so strongly.

173

This is in sharp contrast to the reticence and gentleness displayed by the affable Arne."

"Well, well! There would, after all, seem to be something to be said for noting a valid difference between what philosophers of reason are wont to call the 'thing-as-it-appears' and the 'thing-as-it-is' – at least as applied to phenomena such as Richard Titmuss and Martin Arne. You will be surprised to hear what I learnt of these two gentlemen from Shinwell Johnson this morning. Titmuss is a non-violent pacifist, a member of the Vegetarian Society, and a friend, from the latter's student days, of a young man called Gandhi who, by all accounts, has been making a fairly substantial nuisance of himself with the authorities in Natal in South Africa. Men like Titmuss are given to being monsters in theory and angels in practice, in an inversion of the more usual criminal propensity to be angels in theory and monsters in practice."

"Like that terrible murderer, Bert Stevens, who wanted us to get him off in '87? I remember your once saying *was there ever a more mild-mannered, Sunday school young man?*'"

"Well, that is quite the mold in which Arne is cast. Johnson tells me that Arne has for long been a member in good standing of a violent, racialist freemasonry called the Norwood League, and is an important (if clandestine) office-bearer of one of the League's more vicious branch organizations, whose members are known by the name of The White Knights of Britain or, more informally, simply as The Hooded Men. This is an execrable organization, whose philosophy – if such it can be called – is styled on the beliefs of the infamous Ku Klux Klan of the New World."

"This is shocking, Holmes."

"And it gets worse, Watson. Martin Arne's brother is a personal secretary of the haughty old nobleman whose disapproval of us mere mortals was so much in evidence in the course of our endeavour to track down that letter which went missing from the Home Secretary's possession. I refer to the former Premier, Lord Bellinger. Arne's connection with Lord Bellinger is no accident. I regret to say that they find common cause in their racialist prejudices. It is a matter of shame that of Cursetji's unsuccessful campaign in the '86 Election, Bellinger actually said something along the following lines: '*However great the progress of mankind has been, and however far we have advanced in overcoming our prejudices, I doubt if we have yet got to the point of view where a British constituency would elect a black man.*' This rightly elicited the following riposte from a political opponent: '*Well, if Cursetji is black, he is not a blackguard like a certain aristocrat we know.*' Of immediate relevance to us is the intelligence which Shinwell Johnson has gathered, to the effect that there is to be an armed attack upon the person of Cursetji after his public address at the Lighthouse Church in Walthamstow, orchestrated by Arne's organization."

"It must be stopped, Holmes!"

"Good old Watson! Of course it must be stopped. Hence the need to have a word with Inspector Lestrade. Here we are. Watson, wait in the cab for me. I shall not be quite five minutes. After I've spoken to Lestrade, the cab will take us to King's Cross where we shall take the train to St James's Park Station. From there, the Lighthouse Methodist Church is but a short walk away."

My mind was occupied by the most perplexing questions as I waited for Holmes to speak to Lestrade and return to the cab. Soon we were on the train to Walthamstow, but in response to my eager queries, Holmes counselled patience, promising that he would let me have a complete account of the case after Cursetji's lecture was over. I had no option but to keep my irritable quest for information and explanation at bay.

Arrived at St James's Park Station, it took us less than five minutes to walk up to the Lighthouse Methodist Church on Markhouse Road. It was a very new construction, built as recently as 1893 according to a design furnished by the architect Dunford. The Church presented a most interesting and impressive red-brick exterior, and its distinctive feature was the lighthouse tower on the corner of Markhouse Road and Downsfield Road. We were just in time for the beginning of Cursetji's well-attended lecture, which was held in the Church's auditorium. The speaker was concerned to explore the economic consequences of British rule in India. He spoke with clarity and passion, and I still have with me the notes I took down on the concluding part of his address:

> *The economic consequences for India are summed up in the declaration of Lord Bellinger himself that India must be "bled," and is the principle on which the whole present system of Indian government is based. Lord Bellinger has coolly and deliberately . . . admitted that India was injured by the drain that was constantly going on in the way of the exportation of so much revenue without any direct equivalent, and has gone on to say that as the great mass of the people, the agricultural community, have no more blood remaining in them, the lancet should be applied to those parts where the blood was congested or at least sufficient. I have said enough, I think, to show how the unhappy Indian Natives are regarded by Anglo-Indian officials.*

175

The lot of the former, indeed, is somewhat worse than that of the slaves in America in old days, for the masters had an interest in keeping them alive, if only that they had a money value. But if an Indian dies, or if a million die, there is another or there are a million others ready to take his or their places and to be the slaves of British officials in their turn . . . . The British people are so taken up at present by the extension of their Empire that they little dream of a day which might come at any moment when their existing Empire might suffer an upheaval and explosion which would shatter it to pieces. I hold out no threats, but that would be the natural consequence of an iniquitous and unjust system of government, as has been declared by Lord Bellinger when he says that injustice would bring down the mightiest kingdom. [1]

With the courageous little man's eloquent words still ringing in our ears, Holmes and I waited at the door to congratulate Cursetji on his way out. As we accompanied him outside the Church gates, one on either side of him, Holmes suddenly yelled out, "Protect him, Watson! And guard that bag in your hand. It contains the anonymous letter, and the scoundrels are after it!" He had barely finished speaking and I had instinctively drawn Cursetji into the protection of my shoulder, when I felt a stinging blow to my wrist. Painful though it was, I was mindful of Holmes's warning, rapidly transferring the bag to the hand that still held Cursetji in a semi-embrace, I let fly with my injured left fist, and had the satisfaction of hearing it land with a resounding smack on my assailant's jaw. I pack a certain chunky power in my arm, if I do say so myself, and I experienced the profound contentment of seeing my antagonist stagger back and suddenly sit down with a bump upon the ground.

Meanwhile, I saw out of the corner of my eye that Holmes was fending off two ruffians with his cane. It was an object lesson in the single-stick expert's artistry that was on display in my friend's skilled defence and subtle but telling attack against a couple of wildly slogging ruffians. Even so, I could tell it was tough going for Holmes. It was not a moment too soon that Lestrade's men closed in and took custody of the three hooligans that had attacked us. Holmes's first concern was for the safety of Cursetji, who was shaken but otherwise completely unharmed. He was safely entrusted to the protection of his friends and colleagues, who made sure that he was securely accompanied to his home.

Holmes then turned to me, his face twitching with anxious concern. "Tell me, my dear fellow, that the sound of a snapping bone which I

176

heard was not your wrist's. If any harm should have come to you, I could never blame myself enough. Tell me you are all right, Watson!" It was but rarely that the mask slipped from that cold, aloof visage, but it was worth waiting for those rare moments to see the depth of my friend's loyalty and affection. "Have no fear, Holmes. I'll admit it was a nasty crack. I have an impressive swelling of the wrist to prove it, but nothing that will not respond to an ice-pack. And if there were any fractures involved, I'm inclined to believe it is that villain who has sustained a broken jaw!"

"Thank God, Watson, thank God!" said Holmes as, putting his arm around me, he walked me back to the station.

By the time we got back to our quarters, we found that Professor Bradshaw, accompanied by Dr. Martin Arne, had already been let in by Mrs. Hudson.

"You have news for me, Mr. Holmes?" asked the Professor eagerly. "Have you cleared up the matter? I may add that I have taken the liberty of requesting Dr. Arne to accompany me, for moral support, as it were."

"I am not sure that that is what you might reasonably expect from this gentleman," said Holmes drily, gesturing toward Arne. "As for your question, Professor Bradshaw: Yes, I do have news for you. I have, I believe, solved the mystery. But before we get to that, tell me – would you say that the culprit is he on whose person the amended draft Evaluation Report was, at the time that the four of you left your study last evening?"

"Yes, of course, though I do not see how the amended draft could have left the room."

"Nevertheless, we know that it did, and I take it that, in your view, the one in whose possession it was as you emerged from your study is the culprit?"

"Yes, yes, I have already said so."

"In that case, Professor Bradshaw, I find myself compelled to point to you as the culprit."

"What tom-foolery is this, Mr. Holmes? Your jokes are as ill-timed as they are in bad taste."

"And yet it is you, Professor, who have insisted that the culprit is to be identified by the fact of possession of the amended draft at the time of your combined exit from the study."

"Are you suggesting then that I carried the draft out on my person?"

"Why, yes."

"Perhaps you would care to explain, Mr. Holmes? You quite bewilder me, and if it were not for the reputation that you command, I should feel well justified in walking out of that door now."

"I am sure I understand, Dr. Bradshaw. Dr. Watson here will tell you that I do display an occasionally mischievous sense of humour, but having indulged it, and discommoded you quite comically in the bargain, I now owe you an explanation. Here it is. We know that that draft evaluation report did leave your study. Cursetji did have the motive and the opportunity to steal it. He could quite easily have entered your study this morning with the spare key, and made off with the report. But, as he himself pointed out when I spoke to him this afternoon, no man bent upon hanging himself could have done a more thorough job of it than he, if he had indeed been the thief. It was unthinkable. There had to be another way, another explanation, another person.

"Watson will tell you that it is a pet dictum with me that when you have eliminated everything that is possible, then whatever remains, however improbable, must be the truth. If we rule out a wildly implausible three-way collusion, then – in view of the searches conducted by each of your colleagues on the other two – it is clear that the draft was not in the possession of any of your colleagues when the four of you left your study last evening. I ruled out an unintelligent and suicidal self-incrimination on Cursetji's part, and allowing for his natural disposition toward orderliness and caution, I also ruled out the possibility of his having left the spare key lying about carelessly for anyone else to pick up. Further, your study offered neither any easy means nor evident signs of having been broken in upon. Having eliminated the possible, we are left with the improbable solution that it was *you*, Professor Bradshaw, that carried the draft report out with you last evening."

"But how could that have happened, Mr. Holmes, without my knowledge?"

"The *modus operandi* is astonishingly simple, when one comes to think of it. Let us call the culprit *X*. As you yourself said, Professor, when the meeting concluded, it was quite two or three minutes before all four of you gathered at the refreshments table. *X* tarries behind for a bit at your desk. With his back turned on his colleagues' backs as they make for the refreshments at the far corner of the study, it should be no more than a moment's work for *X* to abstract the draft report from its buff-coloured cover, to replace the empty cover exactly where it was under those three books next to the pen-holder and with just the corner sticking out, and to shove the draft report into a pale-blue cover he is carrying in his coat-pocket. He then saunters over to join the rest of you for sherry, and hands over the pale-blue cover to you, Professor Bradshaw, with the intelligence that it contains his article on the provenance of the Norse legend – "

178

"How dare you, you damned busy-bodied lover of inferior elements of the human species?" sputtered Dr. Martin Arne, his lips distorted in a snarl, his eyes glaring, his face a mask of hatred, in a complete and shocking reversal of his usual mien of tolerant affability.

" – The Norse legend, I was saying," continued Holmes imperturbably, "of Fenrir the Wolf. You, Professor Bradshaw, and Dr. Titmuss and Dr. Arne, leave your coats on the coat-rack in the hallway leading up to the Senior Common Room. Dr. Arne – he seems to have deduced that he is the X in the equation – has a copy of his article in his pigeon-hole in the Common Room. He knows from experience that the Professor will stay for at least a half-hour chatting with his friends. Twenty-five minutes after your arrival in the Common Room, Dr. Arne leaves, taking his article with him. On his way out at the hallway, it is again a moment's work for him to withdraw the draft evaluation report from its blue cover in the breast pocket of the Professor's coat, and to replace it with his own paper on the Norse legend. Back home, he copies the draft confidential report, cuts out bits from *The Finsbury Gazetteer*, sticks that message from the *Avesta* to a sheet of paper, and next morning (that is, this morning), conveys the draft report, along with the message, to Professor Bradshaw's pigeon-hole."

With his face creased in loathing, Arne hissed, "Do you have any evidence for this farrago of lies you have just uttered? Or are we, simply, expected to swallow your fairy-tales whole?"

"If you did not suspect that a trained expert like myself might detect some evidence from the anonymous message, why were you so keen to recover it by force from Dr. Watson?" Taking the bag from me, Holmes brought out the message, and invited each of us to examine it under his concave lens. Under magnification one could see, sticking in the glue which had been employed to paste the words of the message, what looked like a small and scattered distribution of tiny grey filaments or fibres. "Hair, gentlemen. Feline hair," murmured Holmes. "Though not myself a betting man, I should wager a small sum that the hair belongs to a cat called Baldur. Dear me, Mr. Arne, such language, and that too from a respectable linguist! And this is only the least of it. Right now, the three ruffians you had hired in order to maim, if not murder, Dr. Cursetji and to violently steal the evidence in Dr. Watson's bag, must be singing – like canaries, as I have heard the police employ that expression – for the benefit of Inspector Lestrade's shell-like ear. Let him go, Watson, let him go. We have no use for scum like that upon our carpet, however modest a rug it may be."

The man called Martin Arne bolted like a hunted animal out of the room and clattered down the stairs. "If ever there was a fellow deserving a long stretch of penal servitude, it is that scoundrel," said Holmes. "Unfortunately, he is also in possession of those confidential reports. I am afraid it is a matter of mutual deadlock, Professor Bradshaw. You will have cut your losses by asking him to quietly leave the department, with the threat of pressing charges against him with the Official Force if there is ever any sign of a leak of those confidential reports. I am afraid he is in a position to force you to purchase his silence. Still, you now know who the guilty party is, and your Faculty will be well rid of a dangerous and unsavoury specimen of humanity."

"Indeed so, Mr. Holmes," said the absent-minded Professor warmly. "And it is thanks to you that we have apprehended the blackguard. As the Bard observed with such percipience, '*One may smile and smile and be a villain.*' I blame myself for being a poor judge of character. How I ever made the error of trusting a man whose estimation of the time of the Yggdrasil's shuddering was so fundamentally defective is a matter that will forever remain a mystery to me." The good Professor thanked Holmes, and let himself out, shaking his head and muttering to himself.

"I can only hope," muttered Holmes good-humouredly, "that the old fellow will not forget to send me a cheque for services rendered. By the way, Watson, Arne belongs to a vengeful organization. These fellows are not given to forgetting easily. They have already made one attempt upon my papers – for which you, my dear fellow, have had to bear the price of a swollen wrist. They may well try again, for we are in possession of facts and connections and opinions of a most delicately political nature. They also know that you maintain my official archives, so I would urge you to be careful in attending to their – and of course, your own – safety. Should another attempt be made to get at your papers, you have my unreserved permission to give to the public the whole story of the politician, the lighthouse, and the trained cormorant. At least one reader will understand."

"The reference to the politician points to Cursetji," I said, "or perhaps also Bellinger. The reference to the lighthouse suggests the Lighthouse Methodist Church. But the trained cormorant, Holmes? What does that signify?"

"As I said Watson," replied Holmes with a smile, "At least one reader will understand. The reader I have in mind is Arne. Do not forget his passion for crossword puzzles. Does the phrase '*trained cormorant*' suggest anything in the light of that?"

I brooded and puzzled over what Holmes had said for a full half-hour, before I let out a yell of triumph. "I do believe I have got it, Holmes," said I. "'*Trained cormorant*' is an anagram for '*Doctor Martin Arne*'!"

"Bravo, Watson! You scintillate!"

And with that, I must bring the curtain down upon the drama of the politician, the lighthouse, and the trained cormorant.

> *The discretion and high sense of professional honour which have always distinguished my friend are still at work in the choice of these memoirs, and no confidence will be abused. I deprecate, however, in the strongest way the attempts which have been made lately to get at and to destroy these papers. The source of these outrages is known, and if they are repeated I have Mr. Holmes's authority for saying that the whole story concerning the politician, the lighthouse, and the trained cormorant will be given to the public. There is at least one reader who will understand.*

Dr. John H. Watson – "The Veiled Lodger"

NOTE

The speech attributed to Cursetji is in fact substantially a part of the text of a lecture delivered by Dadabhai Naoroji at Westbourne Park Chapel in London on May 29th, 1899. See 'The Condition of India' (pp. 636-642, especially p. 641) in Poverty and Un-British Rule in India *by Dadabhai Naoroji, published by Swan Sonnenschein & Co., Lim., (London, 1901). This is available on the web at:*

http://www.archive.org/details/povertyunbritish00naoruoft

It may be added that many Sherlockians have identified Lord Bellinger of "The Adventure of the Second Stain" *with Robert Gascoyne-Cecil, 3rd Marquess of Salisbury. The story draws on other real-life persons and events and organizations but, being a work of fiction, it takes many liberties with these and their timelines. – S. S.*

The Abernetty Transactions
by Jim French

T*his script has never been published in text form, and was initially performed as a radio drama on September 23, 2012. The broadcast was Episode No. 106 of* The Further Adventures of Sherlock Holmes, *one of the recurring series featured on the nationally syndicated* Imagination Theatre. *Founded by Jim French, the company produced over one-thousand multi-series episodes, including one-hundred-twenty-eight Sherlock Holmes pastiches – along with later "bonus" episodes. In addition, Imagination Theatre also recorded the entire Holmes Canon, featured as* The Classic Adventures of Sherlock Holmes, *the only version with all episodes to have been written by the same writer, Matthew J. Elliott, and with the same two actors, John Patrick Lowrie and Lawrence Albert, portraying Holmes and Watson, respectively. Mr. French passed away at the age of eighty-nine on December 20*[th]*, 2017.*

This script is protected by copyright.

CHARACTERS

- SHERLOCK HOLMES
- DR. JOHN WATSON
- INSPECTOR STANLEY HOPKINS
- RUDOLPH ABERNETTY
- URSULA ABERNETTY
- CABBIE
- *MAITRE'D*

SOUND EFFECT: OPENING SEQUENCE, BIG BEN

ANNOUNCER: *The Further Adventures of Sherlock Holmes*, featuring John Patrick Lowrie as Sherlock Holmes, and Lawrence Albert as Dr. Watson.

MUSIC: *DANSE MACABRE* (UP AND UNDER)

WATSON: My name is Doctor John H. Watson, and the tale I have for you tonight concerns a mystery that came to our attention in the summer of 1895. As you may remember, Sherlock Holmes had solved the murder of the notorious sea captain known as Black

182

Peter in July of that year, a case that Scotland Yard had assigned to Inspector Stanley Hopkins. Less than a fortnight later, Hopkins arrived at our Baker Street rooms unannounced, his normally sallow face flushed and red, and his collar and necktie in disarray. It was one of the hottest afternoons on record, and his appearance and general exhaustion gave me immediate concern. I'd never seen him appear so spent!

SOUND EFFECT: 221b BAKER STREET, WINDOWS OPEN TO THE STREET

HOPKINS: Gentlemen, may I intrude upon you for a few minutes? I was in the neighborhood, and . . . .

WATSON: You're not intruding at all, Inspector. Come in and sit down.

HOPKINS: Thank you, I will. (HE SITS, WITH A SIGH OF RELIEF)

HOLMES: You look unwell, Hopkins. Watson, what advice can you give our friend to help him survive this beastly heat?

WATSON: Advice it will be hard for you to follow, I'm afraid, Inspector. You should stay indoors, drink plenty of water, wear as few articles of clothing as possible, bathe your feet, your wrists, and the back of your neck in cool water, and sit before a shaded open window to catch any available breeze. That is what you should do.

HOLMES: Or you could go for a cruise on the Thames, hire a cab to create a breeze, or spend the afternoon in the British Museum where the temperature never gets above sixty.

WATSON: Seriously though, you need to drink plenty of liquids. Mrs. Hudson has been bringing us iced tea every hour, and we'll be happy to share it with you.

HOPKINS: Well . . . I'm most grateful. Perhaps I will stay for a few minutes, then, and thank you.

WATSON: Here, take a glass.

SOUND EFFECT: WATER POURED FROM PITCHER INTO GLASS

HOLMES: And when you feel up to it, let's hear what brings you out in this heat.

HOPKINS: (HE TAKES A SIP, RELISHING IT) It's a missing persons case. Four people from Hertford who came to London on Monday to do some business seem to have disappeared.

WATSON: Something easily done, in a city of more than a million.

HOPKINS: True, but this case does have an exceptional twist to it. It seems the four are from a family of dairy farmers – the Abernettys – who came to town on Monday to find a buyer for their goods. The Hertford constable said that Monday afternoon they had wired their farm manager that they would be returning that same evening, but they weren't on any train Monday night or the next day, and nothing further has been heard from them.

WATSON: Then why didn't the alarm go out on Tuesday?

HOPKINS: (HE TAKES ANOTHER SIP) You'd have to ask Constable Tucker at Hertford. He expected them to show up on Tuesday, but when they weren't on the last train from London yesterday, he wired Scotland Yard this morning.

HOLMES: And what progress have you made so far?

HOPKINS: I have the name of the firm they were to have visited: Burkhill Wholesalers on Kinross Street. Their offices are about a mile from here, and I was on my way there when I felt the need to get out of the sun for a few minutes.

HOLMES: Why were you on foot? Surely the cabs are still running, and Scotland Yard would repay the expense.

HOPKINS: I'm embarrassed to say it, Mr. Holmes, but I didn't have a farthing in my pocket! I left my rooms in such a hurry this morning, I neglected to bring any money.

HOLMES: Take our Bradshaw, Watson, and find where trains stop between here and Hertford on night runs.

HOPKINS: I've done that, Mr. Holmes. (PAUSE)

HOPKIINS: On Monday night there were two northbound trains. One had a flag stop at Enfield, and the last train of the day, which left Paddington at ten past eleven, stops at Epping and Waltham Abbey.

WATSON: So they could have gotten off the train at any of those places.

HOPKINS: Yes, but why would they, especially after wiring that they would be home Monday night?

HOLMES: Why would four of them go to London if their sole purpose was to conduct business? And were they successful? Might they have been paid a large sum of money at Burkhill's, making them a target for robbers?

HOPKINS: I don't know any of those things yet. It's early days.

HOLMES: And you have much ground to cover.

WATSON: But you really should stay out of the sun until your body replenishes itself, Inspector, for your own good.

HOLMES: What can you tell us about these missing people?

HOPKINS: Well, I have their names . . . . (CONSULTS NOTEBOOK) The eldest is Rudolph Abernetty, then his two sons, Roscoe and Albert, and Albert's wife, Ursula Abernetty.

HOLMES: Have you their photographs?

HOPKINS: I'm afraid not, not yet. You have to understand, I just got this case, Mr. Holmes.

HOLMES: I do understand, and I beg your pardon if I seem too insistent on details, Inspector, but it seems to me that on a case involving four missing persons, Scotland Yard could spare a second man. Where is Inspector Lestrade?

HOPKINS: On holiday for a week.

185

WATSON: What about this constable in Hertford? Do you think he's reliable?

HOPKINS: But that's just it, you see? I need to interview him and get what intelligence I can from him, but he has no telephone, so I'd have to go there by train, while at the same time I should talk to whoever did business with the Abernettys at the Burkhill works here in London. I can't be in two places at once.

WATSON: Then I have a solution. I could make an inquiry at the Burkhill Company while you rest here and drink all the fluids you can hold.

HOPKINS: I couldn't let you do that!

WATSON: How many times have we assisted in your investigations?

HOPKINS: Many times, and I'm very grateful –

WATSON: Give me Burkhill's address and I'll be on my way. Coming with me, Holmes?

HOLMES: You would be far more useful remaining here, Watson, keeping an eye on Hopkins' physical condition. I will visit the Burkhill works myself.

MUSIC: UNDERCURRENT

WATSON: And so Holmes left me to care for the overheated inspector. His heart rate was still too high and his breathing was too shallow for him to safely return to his duties. An hour passed, and at last Hopkins began to sweat, which was the good sign I had been waiting for. By now his body temperature was nearly normal and he seemed to be refreshed. When Holmes returned, he threw himself into his chair by the window.

MUSIC: OUT

SOUND EFFECT: STREET NOISES

HOLMES: It is ninety-seven degrees outside! I saw a poor horse lying dead in its harness on the way back from Burkhill Wholesalers. And where is Hopkins? Don't tell me you let him go back outside? It's even hotter now than it was an hour ago, and may reach a hundred this afternoon!

WATSON: He's asleep in my bedroom. Now, what did you find out at Burkhill's?

HOLMES: Let's wait until Hopkins is awake. He needs to hear this.

SOUND EFFECT: DOOR OPENS

HOPKINS: (OFF) I am awake, Mr. Holmes, and anxious to hear what you found out.

HOLMES: Ah! You do look more normal.

HOPKINS: And I'm forever in your debt, to both of you.

HOLMES: Now: it seems Burkhill's is in the business of trading and selling farm products. I spoke with Burkhill himself. He told me that the Abernetty brothers have invented a new process for condensing milk. They have a large herd of dairy cows and Burkhill has a cannery, and intends to sell the milk in tins under his own label. So the reason Rudolph Abernetty came to London was to sign a contract with Burkhill, which he did on Monday morning. Rudolph's two sons witnessed the signing, as did Albert Abernetty's wife, Ursula.

WATSON: Did Burkhill give them any cash?

HOLMES: Two-hundred pounds to seal their agreement. Then Burkhill produced a bottle of champagne and toasts were drunk all round. After Roscoe, the older brother, had consumed his third glass, which emptied the bottle, Burkhill opened another bottle, much of which was consumed by Roscoe before the others urged him to stop, after which the four of them departed. And that was the sum total of Burkhill's recollection of the event.

HOPKINS: How can I ever thank you, Mr. Holmes?

HOLMES: And take these two-pounds and hire a cab to take you where you want to go next.

HOPKINS: Mr. Holmes!

HOLMES: You may repay me later.

SOUND EFFECT: STREET NOISES (FADE OUT); (FADE IN) THUNDER

WATSON: Later, as evening came, a thunderstorm rolled in across the city, bringing a downpour of rain and the distinctive smell of ozone. It had grown quite black outside and a wind had come up when a knock came at the door.

SOUND EFFECT: BAKER STREET AND CLOCK

HOLMES: Come!

SOUND EFFECT: DOOR OPENS

HOPKINS: (OFF) I'm afraid it's Hopkins again, Mr. Holmes.

HOLMES: Come in, Inspector. What's the news?

SOUND EFFECT: HOPKINS ENTERS, DOOR CLOSES

HOPKINS: I'm afraid the news is bad.

HOLMES: What is it?

HOPKINS: After the storm began, I was called to Regents Park where a bobby had sent out an alarm. A body had been found beneath a hedge by the broad walk. It was Ursula Abernetty!

MUSIC: STING

HOLMES: Ursula Abernetty? Give us the particulars.

HOPKINS: I'll tell you all I know. Her body was under a hedge along Broad Walk in Regents Park. It wasn't visible from the road. It must have been there two or three days, judging from the condition of it, the hot weather and all.

HOLMES: Who identified her?

HOPKINS: Actually, no identification was necessary. This was tucked in her bodice. One of the morgue attendants found it. It's a railway ticket with her name written on it in pencil.

HOLMES: So I see. Paddington to Hertford, Monday the eighteenth. Her return ticket, never used. But why was her name written on it? Her full name. *"Mrs. Ursula Abernetty"*.

HOPKINS: We know a group of four tickets were purchased at Paddington, probably by the elder Mr. Abernetty, and he might have written their names on them for some reason.

WATSON: But what would be the point, if they were all identical?

HOPKINS: Well, it occurred to me that Ursula might have written her name on her ticket, so she could claim it if it got lost or stolen. It will be simple enough to compare the writing if we can get our hands on another sample of her penmanship.

WATSON: What perplexes me is where the four of them got to, if they knew they were traveling back north that evening!

HOPKINS: Well, we're not absolutely sure they would have known. That would depend on who bought the tickets, and who sent the wire back to Hertford. I'm assuming it was Rudolph, the father. But suppose, after the contract was signed at Burkhill's, they went somewhere as a group – maybe to celebrate.

HOLMES: Which still begs the question, when did the group become four separate individuals – and why?

WATSON: And why was Ursula on her own in Regents Park, and not with her husband? It would have been his duty to accompany her wherever she wanted to go.

HOLMES: We can assume nothing at this point, Watson. Inspector, you have presented us with a challenging puzzle. This case intrigues me!

MUSIC: UNDERCURRENT

WATSON: And so Holmes and I proceeded on our own. We began with a trip to the morgue, to view Ursula Abernetty's remains, an unpleasant but necessary task.

MUSIC: OUT

SOUND EFFECT: ADD MORGUE REVERBERATION

CORONER: Easy to see what killed her. She was choked to death.

HOLMES: Yes, I see. The marks on her neck are still visible.

CORONER: I estimate – given the extreme temperatures of the last three days – she must have died some time Monday. Heat of course speeds the deterioration.

WATSON: The poor woman might have been quite attractive in life, but two days in our blazing temperatures took care of that. I doubt her closest relatives could recognize her now.

HOLMES: Doctor, have you determined whether she was molested?

CORONER: No sign of that. Whoever killed her took only her life.

SOUND EFFECT: (FADE IN) MOVING TRAIN

WATSON: (NARRATING) Holmes was now as absorbed in the case as if he had been commissioned to solve it. When we took the train that afternoon to Hertford, his eager impatience that was part of his usual manner while on scent made him lean forward in his seat, as if urging the engine to go ever faster. I reminded him that his efforts wouldn't be paid for.

HOLMES: You know that I take only those cases that interest me, paid for or not, and this one presents a unique challenge. Now Constable Tucker may not be able to shed any light on the Abernettys' disappearance, but he can describe them to us, so – in the absence of photographs of the missing men – I plan to let him ramble.

SOUND EFFECT: TRAIN (FADE OUT); (FADE IN) COUNTRY BACKGROUND

TUCKER: Here's all I know, gents: Abernetty's got a big dairy farm. You can see part of the pasture from here.

WATSON: Where is the farmhouse?

TUCKER: It's a good walk down by the river on the other side of the hill.

HOLMES: What can you tell me about the Abernetty men?

TUCKER: Well, the two boys you're lookin' for –

HOLMES: Roscoe and Albert?

TUCKER: Aye. Albert's the younger. He's the one what invented a way to thicken up milk so as it would keep.

HOLMES: Yes, it's called condensing. Go on.

TUCKER: And Roscoe, he's a big 'un, a mechanic. Knows about machines and the like. Keeps to himself. Have to run 'im in now and then when he drinks too much at the pub.

WATSON: And their father? What can you tell us about him?

TUCKER: Big man, Mr. Abernetty. Not afraid of work – works right alongside the help. One day he'll be in the milkin' shed with the others, milkin' fifty, sixty cow. Next you'll see him throwin' hay bales into a wagon or heftin' ten gallon milk jugs like a man half his age. Wouldn't want to tangle with him nor Roscoe. Now Albert, he's the educated one. More brainy than his brother. When he got married, he moved to a little house away from the farm – him and his bride.

HOLMES: And their habits?

TUCKER: Their habits? I don't know as to the old man. He works, he eats, he sleeps. The boys? Young Albert's the one dreamed up the milk condenser. Fair skinned – not delicate, but not heavy like his brother.

HOLMES: And Albert's wife?

191

TUCKER: Ursula? Fair, like her husband Albert. Her family's from German stock.

HOLMES: Do you still have the telegram they sent?

TUCKER: Sure do. Filed it away. You want to see it?

HOLMES: Yes, if we may.

TUCKER: Just a minute . . . .

<u>SOUND EFFECT: HE GOES THROUGH PAPERS IN A DRAWER</u>

TUCKER: Here it is.

HOLMES: Thank you. (READS) *"Contract signed. Home tonight, last train. Signed, R."* Thank you, Constable, you've been very helpful. Now there's just one thing more. We need photographs of the missing family. Can you help us with that?

TUCKER: Well, they'll be on the streets in London tonight.

WATSON: What?

TUCKER: The reporter from *The Evening Standard* was here last night. Asked the way to the Abernetty farm, borrowed my bicycle, and rode right out to the farm and came back with four pictures. Said they'd be in his paper tonight. Then he took the milk train back to London.

<u>SOUND EFFECT: BACKGROUND (FADE OUT); (FADE IN) TRAIN RUNNING</u>

HOLMES: An enterprising reporter and the half-tone printing process.

WATSON: Eh? What did you say?

HOLMES: You were wondering how a newspaper could print photographs so quickly nowadays, and I simply answered your unspoken question. Engraving is being replaced by the half-tone printing process. What used to take a day now takes minutes.

WATSON: How in the world did you know what I was thinking?

HOLMES: Your look of wonderment tinged with disappointment, and the mournful shake of your head. But our journey wasn't wasted. We now have character descriptions of the missing men that we'll pass on to Hopkins. And now that we're going to see what the Abernettys look like, I think we must visit the morgue again, on the chance that one of them may have turned up.

SOUND EFFECT: TRAIN (FADE OUT); ADD MORGUE REVERBERATION

CORONER: Oh yes, I've got my copy of *The Evening Standard* right here. Got your name in the paper again, I see. But it doesn't mention your name, Dr. Watson.

HOLMES: Let me see that!

SOUND EFFECT: HE GRABS THE PAPER

HOLMES: (READS) *"Assisting the investigation is the famous detective Mr. Sherlock Holmes . . . ."*

SOUND EFFECT: HE THROWS THE PAPER DOWN

WATSON: I wonder how the paper got that information?

HOLMES: You know Hopkins. He told them himself. He's honest and slightly naïve – sometimes to his detriment.

CORONER: Well, I've received seven new clients so far today, but all of them were identified and none of them resemble any of the men in the pictures. But you're welcome to look them over. The freshest ones are here on this end.

SOUND EFFECT: REVERBERATION OUT; (FADE IN) HANSOM CAB (BACKGROUND)

WATSON: Holmes, I've been thinking. Has it occurred to you that they may not want to be found?

HOLMES: Hardly. They've signed a contract with the Burkhill people that should mean a good deal of money for them, and they have a large farm to run. No, I can't believe they would walk away from all that and disappear, for whatever reason.

WATSON: It's surely connected in some way to the death of Ursula Abernetty though, don't you think?

HOLMES: Not necessarily. It is tempting to link her murder to the men's disappearance, since they both happened at roughly the same time, but the chain of evidence between the missing men and the dead woman is lacking several links, any one of which could provide a different explanation.

WATSON: I don't suppose they could have been kidnapped?

HOLMES: Most unlikely. It would be a complicated business to seize and hold three men captive, especially if one of them holds the purse strings if a ransom were demanded. Still, nothing can be ruled out. (UP) Right here, driver. *2-2-1-B*.

SOUND EFFECT: CAB COMES TO A HALT

MUSIC: UNDERCURRENT

WATSON: As we climbed the stairs to our rooms, Mrs. Hudson stopped us to report that our telephone had rung several times during our absence

SOUND EFFECT: DOOR OPENS

HOLMES: Perhaps whoever it was will call again if it was important.

SOUND EFFECT: THEY WALK IN. DOOR CLOSES. STREET, CLOCK BACKGROUND

WATSON: (HEAVES A SIGH) It's been a busy day – exciting and exhausting all at once.

HOLMES: Indeed, and it's not over yet. Perhaps you should relax while you can. I am going to smoke two or three pipefuls.

WATSON: Which he did. His back was to me as he sat in his favourite chair, great clouds of pungent smoke rising every few seconds. The heady aroma of the tobacco and the regularity of his puffs produced an almost hypnotic effect on me, and I felt myself drifting into pleasant oblivion, where I remained until I was awakened by a cry from Holmes. He had sprung from his chair.

MUSIC: OUT

HOLMES: (OFF MICROPHONE) Watson! Get me the *Bacon Atlas*!

WATSON: (A BIT GROGGY) The what?

HOLMES: The new London atlas put out by G. W. Bacon last year! If logic played any part in the movements of the Abernettys after they left Burkhill's office, I may have found the next turn in the maze!

SOUND EFFECT: HEAVY BOOK SLIDES

WATSON: I think this is what you need. Yes, here you are.

HOLMES: And hand me my lens.

WATSON: I don't know where you left it.

HOLMES: On the mantel next to the slipper!

WATSON: Oh yes, here you are.

HOLMES: Good! Now, the West End map . . . .

SOUND EFFECT: HE TURNS PAGES

WATSON: What are we looking for?

HOLMES: Ah, here it is. Kinross Street.

WATSON: But you know Kinross Street. That's where the Burkhill Works are.

HOLMES: I'm ashamed to say I paid little attention to the route the cabbie took to get me there, and the industrial section of west London is one of the few districts I'm not familiar with.

WATSON: Then what do you need to find?

HOLMES: Assuming that these country folk knew little about London, and in light of the fact that they had more than eight hours to while away in a strange city before taking the last train home, where would they have gone, and what would they have wanted to do, after the contract was signed?

WATSON: Eat lunch, I suppose.

HOLMES: And in light of their sudden prosperity, wouldn't they have wanted to eat in an excellent restaurant to celebrate?

WATSON: Well, I know I would.

HOLMES: And, since Burkhill Wholesalers is in a commercial and industrial neighborhood, even country bumpkins would hardly expect to find such a place nearby, so what would they do?

WATSON: Take a cab and ask the cabbie for his recommendation.

HOLMES: And since there were four in their group, they would have taken two cabs.

WATSON: So our task is to find one or both of the cabbies.

SOUND EFFECT: CITY BACKGROUND

CABBIE: You're Mister Sherlock Holmes, aren't you? I've driven you a time or two.

HOLMES: What luck! Tell me, on Monday around twelve noon, did you encounter a group of three men and a woman on Kinross Street who asked you to recommend a good restaurant?

CABBIE: I remember 'em clear as a bell. There were four of 'em, like you say, three men and a woman. They wanted to know where they could get a good meal, and I gave 'em a choice of places. They

196

talked it over and finally they decided they'd go to Kester's Chop House in Bayswater Street. And that's where I took 'em, the two black-bearded men. The other couple stayed behind to wait for another cab.

WATSON: I don't know Kester's Chop House,

CABBIE: I'd be glad to drive you there.

SOUND EFFECT: CITY BACKGROUND (FADE OUT); (FADE IN) BUSY RESTAURANT

MAITRE'D: A party of four, three days ago? Sorry.

HOLMES: What about two sturdy black-bearded men, father and son, bearing a resemblance to each other?

MAITRE'D: Sir; on a good day we feed well over a hundred people here. I can hardly be expected to remember two of them.

HOLMES: One of the men may have appeared to be intoxicated.

MAITRE'D: That could also apply to many of our customers.

SOUND EFFECT: BACKGROUND (FADE OUT); (FADE IN) – EXTERIOR, STREET

HOLMES: Blast the luck! The second cabbie's sick and won't be driving today, so we can't track the movements of Albert and Ursula.

WATSON: Yes, we seem to have struck a dead-end.

HOLMES: Not quite yet. There must be some possibility we have yet to explore. For one thing, who was trying to reach us on the telephone?

WATSON: Oh, that could have been anyone.

HOLMES: Nevertheless, we should go back to our rooms post-haste, to receive whatever information may come our way.

SOUND EFFECT: STREET (FADE OUT)

197

WATSON: Although Holmes would deny it, sometimes it seems that he is subject to moments of precognition, and this was one of such moments. No sooner had we walked into our sitting-room, than we heard the doorbell below, and in a few moments, Inspector Hopkins hurried in, transformed into an excitedly eager presence.

SOUND EFFECT: THEIR ROOM (FADE IN)

HOPKINS: I've caught up with you at last! Gentlemen, I have good news! Or I should say, sad news for some, but good news for many, including us!

HOLMES: You're speaking in riddles.

HOPKINS: I know I am. Forgive me. Here is my news: Ursula Abernetty is alive!

HOLMES: Is this a miracle or a mistake?

HOPKINS: No, it was a case of mistaken identity. The young woman we saw dead in Regents Park has turned out to be a prostitute, identified by some jewelry she was wearing.

WATSON: But what about the train ticket with Ursula Abernetty's name written on it?

HOPKINS: Perhaps Ursula dropped her ticket and the girl found it.

HOLMES: Such a happenstance seems quite unlikely. There is a darker possibility to be investigated.

HOPKINS: What is that?

HOLMES: I'm not prepared to explain it until we learn more about the missing father and sons.

HOPKINS: It seems that we are back where we started, with four people gone missing and little or no progress to report.

HOLMES: I agree there is much that must be discovered, but there is also the element of time. All events happen somewhere and at some

198

time. When we learn the one element, that should lead us to the other.

SOUND EFFECT: BACKGROUND OUT

MUSIC: UNDERCURRENT

WATSON: I have often drawn a comparison between the work of a doctor and that of a detective. The doctor may not be able to create the desired results by ministering to his patient, but must wait for missing symptoms to appear on their own before he can make a reliable diagnosis, and the detective may not be able to solve a case on his own until all missing clues are discovered and evaluated. In the case of the four missing Abernettys, this was proving to be true. Now we played the waiting game, with Holmes smoking his way through nearly an entire packet of cigarettes, while I sat near the open window, trying to clear the air – metaphorically as well as actually. The afternoon wore on in silence, until we heard the doorbell.

MUSIC: OUT

SOUND EFFECT: 221b BACKGROUND (FADE IN); DOORBELL RINGS DOWNSTAIRS

HOLMES: Ah.

WATSON: Hopkins again?

HOLMES: (LISTENING INTENTLY) No . . . not unless he's brought someone with him. These are strangers.

SOUND EFFECT: (PAUSE) A SLOW KNOCK ON DOOR

HOLMES: (CALLS OUT) Who is it?

RUDOLPH: (OFF, THROUGH THE DOOR) My name is Abernetty. I come to see Sherlock Holmes.

WATSON: (LOW) Abernetty! Which Abernetty?

HOLMES: Come in, Mr. Abernetty.

HOLMES: Would you be Rudolph or Roscoe Abernetty?

RUDOLPH: Roscoe's my son. He's out in the hall but he won't come in. I'm Rudolph Abernetty. Are you Sherlock Holmes?

HOLMES: I am, and this is my associate, Doctor John H. Watson.

WATSON: Good afternoon, Mr. Abernetty. Have a seat.

RUDOLPH: I'll stand, thanks. I been trying to get you on the telephone, and then I decided I'd just come here and take my chances. I'm comin' to you instead of the police. I want to tell you my story, and you can decide if Scotland Yard should hear it.

HOLMES: Very well. Tell it.

RUDOLPH: I'm a dairyman from up Hertford. Got two sons, Albert's the other one. Roscoe's got himself in trouble, and Albert's gone missing. So has his wife.

HOLMES: I see.

RUDOLPH: Roscoe's got himself in trouble and he'll have to pay for it with his life, I'm afraid. He's been drunk for three days. It started Monday morning, and it got worse. He lit out and went from pub to pub, spending money by the handful. He found himself a woman, took her for a cab ride, and – well, now she's dead. He didn't mean to do it, but he got mad. And I think you know the rest.

HOLMES: Possibly not. Please continue.

RUDOLPH: He's never been mean. Not 'til his brother married Ursula. Well, after he done what he done, he left the poor woman in a park and took into the streets, cryin' and carryin' on like he was possessed, and maybe he was. Lucky they didn't run him in. Anyway, when his money run out, he come back to the hotel where I was staying, and told me everything. Then the papers put out our pictures and said we was missing. They said it was Ursula who died because her name was on a train ticket. But that ticket was

Roscoe's, and he wrote Ursula's name on it. That's when I knew I'd have to turn him in.

HOLMES: Do you have any idea where Albert and Ursula might be?

RUDOLPH: No idea.

HOLMES: Roscoe will have to tell this to a policeman from Scotland Yard, and I know the very man he should tell it to. His name is Inspector Hopkins.

MUSIC: (FADE IN) (UNDERCURRENT)

WATSON: Roscoe Abernetty and his father remained at 221b until Inspector Hopkins arrived, trailed by reporters from three or four papers. When they left, Holmes looked at the clock.

MUSIC: OUT

SOUND EFFECT: 221b WTH CLOCK

HOLMES: You know, I believe there's a train to Hertford leaving in twenty-five minutes.

WATSON: Why are we going back there?

HOLMES: To confirm that what I have deduced is true. Do you still have your bicycle clips?

SOUND EFFECT: BACKGROUND (FADE OUT); (FADE IN) TRAIN RUNNING INTERIOR

HOLMES: When we get to Hertford, again we'll enlist the help of that sturdy minion of law and order, Constable Tucker, who may be able to scare up a pair of bicycles for us. You remember that he said that was how *The Evening Standard* reporter got from the railway station to the Abernetty farm?

WATSON: And where will we riding?

HOLMES: To the same destination.

HOLMES: (EXERTING BUT NOT WINDED) How are you feeling, old fellow? Enjoying the ride?

WATSON: (A BIT WINDED) I'm enjoying it now, since it's mostly downhill, but if we have to come back the same way . . . well, it's been a long time since I was thin and played rugby for Blackheath.

HOLMES: I understand. But console yourself. If nothing goes awry, you'll be at home in your bed with this whole adventure behind you by ten o'clock tonight. Ah! Look down to that clump of trees on the right at the bottom of the hill.

WATSON: I see. Is that their cottage?

HOLMES: If Constable Tucker's directions were correct. I think we had better dismount here and leave our bicycles in the ivy, and approach on foot.

SOUND EFFECT: VARIOUS CRUNCHES UNDERFOOT; CLATTER OF SPOKES IN FOLIAGE. THEN, TWO MEN WALKING IN GRAVEL

HOLMES: There's no smoke from the chimney. We'll knock at the front door, and if they're in, I'll do the talking.

SOUND EFFECT: A FEW MORE STEPS, THEN HOLMES KNOCKS ON THE DOOR, WAITS, KNOCKS AGAIN

HOLMES: Nobody home and no watchdog on duty.

SOUND EFFECT: FIDDLING WITH KEY AND LOCK PICK

SOUND EFFECT: CREAKY DOOR OPENS

HOLMES: (CALLS) Hello! (PAUSE) Anybody here? (DOWN) Evidently not. Come in, Doctor. Consider this a house call.

WATSON: You have deuce of a sense of humour at times. Where are you going?

202

HOLMES: To the pantry.

SOUND EFFECT: TWO MEN WALK STEALTHILY ON WOOD
FLOOR

WATSON: Well? What are you looking for?

SOUND EFFECT: STEPS STOP

WATSON: Look here on the table. Two place settings.

HOLMES: And a butter dish with fresh butter and a sprig of parsley.

HOLMES: (LOUDLY) You may come out now, Mr. and Mrs.
Abernetty!

URSULA: (OFF MICROPHONE, SCARED AND ANGRY) Who are
you? What do you want?

HOLMES: Mrs. Ursula Abernetty?

URSULA: Who are you? Did you come to steal from us?

HOLMES: Not at all. Actually, you've just given us what we want. My
name is Sherlock Holmes, and this is my friend, Dr. John H
Watson.

WATSON: Do you know that all of London is looking for you?

URSULA: (HESITANT) No . . . .

HOLMES: After you left the Burkhill Works on Monday, instead of
taking the last train back to Hertford as your father-in-law had
wired, you must have gone straight to the railway station and caught
the same train back to Hertford that Dr. Watson and I caught this
afternoon.

URSULA: Mr. Abernetty didn't send that wire. Roscoe did. He wanted
to get me alone with him. That's why we left early. He's been
bothering me ever since Albert and I announced our engagement.
He's a terrible, jealous man!

203

WATSON: Well, he won't be bothering you again, Mrs. Abernetty.

HOLMES: In fact, you'll never see him again, if the Crown has its way.

URSULA: But I don't understand how you knew we had been here these three days.

HOLMES: The parsley on your butter told me. I happened to know about the old German tradition of decorating fresh butter with a sprig of parsley. It's been so hot here the last two or three days, the parsley would have melted into the butter – which would indicate that you'd been away long enough for the butter to spoil if it weren't looked after. But your butter looks sweet and fresh.

WATSON: Which could also describe its keeper.

HOLMES: Watson!

MUSIC: *DANSE MACABRE* (THEME UP AND UNDER)

WATSON: This is Dr. John H. Watson. I've had many more adventures with Sherlock Holmes, and I'll tell you another one . . . *when next we meet!*

MUSIC: (FADE OUT)

> *"You will remember, Watson, how the dreadful business of the Abernetty family was first brought to my notice by the depth which the parsley had sunk into the butter upon a hot day."*

> Sherlock Holmes – "The Adventure of the Six Napoleons"

Dr. Agar and the Dinosaur
by Robert Stapleton

When relating "The Adventure of the Devil's Foot", I promised to tell the story of how my friend, Sherlock Holmes, first made the acquaintance of Harley Street physician, Dr. Moore Agar. It is a story I have described as dramatic. And so it proved, as it nearly resulted in the deaths of all three of us. With my notes open before me, I now take up my pen to fulfil my promise to give the story in full.

Following the loss of my dear wife and the sale of my medical practice, my world once more revolved around 221b, and the eccentric man with whom I shared rooms there. The years following the return of Sherlock Holmes, as though from the dead, turned out to be busy and demanding on both of us, and the summer of 1895 proved no exception.

From his place in the armchair beside the empty grate in our sitting room, Holmes looked up from his reading of the morning newspaper. "Now, there is a singular matter, Watson."

"You have the advantage of me, Holmes," I replied.

"Why, the theft of a skull."

I failed to share his enthusiasm. "You are telling me somebody likes old bones. Why is that so remarkable?"

"Because, Watson, the skull belonged to a long extinct species of dinosaur."

I returned his gaze, with surprise. "Here in London?"

"Precisely. According to the article, it had been sent to this country on temporary loan from a museum in Washington, D.C."

"And now it has gone missing."

"And the police have drawn a blank in their investigations of the matter."

I chuckled. "I can imagine Lestrade scratching his head over this business."

Holmes sat back, and stretched out his legs. "I expect we shall find out presently."

Almost at once, we heard a vehicle draw to a halt in the roadway outside. Holmes, still in his purple dressing gown, took his stand beside the hearth, facing the doorway. And waited.

The door opened, and Mrs. Hudson stepped inside.

"Excuse me, Mr. Holmes," she began. "But you have a visitor. A very important man, sir." She passed a visiting card to Holmes, and waited.

Holmes read it, and looked up. "Thank you, Mrs. Hudson. Please show Dr. Agar in."

I expressed my surprised. "Not a visit from Scotland Yard, then."

"Apparently not," returned Holmes. "At least, not directly."

A man walked in. He was in mid-life, of medium height and weight, with thinning gray hair and bushy side-whiskers. He carried himself with a slight stoop, and his sad brown eyes betrayed a troubled mind. Even in the middle of the morning, he presented a less-than-perfect appearance.

"You are Dr. Moore Agar, of Harley Street," noted Holmes.

"The same," replied our visitor. "And you, I hope, are Mr. Sherlock Holmes."

"I have that honor. And this is my colleague, Dr. Watson."

The visitor and I exchanged nods.

"Please take a seat," said Holmes, indicating a chair he had conveniently placed opposite his own beside the fireplace. "I see you are a man preoccupied with antiquities," Holmes continued. "More so perhaps than with the care of your more general appearance. Cufflinks of carved bone faded with age, and a watch-chain fob fashioned from an ancient Greek coin. You had time to attend to those items this morning, yet you have not found occasion to brush down your coat or polish your boots."

Dr. Agar appeared embarrassed by the comments.

"Forgive me, Dr. Agar," continued Holmes. "I merely voice my observations."

"But I do not neglect my patients, Mr. Holmes."

"Indeed not," replied Holmes, affably. "Come now, tell us about your missing dinosaur skull." I noticed a hint of mirth play about my friend's countenance. "For that is the purpose of your visit here, is it not?"

Dr. Agar leaned forward in his seat, and fixed Holmes with a penetrating stare. "A few months ago, I accepted an invitation from a colleague in the United States to present a series of lectures there on recent developments in Medicine and Surgery in this country."

Holmes nodded.

"He knew of my interest in ancient history, so whilst I was in his country, my associate took me to visit a number of museums. One I found particularly fascinating. The place was filled with the most amazing skeletons of long-extinct creatures. We have our own exhibits in this country, but I had never seen anything remotely like this. A member of the museum staff told me about the discoveries made in recent years in Colorado and Wyoming, of the remains of huge creatures from the Cretaceous period of pre-history. He told me of men in the United States who set great store by collecting and exhibiting such things. These men expend huge sums of money on securing the remains of these ancient creatures."

"An object of such curiosity might well attract the interest of people in this country as well," said Holmes, soberly.

"Precisely my thinking, Mr. Holmes. I wanted to learn more, so he introduced me to an official at the Smithsonian Institution in Washington, D.C. This gentleman took me to see some of the latest fossil remains they had uncovered, and are even now in the process of restoring. Among these remains, I discovered the huge skull of a horned dinosaur. A creature they are now calling *Triceratops*." Dr. Agar's eyes glittered with animation. "Each has two genuine horns. Huge, deadly things. In 1842, Sir Richard Owen proposed the name *Dinosaur*, meaning 'terrible lizard'. The moment I first cast my eyes on this monster, I understood how apt the name was. The sight of it filled me with awe, Mr. Holmes. At that moment, I knew I had to have this very skull for exhibition here in London."

Dr. Agar paused in his telling of the tale. With the warm summer weather, and the enthusiasm with which he spoke, Dr. Agar took out a white handkerchief and wiped his moist forehead.

All this time, Holmes had been listening with rapt attention. "Pray, continue with your story, Dr. Agar."

"Before I left," continued Dr. Agar, "I had a meal with my new acquaintance at the Smithsonian. The drinks flowed, and before the end of the evening, he had signed an agreement allowing me to borrow one of these skulls. He also undertook to ship it across the Atlantic as soon as I had found a suitable venue for the exhibition."

Dr. Agar turned his gaze upon me. "I had been planning to organize an exhibition of my own inadequate collection, and I realized this dinosaur would be the highlight of the event. The focus of publicity."

"I have seen the model dinosaurs at the Crystal Palace gardens in Sydenham," I told him.

"An imaginative attempt by Waterhouse Hawkins to popularize and set in concrete the extent of Sir Richard's limited research at that time," he retorted with a smile. "But I am talking about the real thing – genuine fossilized bones of gigantic creatures."

"And you managed to arrange a suitable venue," noted Holmes, returning to the subject in hand.

"I was lucky," said Dr. Agar. "I managed to hire a room at the Museum of Practical Geology, here in London. The Museum agreed to receive the crate containing the skull and have it ready for me to inspect the moment I was free from my medical commitments."

"And this dinosaur duly arrived," I concluded.

"Two days ago, the crate was unloaded at the Port of London docks, exactly as agreed. The Geology Museum's own contractors collected it that afternoon, and delivered it to the room assigned to me. The American museum had also sent a courier to accompany the skull. He took a room at a local hotel. All seemed well. When I received the news that the crate had arrived, I was delighted. I was delayed by my work, and arrived first thing the following morning. Then I opened the crate." Dr. Agar's expression fell. "To my horror, I discovered that it contained nothing more than a shapeless lump of rock. But of the skull, I could find absolutely no trace whatsoever."

"And what did the courier have to say?" asked Holmes.

"He assured us the Triceratops skull had been packed, and that the crate had not been tampered with in any way since the moment it left Washington."

"To summarize," said Holmes, leaning back in his chair, and cupping his hands behind his head. "At some point between the crate leaving America and your inspecting it, the skull vanished."

Dr. Agar took a deep breath, and let it out slowly. "So it seems, Mr. Holmes. But how could something that big simply disappear into thin air? And, if somebody stole it, what reason might they have had?"

"The reason for such a theft, you mentioned yourself, Dr. Agar. The skull must be worth a great deal of money to whoever took it. To collectors in America, and other museums across the world."

"The biggest mystery of all is how the thief managed to accomplish such a feat. The skull itself weighs more than a ton."

Holmes pursed his lips in thought. "That remains to be seen," he said. "But whatever can be delivered can just as easily be removed."

Dr. Agar looked pleadingly at Holmes. "Neither the Museum nor Scotland Yard seems able to trace the skull. I'm at my wits end about this matter, Mr. Holmes. You're my final hope."

"I can promise nothing," said Holmes, smiling modestly. "I merely make deductions based upon the facts presented to me."

"Then allow me to present you with the starkest of facts, Mr. Holmes. Come with me to the Geology Museum, and see what deductions you can make of this matter."

Dr. Moore Agar's four-wheeler took us to Piccadilly, and then round the corner into Jermyn Street, where it dropped us off at the entrance to the Museum of Practical Geology.

In the doorway, we encountered a familiar figure waiting for us.

"I'm surprised you consider this business merits your attention, Mr. Holmes," said Inspector Lestrade.

"On the contrary, Lestrade," replied Holmes. "Any case considered too demanding for Scotland Yard is something I am always willing to consider. And, as for this present matter, I find it curiously compelling."

We followed Dr. Agar along echoing corridors to a room empty of all but a small desk and table set beside the wall, and a single wooden crate standing alone in the centre of the floor-space.

The crate measured approximately seven feet in length by five feet in both width and height. The lid had been removed and stood on the floor, propped up against one side of the crate. Holmes and I looked inside, and discovered a rough-hewn boulder of white rock.

"Hmm," mused Holmes. "My knowledge of Geology suggests this stone comes from no farther away than northern France."

"Instead of a skull recently transported from America," said Lestrade.

Holmes turned to Dr. Agar. "Can you show us what it ought to look like?"

"Certainly," replied Dr. Agar, collecting a line drawing from a folder on the adjacent desk, and spreading it out upon the table top.

We all looked down at the image of a skeleton – a huge horned dinosaur. "An intimidating monster," I said.

"Even more in the flesh, so to speak," said Dr. Agar.

"And when exactly was this delivery made?" asked Holmes.

"As I said, I called in yesterday morning, and discovered what you now see."

"You say the Museum's own contractors delivered it," said Holmes.

"That's correct," said Lestrade. "The Museum is occasionally obliged to receive and dispatch items of great size and weight. The contractors collected it from the docks, and brought it here late in the afternoon."

"And what about the other crate?" Holmes asked, with eyebrows raised in enquiry.

Lestrade looked at Holmes, with furrowed brow. "What other crate are you talking about, Mr. Holmes?"

"An elementary matter," replied Holmes. "If the crate was delivered in the same condition in which it was sealed, then it follows that there must have been a second crate delivered to the Museum." He knelt on the floor, and examined the floorboards on all sides of the crate. "Although the floor naturally shows a great deal of wear, it is quite evident that another crate stood here in the recent past. Within a matter of days, in fact."

"In that case," said Lestrade, looking intrigued, "I suggest we speak with the delivery staff."

"Yes," said one of the Museum's workmen. "We placed a heavy crate on the floor here two days ago."

"Did you find anything else in the room?" asked Holmes.

"No, sir. The room looked exactly as it appears now."

"No other crate?"

"No, just the one."

"And yet, another crate was here, either before or after you undertook your delivery," said Holmes. "The indentations in the floorboards, together with minute specks of wood shavings, settle the matter."

Dr. Agar shook his head in dismay. "I can hardly imagine a thief coming in here and walking out with something so heavy."

"Maybe not on his own," replied Holmes, "but I can imagine a legitimate firm being employed to come in and remove it." He turned to Lestrade. "I suggest that he pay another visit to the Museum office. They might have a record showing who came to remove a heavy item between the delivery of the crate and Dr. Agar's arrival here the following morning."

We made our way to the Secretary's office.

"We keep a record of everything that comes in and goes out," said the Secretary, consulting the daybook. "At five o'clock that evening, our contracted workmen delivered a crate they had collected from the docks."

"That confirms what we already know," said Holmes. "A crate was delivered. And then?"

"Only two hours later, another wagon arrived, to deliver a second wooden crate."

"Now we are getting somewhere," said Holmes.

"They had paperwork which appeared to be legitimate."

Holmes nodded. "And did they leave a name and address?"

"Indeed they did," replied the Secretary. "We insist upon it. They gave their name as Jenitsen and Nephew, and gave an address we can only assume to be authentic."

Holmes turned to Lestrade. "We need to find these people, Lestrade, and I suggest this is a job for the Metropolitan Police."

210

"Leave it to us, Mr. Holmes," replied Lestrade. "We'll find this man, Jenitsen, and bring him along to Baker Street so you can see what you make of him."

Dr. Agar turned to the door. "In the meantime, gentlemen, I must return to Harley Street. I have patients waiting for me."

"Of course," said Holmes. "And yet, judging by the way this matter is shaping, it might be wise for you to clear your diary for the next few days."

By the middle of the afternoon, Holmes was ready to interview the owner of the removal firm.

"Now, Mr. Jenitsen," he began, standing once more in front of the empty hearth in Baker Street. "You admit it was you who came to the Geology Museum two nights ago."

"That's right, Mr. Holmes," said the little man standing before him. "I have neither wish nor need to deny the fact." Jenitsen was not a tall man, but what he lacked in height he made up for in muscular strength. Even so, with two burly constables flanking him, he looked like a man who had come to meet his doom.

"Then, kindly furnish us with the details of your purpose in being there."

"Well, Mr. Holmes," he began. "It all started when this bloke came into our office a week ago."

"Can you describe the man?"

"Foreign. In expression, language, and clothing."

"European?"

"No."

"American?"

"Not like any I've ever met."

"Please continue."

"Well, this bloke told me he had a job for me. He would pay me up-front. Handsomely, like. I wasn't going to turn down a job like that now, was I?"

Holmes was becoming impatient. "Of course not. Now, please tell us about the job he wanted you to undertake for him."

"That's what I'm coming to, Mr. Holmes. He wanted me and my brother's lad to collect a heavy wooden crate from a train due to arrive at Charing Cross from Paris. We were to take the box direct to the Museum of Practical Geology, in Jermyn Street. He gave us the time and place for both collecting and delivering."

"And you did that."

"Of course. Mind you, with the crate being so heavy, we needed to hire in a few other lads to help. But we got the job done. We collected the crate, and took it to the Museum at exactly seven o'clock that same evening. Just like the fellow told us. Odd that, weren't it, him being so precise about the time?"

"Where did you leave the crate?"

"We wheeled it to a room along one wing of the building. It was a heavy job, I can tell you. But we got it there, and signed that it had been delivered."

"And the other crate?"

"Ah, yes," Mr. Jenitsen rubbed his chin thoughtfully. "That was the other part of the job. We put the crate down on the floor, directly beside another wooden box that was already there. Same size. Same shape. And the same weight, as we found out when we carried the blooming thing out to the wagon."

"And what happened to this other crate?"

"We took it all the way back to Charing Cross station, and put it back on the very same train we'd taken the other one off."

"Did the crate carry any identification?"

"Only what I fastened onto it. The bloke who hired us gave me a luggage label to fix on."

"Do you remember what it said?"

"It's my job to make sure everything gets to where it should be. It said, '*The Gare du Nord, Paris. To be collected*'. That's all I can tell you, Mr. Holmes, and that's the truth of it."

"Nothing more?"

"Oh, wait a minute. The back of the label had a picture."

"Of what?"

"Of a spider."

Holmes turned, and rummaged through his collection of newspaper cuttings. For several minutes, he paid no attention to anyone else in the room. Then, as Lestrade was about to turn and leave, Holmes stood up, holding a sheet of newsprint in his hand.

"Mr. Jenitsen," said Holmes. "You said this man gave you a label bearing the image of a spider."

"That's right, Mr. Holmes."

Holmes passed him the cutting. "Then kindly look at this picture."

Jenitsen studied it for a moment, and then looked up again, wide eyed with amazement. "Yes, Mr. Holmes. That's the exact one I saw on the label."

Holmes took back the cutting and looked around triumphantly. "This is an advertisement from a couple of years ago. It invites collectors of antiquities to gather for a private auction, in Paris."

"Does it give an address?" asked Lestrade.

"It asks anyone interested to contact the Proprietor, Rue St. Martinot, Paris."

"And is this relevant to the present business?"

"A picture of a spider links this advertisement with our present case. I think that makes it of enormous interest. Our search for the dinosaur skull must now take us across the Channel to Paris."

I consulted our Bradshaw. "A train is due to leave Charing Cross for Paris by way of Calais first thing in the morning," I told him.

"Then we should be in Paris by the late afternoon, in time to reach the Rue St. Martinot before the end of the day."

"I'll get in touch with the Paris Police," said Lestrade, "and warn them that you're on your way."

"Watson," continued Holmes, "get our things packed, and tell Dr. Agar to be at Charing Cross in time to catch that train. In the meantime, I need to think." So saying, Holmes took his seat beside the window, and lit up his old and oily clay pipe.

Dressed in his gray traveling cloak, Holmes set his face with determination as we journeyed to Paris the following day. He said nothing for most of the time, whilst Dr. Agar and I shared tales of our various experiences in the medical profession. We had more than enough stories to last the whole journey.

When we alighted from the train at the Gare du Nord, Holmes made immediate enquiries about the crate labelled "*To be collected*".

It had indeed been collected, but the station officials could tell us no more, other than that the man who collected it had been neither French nor European.

"Sounds like the same fellow Jenitsen described," I told Holmes.

"I am sure you are right," he replied.

"The only address we have is Rue St. Martinot," I added. "It might be busy at this time of day, but it should be easy enough to find."

"Then it is there we must extend our search. I fancy the game is now afoot, Watson."

We took a cab through the rush-hour streets of the French capital city, and ten minutes later, our cab dismissed, the three of us were standing at the end of a narrow street, which matched our expectations only in its nameplate.

Holmes wandered slowly along the lonely street, looking carefully at each and every entrance in turn. When he reached the far end, he stopped, looked back at us, and beckoned for us to join him there. Carrying our bags, I made heavier weather of it than either of my companions.

I soon found myself standing before a forbidding front door with a mixture of curiosity and trepidation. What was this place? What secrets lay concealed beyond its gloomy entrance?

"I'll wager this is what we want," said Holmes as he stepped up to the door and pressed the bell-button. A sharp jangling sound deep inside the property was followed a few seconds later by the door opening. An elderly woman stood in the doorway, a creature shrivelled and bent with age. Her skin looked as yellow as parchment and her mouth displayed a scattering of broken teeth, but her expression looked as sharp as the doorbell itself. The old woman reminded me of Madame Defarge, whom Dickens describes in his novel *A Tale of Two Cities* as sitting, knitting, beside the guillotine, with a vengeful eye which showed no hint of pity.

Madame Defarge grunted something in deep guttural French.

"We have come to speak to the proprietor," explained Holmes. "So I suggest that you invite us inside."

The woman in the doorway nodded slowly but remained where she stood.

"I know all about the spider," added Holmes, fixing her with a penetrating stare.

"Do you, indeed?" She sounded mildly impressed.

Slowly, the woman stepped aside, and Dr. Agar and I followed Holmes into the entrance hall. Madame Defarge closed the door and led us along a dark passageway, towards a closed door at the far end.

"Leave your bags out here," croaked the old woman, opening the door.

I pushed them into one corner of the passageway and followed Holmes, Dr. Agar, and the woman in through the door.

At first glance, the room appeared empty. But as we watched, a man emerged from the shadows at the far end of the room, tall in stature, dark in countenance and hair colouring, and with angular facial features.

The man grinned. "Welcome to my parlour, said the spider to the flies. Permit me to introduce myself, gentlemen. *I* am the spider."

But I recognized the man by a different name.

"Khan!"

"Dr. John Watson," the man said, with a sneer in his voice. "The famous companion of Mr. Sherlock Holmes, here."

214

"And now a colleague also of Dr. Moore Agar of Harley Street," I said, indicating my other companion.

"It is indeed fortuitous that we meet again after so long, Dr. Watson."

"Do you know this man?" enquired Holmes.

"Sadly, I have to admit that I do," I told him. "Although he looks older than the last time we met."

"The years have changed us both," said Khan. "But perhaps not on the inside."

I half-turned towards Holmes. "I came to know this man during my time with the Army in Afghanistan. We all knew him then as 'Khan of the Mountains'. He was one of the bandits who waged blood-soaked war upon our soldiers. He is personally responsible for the deaths of many fine young men. I'll wager a pretty penny that the revolver he is now holding was taken from the hand of one of our soldiers as he lay dying, or perhaps suffering terrible torture."

Khan gave a nasty grin. "Tell them about the last time we met."

"I was on patrol with a party of soldiers. We had made camp for the night when, out of the darkness, a band of these villains descended with deadly ferocity. Half of our men were dead before they could take up their firearms. It was a massacre. I fled, together with three other men, leaving the dead behind, but with Khan and his ruffians in hot pursuit. We reached a ravine, with only one way across: A rope bridge so flimsy that we hesitated before committing our lives to such a contraption. But we had no choice. As the others crossed, I kept our attackers at bay with my revolver. Eventually, despite Khan's threats and insults, I also crossed the ravine. Had it not been for the darkness, I have no doubt this fellow would have shot me dead. The moment I reached the far side, I cut the rope securing the bridge, and allowed it to plummet into the gorge below."

Khan added, "I predicted that we would meet again one day. And, on that day, one of us would surely die."

"You were always prolific with your threats, Khan," I told him.

Khan laughed. "But first, to business. It is no doubt your search for that skull that brings you to my doorstep."

"Indeed," said Holmes. "I am working with Scotland Yard to find that stolen skull and bring the thief to justice."

"Scotland Yard has no jurisdiction here," said Khan.

"No, but the Paris Sûreté certainly does."

"In that case, I have to disappoint you, gentlemen," said Khan. "I do indeed have the item you seek, but it is not here."

"Then what have you done with my Triceratops?" demanded Dr. Agar, stepping forward to confront Khan.

"It is somewhere safe," returned Khan, standing firm. He turned to Holmes. "I can only assume, Mr. Holmes, that your skills of detection brought you here this evening."

"Together with your advertisement," said Holmes, holding up the newspaper cutting.

"Ah, yes. The advertisement. I initially needed to go public in order to build up my web of purchasers, dealers, and agents. Since then, it has grown by word of mouth."

"If nothing else, I have to admire your organizational skills," said Holmes.

"My genius," replied Khan, "is to persuade people across the world to do little jobs for me, not realizing they are part of a greater web of deception. An American contact of mine told me about the skull several months ago. I organized the construction of an identical crate, then traveled to England to organize its exchange of the other. As I told you, I am the spider."

"I wish you had remained in Afghanistan," I told him.

"I left because I considered my talents wasted there. Fighting the invaders was a laudable occupation, but it hardly made me a wealthy man. I quickly became involved in the selling of antiquities. Whether legitimate or stolen, I chose not to ask. I now provide a service to people who wish both to sell and purchase such objects. I decided to go worldwide. Hence my advertisement, which was placed in newspapers across the globe."

"And why do you dare to tell us all this now?" asked Holmes.

"Because you will not live long enough to share it with anyone else," said Khan.

"When do you plan to sell the skull?" demanded Dr. Agar.

"Tonight. Within the next few hours, men from across the world will gather to bid for it. To the right people, it is worth a fortune. And since I am the one who has now acquired the thing, I shall be a very rich man before dawn tomorrow."

"You fiend!" cried Dr. Agar, once more advancing towards Khan.

"Stay where you are!" growled Khan, raising the revolver. "Time is going on, and I must deal with you three before I leave."

He looked to me. "Dr. Watson, remove your gun, and drop it into the left-hand drawer of the table in the corner of the room."

I removed the revolver from my pocket, and pushed it into the indicated drawer. Now we were without any form of protection.

216

"Turn round," said Khan, "and go out through the door by which you came entered. Then turn left, and follow the flight of steps down."

We turned, and noticed the woman we had first met at the doorway. Holding a lighted lantern, she led the way down into the depths of the building's foundations.

Behind me, Holmes remained silent as he descended the steps. Only the tapping of his cane upon the stone stairs told me he was there.

We finally came to a halt outside a closed wooden door.

"Dr. Agar," came Khan's voice from the rear of this bizarre procession. "Kindly open the door, and lead the way inside."

By the light of the lantern, we saw that the room was unlit, and roofed with a vaulted stone ceiling. The place smelled of mildew – clearly a place of some antiquity. Worst of all, as we stepped down into the room, we discovered the place was flooded, with water submerging us to waist height.

"What is this place?" I demanded.

"The place of your demise, Dr. Watson," came Khan's voice from the doorway. "You will live only so long as you can remain awake. The moment you submit to sleep, you will drown. Nobody will ever find your bodies down here. Now, I wish you all *adieu*."

Khan laughed and closed the door, plunging the flooded room into the most profound darkness.

Dr. Agar gave a deep sigh. "I must apologize to you, gentlemen, for leading you into such a dreadful predicament."

"It is hardly your fault," I told him.

"But we will all be dead within a couple of hours, either from drowning or from hypothermia."

I felt something bump against me. A bulky object, floating in the water. "Holmes," I said. "I have found a body."

Dr. Agar took out a matchbox and struck a match. It flared in the darkness, and we looked down at the corpse as Holmes turned it over onto its back.

"Poor fellow," he breathed.

"I recognize him," said Dr. Agar, grimly. "It's the American courier. But what is he doing here?"

In the light of a second match, Holmes searched the man's pockets, and brought out a card. "This declares him to be a Pinkerton agent. Now it makes sense."

"How?"

"The Americans must already have known about Khan's network, and decided to take the opportunity to send their agent to investigate. We can only assume he walked into a trap."

"Just as we did."

"There is nothing we can do for him now," said Homes, "so let us consider our situation. I suggest we return to the doorway."

In the light of another match, Holmes examined the stone steps down which we had so recently entered this accursed room.

"I would draw your attention," said Holmes, "to the fact that the steps above the level of the water are dry." Holmes allowed the match to burn itself out. "Before entering this building, I noticed the river close by. It seems reasonable to conclude that the level of water in here it the same as that of the river outside. And therefore that the quantity of water coming into the room is balanced precisely by the quantity of water leaving it."

"How is that significant?" I asked.

"If you listen carefully, you can detect the sound of water running in, no doubt from some freshwater spring the builders broke into during the construction of the foundations. The water is also finding some way of escaping from the room, and flowing into the river. Presumably through a gap between the stone blocks making up the wall."

Our wet clothing was already draining the warmth from our bodies, and I wondered how long we could last. But I said nothing as Holmes began to rap the stonework of the walls with the top of his cane. After a few minutes, he paused in his work.

"A-ha!" he cried. "Here we have a different sound. Behind this stone, I detect a space. Dr. Agar, another match, if you please."

In the brief, flickering light of the match, Holmes handed me his cane, took out his pocket knife, and began to chip away at the mortar surrounding one of the blocks. "We shall have to pull it out together," he said.

Our three pairs of hands fought for purchase along the edges of the stone, a few inches below the waterline, and pulled. In the darkness, I could feel the wet, rough stonework chafing my fingers. But a grating sound of stone against stone suggested we were making progress. As soon as the block had moved out sufficiently, we placed our hands beneath it and lifted. In this way, we eased the stone away from its resting place until it was free, and allowed it to sink to the floor of the flooded room.

Looking through the gap in the wall, I could see a half-submerged water-channel, leading off into the distance, with subdued light now filtering in along its length. The gap allowed sufficient room for Holmes to climb through. He stopped, and looked up. "This must be the bottom of some inspection shaft," he called back, "although it has not been visited for many years."

"Can you find any way of climbing out?" I enquired.

"Indeed I can. A series of corroded iron rungs are fixed into the wall directly above me. They lead up perhaps twenty feet to floor level, judging by the number of steps we took coming down here. You wait here with Dr. Agar."

Ignoring the scurrying of rats, disturbed by our unexpected disturbance of their world, I watched Holmes climb up until he disappeared into deeper darkness.

A few minutes later, we heard a sound from the other side of the door. We stood back as it burst open, flooding light into the underground room.

"Are you alright, Watson?" came Holmes's voice.

"Yes. How about you?"

"Encouraged. And how is Dr. Agar?"

"Cold," the Harley Street doctor replied.

"In that case, come up and meet Inspector Albert of the Paris Sûreté. It seems Lestrade remembered to tell the Paris police that we were coming."

The French policeman greeted us warmly and insisted we change out of our soaking wet clothes. "We have your luggage," he told us, "and I am sure we can supply anything else you might need."

As we changed into dry clothing, Holmes explained to Inspector Albert about Khan and the stolen dinosaur.

"Inspector Lestrade appeared confused," said Albert, "but I followed you here and now that I have the full story, I am ready to help in any way I can."

"But where has Khan gone?" Dr. Agar sounded exasperated. "He is planning to sell the dinosaur skull tonight, presumably by auction to the highest international bidder. If he does that, we might never find it. Our American cousins will never trust us again."

"As we were climbing down to the cellar," said Holmes, "I happened to notice a detectable smell about Khan's clothing. Tobacco. I am willing to hazard a guess that he had been in a tobacco warehouse not long before we met him."

I turned to Albert. "Do you know of such a place, Inspector?"

"I know of several, all within a short distance of each other," said the French policeman.

"But we can narrow down the search," Holmes stated. He turned to a figure standing almost unnoticed in the shadows, the woman that I had called "Madame Defarge". "Can you tell us where Khan has gone?"

The old woman sneered back, "I will never tell you, *Monsieur*."

219

As she turned away, the old woman cast a glance toward a bureau standing at the far side of the room. Holmes immediately strode over to the bureau, opened it up, and began to rummage through the contents of its drawers and alcoves. A moment later, he stood back, holding a carved wooden printing block, nearly six inches in length, and a pad of black ink.

"I suggest that here we have the answer to our problem," he said. "But we shall see. Watson? Paper, if you please."

From the same bureau, I took out a blank sheet of paper and spread it out upon the table in front of Holmes. He inked the block and pressed it to the paper. The image of a spider lay before us, the exact replica of the one on the advertisement, only somewhat larger.

Holmes turned to Albert. "Inspector, I suggest your men search for a warehouse displaying this image of a spider. We may also assume the road outside will be congested with parked vehicles."

Inspector Albert turned and gave a few instructions to his assistant, who turned and hurried away. "That should be easy enough to find, *Monsieur* Holmes. I have a coach waiting outside. Shall we go?"

The coachman took us to an area of the city lined with warehouses and stopped when a man in uniform waved us down. After Inspector Albert had received the man's report, we turned another corner and drew up outside one building that looked no different from any other.

"See," said the inspector. "The poster on the door. The spider, *Monsieur* Holmes. This has to be the right place."

"And, judging by the number of other conveyances parked outside, I would tend to agree," replied Holmes.

Albert looked around as three other vehicles arrived, and uniformed officers spilled out into the street. "While you were changing, I called in some more of our men."

This time, we entered the building without knocking, and soon found ourselves in a large interior room. The air held an all-pervasive smell of raw tobacco leaf. I became aware of people all around me who pulled back into the shadows as we entered. If I hadn't already been assured by Holmes, I would now be certain we had reached the correct place.

In the centre of the room, I saw Khan. And, next to him, a thing which at the same time both echoed my darkest nightmares and thrilled me to the core. A massive skull, approximately six feet in length, with a frill behind the head, and the bony cores of two lethal-looking spiked horns. The jaws held a multitude of grinding teeth, and the face ended in a vicious beak, with a smaller horn on the snout.

"Isn't she magnificent, Dr. Watson?" gushed Dr. Agar. "A Triceratops, in all her splendour!"

Khan stepped towards us. "This is a private gathering," he shouted. "I demand that you remove yourselves forthwith."

Inspector Albert, flanked by two uniformed policemen, confronted Khan. "You must come with me, *Monsieur*. You must answer questions about the theft of this skull. And murder."

With a sneer distorting his severe expression, Khan pulled his revolver from beneath his coat, and leveled it at me. At the very moment he pulled the trigger, one of Albert's men threw himself toward the gunman, and caught the full force of the gun's discharge.

I reached for my own gun, but remembered I had forgotten to collect it from the drawer at the Rue St. Martinot. Instead, I heard another revolver fire from close beside me. I saw Khan stagger back, with pain and shock showing on his face, and blood staining the right shoulder of his jacket.

As Khan retreated another step, I watched him trip, and fall heavily against the skull of the Triceratops. Hardly believing what I was witnessing, I watched as one horn of the dinosaur emerged, covered in blood, through the centre of Khan's chest.

The grotesque and blood-soaked scene reminded me of a gargantuan beetle mounted in the collection of some eccentric entomologist.

I broke off my attention, looked around, and saw Dr. Agar standing behind me, holding my own gun.

"You left it behind," he told me, "so I brought it along in case it turned out to be useful."

As I bent down to care for the fallen policeman, and call for his colleagues to consign the badly injured officer to hospital, Dr. Agar examined the man he had shot. None of us had any doubt that the man who had stolen the dinosaur now lay dead, impaled by the very object of his criminality.

Inspector Albert immediately took charge of the situation, and arranged for each person present to account, in writing, for his presence there that night.

At least one newspaper headline the following day read, "*Man Killed by Dinosaur in Paris*".

With such publicity, Dr. Agar's exhibition at the Museum of Practical Geology in London proved a tremendous success. Private donations flooded in, and fully paid the costs of transporting and exhibiting the dinosaur skull.

Sherlock Holmes turned down the invitation to be guest of honor at the opening. But despite his protestations, and out of respect for Dr. Agar, he did agree to stand beside the dinosaur for a photograph. I have it before me now, and slip it once more between the pages of my notebook, as I finally conclude my story of Dr. Agar and the Dinosaur.

> . . . *Dr. Moore Agar, of Harley Street, whose dramatic introduction to Holmes I may some day recount . . . .*

Dr. John H. Watson – "The Devil's Foot"

The Giant Rat of Sumatra
by Nick Cardillo

"Life is infinitely stranger than anything the mind of man could invent," Sherlock Holmes once remarked. Both my friend's chosen profession and an inherent predilection towards the bizarre proved his point to be an accurate one almost every day of the many years which we spent together, yet I can think of no better way to introduce the tale which I am about to tell than by referencing the detective's words. Never, I must admit, have I ever encountered a problem in my life quite so unbelievable and grotesque as the one I am about to relate. For many years, I deemed it a story for which the reading public at large would never believe. Perhaps in setting down the account to paper I am being too presumptuous, I tell myself even now, and maybe it would be for the best if this most singular adventure never did see the light of day.

It all began in that prestigious year of 1895, a span of twelve months which found Sherlock Holmes in more demand than ever before. There were few days when my friend was not roused from his bed early in the morning by a caller upon the doorstep, and there were even fewer evenings where we both found ourselves sitting idly by the fire of 221b Baker Street. At the beginning of this particular tale, Holmes and I had been called away from London to the seaside to investigate a series of seemingly unexplainable goings-on at Whitby Abbey. The case proved to have a completely benign explanation, and I feared Holmes may have resented being summoned from the city, but he was in a good humor that evening as we sat across from each other in our hotel room, blissfully unaware of what was to come.

The following morning, Holmes and I both rose early with the intent on taking the first train back to London. Despite my friend's mild protestations, I cajoled him to break his fast, knowing that the long train ride would be an arduous one on an empty stomach, and as we sat together sipping from freshly brewed tea and indulging in some delightful home-made marmalade (courtesy of the innkeeper's wife), I suddenly took notice of a young man rushing up the path towards the inn. He was dressed in the attire of a priest, but I was unable to make out much about him until he bustled into the dining room of the lobby, wringing his hands, and speaking in hushed, conspiratorial tones to the innkeeper. I saw the man point in our direction, and before I even had time to warn Holmes – who was surely watching the scene play out with just as much interest as me – the young priest was upon us.

"Mr. Sherlock Holmes?"

"That would be me," my friend replied courteously, "but I am afraid that now you have the advantage of me."

Holmes gestured for the young man to take the empty seat beside him, which he claimed only too readily.

"My name is Father Michael Frobisher," he began, "and I come in desperate need of your help. The local police have already begun an investigation, but when I learned that Mr. Sherlock Holmes, the great detective himself, was in town, I simply couldn't pass up the chance to come to you. Something ghastly has happened, Mr. Holmes, something I can only suspect that the devil had a hand in."

"Then I should imagine that you would be far more able than I to handle such a situation," Holmes replied.

"Oh, you must forgive my poetic license," Father Frobisher replied. "However, you must not underestimate the severity of this state of affairs, sir. I believe you to be the only man on earth who can help us."

Holmes flashed a knowing grin. "Then, pray, lay all of the facts before me, Father, and omit nothing, no matter how insignificant they may seem."

The young priest sat upright and adjusted the delicate pince-nez which were clipped to the end of his pointed nose. "Simply put, Mr. Holmes, it is murder. Two men of this community – a thoroughly disreputable lot by the name of the Connolly twins – were found murdered this morning, savaged by a hand which cannot be entirely human. I know this only as I am unfortunate enough to be the man to have found their bodies."

The color drained from Father Frobisher's face, and I pushed a cup of tea in his direction. He accepted with a thankful smile.

"I do not wish to speak ill of the dead," he continued, "but the Connolly's were not revered. It was well-known that they could be paid to commit any sort of indiscretion, so it was little surprise that they were discovered within the church's cemetery. They appeared to have been killed in the midst of attempting to desecrate a grave."

Holmes's ears perked up at such a detail and he leaned forward on the table, all the better to absorb all the facts of Father Frobisher's story.

"Whose grave?"

"That of the late Charles Morrison, the shipping magnate who died a little less than a month ago."

"Aside from the obvious signs of violence upon their bodies, what else did the scene yield?"

Frobisher shook his head. "I am afraid that I cannot say with any certainty. After I reported to the police what had happened and answered their questions as best I could, they sent me on my way. I confess that I do have something of a reputation for being a busybody in town, and I suspect that the authorities thought of me only as a burden to their investigation."

Holmes considered for a moment. "Clarify one point for me, Father: When you say that the two men were *savaged by a hand which cannot be entirely human*, what, precisely, do you mean?"

Frobisher drew in a deep breath. "Both of the Connollys – Edwin and Jeffrey – had had their throats torn out. On their faces were looks of extreme terror which I have never seen in another man, alive or dead. Something perhaps too ghastly to contemplate killed the two men, worrying them like a wild animal."

"Perhaps it *was* a wild animal," I suggested. "One hears tales nowadays of wolves being spotted in parts of England and Wales. Perhaps the Connolly twins, faced with such a creature, fell victim to its unfamiliarity with human beings."

"A sound theory, Watson," Holmes replied, "and one to which I shall return as we progress." Turning back to the priest, Holmes added, "I shall do all in my power to bring this matter to a close, Father Frobisher. I greatly appreciate your bringing this ghoulish business to my attention, and in such a timely manner too. Perhaps you can provide me with the name of your local inspector?"

"The man assigned to the case this morning was Inspector Seward," Frobisher replied.

"Excellent," the detective answered. "I shall seek him out as soon as we conclude here. Before we go, however, I should like to return to the matter of the grave. You say that Charles Morrison died less than a month ago?"

I was unsurprised by Holmes's ignorance on the matter, for he had been consumed with a perplexing case at the time that the magnate's death had reached the headlines. Morrison had done more than any man in English history to single-handedly perpetuate trade between Great Britain and the island of Sumatra, and it was estimated that over a quarter of all teas, coffees, and spices imported from the island were through Morrison's shipping company. His death had been a severe blow to the morale of the caste of society who inhabited Morrison's sphere, but much was made of the fact that his two sons, Archibald and Nicholas, were on hand to carry on his legacy.

In response to Holmes's question, Frobisher nodded wordlessly.

225

"Can you think of any reason that the Connolly twins should wish to rob his grave in particular?"

"It's relative freshness?" I suggested. "Burke and Hare, after all, robbed graves to supply to medical schools for dissection. I am happy to say that the state of things is different now, and lecturers are not required to seek the *services* of resurrectionists, but one nevertheless hears horror stories."

"Is Morrison's the most recently dug grave in the cemetery?" Holmes asked.

"An elderly woman, Mrs. Hoffman, died less than a week ago and was buried on Monday last," Frobisher replied.

"Then I am afraid that that disproves the Doctor's theory," Holmes mused aloud. He tapped his long index finger to his lips in a moment of concentration before he abruptly stood, shrugging into his coat. "I'm afraid that we shall yield nothing sitting here, gentlemen. Come, let us go to the cemetery and see what we can glean from there."

We made our way outside, I'm sure cutting a set of peculiar figures along the way, with Holmes leading us through the streets of the ancient seaside city, the young priest at his side, and I following them closely behind. The morning had taken a turn for the cold and, though the sun hung in the sky, its beams doing their utmost to penetrate the grey clouds which worked to blot it out, I still felt a shiver pass up and down my body. Holmes, as usual, seemed to pay the cold no heed and pressed on with Father Frobisher, instructing him where to go along the way. We had soon left the town itself and made for a hilly, stone crag, on top of which was perched the church. Father Frobisher led us up a narrow stone staircase towards the building, and then pointed towards the small gathering of headstones which formed the cemetery.

Had the markers of the graves not been visible to us, we would have still known that something was amiss. A group of men – two uniformed constables and an inspector dressed in a greatcoat – stood together deep in conversation. The inspector looked up, perceiving our approach and visibly rolled his eyes at the approach of Father Frobisher.

"I thought we told you that we did not need any further insistence, Father," Seward remarked coldly.

"Yes, yes," Father Frobisher replied nervously, wringing his hands in his habitual manner. "Be that as it may, I had word that Sherlock Holmes and Dr. Watson were staying at the inn in town, and I thought –"

The inspector silenced the priest with a look. He then turned to Holmes and me. "You gentlemen are Sherlock Holmes and Dr. Watson?"

"Indeed," Holmes replied with a polite tip of his hat. "And if Father Frobisher is to be believed – and I do not doubt his word – you would be Inspector Seward."

"Yes," Seward replied gruffly. "As exciting as it is to meet you, Mr. Holmes – we here are admirers of Dr. Watson's accounts of your work – I do not believe that your assistance is necessary in this matter."

"How do you explain the gruesome deaths of the Connolly twins, then?" I asked.

"Though it chills my blood to suggest such a thing," Inspector Seward began, "I am of the opinion that the Connolly's were joined by a third confederate in their grave-robbing expedition. A disagreement between this third party and the brothers broke out, and the third man killed them and escaped."

"This disagreement that arose between the twins and their cold-blooded accomplice," Holmes began. "What did it concern?"

Seward stammered. "Money, certainly," he replied. "What else are most disagreements about?"

"It is then your opinion that the Connollys were employed by someone to dig up graves in order to supply a specimen for some other purpose? Perhaps, as Dr. Watson suggested this morning, they were employed by a member of the medical fraternity to supply a cadaver for dissection?"

"That is precisely my supposition," Inspector Seward replied. "This third man was obviously far more unhinged than either of the twins suspected and, when they could not agree on a manner to distribute their earnings from this illegal task, he turned on them and killed them."

Holmes stared at the ground and considered for a moment. "Your theory is a sound one, Inspector," he said at length. I arched an eyebrow at how readily Holmes was willing to accept Seward's theory, especially as I almost discounted it outright earlier that morning. "Do you have any leads on finding this man?"

Seward smirked. "We have our methods, Mr. Holmes. I shall spend much of the day questioning doctors at the local hospital."

"But what need would they have for cadavers?" I interrupted.

Holmes silenced me. "Watson, please. Inspector Seward's theory holds water for the time being. I should very much like to hear of his progress throughout the day, if he feels so inclined."

"Should you wish it, I would be happy to keep you abreast of developments."

"In the meantime," Holmes replied, "would you and your officers be averse to me acquainting myself with the ground for a more thorough examination?"

227

Inspector Seward shrugged his shoulders. "I don't see why not. We do have to be going, so if you do not mind – "

"Please, do not allow us to detain you any further, Inspector."

Cordially, Holmes extended a hand and shook Seward's warmly. Once the three representatives of the law had disappeared, my companion turned to Father Frobisher and dismissed him with a few polite words. Left alone, Sherlock Holmes burst into laughter – an act I found rather distasteful, considering our current environs.

"What could possibly be so amusing?!"

"I don't know how much longer I could act the part of the unknowing fool," the detective replied. "I was sure from the instant that I saw the inspector standing over-confidently before his constables that he could not be more in the dark. However, I wished to institute myself into his good graces so that he might leave us be and we could gather some actual data. I do hope, my dear fellow, that you did not take too much umbrage with me silencing you as quickly as I did."

I waved away the notion. Then, crouching down, Holmes withdrew his convex lens from his inner pockets and scanned the ground in our immediate vicinity. He moved, carefully, towards the grave of Charles Morrison, his eye to the lens at all times. Once he was before the grave, he sprawled himself out on his stomach, sifting his long, dexterous fingers through the soft dirt and grass. He did this for perhaps five minutes or more before he returned to a kneeling position, fished inside his coat pocket, and withdrew a small envelope. He then plucked something off the ground and placed it inside the envelope, wordlessly returning it to its original place next to his breast.

"Well?"

"It is a starting point," Holmes cryptically replied. "I should like to make directly for the morgue and, using our good graces with Inspector Seward as a skeleton key, examine the bodies of the Connolly twins."

The constabulary was located in a small, stone structure off the main thoroughfare, and once inside, Holmes dropped Seward's name to the desk sergeant who sat just within the building's front door. Stretching the truth to its extreme, Holmes said that we had come on Seward's behalf to make an examination of the bodies of Edwin and Jeffrey Connolly. The desk sergeant led us – at first with trepidation – towards the back of the building to a low, tiled room which served as a place for the dead. Laid out on two identical slabs were the identical figures of the Connolly brothers who, I am sure, led similar lives and died similar deaths.

Both men were of average height and build with flaxen hair. Their pale corpses were scored with deep wounds, just as Father Frobisher had said, their throats having sustained the majority of the violence. It was a sorry sight, indeed, and even if the twins had had a reputation of little repute within the town, such grim ends were most certainly not warranted. Holmes and I approached them with some reverence. I leaned over them to make a cursory examination of their wounds. It did not take me long to make a startling pronouncement:

"Inspector Seward could not be further off the mark. No man could have inflicted these wounds, Holmes. These scratches look more like claw marks than anything else."

However, Holmes seemed to have taken little notice of my words. He was instead focusing all of his attention on the dead men's fingernails. He wordlessly went about a minute examination of their hands before straightening himself with a self-satisfied smirk.

"Claw marks, you say?" he asked, seemingly only half interested. "Your theory of a wild wolf does seem plausible then, does it not?"

"Perhaps," I said, "but I'm surprised at you, Holmes. Surely you would normally scold me for theorizing before I'm in possession of all the facts. Is that not your maxim?"

"It is," Holmes replied. "However, at present, I must admit that my mind is preoccupied. The manner of the Connolly twins' deaths is only of secondary importance right now."

"Oh? And what is of *primary importance*, then?"

"Charles Morrison," Holmes replied. He extracted his watch from his waistcoat pocket and scrutinized it. "Ah, just as I suspected: We have missed our train for London. Well, if we are to be stuck here for a few hours more, then there should be nothing preventing us from calling on the new patriarch of the Morrison household. Come, let us hail a cab and have a few words with Mr. Archibald Morrison."

The home of the Morrison family was by far the grandest on the seaside, a three-story stone edifice with vines of ivy adhering to its aged exterior. It was the kind of house which I knew, as our cab rattled up the gravel drive towards it, had a history. The nature of that history was lost to me, but there was an inherent romanticism in the place which excited me. Sherlock Holmes, on the other hand, seemed to take no notice of the structure which looked as if it had been plucked from an earlier century and placed where it now stood. Beneath the brim of his ear-flapped traveling cap, his inscrutable grey eyes were set with their customary determination, and he was drumming his fingers restlessly upon his knee. Our cab rattled to a halt and we approached the grand double-doors beneath an ornate portico. No sooner had we made to ring the bell,

229

however, was the door opened from within and we stood face-to-face with a young man who smiled nervously at us.

"Can I help you, gentlemen?"

"Mr. Nicholas Morrison, I presume?" Holmes said. The young man was utterly taken aback.

"Yes. But . . . how did you – "

"That is beside the point. My name is Sherlock Holmes, and this is my friend and colleague, Dr. Watson. We would like to have a few words with you and your brother."

Nicholas Morrison breathed heavily. "Is this about that unfortunate matter at the cemetery this morning? Archie and I were informed by Inspector Seward only a few hours ago."

"Yes, Mr. Morrison. I do believe that you and your brother could be quite useful in helping Mr. Holmes and I sort this matter out," I replied.

Morrison opened the door wider for us and we stepped inside. He divested us of our hats and coats.

"Do forgive the informality," he said, laying our garments on an ornate chest within the foyer, "but we have recently lost our housekeeper and servant of many years a few weeks ago. Archie and I have been quite lost without them."

"You have not been burdened with further grievances?" I asked.

"Oh, no," Morrison replied. "However, they turned in their notices a few days before my father's death. But, please, come in. I believe Archie is handling some business in the study."

We crossed a polished marble floor deeper into the house, past a sprawling sitting room, and into a wide-open room overflowing with books. Seated behind a large desk crowded with ledgers and papers was a young man bearing the familial resemblance to Nicholas Morrison. He was a few years older than Nicholas, his temples having already begun to gray, and there was something haughty about his demeanor which was not reflected in the countenance of the younger Morrison son. This man, whom I took to be Archibald Morrison, was engrossed in the contents of the papers spread out on the desk as he puffed contentedly upon a pipe.

"Archie," announced Nicholas, "we have guests."

Archibald Morrison peered up at us and arched an eyebrow. "Who are these men?"

"Sherlock Holmes and Dr. Watson," Nicholas replied. "They're here about the tragedy in the cemetery this morning."

"We have already told that numb-skull inspector everything there is to know," Archibald Morrison retorted. "Besides, what could we know about any of this? Father's grave was untouched, and that is the only help that we can be."

"I beg to differ on that point," Holmes said. He stepped further into the room, his hawk-like head shifting from side to side, taking in the chamber with his habitually penetrating, all-seeing gaze. "For instance, perhaps you could tell the Doctor and me why anyone should wish to desecrate your father's grave."

"How should I know that?" Archibald Morrison returned his attention to the papers on his desk. "Now, if you will excuse me, gentlemen, I am extremely busy this morning and, though I would be happy to help you with your investigation, there is little that I can do to assist you. Nicholas, on their way out, please apologize to Mr. Holmes and Dr. Watson that we couldn't be of more help to them."

And with that, Archibald Morrison returned his attention entirely to the work on his desk. Muttering a curt thanks, Holmes turned and walked out of the room. Nicholas Morrison and I found him standing in the hallway outside the study, examining an oil painting hanging upon the wall.

"This is, of course, an original?" he said turning to us as we approached.

"Yes. My father was a great appreciator of art. A number by that artist can be found throughout our home. And I do apologize on my brother's behalf, Mr. Holmes. His rude behavior was not warranted, but he has been under a great deal of stress of late. Our father's death pushed the responsibility onto Archie's shoulders quite suddenly, and though he spent many an hour at my father's side in that study learning his business practices, surely those hours alone were not enough."

"Your brother's predicament is an understandable one," I remarked.

"What was your brother doing when we interrupted him?"

"It appeared as though he was going over a record of the latest imported cargo. Only last evening, one of our trading ships – the *Matilda Briggs* from Sumatra – put into port. Onboard were crates full of spices, teas, and coffees."

"Sumatra is one of your most frequent suppliers, is it not?" Holmes asked.

"Oh, indeed!" Morrison replied, his eyes twinkling. "Some say that my father opened trade with that country by himself."

"Quite an accomplishment." Holmes returned his attention to the painting and then suddenly spun around on his heel. "Dr. Watson and I must be taking our leave, but you have been very helpful, Mr. Morrison."

So saying, my companion strode off, leaving me to apologize for his curious behavior. I caught up with Holmes outside as he was shrugging on his Inverness and starting down the gravel drive on foot.

231

"I do not understand you at times," I said as I fell into step alongside him. "This morning, we are handed a case in which two men are brutally murdered, and you regard it with only passing interest. Yet you find the machinations of a family – who seem to be only tangentially related to the matter – to be of the utmost importance. You know something that I do not."

Sherlock Holmes smiled knowingly. Instead of answering me directly, he said cryptically: "You know of my habit of eliminating from my mind all manner of thoughts, fancies, and facts which I do not deem relevant?"

"Yes," I retorted, "like how the Earth revolves around the sun!"

Holmes silenced me with a wave of his hand. "There are times, however, when something will stick to my mental fly paper and simply will not yield. I am suffering from just such a preoccupation now, and if I am correct, this matter shall hold unexpected surprises for us both."

I took a hold of Holmes's sleeve, stopping him. "What do you mean?" I asked gravely.

"Something of which men of science have only just begun to probe may be inextricably linked to both the death of the Connolly twins and the Morrison family. I have an idea of what we seek, but I must pursue a few arcane zoological texts in order to prove my hypothesis. I fancy that I shall be spending the remainder of the day behind the stacks of the local library."

"And what shall I be doing, then?"

"You, my dear Watson? First, procure for us our rooms at the inn for the rest of the night. We shall not be leaving Whitby before midday on the morrow at the earliest. Then, stop 'round to the telegraph office and wire Lestrade. Tell him to fetch Toby from Pinchin Lane, and instruct him to board the first train to the coast as soon as he has done so. We shall be in need of both the dog and his revolver tonight. You, too, have your revolver?"

"Of course."

"Excellent. After you have carried out those errands, I suggest that you get some rest. It shall be a late night for the three of us and, at the end of it, I fear that we may emerge lesser men because of it."

With these daunting words ringing in my ears, Sherlock Holmes and I parted ways.

I had no idea just how true his premonition of doom was to be.

By two in the morning, the damp chill of the autumn day by the sea had given way to a bone-freezing cold. There was little that I could do other than wrap my great coat around me tighter and massage my fingers through my gloves. I took some solace in the fact that Inspector Lestrade seemed to have been just as perturbed as I by the cold. Holmes, however, couldn't have cared any less.

Our evening had been one full of activity. After I sent off word to Lestrade at Holmes's request, I heeded his words and returned to the inn, where I willed myself to sleep, and was only roused when my friend returned from his mission. He told me little of what he had been doing (as was his irritating custom) and insisted that if Lestrade had followed his instructions to the letter, then we ought to meet him soon. As we made our way to the Whitby station, the sun was already beginning to disappear over the sea, its orange rays mixing on the water like colors in an artist's pallet.

Considering the relative lateness of the hour, it was hardly surprising when few others disembarked alongside Inspector Lestrade from the sparsely-populated carriage. He led Toby, somewhat unwillingly, by the leash, and seemed only too happy to turn the animal over to Holmes when he clapped eyes on us. I exchanged a laugh with the little policeman at his words concerning the mercurial Mr. Sherman, Toby's keeper, who threatened Lestrade with bodily harm before he used Holmes's name as a passkey, as I had encountered the exact same scenario when I had first procured the bloodhound some years before.

Our party returned to the inn where Holmes insisted that we eat and, after we had concluded our meal and drained our glasses of port, we returned to our room where we sat in relative silence. It was nearly midnight when Holmes announced that it was time to venture out into the night. From his coat pocket, he produced the small envelope containing whatever he had found at the scene of the twins' murder, and wafted its unseen contents beneath Toby's nose. The dog perked up at the stimulus and broke into an all-out run by the time we hit the street.

I could only marvel at the labyrinth-like path we traversed that night, rushing hither and thither across hilly embankments and up and down flights of steps. At times, it seemed that we were traveling merely in circles, yet Holmes did not seem concerned by the randomness of our journey. If anything, he seemed pleased, murmuring time and time again, "Yes, just as I suspected." Lestrade and I shared a number of curious glances, but we knew that Holmes would only divulge the truth of the matter when he saw fit. In time, we found ourselves at the quayside. The cold intensified as we walked by the docked ships, listening to the water lapping at their hulls. Toby stopped before the moored *Matilda Briggs*, and Holmes stopped and considered it for some time before he gave the canine another whiff of his peculiar discovery, and we were off again.

We had not ventured far when Toby stopped dead in his tracks and issued a series of savage barks into the night. Holmes stopped too, and his pale countenance took on an even greyer pallor as we stood in the light of the moon. Wordlessly, he gestured for Lestrade and me to take up our revolvers. We did so and I felt comforted by the weight of the Webley in my hand, that cold, dead steel giving me some much-needed reassurance as I watched this strange tableau unfold.

"Gentlemen," Holmes whispered, his voice breaking the eerie silence and stillness which had descended over us, "I very much suspect that we are about to encounter something the likes of which we have never seen. Keep your wits about you."

I know that it was not only the cold which sent a shiver down my spine at Holmes's words. I had little time to linger on their potential meaning, however, for Toby began to bark once more – his wails increasing in volume and aggression – and that was when I divined a shape emerging out of the blackness and slowly, stealthily advancing toward us.

I could not at first believe what I saw, but as the thing stepped towards us, its form became ever more evident to my unbelieving eyes. I mistook it at first for a dog, for it was about the same size as Toby. However, I saw at once that it was much lower to the ground than a canine, and its body was far more elongated and sharper than any dog which I had ever seen. A large, snout-like nose protruded arrow-like from the front of its face, and two beady, black eyes stared at us, their sheen being caught in the light and looking even blacker and more bottomless than I knew they actually were. As I stared at it longer – in a second which felt like eternity – I realized that this was a creature which I had seen countless time scurrying through the streets of the city but never paid much heed. Yes, I realized, as mad as it seemed, this creature was a rat, but of a size that mortal eye had never rested upon.

The giant rat opened its mouth, revealing a series of sharp teeth, and the creature issued some kind of snarl which could have emanated just as easily from the depths of hell as it did the back of the beast's throat. Toby unleashed another series of angry barks towards the thing which seemed to break all of us from our dazed reverie. Even Holmes – whom I suspected knew full well what we were about to encounter – was rooted to the spot where he stood, simply unable to fathom the apparition before us. Toby's fuming outburst must have had much the same effect on the creature itself, for it rushed at us. As one, we all jumped back and the creature scurried past us, neither Lestrade nor I having had time to squeeze off a shot at the thing's retreating back.

"Come, gentlemen!" Holmes cried after what seemed like another eternity, "We mustn't let it get away!"

I reckon that that night we were all men who were fleet of foot, but the giant rat had the advantage on us, its short, stubby legs inexplicably carrying it faster than we could run. The cold wind biting at my lungs, I felt myself beginning to weaken almost from the start of the chase. However, I knew that I must keep pace with Holmes and Lestrade. I would not allow myself to be blamed for letting the monster – for that is what it truly was – get away.

The next few moments passed by in a daze, but I was next aware of the three of us charging up a frighteningly steep stone staircase, the process seeming to me in the moment to be very much like trying to scale a cliff-face. It was a relief to come to the top of the steps, but we had little time to collect ourselves once more for we were still hot on the heels of the giant rat. Huffing and puffing, we continued after it. My whole chest was beginning to burn now, and I felt drops of sweat accumulating on my brow. All at once, I felt my legs give way and I stumbled, collapsing to the ground. Helpless, like a ragdoll, I endeavored to right myself and looked up into the concerned face of Inspector Lestrade, who extended a hand to help me to my feet.

I looked around and saw that both Holmes and Toby were some yards off, the dog having now fully joined the hunt as much as his master. The over-zealous creature was suddenly out of Holmes's grip, however, and it bounded after the rat and was instantly upon its back. I watched dumbly as the two animals wrestled, clawing at each other, both snarling like feral beasts. I had enough sense to rush forward – exerting all of my remaining strength – and pull my revolver from my pocket, aim, and fire. The bullet met is mark, the giant rat issuing a great gasp of pain as it was wounded. At the sound of the shot, Toby backed away, leaving Lestrade and me to unload round after round into the seemingly undying creature's flank.

The end came quickly for the giant rat and it lulled to one side, quite dead. We collectively heaved a great sigh of relief.

"I still cannot believe my eyes," Lestrade said at length as we stood over the body of the dead creature. "What is it?"

"A true miracle and nothing short of that," Holmes replied. "This oversized rodent – *Coryphomys* – is the largest of its size to have ever lived. I must confess, gentlemen, that even I underestimated its size. I suspected a creature, yes, but something as large and ferocious as this would have gone extinct with the dinosaurs. Its existence is nothing short of truly incredible."

"And this . . . monster . . . is what was responsible for the deaths of Edwin and Jeffrey Connolly?"

"Yes, Watson," Holmes replied. "We have brought their murderer to justice, though I never anticipated the toll which doing so would have on all of us. I suspect that I have kept you both in the dark for long enough, and I have some explaining to do. Let us retire to the inn and steady our nerves with some drinks. I shall endeavor to lay everything before you both, and we shall tend to Toby, who I fear is just as shaken as we are."

"But what about the rat, Holmes?" I asked. "We simply cannot leave it here."

Holmes considered. He picked up the beast and carried it by himself – how he managed I daresay that I shall never know – once more to the water's edge, where he tossed the thing into the ocean.

"Perhaps it is for the best that the civilized world never knows of the existence of the giant rat of Sumatra. Now, let us be off. It is, after all, exceedingly cold out here."

Half-an-hour later, we three were thankfully ensconced in the warmth of our room at the inn, sitting comfortably before the fire. We all nursed glasses of brandy, while Toby sat curled up in a ball upon the floor, letting the warmth from the dancing flames of the fireplace warm him all over. Holmes downed his drink and lit a cigarette, and I perceived that his hand was still not entirely steady after what we had all endured. He smirked at his own jittery fingers, and tossed his match into the fire. He then strode up and down the room in what I thought to be an attempt to regain his composure.

"I admit," he began, "that I was biased from the beginning by Father Michael Frobisher's words when he said that no human hand could have been responsible for the Connolly twins' murder. With that hypothesis in mind, then, I made an examination of the cemetery in which they were found for evidence to support this claim. I was particularly on the lookout for footprints which would have proved that a wild animal was on the loose, and the two men were unfortunate enough to run afoul of the beast. However, I soon found myself out of luck, for the Whitby constabulary, it seemed, were just as adept at obliterating evidence as Scotland Yard. No offense to you, Inspector."

"None taken, Mr. Holmes," Lestrade replied, and took a long gulp of his drink.

"However, what I did manage to find proved to be even more helpful."

From the end table at his side, Holmes plucked the small envelope which he had used at the cemetery, and for the first time withdrew its unseen contents. In his fingers he held a few tufts of hair.

"I was certain, as soon as I found these hairs," Holmes continued, "that it *was* a wild animal which was responsible for the Connolly's deaths. When Watson and I made an examination of the two men's corpses in the mortuary, I played a hunch and devoted myself to a study of their fingernails. Just as I had suspected, I found a few strands of the same hair beneath the dead men's fingers. Obviously some kind of struggle had broken out between the twins and their killer.

"From there, gentlemen, my task was a comparatively simple one. I had read once some years ago of a zoological expedition which was mounted into the darkest jungles of the Sumatran rain forest. In doing so, the men of the team had observed oversized rodents in their natural habit: Creatures which modern English society still knows little of. It didn't take me long to determine that the hairs which I had discovered at the cemetery belonged to a rodent and, after availing myself to a microscope, I was able to conclusively determine the rat's point of origin. However, as I said earlier, I had no idea that the creature would be quite so large. For never considering such an eventuality and subjecting you gentlemen to such a scene, I do apologize."

"Save your apologies, Mr. Holmes," Lestrade said. "The Doctor and I are made of stronger stuff than that."

Holmes nodded in thanks at the inspector and puffed on his cigarette.

"But how the devil did the giant rat get to our shores in the first place?" I asked.

"Have you not put two and two together yet, Watson? The giant rat was obviously a stowaway aboard the trading ship, *Matilda Briggs*, which put into port from Sumatra on the night of the murders. If I were the Morrison's, I would surely reprimand the ship's captain for being careless enough to let such a fearsome, unwanted passenger aboard in the first place."

"So I suppose that explains your inexplicable fascination with the Morrison family, then?"

"On the contrary, my dear fellow," Holmes responded. "In fact, my approach to this case has been – almost from the beginning – that the real heart of this mystery lies with the Morrison family, and that the deaths of the Connolly twins were an unfortunate consequence."

I confessed that Holmes had quite lost me. He responded with another mirthless grin.

"I shall elucidate later, Watson. For now, I suggest that we all attempt to get some sleep. It has been an arduous day for all of us. Tomorrow morning we can bring this business to a successful conclusion."

237

So saying, Holmes dropped all discussion of the matter. We sat in silence for some time before taking his advice and we all dropped off to sleep, Holmes and I in our beds, while Lestrade made do with his armchair before the fire. It was a fitful sleep which greeted me that night, and I was only too glad when the first rays of morning sunshine began to peek through the shutters. I roused myself early, not having to wait long before both Holmes and Lestrade joined me in the inn's front room for breakfast. I could only imagine how much pain Lestrade was made to endure sitting in his armchair all night and asked him as much once he had downed a cup of coffee.

"I have fared better, to say the very least, Doctor."

"I hope that we didn't incommode you enough that you will be unable to accompany Watson and me to the Morrison home, Lestrade. I can assure you that your presence there shall make my task a much simpler one."

"I've come this far," Lestrade retorted, not without some jollity, "that I might as well see this business through to the end."

Within the hour, we three were once more making our way up the gravel drive towards the Morrison home. Nicholas Morrison greeted us at the door, and drew Holmes aside once we had stepped into the foyer.

"I am afraid that my brother is in just as much of a state today," he said. "You may not wish to disturb him."

"Disturb him, we shall," Holmes rebuked. Wordlessly, my friend bounded off down the corridor towards the study, rapping on the door and hardly giving the room's occupant enough time to answer before he had entered. Lestrade I bustled in after the detective, with Nicholas Morrison following on our heels. Archibald Morrison scowled at Holmes upon our entrance.

"Mr. Sherlock Holmes has returned," he said airily a moment later. "How may I be of service *now*?"

"I would sheath my sarcasm if I were in your position, Mr. Morrison," Holmes said. "I cannot be precise, but I believe that the proper authorities would find grave-robbing a hanging offense."

All the color drained from Morrison's face, yet he seemed to regain his composure when he said, "Why tell me this, Mr. Holmes?"

"Your act is wearing thin, Mr. Morrison. I know beyond a shadow of a doubt, that it was *you* who hired the Connolly twins to dig up your father's grave."

"You dare to defame me!" Morrison cried, slamming his fist onto the table. "What gives you the power to walk in here and make such accusations, Mr. Holmes?"

238

"Admittedly little right, I'll admit, Mr. Morrison," Holmes replied coolly, "but under the present circumstances – and knowing you as I believe I know you – I can come to no other conclusion. Had your father been the last person to die in the village, I would have been more willing to accept the postulation which said that the Connolly's were employed by someone to rob your father's grave and use his body for some nefarious anatomical purpose. However, any skilled grave-robber would have selected the grave of the elderly woman whose death followed your father's by several weeks. Therefore, there must have been another motive behind the attempted grave-robbing."

Holmes suddenly turned and posed a question to the younger Morrison. "Mr. Morrison, to the best of your knowledge, is there anything missing from this room?"

Nicholas Morrison looked around in his habitual nervous manner. "No," he said, "not that I can notice."

"However. I imagine if you had spent more time in this study – as you yourself said that your brother did in the days before your father's death – then you might be even more familiar with its contents. I, myself, noticed the disturbed dust atop that safe in the corner of the room when I first entered yesterday afternoon. Clearly, something sat atop that safe for some time until recently. I learned that it was a chest which your father used for keeping additional money. Perhaps it was even a collection meant especially for you. Am I not correct, Mr. Morrison?"

Archibald Morrison stood fast, unmoving and unspeaking.

"As I discovered yesterday," Holmes continued, "your father knew of your lewd behavior, Mr. Morrison. Yes, I speak to the incident surrounding the resignation of your former housekeeper and manservant. I was quite happy to get wind of some local gossip at the public house where your reputation as a cad precedes you. From there, I was able to locate the housekeeper, who told me of the chest, and where it went. Obviously, your father learned of the true nature for their leaving and, as a means of punishment to you, instructed that he be buried with that stash of money so that you might never get your hands on it. I'll warrant that he regretted, in the end, the lavish style of living in which he raised you, and was prepared to teach you something of a lesson from beyond the grave.

"Once your father was buried, you discovered what he had done and – being the greedy man you are – took it upon yourself to reclaim the money. You hired the Connolly twins who, for the right price, would be willing to execute any odd job given to them, and sent them off to stage the robbing of your father's grave. By a cruel twist of fate, they happened to be in the wrong place at the wrong time and met their fates by one of Mother Nature's most aberrant creations which, ironically, you helped to inadvertently bring into this country."

Both Morrison brothers looked to the detective on that last point, but he shut down any of their attempts at questioning him with a stern look. He then left the two Morrison brothers to stare blankly at each other.

"I knew that you were one to stoop low, Archie," Nicholas Morrison said, "but I never suspected that you would do something so . . . so *horrible.*"

"What punishment shall you put to me, Mr. Holmes?" Archibald Morrison asked.

Holmes stared at a spot on the floor and drew in a deep breath. "Considering that you did not actually succeed in robbing the grave or stealing the money, I believe that it is for the best that this incident does not come to light. I am not blind to the importance of the Morrison business, and should your trading company fall, so should your solicitors' and other branches of this great enterprise. I would not wish such a fate upon so many for your petulant and dangerous behavior alone, Mr. Morrison."

Archibald Morrison could hardly make his eyes meet Holmes's. "Thank you, sir."

"I believe, then, that this concludes our business here," Holmes said suddenly. "If Inspector Lestrade, the Good Doctor, and I are to make it to London, we must make haste. We shall show ourselves out, Mr. Morrison."

Once we were outside, leaving the Morrison home behind us, I turned to Holmes and asked, "Shall we not explain this business to Inspector Seward?"

"If we are to tell the inspector anything, Watson, then let us give him a fabricated version of the truth. He would never believe the reality of this case, and if I am quite of the opinion that this is a matter for which the world is not yet prepared."

> "Matilda Briggs *was not the name of a young woman, Watson,*" said Holmes in a reminiscent voice. "*It was a ship which was associated with the giant rat of Sumatra, a story for which the world is not yet prepared.*"
>
> Sherlock Holmes – "The Sussex Vampire"

The Adventure of the
Black Plague
by Paul D. Gilbert

As I look back through my notes for the autumn of 1895, I realise that the glut of cases with which my good friend Sherlock Holmes and I had been inundated will provide me with enough source material for my humble literary offerings for some time to come.

A brief respite had allowed Holmes the opportunity to resume his violin compositions, but that was a process that didn't exactly induce an atmosphere in which I could proceed with my own form of creativity. I tried my best to block out the discordant screeching that his beleaguered instrument had been continuously forced to produce. However, I soon realised that my references to the cases of the Nervous Mariner and The Armour of Charlemagne would remain as nothing more than that unless my friend postponed his torturous recitals!

"Really, Holmes, I am certain that even Beethoven must have given himself and those around him an occasional recess from his great works!" I protested while slamming my notebook shut with violent frustration. I was relieved and surprised to note that he was prepared to respond to my outburst in an unexpectedly affable manner.

"Oh, my dear fellow! I did not realise that my harmless attempts at musical composition would provide you with such distress. Naturally, I shall cease at once." He smiled while placing his violin back upon its rest.

"Holmes, I do apologise, but you must realise that you were making it impossible for me to concentrate upon my notes."

He dismissed my attempt at appeasement with a dramatic flourish of his arm as he moved over to the fireplace. From there he collected together all the plugs and dottles from his smokes of the previous evening and then put a light to this, his first pipe of the day.

I am ashamed to admit that it was almost noon before our breakfast table was finally cleared that day and Holmes was still clad in his favourite purple dressing gown. Although it is true to say that, when not gainfully employed, Holmes and I tended to keep the most Bohemian of hours, on this occasion I fear that we had overstepped the mark somewhat.

Then I noticed that Holmes was employing his cherry-wood pipe and I knew at once that I could expect a rather disputatious conversation from my friend. In this, I was not to be disappointed.

"So, Doctor, which of our recent adventures do you intend to embellish and romanticise before inflicting the results upon your long suffering readers?" I could tell from his tone that Holmes was determined to take out his creative frustrations upon my own humble efforts.

Nevertheless, I was not going to sit idly by while he censured my writing skills once again.

"Holmes, I do not consider my attempts at making your demonstrations less dry and more readable as embellishments! Surely you cannot raise any objections at having our adventures, when published, reach a wider readership?"

"What difference does it make so long as this larger audience of yours fails to appreciate the subtleties and nuances of the science of deduction? Your intention should be to broaden the understanding of observation and reason, rather than to diminish it. I mean to say, just look at this!" Holmes snarled whilst throwing down my recently completed manuscript for *The Giant Rat of Sumatra* upon the dining table.

"You have me here, for example, slithering around upon the deck of the *Matilda Briggs* like some predatory reptile, whereas in actual fact I was engaged in the most intricate exercise of observation and deduction. You describe the weather in the most engaging and dramatic fashion whilst, all the while, I was below deck delving into the unlocked secrets contained within the bowels of that most mysterious and tragic ship. Thrill your readers if you must, but do not denigrate my art and science by passing them off as some form of cheap theatrical display!"

I was so completely taken aback by this, Holmes's most violent attack to date, that I could not, in all honesty, offer a single word of response in my own defence.

"Well, I'm certain that my sorely put-upon public will appreciate your considered and valued critique!" I am ashamed to admit that this feeble and sarcastic response was all that I was able to muster.

Mercifully, this acerbic encounter of ours was brought to a premature but welcomed conclusion by Mrs. Hudson announcing the arrival of our former antagonist, Inspector Lestrade of Scotland Yard.

I say 'former antagonist' because, by this stage in our association, both Holmes and the inspector had garnered a form of mutual respect from the other. Ever the since the investigation into the most singular events of the Norwood Builder, Holmes was made to realise that Scotland Yard no longer felt any resentment at his interventions.

On this occasion, Lestrade's normally drawn and hangdog features were further contorted by an anxiety that I had not previously witnessed upon them. Recognising this at once, Holmes immediately showed the troubled inspector over to a chair by the fire with a dramatic flourish of his right arm and then, despite the hour, he poured him out a generous measure from our port decanter and offered him a cigar. Lestrade readily accepted them both.

Holmes allowed the inspector time enough to relish both offerings before broaching the subject of his reasons for this unexpected visit.

"So, Inspector Lestrade, I perceive that we are not being honoured by a social visit on this occasion," Holmes declared by pointing towards the policeman's notebook, which was protruding rather precariously from the top of his coat pocket.

Lestrade was visibly embarrassed by Holmes's declaration, and he did not hesitate for a moment in confirming the accuracy of Holmes's observation. He nodded emphatically while putting a light to his cigar.

"I would have been glad had it been a social visit, Mr. Holmes, but sadly nothing could be further from the truth."

After a sip or two from his port, Lestrade became more conducive to the idea of voicing his concerns.

"What do you know of the individual who goes by the name of Wilson the Canary Trainer?" he asked bluntly.

Holmes jerked his head in the direction of the shelf that contained our indexes. I pulled down the file marked "*W*" and began to turn over those well-thumbed leaves. I slapped my hand upon the relevant page to confirm my success.

"I have it!" I announced. "It states simply: '*Wilson, the notorious canary trainer, who is also known as "The Black Plague of East London"*'."

"Oh, so you already know him as such?" Lestrade asked, clearly surprised by the data that was at our disposal.

"It is our business to have as clear an understanding of the criminal world as is possible." I said proudly while returning the index to its shelf.

"I also seem to recollect that you placed him under arrest a full year ago, Inspector! I fail to see why you have come to us upon the matter at this late stage," Holmes stated sharply while turning abruptly towards the troubled policeman.

Lestrade was clearly uncomfortable with this revelation and he shifted in his chair several times before replying.

"That is true, Mr. Holmes, but unfortunately the evidence against him was insufficient for a conviction. The man is the vilest exponent of extortion, and he utilizes every sort of threat and violence in order to obtain his ill-gotten gains. Obviously his canary emporium is but a facade for his real trade. He employs the worst kind of hoodlum to visit every tradesman in the area on the last day of every month.

"He sets a price based on the type of business concerned, but if the payment is not immediately forthcoming, his men are instructed to cause as much damage to the premises as is possible. Unfortunately, if his men continue to return empty-handed, then it is the proprietor himself who feels his wrath!

"The rogue makes no secret of his malicious profession, so a warrant for his arrest is never hard to obtain. However, by the time that the case finally comes to court, each witness receives another visit and is left in no doubt as to the dire consequences of his giving evidence against Wilson or his men. Subsequently, each case against him breaks down as soon as a witness is called. No one dare say a word against him, and my superiors are unrelenting in their demands for a conviction, I don't mind telling you.

"So I have come to you, Mr. Holmes, as I have on so many previous occasions, in the hope that you might find a solution to my dilemma." Lestrade was red-faced and almost breathless by the time that he had made his plea for help to my friend.

Holmes smiled sympathetically once Lestrade had concluded his statement and he immediately swapped his cherry-wood pipe for his old clay. He drew on this long and hard for a moment or two before responding to Lestade's request.

"I sincerely have the utmost sympathy for you, Lestrade, but I fail to see what it is that you expect me to do. Clearly there is no new evidence that I can accrue on your behalf, and I certainly cannot force your witnesses to give evidence against their will. Yet such a creature cannot and must not be allowed to continue," Holmes said with quiet thoughtfulness.

"The scoundrel!" I blurted out, my indignation with understandable ferocity, but Holmes hushed me with a movement of his hand. He moved slowly over to the window and smoked in silence, clearly lost in concentration.

"There is nothing else for it . . . ." He said this more to himself than to us, and he was barely audible.

Suddenly he returned to the centre of the room and his eyes flared with excitement. He pulled Lestrade back up onto his feet and began to usher him towards the door.

"Inspector, you shall hear from me within forty-eight hours, but I warn you that a long and dangerous night's work will lie ahead of you!"

The inspector appealed to me for an explanation as he opened the door to leave, but I merely shrugged my shoulders, for I had none. Upon Lestrade's departure, Holmes wasted no time in dashing off to his room with the door slammed resoundingly behind him.

For a few minutes, a perplexing cacophony of violent sounds reverberated from behind the door, while Holmes conducted a hurried and haphazard search through his drawers and cupboards. When he did eventually emerge, his transformation was as startling as it had been complete.

Indeed, his mutation had been so thorough that his laugh upon seeing my look of amazement was that of a bucolic and elderly tinker! He had a taken a full six inches off of his height, and somehow his self-imposed stoop conjured up the hump-back of a man used to bending over for hours on end while he went about his craft.

Holmes's hair now protruded below the rim of his crumpled, old brown hat, and it was a dirty silver grey in colour. His elongated nose sported a lacerated and congealing boil, and his lips were cracked and red. He sported a battered old greatcoat and a stained tinker's overall. The final touch was a bent pair of steel-rimmed spectacles that were perched precariously on the edge of his nose. When he smiled, however, he was unmistakable to me, even through this disguise.

"So, Watson, do you find my new persona satisfactory?" he asked superfluously.

"It is wondrous, Holmes, as well you know, and I would not recognise you had I not been witness to this miracle. For the life of me, however, I cannot imagine why you have gone to such lengths," I ventured, although without any real hope of receiving an explanation from my friend.

"Very likely not, but suffice it to say that you would certainly not approve were you to be privy to my intention. I cannot venture a time for my return, but I would strongly advise you to take all necessary precautions during my absence." By this I knew him to mean that I should clean and load my old army revolver in preparation for an imminent, but as yet, unidentifiable new adventure.

Then, without another word or a moment's further delay, Holmes was gone and I went upstairs to fetch my weapon from its drawer. The next twenty-four hours passed very slowly indeed, and I lost count of the number of times that I cleaned my revolver during that long wait.

My meals and Mrs. Hudson came and went with regularity and the papers were without any real points of interest. The cold, damp weather precluded any thoughts of a long walk and I had not the patience for a book. Twenty-four hours slowly became forty-eight and finally, when I was beginning to despair of ever seeing my friend again, my lonely reverie was broken by a terrible commotion at the street door.

I raced down the stairs and I was immediately met by a sight that shook me to the core! Sherlock Holmes was actually leaning upon the shoulder of Mrs. Hudson for support, and even with her assistance, I struggled to heave his listless form up the stairs to our rooms.

I could see Holmes attempt an ironic smile at the sight of my concern and, despite the visual evidence to the contrary, he insisted that his appearance should be of no cause for concern. Obviously I begged to differ and immediately set to work at removing the vestiges of his bedraggled disguise while causing as little further damage as possible.

His wounds were many, but thankfully mostly superficial. His coat was stained with blood down one side, where he had obviously taken a kick or two from a steel capped boot. There was severe bruising around and above both eyes, and his lips were a bloody pulpy mess.

Clearly he was in no condition to answer any of my myriad of obvious questions, so I worked upon him in silence with my bottle of iodine, some lint, and bandages. Finally, I completed my treatment with a generous helping of brandy, which I fed to him slowly where he lay upon the chez-lounge.

As a precaution, I decided to leave him there overnight, rather than to force him to struggle into his room. To my surprise, he was still there the following morning and his wounds were already well on the mend. Holmes sat up to greet me and he was clearly aware of the progress that he had made.

"Watson, you are a most excellent doctor, I must say!" He smiled.

"Thank you, Holmes, although I must say that your remarkable recuperative powers deserve as much credit as I do."

"You do not do your skills full justice, Watson, and on further consideration I must confess that my assessment of your writing abilities may have been somewhat wide of the mark," he admitted sheepishly. Then he paused for a moment, as if lost in deep thought.

"My dear Watson, although your concern for my welfare is undoubtedly most admirable, one should not lose sight of the fact that the process of actually *caring* is detrimental to the pursuit of pure logical progression," he stated simply.

Naturally I was on the point of raising my objections to Holmes's flagrant dismissal of the virtues of human compassion when, to my surprise, he suddenly expressed an unusual eagerness for his breakfast. When it did finally appear, he devoured his ham and eggs voraciously.

"Nothing quite builds up an appetite like a sound thrashing!" He laughed in acknowledgement of my look of surprise.

"Well, I must confess that I would rather not eat for a week than endure what you have been through," I responded. Holmes dismissed this with an ironic smile.

It was only when the breakfast things had been removed and we were both lighting our cigarettes that Holmes decided to divulge the chain of events that had led to his sorry condition of the evening before.

"As you know, my knowledge of the geography of our beloved city is second to none, so I immediately made for a sector of the East End where I knew a large number of small shops and business premises existed. My research at these establishments revealed two key facts that have since proven to be invaluable. Firstly, I was soon made to realise that the threat posed to these proprietors was very real and that it ran deep. Everyone to whom I spoke expressed a grave fear of even discussing these matters with me, much less providing me with any tangible assistance.

"I was also soon made aware of the fact that the radius of Wilson's influence was far wider than anything that I could have imagined. The dramatic and vivid description of his being 'the black plague' is not so far from the truth. However, this realisation also helped me with my task, because I knew of a small tinker's workshop that is located on the very fringes of Wilson's self-imposed boundaries.

"As you can imagine, I made for this workshop without a moment's delay, and I soon arrived on the door-step of Jacob Dobson, an elderly gentleman with grey sparkling eyes and the heart of a lion. He greeted me with a broad toothless smile and a mug of tea that proved to be as tepid as it was toxic.

"Once I had recovered from my first and only sip of that noxious brew, I explained to Mr. Dobson the intention behind my visit. He was surprisingly agreeable to my scheme, and it was soon agreed that I should stand in his stead that very evening when Wilson's men were due to arrive for their regular payment. He entrusted me with his keys, and I advised him to remain as far away from his workshop as possible for the next forty-eight hours.

"I settled myself down for a long and thankless evening with my only companion, a liberal supply of my old shag. A battered carriage clock, cloaked in a thick layer of metal dust, told me of the slow progress of the evening, but all inclinations for sleep were stifled by the rush of expectation that ran through me.

"That feeling was heightened when the old time piece chimed out the news that it was now eleven o'clock at night – the appointed time of arrival for Wilson's henchmen. A loud single rap upon the back door had

247

alerted me to their punctuality, and I stood up slowly and gingerly in order that I attain the movements of my assumed characterisation.

"Watson, you can imagine their surprise upon finding me standing there, instead of their intended victim, when I did eventually open the door. They pushed passed me with an almighty shove against the wall as they burst in. They immediately demanded to know the whereabouts of 'the other gentlemen'.

"I explained that 'my cousin' had been taken poorly and that he had asked me to meet with them in his stead. To this substitution they did not raise a single word of objection. However, it was a different matter when their demands for payment were met by an empty hand and an abject refusal to pay.

"I told them that the funds would not be available until the following evening, and that if it had been up to me there would have been be no payment forthcoming whatsoever! The results of my lack of funds and those words of bravado were somewhat more painful than I could have anticipated, and I was left lying there in the condition in which you found me."

"Good heavens!" I protested. "Do you have absolutely no regard for your own well-being?"

"What other recourse did I have?" Holmes implored. "After all, in order that I maintain the integrity of my assumed identity, I could hardly resist or fight back. Although in truth, even should I have not been in character, any resistance on my part against such large and formidable foes would undoubtedly have had the same dire and painful outcome.

"I was left in little doubt as to the consequences of any further refusal to pay when these jovial gentlemen dismantled poor Dobson's rear door with just a few blows from their enormous boots! I was also threatened with the honour of meeting Wilson himself on the occasion of their next visit to Dobson's, at midnight tonight."

"But that is barely twelve hours from now!"

"Exactly. I really must get that wire off to Lestrade without a second's delay! Mrs. Hudson!"

As soon as our harassed landlady had bustled off with Holmes's message, my friend requested a full nine hours of quiet and complete rest. As both his friend and doctor, I wholeheartedly approved of that, at least.

At precisely nine o'clock on that very same evening, Holmes finally emerged from his room dressed in his overcoat and hat while brandishing his weight-loaded cane. His transformation had been a remarkable one and his cheery laugh showed me that he viewed our impending adventure with an unjustifiable relish. I touched my revolver reassuringly as it sat securely in my coat pocket.

We were greeted at the street door by our old friend and ally, the cabby, Dave "Gunner" King, who sped us along to the same address that Holmes had already furnished to Lestrade, one among a labyrinth of small side streets that run behind Petticoat Lane. King steered his cab along a narrow, muddy, and uneven alleyway that led us to the rear of Dobson's workshop, our point of rendezvous, before ensuring that he and his vehicle remained out of sight until next called upon.

The damage caused to the door by Holmes's assailants was obvious, although Holmes had subsequently arranged for a makeshift repair to ensure the security of Dobson's premises in his absence.

We synchronised our time pieces and realised that our early arrival gave us the opportunity for a cigarette or two before taking up our positions. Holmes then led Lestrade and me to a dusty old screen behind which we could remain out of sight, although a jagged tear down its centre afforded us a clear view of the remnants of the back door as Holmes had anticipated.

Once Holmes was satisfied with his arrangements, he allowed one of Lestrade's constables to enter with Mr. Dobson, who had been securely escorted from his temporary bolt hole, in time to meet his irrevocable appointment. The genial old man seemed to be surprisingly underwhelmed by the dramatic events that were soon to unfold before him, and he was attentive to every letter of Holmes's detailed instructions.

Holmes's attention to detail was most admirable, and he even counted and then recounted the amount of money that Dobson had brought with him, to ensure that the old man's safety should not be jeopardised by a simple miscalculation. He thought it to be more natural for Dobson to be working on repairs to his backdoor, at the time of Wilson's arrival, rather than having him waiting nervously for him in the dark. Holmes lit a lantern at the rear of the workshop to aid him in this, and also to ensure that Lestrade had a clear view of all that was soon to transpire. Dobson dutifully set to his task while Holmes positioned two more of Lestrade's men in a shadowy doorway on the opposite side of the alley.

By now, the time had crept along to five minutes before midnight and, satisfied with his preparations, Holmes crept over to his position deep within the shadows of the old workshop. Then we waited.

Wilson and his men were agonisingly late and the chimes of midnight were more strident as a consequence of our strained apprehension. Had it not been for the constant tapping of Dobson's hammer upon his door, the silence that followed would have been excruciating. As it was, we all held our stoic stillness and the hands on the old clock seemed to have ground to a halt.

We all hoped that Dobson would keep his nerve and continue with his work, for he had begun to glance anxiously over his shoulder towards Holmes's position as the hour progressed. Finally, at the very moment when I feared that our game was surely up, we were rewarded by the sound of three sets of boots walking slowly and deliberately along the alleyway towards where we were lying in wait.

Dobson continued bravely with his work, right up to the moment that the three shadows appeared in the doorway. Two of the shadows were pretty much as I had imagined them to be – tall, hulking, and ungainly. The third, however, would remain indeterminate until it came within the coverage of the small lantern.

The larger shadows remained at the doorway, but the sight of the third caused in me an involuntary shudder. Never before had I been witness to the very epitome of pure evil. The figure was short and slight, dressed impeccably in a fine mohair coat, a lustrous top hat, and a pair of shoes that shone, despite the dismal light. It says much of a man's nature, however, when he attached far more importance to his outward appearance than he did to his inner sanctity.

Even from my current distance, the stench that wafted from this most disreputable of men was over-powering. His unwashed face and hair were obvious signs of his lack of self-respect and indicative of his priorities. However, it was when he broke into a sinister smile and then spoke that his true nature became manifest. His teeth were black, uneven, and sparse. His eyes were dark and lifeless, and when he spoke, his thin ulcerated lips seeped blood. His voice was surprisingly deep, guttural and full of mucous.

"Ah, Mr. Dobson, I am glad to see that you are well again, and that you have removed your idiotic cousin from our little business transaction." Then Wilson's voice changed suddenly and horrendously, almost into a hellish shriek. "He was lucky to have escaped with his life, and so are you!"

Dobson dropped his hammer and took several steps back, so shocked was he by Wilson's unfeasible transformation, but he held his nerve, knowing full well that we could not yet make our move.

"Let me now make matters as clear to you as I possibly can, Mr. Dobson, in order that there should be no future ambiguity or misunderstanding between the two of us, of course," Wilson continued in his higher octave.

"You should be glad to know that the arrangements between us will continue exactly as before. There shall be no punishment levied, despite your unforgivable behaviour. However, should you ever try to trick me again, I assure you that your life will never be the same. My colleagues outside are more than capable of levelling this place to the ground with just a few well-placed blows. Even were you able to return your trade to its nomadic roots, I am sure that your skills would be harder to employ were you to be without both of your hands!" The pitch of Wilson's voice reached a crescendo, and one could almost hear Dobson's voice crying out for help. Mercifully, he maintained his silence.

Wilson clicked his fingers and the two lumbering forms moved forward and through the doorway. He laughed manically and then held his hand out threateningly towards the quivering Dobson.

"So, Mr. Dobson, as you have probably realised, it is now time for you to hand me my money," he invited with an odious smile. Our vigilance had been rewarded at last, and I sensed Lestrade's hand move slowly towards his revolver, an action that mirrored my own.

Each man was ready to pounce at a moment's notice and we were attentive to each of Dobson's movements. As Dobson's money passed from hand to hand, Lestrade signalled his men with a short blast from his whistle and they crossed the alley in a second.

Wilson's curses were violent and unrepeatable, and he wrapped his right hand around Dobson's throat with a manic delight.

"One more move from any one of you and I assure you that I would not hesitate for an instant in choking the life out of this imbecile!" Wilson declared, and there was not one of us who did not believe him.

We all stood our ground and replaced our guns, but at that moment a scuffle that had ensued outside between the constables and one of Wilson's henchmen exploded unexpectedly into the workshop. One of the constables was hurled through the shattered doorway and collided violently with Wilson's legs. His grip on Dobson's neck was immediately released, and we moved towards him with our guns at the ready.

One of Wilson's men was stupid enough to rush towards us, and Lestrade brought him down with a single shot. The other made a bolt for it down the alley, but with both constables in immediate pursuit. The result of this chase was inevitable – not least because King had pulled up his cab at the opposite end of the alley.

Wilson's resistance was over and he held up his clasped hands in anticipation of Lestrade's handcuffs. The inspector did not hesitate for a second in applying them to him.

"Well, well, my old adversary, Inspector Lestrade! You have finally undone me, but not without a little help I fancy, eh?" Wilson jerked his head towards a movement in the shadows and my friend finally made himself known. "I should have known that you were neither brave enough nor intelligent enough to have devised this scheme for yourself. I congratulate you, Mr. Sherlock Holmes!" Wilson cackled.

"I have never felt less deserving of congratulations, I assure you. There is no less noble a task than bringing down a creature such as you." Holmes spat out these words in disgust and he turned on his heels as Wilson was being led away.

"It is a waste of time, Mr. Holmes. You must already know that I shall be back before very long."

"I think you will find that we have more than enough reliable and willing witnesses on this occasion. I will see to it that you shall never see the light of day again," Holmes declared with a dismissive wave of his hand.

As the hapless Wilson was being dragged unceremoniously from the room, I noticed Lestrade walk towards Holmes with an outstretched hand.

"Thank you, Mr. Holmes." he said simply. "This time you have sacrificed and risked much in your pursuit of justice, and in doing so, you have eliminated a dark entity from our streets once and for all."

The effects of the last few days finally took their toll on my friend and, once Lestrade had left the room, Holmes let out a deep sigh and leaned against the dank wall for support. Fortunately King's cab pulled up outside at that moment, and between us we helped Holmes climb aboard.

The journey back to Baker Street was completed in silence and Holmes was asleep within an instant. However, it was gratifying to observe that he had fallen into unconsciousness with a smile of satisfaction upon his wounded and sallow face.

In this memorable year '95, a curious and incongruous succession of cases had engaged his attention, ranging . . . down to his arrest of Wilson, the notorious canary-trainer, which removed a plague-spot from the East-End of London.

Dr. John H. Watson – "The Adventure of Black Peter"

Vigor, the
Hammersmith Wonder
by Mike Hogan

I arrived at 221b Baker Street on a blustery day in January after a successful shopping trip in which I had spent an extravagant (for me) amount of money on a new, high-crowned, curved-rim bowler hat in the very latest style. I justified my purchase as a late, or very early, Christmas present for myself, and a gesture to take my mind off the depressing news on the screaming newspaper placards.

I divested myself of my overcoat and umbrella and admired my new purchase in the hall mirror for what would have been an embarrassing length of time if I'd been observed, before I hung the bowler reverently on the rack where Holmes could not fail to spot it. I clambered up the stairs with my other purchases – a new shaving brush, a pad of letter paper, and the latest *British Medical Journal* – in a packet under my arm.

I had my hand on the door knob of the sitting room when I heard a murmur of voices on the other side. I turned to continue up to my bedroom on the next floor, intending to slip off my shoes, lie back on my bed in comfort, and take my ease with my *Journal*.

The sitting-room door sprang open and Holmes beamed at me. "Watson, I knew your tread on the stairs. (Come in for pity's sake and rescue me)."

Holmes took my arm and all but propelled me into the room, in which a man in clergyman's weeds sat on our sofa, blinking at us. He stood, and Holmes introduced him as Reverend Martindale, Vicar of the St. Matthew's Church in the village of Cussop Dingle on the River Wye in the West Country.

We shook hands, and Holmes insisted that I join him and his guest to hear the intriguing story Reverend Martindale had been relating.

"Since breakfast time," he murmured in my ear.

I remained standing. "As a matter of fact, gentlemen, I have several matters – "

An imperative gesture from Holmes silenced me, and with a sigh I laid my packet on the table and sat in my usual place in front of our crackling fire.

Reverend Martindale took a breath, but Holmes held up an admonitory hand.

"Allow me to summarise, sir, so that I may confirm that I have a complete grasp of the facts of the case." Holmes took his client's consent as given, and he began.

"Two months ago, Myrtle Cottage, a property on the edge of the village of Cussop Dingle usually rented to summer visitors, was occupied by a gentleman and his young nephew. They were Dutch – Vincent van den Hoorn, and the boy, Klaas."

"I passed the cottage on my bicycle a day or so after they moved in, Doctor," Reverend Martindale said, turning to me, "and I heard Klaas singing in a sweet treble and playing the piano with great facility. I entreated him to join my choir. We were short of – "

Holmes again held up his hand. "Reverend Martindale visited his new neighbours as a matter of courtesy and to invite them to join the congregation of St. Matthew's. Mr. van den Hoorn regretfully declined, citing religious scruples."

"The van den Hoorns attended neither the Methodist nor Baptist chapels in Hay-on-Wye, our nearest town," Reverend Martindale added. "I thought our new neighbours might be Calvinists, or even Zwinglians. And there are even more arcane and exclusive religious communities in Holland to which they may have adhered."

Holmes smiled a tight smile. "Reverend Martindale was able to supply Mr. van den Hoorn with the names of local women who would do the cooking, housekeeping, and laundry for the pair, and an introduction to the blacksmith, Mr. Tulliver, at whose livery they rented a horse and bought a pony."

Holmes stood and helped himself to a cigar from my pack on the mantel. "During the short time they resided in the cottage, the van den Hoorns were polite but kept themselves to themselves, and did not settle into the life of the village. Mr. van den Hoorn was a very well-set-up man in his mid-thirties, muscular to the point of caricature, who spent inordinate amounts of time in the cottage garden swinging Indian clubs and flinging them and other heavy objects into the air and catching them.

"His doings were the source of speculation among the females of the village, particularly the post-mistress and her cronies at the village shop – the centre of rumour and gossip, as in every village. The general opinion was, judging by the quantity of best steak delivered to the cottage by the housekeeper, Mrs. Rudge, and the lack of evidence of a wife, that Mr. van den Hoorn was a gentleman of means, and that he was available. A prime catch for the village maidens and widows."

"I say, Mr. Holmes," the vicar expostulated, "I made no such inference."

Holmes smiled. "Reverend Martindale's choir met for practice on Wednesday afternoons. On a particular afternoon in December, a group of choirboys were *en route* to the church when as they passed over a small bridge, Klaas came towards them on his pony. The boy was not part of the church community, he had no status in the village, and he was considered by his peers to be foreign, snooty, and, because of his slight physique and auburn curls, a sissy."

Reverend Martindale sighed. "My wife invited Klaas to tea at the vicarage with several of the village boys, hoping to engender an acquaintance and possibly friendship, but it did not answer. Our boys are a rough and tumble crew, and Klaas was perhaps too nice in his manners."

"On the bridge, words were exchanged between the boy and the gang, particularly their leader Will Tulliver, easily recognised by his unruly blond hair – "

"Will is the son of our blacksmith, a widower, and he and his father are the only fair-haired persons in the village," Reverend Martindale explained. "Until Mr. Hoorn arrived, Mr. Tulliver was considered our local epitome of manly beauty and muscular development." He turned to Holmes. "I say, sir, I cannot accept your use of the term 'gang' with regard to my choir."

"Words were exchanged," Holmes continued, "and as Klaas trotted past on his pony, ignoring the choirboys, one of them picked up a stone and threw it, hitting and alarming the pony. Two more did likewise, and then, hit by a final stone, the pony reared, unseating his rider onto the verge beside the bridge. The horse bolted, and the choirboys ran off to the church, laughing and hooting, leaving Klaas on the grass."

"I interpreted the boys' excitement as pre-Christmas high spirits," Reverend Martindale said sadly. "It was a few days before the feast."

Holmes stood and scrabbled along the mantel for his pipe. "And there we have it, Doctor." He gave me a despairing look as he packed his pipe with tobacco.

"An unprovoked attack," I suggested. "And dashed unsporting at several against one, even if the other boys did not participate in the ragging. I suppose the unsatisfactory ending to the Boer War some years ago and recent news of mistreatment of English women and children by Boers in the Transvaal has made anyone with a Germanic taint a target. Then the Kaiser sent his telegram congratulating the Boers on repelling Dr. Jameson's raid on Johannesburg! German businesses in London have had their windows smashed, and Dutch sailors in the Port of London – "

I looked up and reddened as I saw Holmes and Reverend Martindale

255

looking at me. "The Dutch accent is very like the Afrikaans," I suggested meekly.

"Perhaps I should continue, gentlemen?" Reverend Martindale asked.

Holmes frowned. "I'm not at all sure how I might be able to assist you in this matter, Reverend Martindale. I do not mean to appear self-promoting, but I owe it to myself to inform you that my cases are usually of a more substantial character than a scuffle between schoolboys. Could not their fathers deal with the matter in the usual way, with a belt or hairbrush?"

Reverend Martindale sniffed. "Perhaps I should have mentioned earlier, Mr. Holmes and Doctor Watson, that the matter on which I seek your advice is of graver moment than a mere scuffle. The boy Tulliver may face a very serious charge. Scotland Yard is on the case."

Holmes folded himself into his chair and lit his pipe. "Do go on."

Reverend Martindale clasped his hands together as he collected his thoughts. "The following morning the housekeeper went as usual to Myrtle Cottage to deliver groceries and make the breakfast. She found a note on the kitchen door requesting her to tidy and clean the cottage, then lock it up until further notice. The keys were on the kitchen table amid a mess of bowls and blood-stained bandages. More soiled bandages and towels were on the bathroom floor, and blood stained the sink. Drawers lay open in the bedrooms, but most of Mr. Hoorn's and his nephew's clothes were still in the cupboards, suggesting their absence would be short-lived. Klaas's pony was in the back yard, but Mr. Hoorn's horse, an unusually strong beast to suit his physique, was missing."

Reverend Martindale sighed. "And that was the situation until a week ago. Nothing had been seen or heard of the van den Hoorns."

I stood. "Reverend, may I offer tea, or perhaps something stronger?" I indicated the Tantalus on the sideboard.

"Tea would be most welcome in fact."

I called downstairs to Billy and ordered a pot of tea and whatever we had in the way of biscuits. When I returned to my seat, Holmes was questioning the vicar.

"I interrogated the boys," Reverend Martindale answered. "After some dissimulation on Will Tulliver's part, I discovered that he was the instigator of the assault. He threw both the first stone and the last stone that unseated Klaas."

Reverend Martindale shook his head. "You must understand, gentlemen, that ours is a quiet village. We are unused to violence of any description. Our genial and neighbourly atmosphere had already been affected to a considerable degree by the rivalry the local men felt for the

256

muscular newcomer who seemed to be the object of several ladies' interest – I say *ladies* advisedly, as some are of an age to know very much better."

"Was there any evidence that Mr. van den Hoorn appreciated their attentions, or responded to any particular lady?" Holmes asked.

"None."

"So, the local ladies were in a flutter," Holmes said, "and their swains were jealous of Mr. van Hoorn's manly attributes. The blacksmith's son may have picked up on his father's disdain for the newcomers, in which case the police may have grounds to allege premeditation in the assault."

Billy brought in the tray, and I helped him serve tea and buttered bread. He closed the door behind him, and Holmes gestured for Reverend Martindale to continue.

"The village was in a state of tension for a week until we received word from the housekeeper that Myrtle Cottage was again occupied. I hurried there and found a knot of villagers in the lane gawping at a line of carriages drawn up outside the cottage. The first was a hired carriage from the station at Hay, the second a fine doctor's brougham, and the last an official van with a police constable standing beside it.

"I made myself and my position known to the constable, who would neither answer my enquiries nor allow me to knock at the door of the cottage. I asked him to inform Mr. Hoorn that I had called and ask whether I might return at two in the afternoon and speak with him."

Reverend Martindale sipped his tea, dabbing his lips with his handkerchief with a prim gesture. "At ten to two, I found Mr. Tulliver and his son with the two other boys implicated in the matter and their fathers waiting outside the rectory. They insisted on accompanying me to Myrtle Cottage, where we were ushered into the sitting room by the constable.

"In the room, Mr. Hoorn and another gentleman who the policeman whispered to me was a Scotland Yard detective were huddled at a table, poring over a stack of papers. As we made to approach them, a very elegant gentleman in a frockcoat came down the stairs and, ignoring us, joined Mr. Hoorn and the inspector. The constable whispered that he was a Harley Street brain specialist. From the doctor's face and demeaner and the reaction of Mr. Hoorn, he clearly carried no welcome news of the boy. The constable confirmed that Klaas was in grave condition and that he had made a statement naming his attackers.

"The doctor broke off his discussion and returned upstairs and Mr. Hoorn faced me, but he did not take my proffered hand. The inspector stood by the table, saying nothing. On my gesture, Mr. Tulliver and the

257

other two fathers, and then the boys (who were in floods of tears) apologised for the incident. Mr. Hoorn said not a word, neither accepting nor rejecting the apologies. He nodded assent when I requested permission to visit Klaas."

"More tea?" I offered.

"No, thank you." Reverend Martindale sighed again. "The boy's head was swathed in bandages, and he was unconscious. A tall cross had been fixed over his bedhead, and candles in brass holders stood on either side of the bed. The doctor looked up when I entered the bedroom and slowly shook his head."

Our visitor related how the three fathers and boys had visited the sickroom, knelt and prayed for Klaas's recovery, and how daily services had been held at his church in the week since that day, attended by almost the whole village.

"The sick child has been in the cottage for a week?" I asked.

"No, Doctor. The day after my visit, the cottage was vacated. I learned from the housekeeper that the boy had died in his uncle's arms during the night."

Reverend Martindale put down his teacup with a shaking hand. "A Sword of Damocles has hung over our village since that terrible day. We are split into acrimonious factions, blaming or supporting Tulliver or Mr. Hoorn. The choir has disbanded."

"You have had no contact with the police?" I asked.

"None."

"Did the fathers of the boys involved not seek legal advice?" Holmes asked.

"Only Tulliver. His solicitor told him to say and do nothing until contacted by Scotland Yard."

"Have you any way to trace Mr. van den Hoorn?" Holmes asked. "Was he a professional man in his dress and deportment, and have you an idea of his avocation?"

"None." Reverend Martindale frowned. "Perhaps I am old-fashioned, and I have obviously not kept up with fashions in the metropolis, but – well, I hardly like to comment on someone so cruelly wronged by our village."

Holmes waved an indulgent hand.

"His dress was a little bright for village tastes, perhaps a touch loud."

"Flash?" Holmes asked.

Reverend Martindale nodded. "And his nephew was also somewhat foppish, thus provoking the boys."

Holmes tapped his pipe stem against his lip in a characteristic gesture. "One last question. Has anyone come to the village asking about the incident? Reporters perhaps, or detectives?"

"Three days ago, two men arrived at Cussop Dingle and identified themselves as private investigators hired by the van den Hoorn family," Reverend Martindale answered. "They took statements from me and from other witnesses. The detectives had marked Dutch accents and, despite the general grief in the village, owing to a prejudice against Boers and to the unfortunate news from the Transvaal, they were not well received. It was at that point that I determined to seek your advice, Mr. Holmes. Mr. Tulliver placed fifty sovereigns in my hands, which I hope will cover fees and so on." Reverend Martindale laid a small leather bag on the table beside his teacup.

Holmes stood. "I have your card, and I will contact you as soon as I have news to impart. Good afternoon." The vicar was swept to the sitting room door.

I intervened and volunteered to accompany Reverend Martindale to the omnibus.

Holmes was lounging in his chair by the fire smoking his pipe when I returned. He blew a stream of smoke across the room. "I came to my conclusions at ten-to-twelve, and only waited for Reverend Martindale to leave us to fill in the blanks with names."

"You have some clues?"

"I have a strong suspicion of the who and I have a notion of the how, but not quite yet the why." Holmes tamped his pipe with a finger. "How likely is it, in your medical opinion, Doctor, that a boy falling from a pony in the manner described by the vicar would suffer death?"

I considered. "Unlikely, but certainly possible."

"He fell onto the grass verge."

"True. But you and I both know how fragile the human body is in certain circumstances and unexpectedly robust in others. Klaas was evidently a slight child. If I were questioned in a court of law, I would maintain a firm opinion that the fall could have resulted in Klaas's death, assuming the medical evidence on the injury supported that conclusion."

I frowned. "And what of the blood and the eminent brain surgeon? And the police inspector? Scotland Yard will surely investigate the matter as a murder inquiry!"

"Will they so?"

"There are puzzling factors," I suggested. "Why has there been no official presence in the village? The coroner must have been informed of an assault resulting in death, so why have the police not instigated enquiries among the villagers?"

259

Holmes threw me one of the morning newspapers, folded to the advertisements. "If Reverend Martindale decides to prolong his stay in London and visit the *Temple of Varieties* in Hammersmith on Saturday, he might solve the case by himself." He leaned back in his chair. "Call down for luncheon, would you, old man? Then I invite you to join me at the music hall."

Our cab stopped outside the ornate façade of the *Temple of Varieties* music hall in King Street, Hammersmith. The doors of the theatre were plastered with notices indicating that the building was under new management and that it would re-open the following Saturday, in three days' time. A billboard promised Vigor the Hammersmith Wonder as the star attraction.

Holmes and I gave our names to a page, and after a short wait we were shown through a grand vestibule ornamented with colourful tiles, and then around the left side of the auditorium along a wide corridor decorated in a chaste design of nymphs in cracked and peeling cream and gold. Dusty gas chandeliers hung from the ceiling, and matching wall sconces adorned the walls. I peeked through the entrances to the auditorium as we passed and saw that the *fauteuils* of the Pit-stalls and Stalls were upholstered in faded ruby velvet, harmonising with the threadbare Brussels carpet.

We passed through an iron door on one side of the stage, up several flights of steps to the office floor, and then to the door to the chairman's room. The page knocked and passed us into an elegantly appointed room decorated in the club style which had clearly seen better days.

A pale, flabby gentleman whose considerable paunch was covered by a broad-cut frockcoat and whose neck was adorned with a flamboyant cravat sat behind a mahogany desk. He heaved himself partly out of his chair and, craving our indulgence, subsided with a moue of discomfort.

"Mr. Holmes and Doctor Watson, how good to see you again. I do apologise for not greeting you properly. I suffer from a twinge in my lumbar regions, which have not been the same since I made the mistake of attempting to separate a trio of 'Flying Verinas' quarrelling with a quartet of Chinese jugglers. I imbibe *Chlorodyne*, Doctor, in heroic doses, but it does not answer."

"Anything over a half-teaspoonful may be injurious," I suggested.

A growl came from Holmes as he sat in one of two mismatched guest chairs pulled up to the gentleman's desk. "I do not believe Mr. Pargeter requested a medical consultation."

260

I instantly recalled Mr. Pargeter, the owner of a small and rather sleazy waxworks, whom Holmes and I had met in a case several years before. I smiled a greeting and sat in the second chair.

"I do beg your pardon, Mr. Holmes," Mr. Pargeter answered. He settled carefully against his seat back. "I am so happy to see you, gentlemen. I have no doubt that you are here at the instigation of our stage manager, who has been running me wretched over the past week, insisting that I lay the matter before you. My reluctance was obviously not the result of any lack of faith in your abilities, sir, but a sense of doubt as to the importance of the matter. I know that you only deal with affairs of the very highest moment."

"I'm not sure I understand, Mr. Pargeter," I suggested. "Mr. Holmes and I are here – "

Holmes laid a hand on my arm and gestured for Mr. Pargeter to continue.

"Perhaps I might begin with a brief survey of my business, which has changed greatly in recent years."

Holmes muttered what I took to be assent, and Mr. Pargeter began his story.

"When we met in '87, gentlemen, I was the sorry possessor of a single wax museum off the Ratcliffe Highway in Limehouse. You will recall that my circumstances were so reduced that my prime exhibit was the death of General Gordon of Khartoum." He sighed. "I shame to admit that business faltered to such an extent in the following year that I fell back on that old chestnut, the Death of Nelson and Kiss me Hardy."

Mr. Pargeter shook his head in chagrin, and then smiled. "However, since then, I have, in a limited way and within my station in life, flourished. I would pat myself on the back and laud my business acumen, but I must admit that my success was absolutely and entirely due to – "

"Jack the Ripper," Holmes said with a sniff.

Mr. Pargeter beamed. "Exactly so, sir. The events of the autumn of 1888, although regrettable from the point of view of the distressed ladies and general public order, were a catalyst (if I may use a scientific term, Doctor?), that brought about a flowering of public interest in murder and mayhem. Oh, forgive me, gentlemen. May I offer you some refreshment?"

I politely refused on our behalf, and Mr. Pargeter continued.

"I should explain that at the apex of our waxworks business is Madame Tussaud's Museum, who pride themselves on the exactitude of the likenesses of the celebrated persons they mould in wax.

"Unencumbered by Madame T's dependence on verisimilitude, I was able to exhibit a likeness of the Whitechapel murderer despite the lack or confusion of evidence. In fact, my modest claim to fame in the affair was my depiction of Jack as a gentleman in a topper and cape and carrying a shiny Gladstone bag in which his dread utensils were concealed.

"My conception of the fiend caught the imagination of the public, and my tableaux of the murders as they occurred, one by one through the dark summer-autumn season from August to early November of that fatal year, attracted record crowds in a most perfect run up to Christmas. You will recall, gentlemen, that interest in the murders was intense, and the Ripper's dramatic displays of gore, his teasing letters to the press and police, intensified that interest into an insatiable thirst for – "

"Blood," said Holmes.

Mr. Pargeter beamed again. "Since then, although we have had a dearth of murders of *quality*, I may surprise you, Mr. Holmes and Doctor Watson, when I say that I now own six waxworks, three north and three (regrettably from the takings point-of-view) south of the river."

"May we come to the point, Mr. Pargeter?" I asked, sensing Holmes growing impatience.

"I have taken the freehold of the *Temple of Varieties*, one of the premier music halls in the city – well, at least in the suburbs – as my first venture into the halls. I flatter myself that I know the waxworks and tableaux business. I know what the public want. I aim to combine the usual fare of the halls with a touch of drama and a thrill of horror."

"A fine old hall," I said.

"And?" Holmes snapped.

"It is kind of you in the extreme to make an effort on my behalf," Mr. Pargeter answered. "Needless to say, I will make it worth your while, Mr. Holmes, in the sum of a hundred guineas, in gold."

I frowned. "What exactly is your problem?"

Mr. Pargeter blinked at me. "We open on Saturday, and I am without my premier act."

He unrolled a coloured poster featuring an immensely muscled strong man with centre-parted hair and a waxed moustache whose arm muscles rippled under a scarlet jerkin and whose legs bulged in white tights. He lifted a chair high above his head on which a very personable young lady sat in a dress that exposed her ankles, and with his other arm he held up a cage in which a huge lion roared.

I stroked my moustache. The lady was quite remarkably pretty.

Holmes glanced at the poster and waved it away.

"'*Vigor the Hammersmith Wonder*'," I read in lurid text. "'*And the Wandsworth Warbler, Miss Arabella LeBeau*'."

262

"The lady and gentleman took a cottage in the country while legal and financial arrangements were being made regarding the change of ownership of the *Temple*," Mr. Pargeter said. "They should have returned here for rehearsals. Vigor and Arabella have been missing for a week. I am at my wits' end."

"Kindly give the details to Doctor Watson." Holmes stood. "Are Vigor and Miss Arabella of Dutch extraction?"

"No, Mr. Holmes, but Arabella has a slight Cape Colony accent that, in these troubled times, she modifies to Scotch. She was born in Johannesburg, and I believe her family reside there. I hope they were not discommoded by recent events. Vigor was born Armend Vigor, anglicised to Albert Vigor, and he is originally from Albania. He affects a generic European accent at press interviews as very few people know of his homeland."

I requested the full names of the missing man and woman, the address of their lodgings, and the places and dates on which they had last been seen. Mr. Pargeter suggested that George, his stage manager, could best answer me and describe the habits of the missing artistes. He mentioned that the cast were assembled for rehearsals that afternoon and would be at the theatre every day until the grand opening in three days' time.

I stood and bid Mr. Pargeter farewell. Holmes waved a languid hand and followed me to the door, then turned. "Did you hire any other investigators to find Vigor and Miss le Beau?"

"I did not." Mr. Pargeter shook his head. "I do not understand it, Mr. Holmes. Vigor is on the cusp of national acclaim and considerable revenues. An American advertising firm hired him to advocate a new breakfast food, offering two-hundred pounds a year and royalties on every box consumed."

"Two-hundred a year, just to use his name? A significant sum," I suggested.

Mr. Pargeter mopped his brow with his handkerchief. "We open on Saturday, willy or nilly, as they say. Without Vigor and Miss Arabella, I shall be the laughing stock of the profession, booed to the rafters by a ravening mob."

"Missing circus strong men and Watford Warblers. Ha!" Holmes said as we followed the page downstairs. "My last missing persons case concerned a royal duke and an imperial duchess. What next? '*Lost:* '*Tiddles*', *Tortoise. Last seen on the roof of 221b Baker Street*'?"

"This strikes me as a wholly legitimate case," I said. "Mr. Pargeter's business will be ruined if the star performers are not on stage for the opening night on Saturday. He offers a perfectly respectable hundred-guinea fee and he deserves the courtesy of your best efforts on his behalf. Just because your finances are in a better condition than they have been for several years – "

"Very well." Holmes rubbed his hands together. "The vicar's case is solved, and a new case opens."

I paused on the stairs and smiled a smug smile. "I believe Reverend Martindale's Klaas was, in actual fact, the Watford Warbler."

"Do you say so?" Holmes cried. "Then could it be that Mr. van den Hoorn is none other than the Hammersmith Wonder?"

I folded my arms across my chest. "You may make as much fun of me as you want, Holmes – "

"Go on, what else?"

"I believe Miss LeBeau died in the accident at Cussop Dingle, and Mr. Vigor is sequestered somewhere, mad with grief."

"I'm sure you are quite right, my dear fellow." Holmes snapped his fingers at the page. "Take us to Mr. George."

The boy chuckled, but he conducted us through the door to the auditorium and to the front row of the Stalls. He indicated a flamboyant figure with a mop of blond curls wearing red-and-white striped tights and a fluffy, white waistcoat who sat in the centre of the row just below the stage, smoking a pipe. I was flabbergasted when George stood to shake our hands and I observed that the stage manager was, notwithstanding the pipe, very obviously from her uxorious figure, a woman.

"Don't bother yourselves with the Watford Warbler," George said after Holmes and I had introduced ourselves. "Arabella is a lady of fervent charm that she spreads generously abroad, but with a small voice and little sense of stagecraft. Vigor paid to have her voice professionally trained, with the result that she is now in tune, but still ineffectual." A dismissive wave of George's thick arm released a cloud of pungent perfume. "She cannot command an audience, gentlemen. Frankly, she is kept merely for her lover's convenience."

"Does Miss Arabella appear with Mr. Vigor?" I asked.

"She does. Vigor will not dance, but he is willing to sway in time with the music. He agreed to the addition of Arabella, who twirls around him while he heaves up various objects. That is how they met. She is a slender girl who amplifies his muscular presence. For his finale, Vigor lifts a chair with Arabella seated on it in one hand, and a piano in the other. Arabella plays a pretty tune on the piano and the curtains close and then open again for numerous curtain calls. Vigor has a large and vociferous following among ladies who admire his manly beauty and curled moustachios."

"A piano? Not a lion?" I asked.

"Animals, no, no. They and children are always trouble." George shuddered. "The lion and cage on our poster are artistic licence, gentlemen, but the depictions of Vigor and Arabella are, within the conventions of the advertising form, exact."

George leaned towards me in another cloud of perfume that tickled my nose. "Vigor is a remarkable performer. He once held Arabella and the piano up for seven curtain calls. Without Vigor, the *Temple's* reputation is in the hands of birdsong imitators and tramp comedians. We thought to contact Chang the Chinese Giant as a substitute, but he is engaged elsewhere. Our last hope is that Mr. D'Oyly Carte will allow us to stage 'With Cat-like Tread' from *The Pirates of Penzance*. We have the pirate and comic policemen costumes left over from a pantomime."

"Could you give us an impression of the performances of Mr. Vigor and Miss Arabella?" I asked.

"Barbells, Indian clubs, tossing a Chubb safe, and finally the piano and Arabella." George shrugged. "We can replace her with one of the chorus line, and good riddance. But don't mistake her, gentlemen. The Watford Warbler is a forceful woman – no blushing violet, she – and Albert is a gentle giant and much put upon."

On Holmes request, I noted the address of Vigor and Arabella's lodgings and enquired about relatives and associates.

"Her people are in South Africa," George said. "Albert's mother resides in a villa in Ruislip. I telegraphed her, but she returned that she had not seen her son recently."

I noted the address, then turned to Holmes and found an empty space beside me. I caught a glimpse of his coattails as he swept out of the room with the page trotting behind him.

I caught up with them outside a dressing room labelled with a faded star and the legend "*Miss LeBeau, the Watford Warbler*". The boy stood beside the open door flicking and catching a sixpence.

Wardrobes full of frilly costumes and a mirrored dressing table covered with jars, bottles, and cosmetic sticks took up most of the room.

"That stage manager, Holmes!" I exclaimed.

"A rather cultured lady. Did you notice Diderot's *Promenade du sceptique* open and face down on the seat beside her?" He peered at a photograph of an arid landscape fixed to the wall, then picked up a book. "*Through the Kalahari Desert, a Journey to Lake N'gami and Back,* by G. A. Farini."

I frowned, "Farini? I know that name."

"Come." Holmes directed the page to show us Mr. Vigor's dressing room.

His was a larger room with a wide armchair before a neatly arranged dressing table. Two brightly coloured, framed posters were fixed to the wall. One was identical to the poster we had been shown by Mr. Pargeter, the other depicted Vigor against an Egyptian themed backdrop. He was dressed as a pharaoh, holding up a pyramid in one hand and a massive bowl of what looked like porridge in the other.

Holmes peered at a line of print along the bottom of the poster. "*The Quaker Oat Company of Ravenna, Ohio. London agents, McQuarrie and Gordon, 110 The Strand.*"

Holmes swept out and led me back the way we had come and outside the theatre. He accosted the uniformed commissionaire smoking under the theatre canopy, introduced himself, and elicited the commissionaire's name.

"What of the stage-door johnnies, Mr. Barker? Did any of them exhibit a particular interest in Miss LeBeau?"

Mr. Barker considered. "She's not a broad lady if you get my meaning," he answered, making a vulgar gesture with his hands, "I like 'em with a bit more body, something you can get your hands on, get a grip like. But each to his own is my motto, and Arabella has a following among them with more petite tastes."

"Was there a particular young man, or older man for that matter, who had a yen for her?"

Mr. Barker considered as the stub of his cigarette burned down to his hand. I was about to warn him when he answered. "The Captain."

"A military gentleman?" I asked.

Mr. Barker flicked the stub aside and drew himself erect. "A h'officer and a gentleman. Navy, as I understand, sir. God bless 'em."

"Indeed." Holmes passed Mr. Barker a coin, and while they murmured together for a few moments, I bought an afternoon paper from a boy shouting "Special edition!" over a placard screaming "*Kaiser Telegram Outrage Latest!*" in blood-red letters.

I flicked through the newspaper and found that the placard was technically correct – the Kaiser had sent a telegram of congratulations to the Boers of the Transvaal for their successful repulse of a British "invasion" of their territory, and a huge number of people of all ranks of society were expressing outrage at the His Imperial Majesty's unwelcome interference in British colonial affairs. In my opinion, the news that we were all annoyed with the Kaiser hardly rated a penny for a special edition.

Holmes jumped aboard our waiting hansom, calling "London Road, the Borough!" to the cabby. I leapt in beside him as the cab moved off.

266

"I run a Christian house," Mrs. Wills, the owner of Mr. Vigor and Miss Arabella's guest house assured us. "But, unlike many a landlady, I do not demand to see marriage lines – I'd lose half my show folk custom else. I make no provision with regard to liaisons, always assuming the proprieties are observed. A couple declaring they are married may take a room together and share a Christian bed, if of clean habits. I am a Blue Ribboned abstinent, gentlemen, and I will allow no alcohol nor bad language on the premises."

She tapped a finger against her nose and continued in a confidential tone. "Now, you may make a fuss if you like, but married or not, I never saw a more devoted spouse than Mr. Vigor. Anything Arabella wants, Arabella gets. Pearl necklace, agate choker, dresses galore – poor Mr. Vigor throws his money at the girl."

"Did Arabella hint at a possible augmentation to the couples' financial position?" I asked.

Mrs. Wills blinked at me.

"Did Arabella say she had money coming?" Holmes translated.

"Hint! She shouted it from the rooftops! How they were going to be rich on account of some oatmeal come from America, and she would move to a house in Belgravia with a carriage-and-four and servants galore. Hint? She trumpeted at Jericho. It was her only topic of conversation at the supper table."

Mrs. Wills sniffed. "I'm used to big talk among the show people, but her going on and on in that shrill voice of hers and grating accent, it spoiled my lodgers' appetite. Mr. McCarthy, the tramp comedian, said she sounded like the Kaiser after a nasty accident. He's a card, is Mr. McCarthy, a hoot and make no mistake!"

Mrs. Wills leaned in close to Holmes and me. "Between us and the bedpost, gentlemen, some might say Mr. V was too devoted to his beloved to see what was going on in front of his nose, and that Arabella was no better than she should be with a certain Navy party." She pursed her lips. "But we all have our little peccadilioes, tiny faults that mar the perfection that is only obtainable through devotion to Him."

I followed Mrs. Wills gaze to the ceiling of the room, on which a crude depiction of the Creation was daubed.

"Mr. Wills," she said in a rapturous tone.

I gaped at her.

"Not devotion to Mr. Wills, silly," Mrs. Wills screeched, slapping my arm. "Mr. Wills painted the ceiling after a picture in *Tit-Bits* of a ceiling somewhere foreign." She blessed herself and looked up, her hands clasped in prayer. "Devotion to *Him*."

"Our picture of the couple is fleshed out," I said as Holmes and I emerged from the lodging house into the London Road. "Although of great physical strength, Vigor is the very paradigm of a henpecked husband. Arabella rules the roost. No doubt it was she who insisted on a house in the country to which the couple might repair during the refurbishment of the music hall. There, she presented herself to the inhabitants of Cussop Dingle as a boy. Why? A whim? We know that in the topsy-turvy world of the halls, men dress as women and vice-versa, but why continue the pretence in public?"

Holmes hailed a cab.

"What of her death?" I said as we settled inside. "Could Vigor have been responsible, taking advantage of the injury?"

"What a suspicious mind you have," said Holmes. "And we have another port of call: I had the *Temple* doorman telegraph from the post office."

"I am more than usually confused by this case," I admitted. "Or cases rather."

"Even after the reverend's description of the visit of the Dutch detectives to Cussop Dingle?"

I frowned at Holmes. "Yes."

Holmes and I sat opposite Mr. Gordon, partner in the London agency for Quaker Oats, a sharp-featured, heavily built young man who lolled in a swivel chair behind his desk in the small and dusty office of the agency. Jars of what I presumed were oats and stacks of coloured boxes stood on shelves behind him.

"Our innovation is this," Mr. Gordon said in a marked American twang. He held up a box about eight inches by six featuring the brightly coloured illustration of Mr. Vigor in Egyptian garb.

"What does the box contain?" I asked.

"Oats." Mr. Gordon shrugged, "Previously you had to buy a scoop of oats from an open barrel or sack at the grocer's, with all the sanitary risks involved – insects and other contaminants. We offer a sealed packet of oats mixture, packed by white women of a Quaker character under the most hygienic conditions."

He smiled. "The image of a Quaker we use in the United States would not do here, particularly not in wartime – and when is it not wartime somewhere within the British Empire? The papers suggest that Her Imperial Majesty of Great Britain will soon be at war with the Kaiser of the German Empire, her grandson."

Mr. Gordon picked up a copy of *The Times*. "'*England will concede nothing to menaces*' *The Times* thunders, '*and will not lie down under insult.*'"

"We must hope that it doesn't come to that," I said with a sniff. "If the Kaiser apologises for sending congratulations to the Boers for repulsing Dr. Jameson's ill-advised escapade, then I am sure cooler heads will prevail."

"It seems hard to believe that the British Government did not condone Dr. Jameson's attack on Johannesburg," Mr. Gordon answered. "I understand three regular British Army colonels were with the raiders."

"Mr. Chamberlain," I said, "our Colonial Secretary, has vigorously denied – "

"How do you intend to market your oats?" Holmes asked, bearing me down.

"We will employ a thousand youths on bicycles to deliver half-ounce sample packages of Vigor Oats to every dwelling in the city."

"Including the East End and south of the river?" Holmes asked.

"*Every* dwelling."

Holmes stood. "I thank you for your time, Mr. Gordon."

"Perhaps when you find Mr. Vigor, you might ask him to contact me?" Mr. Gordon requested. "My last letter to him, care of the *Temple of Varieties*, went unanswered. I do hope he and his lady wife are in good health."

"Surely it would take messenger boys a good while to deliver samples to every house in the metropolis," I suggested as we left Mr. Gordon's office and walked along The Strand towards Charing Cross.

"They might be youths at the start of the enterprise, but they would have beards at its conclusion," Holmes answered. "The proposal is preposterous."

"Typical American brag-and-bounce, I'm afraid. And Mr. Gordon's remarks on the Jameson affair were on the verge of insulting."

"You traduce the hard-headed business sense of our transatlantic cousins," Holmes answered. "No, I do not believe our Mr. Gordon. His attempt at an American accent was risible. There is very much more to this than meets the eye."

"I don't understand, Holmes. What makes this American brand of oats more desirable than our ordinary home-grown Scots or Irish variety?"

"The coloured box."

Holmes gestured to the first cabby in the rank, who walked his horse to us.

"If you were contemplating war with Great Britain," he asked me as we settled on our seats, "which branch of the service would be your first concern to hamper?"

"The Navy, of course."

"Very well. It's time we talked to the senior service, but first to Ruislip. We can take the Metropolitan Line to Harrow from Baker Street Station. You have the address of Mr. Vigor's mother?"

"The British Army is puny compared to our Continental rivals," Holmes said we left Harrow-on-the-Hill Station in a hansom. "If Germany or France, or Russia for that matter, established a toehold on this island and passed across the channel even a part of their vast assembly of troops, we would be defeated and annexed by that Power."

"Not *puny*, Holmes. Obviously fewer than the other Powers, but seasoned professionals, who I am persuaded would give a good account of themselves in battle against foreign conscripts. Anyway, the Navy prevents our neighbours from invading, as it has done for centuries."

We got down on Ruislip village square, and I followed Holmes to the door of a pleasant villa.

"I am Sherlock Holmes, consulting detective, and this is my friend Doctor Watson."

"One has heard of you, of course," the elderly lady who answered our knock said as she peered at us through a door open an inch or two, "but I do not recall when or where." She considered. "Are you good 'uns, or a bad 'uns, that's the question. If bad 'uns, I shall be obliged to shoot you. Armend is most insistent."

She produced an enormous pistol and attempted to cock the hammer with both her thumbs. "The mechanism is a trifle awkward."

"I can assure you, Mrs. Vigor, that we are here with the very best of intentions towards your son," I said. "We have been engaged in his interests by his employer, Mr. Pargeter."

Holmes sniffed impatiently.

"It's a question of oil in the breech," Mrs. Vigor said, frowning at the pistol. "When my husband was alive, he took care of our guns."

"Madam," I said in an urgent tone. "I am a medical doctor."

Mrs. Vigor paused in her efforts and peered at me. "Well, why didn't you say so?"

I reached through the gap in the doorway, gently took the pistol and restored the hammer to its safe position. "Perhaps we might have a word with Mr. Vigor, if he is at home?"

270

Mrs. Vigor opened the door wide and led Holmes and me into a pleasant drawing room. A large, colourised death-photograph of a stern-faced, heavily built man in a dark suit and bowler was over the mantel.

"My late husband," Mrs. Vigor explained. "We met at the *Circus Soullier* at the Prater in Vienna in '64." She indicated a pair of photographs in an alcove. "I was on the high wire, and he juggled."

She looked around the room, seeming flustered. "I shall see about tea." She frowned. "You do drink tea, I suppose? Miss LeBeau prefers coffee and – oh, I am not supposed to mention her name!"

Holmes was flipping through an album of picture postcards on the sideboard by the door, so I answered for us both. "Tea would be very acceptable."

"Thank goodness," Mrs. Vigor said. "Cook has no notion of coffee, and she gets into *such* a fuss. What with all the packing, I don't know where we are."

Holmes threw his arms in the air and marched out. I followed, slipping the heavy pistol into my waistband.

Holmes leapt up the stairs three at a time with the lightness of a cat, then he paused on the landing and listened. "Mr. Vigor?" he called up to the floor above. "Miss LeBeau? My name is Sherlock Holmes, and I am here to help you."

A huge shadow blocked the light from the skylight and a massively built man stood, arms folded, at the top of the stairs.

"Steady, Mr. Vigor," Holmes said softly. "We mean you no harm."

"You mayn't come up."

"We know of the incident in Cussop Dingle," Holmes answered. "Doctor Watson and I are here to help. Mr. Pargeter is concerned for your safety. He and George send their regards."

Mr. Vigor narrowed his eyes. "How is George? He was a little unwell when I last saw him."

"*She* is in fine fettle, Mr. Vigor, but worried about you, and Miss LeBeau of course."

A slim young lady in a yellow, lacey afternoon gown appeared behind Mr. Vigor and slapped him on the arm. "Out of the way, Albert," she said in a voice slightly tinged with a Cape accent.

Mr. Vigor stood aside, and the lady slipped past him, brushed past Holmes and me, giving us a pert look, and tripped into the sitting room. Holmes and I followed her downstairs, with Mr. Vigor trailing behind.

"I hope I did right, letting them in," Mrs. Vigor said as she served tea. "The gentlemen said he was a doctor, but he's not carrying a medical bag. Shall I get the shotgun?"

"You did fine, Ma. These gentlemen are good 'uns."

"That's all right, then. I'll tell Daisy to bring seed cake as well as bread and butter, and I can open a jar of quince jam."

Miss LeBeau stood by the window, looking radiant. Her complexion was milk and honey and her lips a shade of red that no make-up could counterfeit. Her golden curls – Holmes's elbow nudged me, and I returned my attention to Mr. Vigor.

He enveloped the arm chair he sat in, his arm muscles bulging to the point of bursting the shirt he wore, and his broad thighs and hams stretching his trousers. "We thought to disguise Arabella as a boy as a capital way of evading her relations." Mr. Vigor explained to Holmes. "Arabella's father has forbidden her marriage to me, and two of her brothers are here to drag her back to Johannesburg. We got the idea from Lulu – "

"Lulu Farini," Holmes said, "or *El Niño Farini*, as he was known in the sixties as a boy trapeze and high-wire artist. His father thought him a better commercial proposition as a female artiste and had him don a wig and dress. Lulu had quite a following among swells in the seventies until a stage accident in Dublin necessitated a trip to hospital and he was unmasked, much to the consternation of the stage-door johnnies who had sent him flowers, get-well-cards, chocolates, and *billets doux*."

I handed Vigor the revolver.

"Oh dear. Father's pistol. Mother gets a little confused nowadays."

"I believe that the people chasing you are not Miss LeBeau's relatives," Holmes said. "They are the oatmeal agents you contracted with. Their interest is focussed on Miss LeBeau, or more exactly on a Royal Navy officer of her acquaintance."

Miss LeBeau spun around and looked down her nose at Holmes. "I don't know what you are inferring, Mr. Holmes."

"Do you mean the Captain?" Mr. Vigor asked. "He's one of the johnnies who sends chocs and – "

"Quiet, Albert. I'm chatting with the gentlemen."

"Come now, Miss LeBeau," Holmes said. "We know of the Captain from the doorman at the music hall. We know he sent you gifts and that you met with him on several occasions. You dined together at – "

Vigor sprang to his feet and shook a gigantic fist at Holmes. "She did not do so!"

"The page saw her join Captain Maxwell in his cab," Holmes said quietly. "The Captain ordered the cabby to the Café Royal."

"Sit, Albert," Arabella snapped.

"The so-called American businessmen are not who they seem, Mr. Vigor," Holmes said in an urgent tone. "I believe they sought to suborn

272

or coerce Miss LeBeau to give them certain information, or perhaps do a certain act for them – something that is connected with the current crisis in South Africa. Whatever it is, the matter is of sufficient moment for them to have gone to the expense of setting up a fake company and printing the advertising posters for this ridiculous porridge."

Holmes's voice hardened. "They gulled you to gain access to Miss LeBeau. Whether they achieved their purpose, I do not yet know. But I do know that they are on your track. We found you, and so will they. Miss LeBeau's attempt to persuade them of her death in Cussop Dingle was a masterpiece of improvisation, but it didn't fool me for an instant, and it will not fool them for long. They or their minions have made inquiries in the village."

Mr. Vigor frowned. "You mean that charade we played on the villagers? We just thought to pay them back for their rudeness and the attack on Arabella. We got a couple of friends to dress up and we played out a little melodrama. No harm done."

"It was a mean trick," I said. "The villagers are beside themselves."

Holmes addressed Miss LeBeau. "That was your design, madam, and that it was meant to deceive a different audience than the villagers. You knew that your disguise as a boy would not keep you safe for long, so the stone thrown by the blacksmith's boy was an excellent *deux ex machina* for a better plan to disappear altogether. Why?"

Miss LeBeau turned back to the window.

I frowned "Disappear? But what of Mr. Pargeter?"

Mr. Vigor's brows knitted, he lowered his head and balled his fists. "The Café Royal? With the Captain!" He slammed his fist on the table, scattering teacups and tipping the sugar bowl and milk jug onto the floor.

Holmes stood. "Come, Watson."

A rumble of accusation followed us down the garden path, overlain with screeched replies.

"What a minx it is," Holmes said with a grin after he had directed the driver back to Harrow. "She will have some explaining to do to her deceived swain." He glanced out of the cab window and tapped on the roof with his cane. "Wait. There is a van company on the corner. Mrs. Vigor mentioned packing."

Holmes jumped back into the cab a few minutes later. "A carriage and a wagon for six chests and trunks and assorted baggage booked for eight a.m. tomorrow for Waterloo Station. The carter understands tickets have been purchased for a steamer to New York."

"Mr. Pargeter will be disappointed."

273

"I'm afraid so," Holmes said. "The carters were very obliging, allowing me to use their telephone. Imagine, here we are in darkest Ruislip, and the local carters have a telephone apparatus. How swiftly the world is changing."

I frowned a question.

Holmes handed me a postcard showing a warship, a cruiser by her lines. On the reverse was a chatty message sent to Miss LeBeau from Gibraltar and signed Freddy.

"I lifted this from her album. And I called my brother Mycroft, asking for him to obtain the whereabouts of this ship and an introduction for us to the captain. To the first he said that HMS *Cyclops* recently berthed on the Thames at the Embankment as a Navy school ship. He claims she is clearly visible from his bathroom window and he can see the cadets on her deck at cutlass drill – an exaggeration of course. All that is visible from Mycroft's bathroom window is the side wall of the Carlton Club. He says that *Cyclops* was removed from Fleet service and re-assigned as a training ship for midshipmen two months ago.

"Mycroft contacted the ex-commander, Captain Frederick Maxwell, at his club and persuaded him to meet us at the Ordnance Office in Pall Mall. I shall call again from the station for further and better particulars."

Holmes smiled. "Did you notice that Madame Vigor's deceased husband is pictured in exactly the type of bowler you bought this morning? It's strange how fashions come around every few years."

"I was commander of the *Cyclops* until recently, when I was seconded from the Navy as secretary to the Ordnance Office in Chief," Captain Maxwell said as he led Holmes and me along an empty, dusty corridor in the deserted War Office to a door marked *"Ordnance (RN)"*. "I keep an eye on our stocks of gunpowder, shells, and so on."

He ushered us into a cramped, dark space furnished with two battered desks and chairs, a few cupboards, and two threadbare armchairs in front of the unlit fireplace. A telephone apparatus stood on Captain Maxwell's desk. Holmes and I turned the armchairs to face the captain as he lit a pair of gas lamps above the fireplace and an oil lamp on his desk.

"You know Miss Arabella LeBeau of the *Temple of Varieties* in Hammersmith." Holmes said as he settled back in his chair.

Captain Maxwell blanched, his thick, black walrus moustache in sharp contrast to his pale face. "Vaguely." He frowned down at Holmes's business card. "You are detectives?"

"I am a consulting detective, Captain. I am not here at Miss LeBeau's behest, and I have no reason to suppose that your relations with her will cause you any anxiety." He smiled a jaguar smile. "If, that is, you are completely frank with me."

Captain Maxwell seemed to gird his loins. "Very well."

"You took Miss LeBeau to the Café Royal after her performance in the pantomime ten days or so before the Christmas holiday?" Holmes asked.

"I did. She seemed a little off-colour – preoccupied, as you might say. I was somewhat taken aback. We had been acquainted for several months, and I thought I was in for a nasty shock in a certain line, if you know what I mean. But she pepped up. All was well, and we spent a pleasant evening."

"And night?"

"Oh, I say. Can't tell tales out of school and all that rot. I mean, Arabella's not a lady as such, but only a cad would – "

"What did you talk about?" Holmes asked.

Captain Maxwell blinked at Holmes. "Talk?"

Holmes sighed. "You will have mentioned your new position to Miss LeBeau. I'm sure she took a lively interest in your work."

"Well, it's not a seagoing command. I had rather hoped for a ship of the line, but it's dashed important. Let me show you."

He stood and opened a cupboard. "Here is a half-section of a twelve-inch shell, showing the explosive (simulated), and here is a half-section of the propellant, Cordite, replicated by bundles of string."

"Cordite?" Holmes frowned.

"Our latest propellant. Three times more powerful than the previous powder. Its composition is secret."

"It is an explosive?" I asked.

"A slow-burning or *low* explosive that propels our shells at the foe. The shell containing *high* explosive is pushed into the breech, followed by cordite in double silk bags. On command, the cordite is ignited, the shell is lobbed at the enemy, penetrating their armour and hopefully sending a parcel of Frogs to *Paradis*. Or these days, a shipload of Germans to Valhalla."

"You control the supply of this propellant?" Holmes asked.

"We indent from Army stores. We buy silk for the bags, and order brass casings for smaller calibres from various manufacturers. I sit on the committee that tenders for Naval supplies."

Holmes tapped his lip. "The cordite is bagged in silk? Do other nations use silk bags for their propellant?"

"The Germans encase their main charge in a brass cartridge even for their battleship-calibre guns," Captain Maxwell answered. "The cost is enormous, but they have far fewer ships than we do, with smaller guns, and they focus on quality, not quantity. We cannot contemplate the expense." He chuckled. "The French proudly use their own invention, *poudre B,* encased, as I understand, in bags of linen. The *poudre* is a highly volatile, dangerously unstable propellant. Long may they continue to use it."

Captain Maxwell leaned forward and continued in a guarded tone. "We need to keep our wits sharpened, gentlemen. Have you any idea how many French waiters there are in Dover?" He frowned. "Well, I don't know the exact number, but there are a damn sight too many for my liking."

"Hear him," I muttered under my breath.

Captain Maxwell closed the cupboard and sat. "Cordite is manufactured at a secret factory, and the amount in store is confidential. I can just say that we have cordite in plenty."

"What of silk?" Holmes asked.

Captain Maxwell pursed his lips as he considered his answer. "The Japanese and Italians export silk, but their entire production has been bought by the Americans and French for ribbons and frivolities. Our silk is imported from China and sewed into bags in Macclesfield."

Captain Maxwell's voice took on a more serious tone. "With the growing unrest in China, my predecessor was altogether too sanguine about our supply. Without silk, we cannot bag the propellant, and our battleships would be toothless after they had expended their ready-use ammunition. No other material offers the safety advantages of silk in containing the cordite."

Captain Maxwell smiled at my nervous expression. "Not to worry, Doctor. My committee took immediate steps to replenish our stock, and we have a huge consignment of silk on its way."

"Miss LeBeau must have been pleased with your new employment, Captain," Holmes said. "You are now based in London rather than on the high seas."

Captain Maxwell smoothed his moustache. "Indeed so."

"Did you mention to her any details of your work? I am sure she would have been very interested."

Captain Maxwell stood erect and slammed his hands on the table. "I am neither fool nor traitor, sir. I said nothing of our propellant stocks."

"I believe you, Captain."

"What then?"

"Silk," Holmes said in a soft tone.

Captain Maxwell subsided into his chair. "Silk? I may have quipped that I would be able to get her a bolt of raw silk in a week or so, once the *Monsoon* has been unloaded."

"A cargo ship?" Holmes asked. "Where is she now?"

"*Monsoon* left Shanghai on the tenth, then called at Columbo and Calcutta." Captain Maxwell consulted a sheaf of papers. "Let me see, her last port of call was Valetta on the sixth of this month, so she will be in the chops of the Channel by now. I would expect her to berth at London Docks within a day or so."

"What flag does she sail under?" Holmes asked.

"French."

I gasped. "Are we mad?"

Holmes stood. "Thank you, Captain."

I stood with him.

Captain Maxwell jerked to his feet and addressed Holmes. "I say, old man, you cannot suggest that any woman of England would spy for a foreign power!"

"Miss LeBeau is not a woman of England. She was born in Johannesburg."

"My God! I had no idea! She said she was from Glasgow."

Captain Maxwell led us into the corridor, his head lowered and his breathing loud and irregular.

Holmes paused at the door and indicated the apparatus on Captain Maxwell's desk. "Might I use your telephone?"

"The Boers simmer," Captain Maxwell said to me as we waited in the corridor. "They want German involvement in a war to secure their independence. If they convince the Kaiser that Britain's navy is impotent against a sudden attack and that after an initial engagement, we will not have sufficient stocks of silk bags to provide the Fleet with propellant, Germany may strike." He rubbed his hands together and his voice faltered. "We would be open to invasion!"

I suggested he repair to the Red Lion, just along Pall Mall, for a restorative. "Mr. Holmes is on the case," I reassured him. "Trust in him."

"I conferred with my brother," Holmes said as we re-boarded our cab in Pall Mall. "Mycroft was sufficiently moved by my suspicions that he agreed to contact the Admiralty and arrange Naval protection of the *Monsoon*. He hopes the orders will be on their way to the Fleet within the hour, but promises nothing as the Admiralty is closed."

Holmes ordered the driver to The Strand.

"Arabella told the Boers what she knew of our silk stocks!" I said.

"Yes. She was besieged with threats or bribes or both," Holmes said. "She told her muscular swain the fairy tale of revengeful brothers, and he swept her to a place of refuge in Cussop Dingle. The couple took advantage of the attack by the choirboys to create a bloody scenario, and

277

they added a dramatic coda with a fake inspector, doctor, and constable – no doubt their thespian acquaintances.

"The melodrama instantly rang false in every particular, from the strange notion of bringing the sick boy back to the village to die, to the remarkably attentive London brain surgeon and the strangely reticent detective. No, no, I knew immediately that it was a charade cooked up by Arabella to fool her pursuers.

"Mr. Gordon, if that is his name, discovered their whereabouts," Holmes added. "I believe his aim was to scare Arabella and prevent her from going to the authorities. He succeeded."

It was raining when I dropped down from the cab in The Strand and peered through the grimy glass windows of the office we had visited earlier.

I jumped back aboard. "Empty. The posters and oats are gone."

"They will need a substantial boat if they mean to intercept *Monsoon* in the approaches to the Thames in winter," Holmes said, "a vessel capable of taking them to the Continent after the attack."

He tapped on the cab roof. "The Steam Packet Wharf by London Bridge."

We leapt out of our cab at the wharf. The jetty was empty, aside from a small skiff tied to a bollard. Rain slashed across the river, the iron gates were closed and padlocked, and only a single oil lamp glimmered over the door of the wharf attendant's office.

Holmes and I clambered over the fence and I knocked on the office door.

"We must determine when and where *Monsoon* is due to dock," Holmes said as we waited for an answer to my knock.

I banged again, with more urgency, but to no effect.

"Do we act in the name of the Queen, Holmes?" I asked.

Holmes shrugged. "I suppose we do."

I indicated the brass sign on the door: *H.M. Wharf Attendant, Port of London*. "This shed is Her property." I put my shoulder to the door and sprang the lock.

Holmes grinned. "I had not heard the law construed in quite that way, Watson."

We passed inside, and I lit two wall sconces. I adjusted the flame and started at a movement in a shadowed corner of the office.

The wharf attendant lay on the floor, tied hand and foot and gagged with a handkerchief. I untied him, and he staggered to his feet, gasping for air and apoplectic with fury. He drained a half-full cup of tepid tea and poured another from the pot on his desk with a shaking hand. "Six of the damned villains, dressed in black with scarves around their faces and flat caps. They have *Desdemona*, a heavy steam launch on hire from Bishop's Wharf in the Borough."

"Is *Desdemona* capable of a Channel crossing?" Holmes asked.

The attendant gulped his tea. "She is, sir. I know her well. All the larger launches, those capable of a Continental crossing, are obliged to register here. As I overheard, the buggers' intention is to head for Holland after they have done their business, whatever that is."

I turned to Holmes. "Well, they are gone. We must pray we warned the Navy in time."

"Not gone yet, sir," said the attendant. "They are taking on clean water at the water barge. Can't use Thames water or the filters would clog. That won't take long. Next they will load coal from our coaling wharf."

Holmes pounced on a telephone apparatus on the desk. He listened, frowned at the instrument and lifted the connecting lead. It was severed. "Well, my dear fellow," he said. "It's down to us."

Holmes and I turned to a noise outside. My heart raced. The Boers had returned. I glared around the room looking for a weapon, anything that we might use against the rebels, but I saw nothing, aside from a domestic knife and fork.

Holmes doused the gas lamps, and I peered out of the window. "I see police, Holmes!" I frowned. "And pirates."

The door opened, and a head appeared in the doorway. "Ah, Mr. Holmes and Doctor Watson, here you are," said Mr. Pargeter.

The rain had eased. Two heavy waggons stood at the wharf gates disgorging colourfully-dressed show people. A third waggon appeared behind the others and in it the theatre band could be heard tuning up.

"The comic policemen are from Gilbert and Sullivan?" I asked Mr. Pargeter.

"Mr. D'Oyly Carte was most accommodating."

Mr. Vigor appeared from the shadows. He carried an Indian club in one hand and the padlock and chain from the gate in the other. He gave the broken chain to the attendant with apologies. Then he smiled at me and drew his monstrous pistol from his waistband.

"An Albanian bear pistol, Doctor, that belonged to my father. Albanian bears are of exceptional ferocity." Vigor handed the heavy gun to me. "I was tempted to use it on the Captain, but saner counsels prevailed." He brandished his club. "This will suit me for Boers."

I hefted the gun for the second time that day and marvelled at its bore and weight.

279

Captain Maxwell joined us and saluted. "I went to the *Temple of Varieties* to have it out with Miss Arabella," he explained. "I found Vigor there, and I rather thought my time had come. He informed me that he had thrown off his yoke and bid Arabella farewell. Mr. Vigor kindly attaches no blame to me, and he roundly condemns Miss Arabella as a Jezebel. I add the sin of treachery."

"She is no traitor. She is from Johannesburg, not Glasgow," Mr. Vigor growled.

"Johannesburg is under the protection of the Queen," I corrected him. "We are not – currently – at war with the inhabitants of the Transvaal, and they are still Her subjects. That makes them rebels and traitors, and Arabella with them."

Mr. Vigor looked down at his toes, clearly upset, and I regretted my emphatic tone.

Mr. Pargeter quickly intervened. "The Captain concluded that the devils would come here to prepare their launch for sea. He enlisted the help of Madame George, who put the matter before the company during their first dress rehearsal. And here we are."

I smiled at Mr. Vigor, hoping to make amends. "You are Albanian, sir. What quarrel do you have with the inhabitants of the Transvaal?"

He returned my smile. "My mother is from Falmouth. We Cornish cannot abide a Boer."

"Enough," Holmes said. "We must formulate a plan to foil the attack on the *Monsoon*. Can we disable their launch?"

"We charge the launch and thump them," said Mr. Vigor.

"They will be armed."

"We charge the launch, thump them harder, take their weapons, and shoot them."

I blinked at Mr. Vigor, who seemed to have shed his gentle demeaner along with his paramour.

"What does the Navy say?" Holmes asked Captain Maxwell.

"We must disable their launch. I suggest entangling their screw with rope – or better yet, chain." He indicated the padlock and chain held by the wharf attendant.

Holmes nodded. "Both plans have merit. I propose we merge them. Their boat, the *Desdemona*, will dock here to take on coal. *That* we must deny them at all costs. Without fuel, they cannot carry out their attack."

"We will scupper their fiendish plans," Mr. Pargeter said, banging a fist into his hand.

"While they are engaged at the coal yard, we foul the propeller," Holmes continued. "As a last resort, we board via the gangplank and at the same time over the opposite side."

"I would propose myself for the sabotage, but I'm afraid I can't swim," Captain Maxwell admitted. "With your permission, I will command the boarding party in the skiff. We can lurk in the shadow of the barges moored mid-stream. When we hear the signal, we board over the *Desdemona's* starboard gunwale."

"I can swim like a mermaid," said George. "In fact, I portrayed a mermaid at the *Temple*, frolicking in a tank with a porpoise, until the animal matured, developed too amorous a disposition, and grew fractious."

Holmes blinked at her. "Very well. Mr. Vigor's mixed force of tramp comedians and birdsong imitators will take post at the coal yard, under cover. They must construct a rampart and prevent the enemy from obtaining fuel for their boilers."

He turned to the attendant. "Are there other sources of coal nearby?"

"Plenty, sir, but all fenced in against thieves." He tapped his finger against his nose. "And you'd have to know where they are."

Holmes nodded. "The policemen, under the command of the wharf attendant, will take cover in the office, ready to sally forth on hearing the signal and force the gangplank."

He smiled at George. "Miss George and I will sabotage the screws."

"And I, Holmes?"

"Yours is the trickiest job, Watson. You will negotiate with the Boers." He handed me the wharf attendant's speaking horn.

"On what terms?"

"If they disembark, disarm, and swear to return peaceably to their homeland, no further action on our part."

"If not?"

"If they discharge a weapon, we attack. No quarter given or expected."

"What is our signal?" I asked.

"A cannon shot, Mr. Holmes," Mr. Pargeter said. "We have a large bore cannon used as a prop in various military tableaux. George can load the powder, and I will fire the gun."

I frowned at a bevy of girls in feathers and sequined costumes. "The chorus girls?"

"Will form a reserve under Mr. Pargeter," Holmes said. "The orchestra may play stirring martial airs to steady our backbones. Nothing from *Pirates*, of course."

The wharf attendant lit a half-dozen *naptha* lamps that bathed the wharf in their harsh, bright glare.

"Holmes, this is all very well," I said vehemently, "but also extremely silly and dangerous. The Boers are no doubt professional soldiers, and they are armed and determined."

"You forget Napoleon's dictum, 'In war, moral power is to physical as three parts out of four.' We just have to delay them while the Navy bestirs itself. They will be under orders to achieve their aim by stealth rather than in open battle."

I nodded doubtfully, then stiffened as Holmes gripped my shoulder.

A long, low, sinister black shape had detached itself from the river shadows. It glided towards the wharf with a soft chug of its engine.

The crew, six men, all in black, squinted in the naptha light. I recognised Mr. Gordan on the prow of the launch. He called, "Ahoy there."

Silence.

"We don't want any trouble, eh. Let us take our coal and leave. We have money."

The launch nudged the edge of the wharf and two black-clad figures leapt off and secured her to bollards.

"No trouble," Mr. Gordan called again, shading his eyes and scouting the wharf. "We'll pay over the odds."

He nodded to his men and three of them joined the two on the wharf. They drew pistols and moved warily towards the coal yard.

They were instantly engulfed in a hail of coal, and they retreated to the launch pursued by catcalls and the twitter of birdsong.

"Get out of our way, or we open fire!" Mr. Gordon called, waving his pistol.

Vigor stood and propelled a barrel onto the stem of the launch. It burst, smothering the deck with reeking pitch. He picked up another barrel, and Mr. Gordon raised his pistol.

I juggled the speaking horn and the Albanian pistol for a moment, then dropped the horn and ran to the wharfside. Time seemed to slow. I noticed from the corner of my eye that Mr. Pargeter and his girls were rolling a wide-mouthed cannon forward. I reached jetty, steadied my gun with both hands, breathed deeply, and centred my aim on Mr. Gordon. "I must require you to immediately surrender," I cried. "If you do not – "

A huge bang came from behind me, followed by billows of black smoke and a shrill whistling sound as a small boy in a spangled leotard was blasted over my head. He sailed over the launch in a glittering arc, trailing sparks, perfectly visible against the black sky. I and the Boers on the launch followed his flight in blank disbelief until he disappeared into the shadows of the river.

With fearsome howls, police constables erupted from the attendant's office and headed for the launch. At the same moment, pirates, led by Captain Maxwell, swarmed over the farther gunwale of the *Desdemona* with martial cries. Vigor was first aboard, wielding a huge beam of wood and baying in what I presumed was his native tongue.

The Boers retreated to the bow of the launch, guns drawn, white-faced and wide-eyed in the bright light. The police and pirates joined forces and crowded forward uttering menaces and brandishing their weapons.

"Stop!" cried a loud voice. "Stop instantly where you are, and maintain silence!" Holmes called from where he stood, dripping wet, at the stern of the launch.

The piercing voice of Miss George seconded him. "Tableau, ladies and gentlemen. Everyone still, *if* you please."

"If you or any of your men fire, *Kapitein*," Holmes said in the silence, "It will be your last act on this earth. Doctor Watson is a dead shot and his pistol is of Albanian bore. You are surrounded by desperate armed men – and ladies. You have no coal, and your rudder is fouled. Your mission is a dead letter."

The chorus girls rolled the cannon forward, and Mr. Pargeter held a smoking match over its touchhole.

"Surrender your weapons, promise to return home, offering no more mischief, and you may go," I said. "Royal Navy warships have been dispatched to convoy the *Monsoon* into port."

I stiffened to attention as the band played *"Rule Britannia"*.

"The cannon shot was the *coup de grace*, Mr. Pargeter," I said as we watched the disconcerted Boers file from the *Desdemona* and out of the wharf gates. "The enemy – and I admit I myself – were stunned at your ruthlessness – firing a child at them! It sapped their morale."

Mr. Pargeter displayed a sodden, scorch-marked dummy in spangled tights. "The pirates retrieved Archie from the river. The boy lives to fly again."

He leaned close and laid a hand on my arm. "A call to action, Doctor! Better than a pint of *Chlorodyne*. My back is supple, and I have never felt more lithe. But why is that?"

"A very interesting question, Mr. Pargeter, one that puzzles modern medical science."

Holmes and I returned home to our lodgings and found the lights burning in the hall and Billy asleep on the first step of the staircase, grasping two telegram forms.

I woke the boy, sent him to his bed, and joined Holmes in the sitting room.

"From Mycroft. The Navy has at last bestirred itself and sent a cruiser to convoy *Monsoon* to London Port."

He ripped open the second envelope. "And a cable from Pinkerton's in New York. I had the commissionaire at the music hall send the inquiry. A Pinkerton's agent made a telephone connection with the American Cereal Company of Chicago, who manufacture the breakfast food featuring a Quaker on the box. They deny any knowledge of an English agency promoting their product, and they know nothing of Vigor Oats, but they express a wish to contact Mr. Vigor to discuss possibilities."

I made a pencil note on my cuff. "I'll inform him."

Holmes disappeared into his bedroom for a few moments, then emerged in his dressing gown, towelling his hair. He slumped into his chair in front of the fire and jabbed at the embers with a poker. "Imagine, Watson, when a telephone connection across the Atlantic is established, as it is under the Channel, I will be able to make a call to Chicago myself and receive an answer in a few seconds, when the information is still of practical use."

"We live in a remarkable age," I said. My stomach rumbled. "I say, old man. In all the fuss, we missed dinner entirely, and everyone is in bed. I noticed a basket of fresh eggs in the pantry and the butt end of a ham in the larder. I might slip down and cook up a couple of omelettes."

"Stout fellow," Holmes said. "I will open a bottle of our yellow-stoppered Claret and we may celebrate the end of an interesting day with a midnight feast!"

> *I leaned back and took down the great index volume to which he referred. Holmes balanced it on his knee, and his eyes moved slowly and lovingly over the record of old cases, mixed with the accumulated information of a lifetime. ". . . . Vigor, the Hammersmith wonder. Hullo! Hullo! Good old index. You can't beat it . . . ."*

Dr. John H. Watson and Sherlock Holmes –
"The Sussex Vampire"

A Correspondence Concerning
Mr. James Phillimore
by Derrick Belanger

Dear Mr. Holmes,

It is great to hear from you again, my friend. I am happy to learn that all is well with you across the pond and that you're now in the editing stages of *The Whole Art of Detection*. I can't wait to get my hands on a copy of that book! My field of interest may be apiology, but Watson is my favorite writer (with Robert Louis Stevenson a close second), and I look forward to studying your methods and seeing how they can be applied to my Melittology.

That, I confess, is the reason I write to you today. One of my associates, Freddy Olson, a doctoral student who is conducting research alongside me, is also a big fan of the works of Dr. Watson. As we were gathering honey samples the other day, we got into a lively discussion about some of the unwritten cases of Dr. Watson, particularly the case of Mr. James Phillimore. We discussed the logic of the case and agreed that the solution rests on the logical state of "maybe". We know he entered the house to get his umbrella, but after that, we have the unknown or maybe state. *Maybe* he left the house or *maybe* he remained inside. We both agreed that there is not enough data to come to any conclusion for this one. Watson mentioned the case as a mere aside.

Could you elaborate on the details of the case? Though we are not detectives, we are fellow scientists, and we have the technical mindset in which you so often pride yourself. Also, Freddy and I have a bet on which one of us solves the case. I have ten bucks riding on this, Mr. Holmes!

Of course, Mr. Phillimore isn't the sole reason for which I write to you today. I want to thank you for your information pertaining to *Apis dorsata laboriosa*, the giant honey bee of the Himalayas. I'm currently planning an expedition to the area to gather specimens for transport to the Rocky Mountains of Colorado. Your information about the possible healing powers of the insect's royal jelly has allowed me to get some investors to open their wallets. It's my hope to bring back specimens to breed at my camp near the summit of Longs Peak and crossbreed the bees with other native species. The possible medical breakthroughs are limitless.

I'll write more as my team prepares for our journey to the East. As always, your information was and is invaluable.

Sincerely,
Robert Hoffman, Ph.D.
University of Colorado, Boulder

P.S. - If you are ever stateside, you are always welcome to visit our apiary in Colorado. We have a cottage house which you may use for an unlimited time absolutely free of charge.

* * *

Dear Dr. Hoffman,

I am glad to hear that all is well with you. I wish you the best of luck on your voyage to the Orient. I also thank you for your kind invitation to stay in your mountain facility if I return to the states. I do hope to get back to America sometime in the future, but being a centenarian makes travel beyond the front steps of my abode rather difficult.

You aren't the first person to write to me about Mr. Phillimore. Over the years many constables, generals, and armchair detectives have offered their theories, the most outlandish falling in the realm of science fiction. I'm happy to tell you the full details of the case. You and your associate are men of reason, a quality seemingly lacking in the people of the mid-twentieth century, and I fully welcome any theory your minds bring forward.

The details of the case are as follows:

Mr. James Phillimore was a wealthy banker in his late forties who resided in a two-story house in Marleybone. Noted for his shrewd business dealings, the man was respected by his peers. He held no debts at the time of his disappearance. On the contrary, he had just completed his two most successful years for his investments, and he continued to make large profits through his portfolio of stocks and bonds. His wife was a quiet girl, younger than him by over twenty years, but the two, by all accounts, were happy. Despite their wealth, the couple had no live-in servants. Rather, they hired seasonal help when needed and enjoyed dining outside of their home.

On the morning of June first, Mr. and Mrs. Phillimore were preparing to go out for lunch. Mrs. Phillimore had stepped into the Daimler which was parked in the front of the house in the half-circle driveway. Mr. Phillimore crank-started the vehicle and was about to join his wife when he pointed out to her that clouds were forming in the sky, and that he wished to go into the house and get his umbrella. Mrs. Phillimore looked at her pocket watch and noted that the time was 11:53 a.m. and told her husband that they would be late to their 12:15 lunch reservation. He said it would only take a moment. She scolded him for worrying too much about the weather, and he laughed with her, as couples do, before turning around and returning to their house. That was the last time anyone saw Mr. Phillimore in this world.

Mrs. Phillimore waited ten minutes before returning to the house herself. She was rather cross with her husband for taking so long. After entering the home, where they curiously lived without any servants, she called out to him several times, saying that they would now most certainly be late. She received no response. She then searched the premises and found no sign of her husband. Nothing seemed out of place. She went outside and called to her neighbors, and none of them said they had seen her husband leave their home. She was baffled, and she returned to the car, waiting by it for another ten minutes before shutting down the vehicle.

After that, she wondered if perhaps an emergency had come up at the bank. She telephoned and asked, but no one had seen her husband, and none of the employees claimed to have called him. She then called some of his associates, but again, no one had called or seen him.

That evening, having exhausted her patience, Mrs. Phillimore telephoned the police. They did a brief inquiry, and in the end suggested that her husband had run off with another woman. As I'm sure you are aware, this was a common occurrence, even in that era, and I don't fault the police for making this suggestion. What I do fault them on is not following up on some of the most intriguing aspects of the case.

Mr. Phillimore disappeared on a bright spring day with the sun only blocked by intermittent periods of cloud. His neighbors' servants were working in their gardens all morning and afternoon, and it seemed that someone would have seen the man if he tried to escape from the rear of the house. At the time of his disappearance, his wife was waiting in the car at the front, and in the rear, his neighbor's groundskeeper, a Mr. Ellis, was outside mending a fence. The property to the east of the Phillimore's was empty, as the owners were in the process of selling it. However, the gardener of that estate was present, trimming the shrubbery next to the Phillimore's. The manor to the west of the house had a large stone fence between it and the Phillimore home. The Crestone family lived in that house and their two children were playing outside under the care of their nanny during the time of Phillimore's disappearance.

It would have been difficult for Mr. Phillimore to have escaped undetected as there were people around his house when he went missing. Even if he had managed to sneak away, the neighborhood was busy at the time of his disappearance. Many people were out and about, yet no one claimed to have seen him that afternoon.

Of course, if Phillimore hadn't left his house, the only other option was that he was still inside his house. This seemed highly unlikely. Mrs. Phillimore had thoroughly searched the premises, as did the police over the course of the next two days. Nothing was out of place. Despite the police's suggestion that Mr. Phillimore may have run off with another woman, none of his belongings were missing. None of his accounts was touched over the two days as well, and there was no unusual activity related to selling of assets. By all appearances, Phillimore had simply vanished.

I was hired by Mrs. Phillimore a full five days after her husband's disappearance. She was most distraught when she spoke to me. Her husband's accounts were still untouched, and by then the police had interviewed everyone in the neighborhood, and all of Phillimore's contacts. No one had heard from the man since his disappearance.

Mrs. Phillimore also appeared to be telling the truth. I noted that she was giving no physical signs of a liar – no shifting eyes or clenched jaw, and she never contradicted her story. She didn't know what happened to her husband. Eliminating her as a suspect I knew made for a more difficult case to solve. She was the person who had the most to gain financially from her husband's demise – if he was actually dead.

Watson and I went to the Phillimore home, and we conducted a search of the house and the grounds. Unfortunately, in the five days since Phillimore went missing, the groundskeeper had cut the lawn and worked in the garden. Any path that might have been trampled in the grass was lost.

We searched the interior of the premises. As Mrs. Phillimore had told us, none of her husband's items was missing or out of sorts. We checked the house from basement to attic for any signs of hiding spots. We found a few storage spaces in odd locations, but nothing unusual for a house of that age. When we searched these areas, they clearly hadn't been used for a long period of time. Had Phillimore concealed himself in one of these spaces, he would have left some signs in the dust which coated the floor. The dust remained untouched.

Having found no sign of Mr. Phillimore on his property, we then began a thorough interview of his neighbors and associates. We started by interviewing Mr. Laurel, the gardener who was working for the Hendersons, the neighbors to the east who were in the process of selling their home. He was a talkative fellow who was noted for his botanical skills. He knew many of the families in the area, and explained their relationship with Mr. Phillimore in great detail. All of Phillimore's neighbors spoke highly of the man, and he had a good rapport with all of them. The only complaints Mr. Laurel overheard about Phillimore was that he didn't have any servants. This was dismissed as an eccentric behavior – every family had at least one in those days – and wasn't held against him in any way.

Laurel, a man with a long flowing beard who had a slight facial twitch, gave us a tour of the Henderson home. It was empty as the owners prepared to sell it. Again, Watson and I searched for any sign of Mr. Phillimore. The house was completely empty and had been thoroughly cleaned prior to the disappearance. The gardener explained that, had Mr. Phillimore run through the shrubbery where he was trimming, he most certainly would have seen him, and he quite possibly might possibly have run smack right into him.

When we questioned Laurel about his relationship with Phillimore, he explained that they got along fabulously. Mr. Phillimore had an interest in botany and the two talked extensively about the plants in his gardens. In fact, minutes before Mrs. Phillimore's announcement that her husband had vanished, the two men had a conversation about his rose bushes.

Phillimore had called Laurel over to the rose bushes that were on the opposite side of Phillimore's house, asking him to come examine them. Laurel came through the bushes, crossed Phillimore's property, and met him by the stone fence next to the rose bushes. Phillimore explained to the gardener that one of his associates had black spot on his roses, and he wanted Laurel to inspect his bushes to see if he had them too. The gardener did so, explained that the bushes were fine, and that there was nothing to worry about. After the conversation, Laurel crossed back through Phillimore's back yard and returned to working on the shrubbery. That was the last time he saw the banker.

We next questioned Mr. Ellis, the groundskeeper of the Kessels, the neighbors located directly behind the Phillimore's house. Ellis had been outside mending the fence between the properties late that morning, and he'd also had a brief conversation with Phillimore at around ten a.m. – that was his best guess – concerning black spot on roses. He also informed Phillimore that he'd seen no such spots and that the Kessels' roses looked fine. Mr. Phillimore thanked him and then returned to his house. Ellis confirmed that he did see Phillimore speaking with Mr. Laurel right before the disappearance.

One thing I did note was that Ellis wore prescription glasses. I had Watson walk out to the side of the house near the rose bushes and made Ellis describe him from a distance. He thoroughly described him and it was clear that as long as he was wearing his glasses, he could have seen the men interacting.

We then interviewed the Crestone family's nanny. She was a girl, eighteen years of age, who didn't see Phillimore that morning because of the height of the stone fence between his property and that of the Crestone's. She did, however, hear Mr. Phillimore several times that morning, and she overheard his discussion with Laurel. She confirmed that the topic was about Phillimore's concerns about his roses, and she said estimated that the conversation lasted no more than five minutes.

After we completed our interviews with the neighbors, I contacted a number of Phillimore's associates. None of them had heard from Mr. Phillimore for quite a while, as his position made it possible for him to be away from the office on a regular basis. Everyone said how he worked diligently at his job and was highly successful. They feared that something dreadful must have happened to the man because they could not imagine any reason for him to disappear. While I made those inquiries, Watson questioned more people in the neighborhood. Again, we came up empty. No one had seen the man on the day in question.

We spent several days working on the case, seeing if any additional information might be brought to light. It wasn't. And so this case remains unsolved.

I should note that two years after his disappearance, the man was declared dead – somewhat sooner than the law normally required. His wife remarried a year later, and now has a family. She was the only person to have access any of Phillimore's accounts until shortly after her second marriage, when her new husband gained control of them.

Those are the details of the case. I do hope that you and your colleague can shed some light on it. This odd caper is now more than half-a-century old, and one of the cases to which I've always wished that I had more data to help draw it to a conclusion.

Good luck with obtaining the remaining funds for your journey East.

Sincerely,
Sherlock Holmes

* * *

Dear Mr. Holmes,

I can't believe that I am actually writing to you. Ever since I was a boy, I've been a big fan of your work. I've read all of Dr. Watson's stories at least a thousand times each. I've probably read "The Red Headed League" a thousand times more.

It's an honor to send you my thoughts on the case of Mr. Phillimore, and hopefully get ten bucks out of Doc Hoffman as well. Although I can't prove what happened, I do believe I have the solution to the mystery. Perhaps there are declassified records which you can use to verify my theory.

Here it goes. From what you wrote in your letter to Doc Hoffman, I think we can safely say that Phillimore didn't die in his house. If he had, after all these decades, someone would have found some evidence of his remains within the building, and there's no way he'd still be hiding out in there after all of these years. I think that we can also surmise that if Mr. Phillimore remained alive. then he must have had another source of income, since he never used his accounts.

So, if he wasn't in the house, then where did he go? How did Mr. Phillimore slip past so many people in his neighborhood? My thought is that with his intelligence, his shrewd business acumen, and his knowledge of the financial world, there is only one answer: Phillimore was none other than a former spy for the British government.

I think that the discussion about the spots on the roses was a decoy meant to be overheard by another agent. Perhaps it was code that Russians had discovered his whereabouts and that he needed to be moved to safety. As a former spy, the government would have hidden him after the war to keep him safe. He built a new life for himself, made money – possibly with some governmental help – and had a new happy marriage.

My guess is that when Phillimore returned to his house, he changed into clothes which hid his appearance. He then escaped by moving in secret when his neighbors were not watching certain areas of the yard. After all, no one can be watching everything that's going on. Phillimore then met another agent who, I'm sure, had his car parked around the corner from the house. Phillimore was then whisked off to a new life and identity. I wouldn't be surprised to discover that he was just as successful in his new life, earning a high income and taking another younger woman as his wife.

Mr. Holmes, I know from Watson's stories that your brother played a prominent role in the British government, and you assisted them on a number of occasions. I'd bet that if you asked about the file on Mr.

Phillimore, so many years after his disappearance, they would let you see it, and then you would know for sure where the man lived for the remainder of his life.

Even if the case remains classified, please let the Doc Hoffman know if I hit the bull's eye with this one. I'd love to be ten dollars richer.

Sincerely,
Frederic "Freddy" Olson

* * *

Dear Mr. Olson,

I appreciate you writing to me and using such kind words to describe Watson's depictions of my cases. As I've said many times, I find my dear friend's renderings of the cases to be a bit melodramatic, but I can see from your own writing that you share Watson's flair for dramatic storytelling.

As entertaining as it was to read, I'm afraid there are many problems with your explanation of the disappearance of Mr. Phillimore. You have him acting as a secret British agent when it is well established that in the years before the case, he was becoming a well-established banker. You also alluded to the Russians hunting down Phillimore, when this case happened long before the Russians were considered an enemy of the Crown. You would have been better off arguing for the Germans or the Turks.

I believe that you've been reading far too many modern spy novels. This is apparent in your idea of a secret code in the discussion of the spots on the roses. If this was a code, I don't know who would have heard it. Unless you are arguing for one of the neighbors being the government agent, then I'm not certain how someone outside the immediate vicinity could have heard the code, unless Phillimore and Laurel were shouting their discussion for all the world to hear. Even if this were the case, I'm not sure how he could have gotten away without being seen by someone in the neighborhood. He would still have to walk or run a good distance to enter the getaway vehicle, and if another agent – the one who overheard the roses code – was with him, it would have been even more noticeable that two unknown men were sneaking around the neighborhood. Unless Mr. Phillimore had the power to blend in with the shadows or cloud men's minds, I believe this would have been an impossible feat.

I do appreciate your effort in trying to find a solution to this case, however fanciful it may be. Perhaps you might try your hand at writing a novel that is purely in the realm of fiction. Like Watson, you have the gift for fanciful storytelling. All you need is a tough dame, a car chase, and a stolen falcon from Malta added to the plot, and you could have a success.

Again, my gratitude to you in your efforts to solve this fifty-year-old case. Please don't think me rude with my sarcasm. I am simply having a bit of fun, which I believe is warranted at my age.

Sincerely,
Mr. Sherlock Holmes

* * *

Dear Mr. Holmes,

I have exciting news! We have secured all the funding for our expedition to the Himalayas. My team will leave sometime early in September and arrive in the middle of the month. We shall stay through the end of November, conducting our research and gathering the specimens. We considered traveling in March to also collect samples of the bee's spring honey which has some hallucinogenic properties. However, we thought that the warm months of October and November in Bhutan would better suit our purposes.

We will have the bees pollinate a number of flowers in America and see what medicinal properties can be created here, avoiding the negative impacts of the hallucinogens or "Mad Honey". I'm thrilled, though I confess it will be odd having Thanksgiving dinner in another country and away from my Aunt Alice's delightful mashed potatoes.

Your letter to Freddy arrived in the mail, and I agreed with your take on his solution. He certainly took no offense to your sarcasm. On the contrary, I think you lit a fire under the man. He bought himself a typewriter and is working through the night on his novel. It involves stolen plans, an airplane capable of traveling at the speed of sound, and a plot to drop a nuclear bomb on Washington. It is just as you suggested, filled with car chases, romance, and double crosses – a real page turner! It is the kind of drivel which sells well and can be made into a motion picture, so unfortunately, I can see myself needing to find a new assistant for the expedition. We'll see if Freddy completes his Ph.D. or heads for the hills of Hollywood.

293

Now, as for my own proposed solution to the disappearance of Mr. James Phillimore, I have something which, I admit, is not really a solution, but it does shed light on solving the problem. Please know that my solution does not in any way mean to offend you. I ask that you follow my reasoning to my conclusion and see why I make the claim that I do.

I confess that my initial solution to the case wasn't too different from Freddy's. The difference is that I was certain Mr. Phillimore was dead. I couldn't think of a solution to the contrary. He left behind his family and his money. What could drive a man to do such a thing – except for him to no longer being upon this earthly plane?

But then, how could he have died? I thought back to his job at the bank. Perhaps he had discovered some inappropriate funds or some embezzling, or he just had seen something which he wasn't supposed to see. A gangster could have then been hired to assassinate the man. My initial thought was that the gangster somehow had gained access to the house and had hidden himself away in a closet. When Mr. Phillimore returned to his house to get his umbrella, the gangster saw his opportunity. He killed Phillimore, probably by hitting him from behind or strangling him, and then he hid away with the body inside the house. The assassin then waited for night, probably the dead of night, when Mrs. Phillimore and everyone in the neighborhood was asleep. At that point, the man then carried the body right out the front door and buried him in some secluded spot, maybe in a forest or an area of tall grass in the vicinity.

This was the solution I intended to propose to you Mr. Holmes, but as I put pen to paper and actually wrote it down, I instantly began to see cracks in my logic. How did the assassin get into the house? More importantly, how did he drag Mr. Phillimore out of the house without leaving some sign of his presence? There would be some tracks left in dust or some item moved ever so slightly in the house. Also, where did the body end up? If the gangster had killed the man and buried the body close by, surely someone would have come across a newly dug mound of dirt, especially with the police and you, yourself, scanning the area.

So, I was back to square one. I knew that Phillimore couldn't have remained in his house. All logical conclusions pointed away from that solution. And I knew he had to have somehow escaped from his home in a short time frame undetected by everyone in his neighborhood, leaving no trace of himself behind. Looking over the data, this seemed to be impossible unless I went with a somewhat fanciful explanation – the ones you have already nixed as otherworldly or something so incredible that it better fits a dime-store novel. Quite frankly, I couldn't think of a solution which I believed hadn't already crossed your mind and therefore, you had already vetted. Surprisingly, when that realization dawned on me is when I came to know the solution to the case.

It all falls back to logic. As has been written many times in your adventures, you need data to draw your conclusions. The more data you have, the better you can reason. This is true with all logic, though we study it fairly rigidly – the problem with logic isn't what you know, but what you *don't* know. Those little missing pieces of the puzzle which elude someone, almost like completing a thousand-piece puzzle, only to discover there are two missing pieces from the box. You can never have a full picture.

I think you have done that to Freddy and me. I think you have done that to everyone who has written you about this case over all these years. You've purposely left out some of the pieces of the puzzle. Whether you're covering something up or are outright lying about the case, I don't know, but I believe you've purposely misled me and therefore, with the information provided to me, made it impossible for me to solve the case.

I also know you are a great man and there must be a reason behind this non-solution solution. You wouldn't mislead without a clear rationale. Perhaps there is something to Freddy's solution and the case really does involve the Crown. Perhaps it is a personal matter. At this point, I am speculating. As you know, that is never a good thing.

So that is my solution. You have made it so that there is none. I really hope that if I am wrong, you take no offense. You are a man I greatly admire, and I hope you understand that I'm just following the pieces of the puzzle to their logical conclusion.

With kind regards,
Robert Hoffman, Ph. D.
University of Colorado, Boulder

* * *

Dear Dr. Hoffman,

Congratulations on securing your funding for your expedition to the Orient. I look forward to hearing about your trip and about the results of your experiments. If I wasn't in the final stages of completing *The Whole Art of Detection*, then perhaps this centenarian would consider joining you, though I admit a hike through the Himalayas would be slow going at my age.

Attached to this letter, you will find a ten-pound bank note, much more valuable than the ten dollars you bet with your colleague Freddy. It is true that you did not technically solve this puzzle of a case. No matter what I tell you in this letter, Freddy will hold fast to that – as I know with all bets, we leave no wiggle room. However, you did get as far as anyone possibly could with the information which I provided to you. And so, I believe it is warranted for you to be the first person to which I reveal the full truth of the matter. Not even Watson had the pleasure of knowing what you shall now know.

Everything I wrote to you about the case was true. Mr. Phillimore really did disappear when he entered his house to fetch his umbrella, and he was never seen again upon this earth. To be frank, Phillimore was a rather resourceful man. If it wasn't for my work on a previous case, I probably wouldn't have been able to uncover what happened to him. But I am getting ahead of myself.

Like you, I first thought of the possibility of dishonesty when Mrs. Phillimore brought me her case. As the police noted, the most likely explanation involved another woman. I've found that no matter how upstanding a man and no matter how good his marriage, never underestimate his proclivity for extramarital romance. I suspected that for Mr. Phillimore to have suddenly disappeared, he needed assistance from someone, and so I thought it was likely that one of his neighbors was covering for him while he had made his escape.

After Watson and I had ruled out the possibility of Phillimore remaining in his home, we then conducted interviews of the neighbors paying close attention to their behaviors. All appeared to answer their questions honestly, and it seemed that not a one of them was helping to conceal Phillimore's whereabouts. As more time passed, it seemed even more unlikely. If one of them was covering for him, surely with his disappearance spreading into weeks and even months, someone would have spoken up out of concern for the man's well-being.

There was also the issue of money. A man can't survive without it, and it would be very unusual for Phillimore to simply abandon his wealth and life without having a very good reason. I actually did check with my brother and with the police to see if there was any connection with their agencies. There was not. I also made use of my resources in the underworld to see if there was any word about Mr. Phillimore crossing someone or being eliminated. There was nothing. No one, from the top government agents down to my Irregulars, could find any information about the fate of James Phillimore.

Having moved onto other cases, and even having successfully completed a number of them while this one remained unsolved, I decided to have one last review of the evidence before contacting Mrs. Phillimore to declare my defeat. That afternoon, I spent some time sitting comfortably in my chair, smoking my pipe, and visiting my 'chamber of loci', running over the information in my mind, trying to see if there was a key detail I had missed. Alas, nothing stood out.

I ruminated on the case well into the evening hours. I hadn't made any progress and didn't see a path forward when Watson, who was sitting beside me reading the newspaper, made an offhand remark which actually solved the case. When I told Watson I was ready to, as you Americans like to say, "throw in the towel", he said he understood, and that the last time he saw me so baffled by a case was when we had to find the whereabouts of Mr. Neville St. Claire. I jumped out of my chair at this statement and extinguished my pipe, telling Watson that he was the master and I the pupil. As Watson asked what I was on about, and dashed out of our room and down the steps before issuing a reply to my dear friend.

Not long after, I found myself at the small gardener's cottage on the grounds of the Henderson family. I could see from the light in the front window that someone was at home, and I pounded on the front door until it was answered.

Mr. Laurel opened the door wide to see who was causing such a racket. When he saw me, all of his anger deflated. He averted his eyes to the ground and asked quietly, "Does Mrs. Phillimore know?" I told him that she did not. He solemnly nodded his head and replied, "I hope that we can keep it that way. Please, come in."

I entered his domicile, a small two-room abode with the main room containing no more than a small round table, two mismatched chairs, and a stack of books on the subject of botany. We sat at the table and he bluntly asked me, "How?"

"It was your face which gave it away," I explained.

"My face?" he asked.

"Yes, your face and Dr. Watson's most astute observation."

"Please explain."

And thus I did. When Watson and I interviewed Mr. Laurel, I noted that he had a slight facial twitch, a minor abnormality, and I believed nothing more. However, when Watson made the comparison of this case to that of Neville St. Clair, I saw that the twitch would be an excellent addition to an actor playing a character.

Perhaps you recall the case of St. Clair ,which Watson told with his usual flourishes in "The Man with the Twisted Lip". Mr. St. Clair had disappeared, and his wife suspected that Hugh Boone, a dirty beggar with a twisted lip, was responsible. I was able to determine that the beggar and Neville St. Clair were actually the same person. He'd taken to a life of begging in disguise so as not to embarrass his wife, and he was so good at it that he was earning a gentleman's salary.

Laurel, like Boone, was no more than a character. When I interviewed all the neighbors who last saw Mr. Phillimore, they all mentioned the conversation between Laurel and Phillimore. While the Crestone's nanny had merely overheard the conversation between the two men, Mr. Ellis had actually seen them conversing. Then it dawned on me that, from where Ellis was working on the fence, the rose bushes would have been partially obscured by the Phillimore home. So Phillimore had gone back and forth between, using his own voice and that of Laurel. He also traded out his white wig and whiskers to make sure that Mr. Ellis saw him in both roles, so even though Ellis only saw one man at a time, and therefore he believed that he saw both men conversing. The trick was rather ingenious.

I also noted that Phillimore had done an excellent job of taking on the role of Laurel for weeks before he traded lives. Everyone in the neighborhood knew *both* men, so slipping from one life into another became seamless.

Phillimore's acting talents were exemplary. I now understood what Watson meant when he always wrote how the stage lost a great actor when I became a detective. Mr. Phillimore would have been a master of the stage. I confessed that he created the character of Mr. Laurel so well and so convincingly that I didn't realize that the two were separate men. His wife didn't suspect a thing, and again it reminded me of when I would take on roles and have conversations with Watson. The good doctor never knew that the man I was playing and the man I am were one and the same until I revealed the truth. I knew how Phillimore had escaped, but I didn't know why.

"I'l explain it all to you, Mr. Holmes, but let me make one thing perfectly clear. James Phillimore is dead. He disappeared when he went to fetch his umbrella, and he shall never be seen or heard from again."

"Tell your story, Mr. Laurel," I answered, "and as long as your reasons are just, I'll accept your request."

My assurance calmed the man, and he explained his rationale. Phillimore was a highly successful businessman. He'd learned early on that financial markets were incredibly complex as were dealings in the business world. To be an industry leader, he understood that he would have to gain great knowledge, and like a detective, learn to connect details to draw profitable conclusions. So he had created a complex system of mnemonic devices to help him keep track of the markets and his own dealings. He also became an excellent actor, taking on specific

298

roles and personalities most suited to various associates and partners. He would draw out specific information about the people he was meeting, their likes and dislikes, and frame conversations around them. He made people feel at ease, and even friendly with him. Using this approach, it didn't take long for Phillimore to become a wealthy and shrewd businessman.

Because of his success, he was able to marry Mrs. Phillimore with her parents' blessing, despite their age differences. Mr. Phillimore was, as everyone around him saw, leading an idyllic life. But nothing is perfect, and cracks emerged in this paradisic life. Mrs. Phillimore desperately wanted to be a mother. Despite their efforts, she never found herself with child and began to blame herself. This caused great concern for Phillimore, who went to the doctor and discovered that the problem was not with his wife but with himself. The other problem was that Phillimore was rather bored. As successful a businessman as he was, there was no challenge in it for him. He really didn't care about money. He enjoyed a simple life. He didn't even hire servants, preferring to do his own manual labor.

About a year before his disappearance, one of Mr. Phillimore's clients mentioned that he was looking for a good gardener. Ever the one to please his associates, Mr. Phillimore said he knew just the man, a Mr. Laurel. Mr. Phillimore had always had a green thumb, and he thought this would be a fun challenge, to take on the role of a wholly different person. He took a day to plan out the character, decided on the white hair and beard, and to ensure he would not be discovered, developed the twitch in his face. It worked wonderfully, and soon word spread of this excellent gardener.

Mr. Phillimore loved being a gardener. He found the financial industry dull, and managed to arrange his duties so that he spent less and less time at the office, without comment. He found the unpredictability of plants, the changes in weather, and the unforeseen bugs and diseases a real challenge, and he enjoyed seeing the success of his work.

As he enjoyed his new secret life, Phillimore was finding more and more trouble at home. His wife was becoming sullen and distant, beginning to hate herself for remaining without child. The man saw the darkness eating at her and knew that it would eventually consume her. That is when he began to concoct his plan to disappear. He had lived a life that the *world* deemed a success, and now he wanted to end his career and begin a life that *he* personally deemed a success. All he had to do was disappear. His wife would get all of his belongings, was young enough to remarry, and have the life she always wanted. He could go on living as a gardener until the day he died.

So he began to put his plan into place. Mr. Laurel took the job of tending to the Henderson's plants. This put him next door to the Phillimore house, so that Mrs. Phillimore and the neighbors would get used to seeing him. He admitted that he was concerned that his wife would see through his disguise, but so talented an actor was he that she never suspected a thing. As time went by, he continued his role, and on the morning of his disappearance took the step of having Mr. Laurel and Mr. Phillimore conversing in front of the various members of the neighborhood. He hid a change of clothes by the rose bushes out of Mr. Ellis's line of vision. He carefully removed and reapplied his wig and whiskers, and changed, making sure that Ellis could see the two men conversing – but without both men in his sights at the same time. He also changed his voice and spoke loudly, ensuring that the nanny next door would hear the men conversing.

He was proud that he had pulled off this trick, and that was all he had planned for the day. However, when he saw his wife in the automobile and the clouds forming in the sky, he made the decision right then to go ahead and leave the life of Mr. Phillimore behind. Mr. Phillimore went into his house to retrieve his umbrella and was never seen again.

That is the story of the disappearance of Mr. James Phillimore, and Mr. Laurel begged me not to tell a single other soul while he lived.

I sat at the table for several minutes, contemplating all that I'd been told. Then I stood from my seat, pushed in my chair, and headed to the door. Before leaving, I turned and told the man, "Goodbye, Mr. Laurel. Unlike Mr. Phillimore, I do hope to see you again."

I had decided to cede Mr. Laurel's wish, and it was a wise decision on my part. Two years later, Phillimore was declared dead, with a quiet word or two from me to aid the process, and after Mrs. Phillimore underwent the traditional mourning period, she met a Duke closer to her age. The two married and had five children, four boys and a girl. Mr. Laurel continued his gardening. Though never wealthy, he earned a respectable living and, before retiring, he did a little work for a certain beekeeper in the Sussex Downs.

Mr. Laurel died in 1925. Until now, I've never told a soul about the solution to the case. When Watson would say he knew I had more knowledge of the case than I had revealed, I would reply that some stones are better left unturned. He would then give me an understanding eye and wouldn't press the subject.

So there you have it, Dr. Hoffman! While you didn't technically win your bet, you do find yourself ten pounds richer, and now about to embark on a worthy adventure of your own. As to sharing the contents of this letter with Freddy or with any other person, I leave the decision entirely up to you.

Good luck on your expedition. I look forward to hearing more about your progress.

With kind regards,
Sherlock Holmes

Somewhere in the vaults of the bank of Cox and Co., at Charing Cross, there is a travel-worn and battered tin dispatch-box with my name, John H. Watson, M.D., Late Indian Army, painted upon the lid. It is crammed with papers, nearly all of which are records of cases to illustrate the curious problems which Mr. Sherlock Holmes had at various times to examine. Some, and not the least interesting, were complete failures, and as such will hardly bear narrating, since no final explanation is forthcoming. A problem without a solution may interest the student, but can hardly fail to annoy the casual reader. Among these unfinished tales is that of Mr. James Phillimore, who, stepping back into his own house to get his umbrella, was never more seen in this world.

Dr. John H. Watson – "The Problem of Thor Bridge"

The Curious Case of the
Two Coptic Patriarchs
by John Linwood Grant

"It would appear," said Holmes, one cloudy October morning in Baker Street, "that, despite initial success, our troops have fallen back, with losses that include an old acquaintance of yours."

I looked up from the early edition of the newspaper, my mood a match for the weather outside. Opposite me sat the great man, contemplating his empty pipe with no trace of humour in his expression. I sighed.

"You received word before me, Holmes?"

"No, I merely observed your face, my dear fellow, as you read. It betrayed your thoughts, like an open ledger. Come, I am in sympathy. Ladysmith, or possibly Mafeking?"

"Ladysmith." I threw the paper to one side. "You are correct, of course. John French and the Lancers gave the Boer a beating, but had to withdraw. Ladysmith will be surrounded by now."

"Such a foolish struggle, between two peoples who should be equals. And the personal loss?"

"Harry Crane, lately of the 5th Lancers. I knew him in Afghanistan, when he was young. Now missing, presumed dead."

"You were close?"

"Not exactly, but it brings it home. Oh, it brings it home."

"Just so." He glanced at his empty pipe, then at the window, where rain had begun to spatter against the glass. "Perhaps I can engage your thoughts elsewhere for an hour, and let South Africa see to itself."

"A case?"

His long face drew itself into a curious smile. "Well, it is a case, but it is almost closed. It won't make a story for the magazines, mind you. Rather delicate."

He had my interest.

"I didn't know that you were presently engaged."

"I am not. But somewhere in the United States of America this very moment, gentlemen from the Pinkerton Agency will be harrying our prey. I expect success within the month."

I rang for tea, and let Holmes fill his old black pipe in silence, until Mrs. Hudson brought in the tray. Detecting the sombre mood in the room, she picked up the newspaper and folded it neatly, leaving us to it.

302

He lifted the lid from the teapot, and drew in the vapours. "Indian. Still, we cannot expect our good landlady to have mint tea, as they sip in the cafes of Cairo."

"An Egyptian tale?"

"Egypt has much to do with it. It is, in fact, what I described this summer as the case of the two Coptic Patriarchs. You were complaining only last week that I have never shared the details."

"Nor have you," I muttered.

"One reason for not doing so was a sound one – it is not wholly settled, as I said. However, the matter of the Patriarchs themselves is long since concluded. Of course, if you would rather wait until I hear more from the United States . . . ."

I protested that as he had baited me, he should continue. For ease, though not for *The Strand*, I record it here, in my friend's own words . . .

.

You will remember (said Holmes) the unexpected affair of the Dragoman's Son, and my passage across the Red Sea. [1] Making my way to Cairo, and afterwards to Alexandria, I naturally became acquainted with a number of officials in the Administration, both Egyptian and British.

One of those officials was a man named John Eldon Gorst – "Jack" to friends, but simply Eldon Gorst to most. An industrious fellow, he was then in the Egyptian Government's Department of Finance. He interested me, but I was not in Egypt long enough to learn much more about him.

So years later, I was surprised to receive, on an otherwise quiet day, a note signed "Jack Gorst". Would I come to the Foreign Office in London, to consult with him on an urgent matter?

You might be forgiven for assuming that personal tragedy must be in the wind for Gorst, but I dismissed this. We would not be meeting at the Foreign Office, a place of sharp ears and active tongues, if that were so. I took the use of "Jack" as a sign that the matter was seriously bothering him.

I despatched a note to say that I would be there shortly, and not long before noon I took myself off to find out what might have rattled the fellow. It was a pleasant day, and I walked via Horse Guards, arriving a few minutes early. At the Foreign Office, I was shown up to a small oak-panelled meeting room deep within the building.

Gorst joined me within moments. We shook hands, and he mentioned a couple of names from Alexandria, but he seemed unusually agitated. He still had, six years since I had last seen him, the habit of tugging first at one end of his moustache and then the other when he was nervous.

"See here, Holmes, I have a fine mess, and it's none of my doing."

He explained that he had taken up the post of Financial Adviser to the Egyptians the year before, and had retained a certain role in advising the Interior Ministry.

"Do you know anything of the Copts?" he asked abruptly.

I indicated that I had a passing knowledge of those people, the Christians of Egypt and the Sudan. A venerable church, differing in its ways from the Holy See in Rome, but staunchly Christian nonetheless.

"Good. That will help." He frowned. "It's a ridiculous affair, but a matter of face, of reputation."

"Yours, Gorst?" I enquired.

"The Government's reputation, for the most part. Two Governments, in fact."

He explained that there were preparations underway for Rome to re-establish the Coptic Catholic Patriarchy in Alexandria the following month. It had long been mooted, and was now to become a reality.

"The Egyptian Administration is displeased?"

"Not sure they care, as such. Not on religious grounds, certainly – they're mostly Muhammedans, of course, and a few Catholics here and there make no difference to them. The delicacy is with the Coptic *Orthodox* Patriarchy, the majority of the Christians out there. Inheritors of St. Mark and *not* St. Peter – you know the score."

He sat down, and I took a place opposite him at the long table. The tugging of his moustache had intensified.

"Go on. Spare me no detail."

"The devil is in the details, Holmes. All parties are agreed that the Catholic Patriarchy is to be revived, and as a gesture of goodwill towards the Orthodox Patriarch, the British Government offered to return a number of important Coptic antiquities to Egypt. In particular, a collection of very early liturgical writings held by the British Museum."

"Valuable?"

"To some, perhaps, but of most value to the Coptic Orthodox Church."

"And these writings have been stolen, I imagine – quite recently."

Gorst sat back, still grasping his whiskers.

"You have heard, then?"

"No, but it seems likely that such an event would prompt you to contact me. Those good fellows at Scotland Yard would be out of their depth, and open news of the theft would cause diplomatic ripples. I

304

would make a poor ecumenical representative, but as a discreet consulting detective, however . . . ."

"You are as shrewd as people say, Holmes. Yes, they were stolen two nights ago, from the British Museum annexe at Laughton House. The Orthodox Patriarch Cyril V, or 'Kyrillos' as they call him, is seventy-two years old, dogmatic, and yet still a force in the country. The antiquities were promised to him, and a place has already been constructed for them in the main Orthodox Church in Alexandria.

"*HMS Aconite* is to sail in four days' time, with myself and the writings, known as the St. Anthony Texts, on board. A major ceremonial act, now placed in total jeopardy. If we admit we have lost them, the British Government will look foolish, the Egyptians will use it as an excuse to criticise us, and this new period of two Coptic Patriarchs will be off to a damned awkward start. Apart from that, as I was charged with overseeing the whole thing until the texts were in the hands of the Copts . . . ."

I nodded. "Two nights ago, but you did not contact me until today?"

"There were complications. Let me hand you over to someone who can explain."

He took me down to a ground floor office, where a young man was waiting for us, Derby in hand. He had a strong jawline, emphasised by mutton-chop whiskers and clear grey eyes.

"Inspector Dominick here is on secondment to Melville's lot – you know, this 'Special Branch'," said Gorst. "He knows as much as I do about the British end of the situation." The civil servant pulled out his watch. "I am needed by my own masters here, Holmes. Can I hope that you will investigate on the Government's behalf – and mine?"

"I shall wait to hear what the inspector has to say, but I am sure that I will be able to shed some light on the matter."

Gorst looked relieved. "Damn good of you."

Left alone with Dominick, I took out my cigarette case and offered him one of the Turkish cigarettes I get from George Salman's little establishment. He thanked me, and we lit up.

"Fenians seem unlikely," I said, conversationally. "This is neither direct nor showy enough to interest the Irish."

He agreed.

"Russian have ambitions around the Mediterranean, but the Copts are closest to their own Orthodox Church, and they have no quarrel with them. Not an official act, then. That leaves anarchists – even less likely that Fenians – or . . . ." I blew a hazy stream of blue smoke into a shaft of sunlight from the window. "Egyptian Nationalists."

305

He nodded appreciatively. "You have it, Mr. Holmes. The seeming of it, anyway."

His remark, and the sharpness in his eye, interested me.

"To Laughton House, then, Inspector. Let us view the scene of the crime."

The annexe was situated off Tottenham Court Road, a few minutes' walk from the British Museum itself – an unimposing building with a uniformed constable by the main entrance.

Dominick nodded to the constable and guided me down to the main basement, along a corridor which led into a large, low-ceilinged room full of crates and boxes of every description. He waved to another unhappy-looking constable outside and closed the door. Nearest the door all was orderly, the containers stacked on wooden shelves, each one displaying a neat label in one hand or another. The writing had faded on some, and could barely be deciphered.

We passed a long, ceiling-high stack which almost divided the room and came upon disorder – some crates were tilted at an angle, others sitting across the aisles. A man in a brown suit was tutting as he leafed through the contents of a damaged pasteboard box.

The inspector introduced us. "Mr. Maltwood, one of the Assistant Curators."

Maltwood had reddened, watery eyes and a pronounced sinus condition. He blew his nose and stood up. I murmured my sympathy, but there were far more important sights to take in. A set of shelves had been pulled away from the back wall, and lines of Arabic were painted on the bare plaster.

Maltwood saw the direction of my gaze.

"It says, '*We need no Empire. Only Justice*', and below that, '*Rise up, brothers. Take back what is ours, with the sword.*'"

"You have an inventory of what was taken, Mr. Maltwood?"

"Partial, Mr. Holmes. I am yet checking to see if other boxes contain all they should. It will take some time."

"But in the main . . . ."

"An apparently random selection of papers, mostly obscure. A box of broken *ushabtis* – little figurines – and such trinkets. However, we are also missing an important vellum text, copied out by a Greek monk and bound in brass and leather some time before the Crusades. It is written in both Greek and Coptic, detailing the acts of St. Anthony and of St. Pachomius. Reputed to be an account by witnesses who personally knew the saintly gentlemen in question. Fascinating, really."

I walked over to where a large patch of a rusty red colour stained the wooden floor.

"Blood?"

The inspector nodded. He reached into his jacket and brought out a photograph. "Blood and more, sir."

I would not say that I was shocked, but the photograph did give me pause. It showed, quite clearly, a severed human hand in a pool of blood, in the same position where the stain could still be seen. Around the hand were fragments of torn cloth, and in front of it lay a curved Arab blade. Several crates in the background had toppled, as if there had been a struggle in the vicinity.

"This is what one of the attendants found when he opened up the next morning, wondering where Welby had got to. The police photographer arrived with an hour of it being reported."

"Welby?"

The night-watchman." Dominick glanced at the photograph. "Charles Welby is . . . missing, let us say. I prefer that you see the details, and come to your own conclusions. The hand is being held by E Division, at the Bow Street Station, packed around with ice. The knife and scraps are also there."

This was an irritating turn of events.

"You realise that I should have seen all this *in situ*, immediately it was discovered?"

Dominick looked unabashed. "It was not my case until yesterday, Mr. Holmes. I was requested to attend only after the graffiti had been deciphered."

"I see." I bent low. "There is more writing here, but it is not Arabic."

Crude hieroglyphs had been painted on the floor, presumably with more of the blood.

"I translate them as '*Sobek has him*'," said Maltwood. "That being . . . um, Sobek, the crocodile God of the Nile."

I asked the two of them to wait outside, and conducted a thorough examination of what had been left to me. The floor was scuffed, and any hope of finding distinctive footprints had been lost. It appeared that boxes had been moved since the event, confusing matters further. It was difficult to imagine a more muddled crime scene.

You know my methods when it comes to these matters. I paid more attention to the less-used "corridors" between the stacks, in case our intruders had loitered there. The air was dry, and under the strong odour of dusty papers and scrolls, I thought I detected another fragrance.

307

The writing on the wall had been done hastily, by the look of it, and in common black paint. I doubted that it would yield anything of interest beyond its stated meaning. On my knees, I quartered the area, discovering something that no one had yet mentioned – other stains on the floor by the nearest untouched stack, a dark, yellowish-brown. A few small, discoloured patches over an area of a few feet, and traces of fibrous matter.

Dominick and Maltwood were in the corridor outside.

"How did the perpetrators enter?"

"We don't know," said Dominick. "No doors or windows were forced. I have also ascertained that no one may leave the building without their baggage thoroughly being checked. Scholars are forgetful, and some of the items are valuable."

I examined the small rear entrance, and the large double doors onto the street. There were no marks other than those which might have been made by a fumbled attempt to get a key in the locks.

"Duplicate keys, then, or a very skilful lock-pick. No matter."

I looked at the Assistant Curator. "By the way, do you have any female staff, Mr. Maltwood, or visiting associates of that sex?"

"Not a one, sir."

"Then I shall have a word with your other staff, if I may."

This took over an hour, and I was in a poor mood as Dominick and I headed towards Bow Street.

"I recall that there was an attempt to plant a small bomb near Parliament in April. Made much of by the papers. Two Egyptians, who said they served Urabi Pasha."

"There was, Mr. Holmes. But Urabi Pasha is in exile, in Ceylon, and said that he knew nothing of these fellows – the need for action was by the Nile, not by the Thames, he stated. The authorities are inclined to believe his statement – on those who were taken, I mean."

"Hmm."

"Besides, those two men were Muhammedan, not of the Coptic persuasion. Where the Egyptian Christians fit in is presently beyond me."

The fellow seemed clear-thinking enough.

"You are on secondment to Special Branch, I am told."

He nodded. "The work interests me, and their scope increases. I hope for a permanent position. Rather an anarchist ring than a domestic dispute in Putney."

"A sentiment I can understand. Now, to business. I must examine that evidence which someone saw fit to remove from its proper setting."

The Bow Street police had at least kept everything in good order. The hand was – as you might expect – an unpleasant object. I lifted it from the ice-filled sackcloth which surrounded it.

"You have a description of Welby, the missing man?"

"Of above average height," said Dominic. "Sturdy, clean-shaven, and with dark hair. Been with the museum for about a year."

On the third finger was a gilt ring worth a couple of shillings, possibly less. I drew out a magnifying glass and looked close at the hand – into the furrows, under the fingernails. There were dark hairs along the back of the object.

"Tell me about this ring, inspector."

"It was one reason they were sure it was Welby's hand. I did ask around, in case they were mistaken. He told his colleagues, who saw little enough of him, that it was a token of a former marriage, but that his wife had died tragically under a train, having fallen off the platform whilst bearing their child."

"I imagine that they heard this story quite recently, did they not?"

"I'm told that he mentioned it only last week, whilst coming off his shift."

"Capital."

A tin next to the hand contained more scraps of cloth – coarse serge in dark blue.

"Torn from the standard garb of a night-watchman, I presume?"

"Exactly so, Mr. Holmes. None of the other uniforms stored at Laughton House show any signs of damage, and none but his are missing."

The knife was caked with dried blood, including the wire-bound hilt. A typical *jambiya*, the curved blade found in many Arab lands. Along with the knife were Welby's keys, equally spattered in blood. I used a pocket glass to examine those as well.

"I believe that I have seen enough," I said. "Inspector, you might indulge me by sending some of your men out to make enquiries."

Dominick hesitated. "I don't have any men as such. I can request officers from E Division, if it is deemed important enough."

"Mr. John Eldon Gorst would consider it so. If I might have pen and paper . . . ."

I wrote out a number of specific requirements, and handed it to him.

I can admire efficiency when it sprouts in an unlikely field. The officers of Bow Street threw themselves enthusiastically into the tasks assigned them.

"The lads do like a change, Mr. Holmes," said the elderly desk sergeant as he led me to an office where I could have a quiet smoke and

309

ponder this odd case. "They will be boasting tonight that they have been a-working for that Mr. Sherlock Holmes."

Dominick was with me for a few minutes, but soon took my silence to mean exactly what it indicated – that I did not require company. He left to co-ordinate the footwork, and at length I informed the sergeant I would be leaving. I had my own records to check, and I required certain equipment. The inspector was to find me the following day, at Baker Street.

Once home, I spent most of the night with my files, my slides, and my microscope, pausing to make a couple of crucial telephone calls at one point. I had little doubt that I could solve the case, but there were now only three days until the *Aconite* must sail. You will see that I had to rely on the police, rather than undertaking certain aspects of the investigation myself. Not an ideal situation. If Dominick's men moved swiftly, and asked exactly the questions I had posed, then all might still be well. If not . . . .

The inspector arrived at Baker Street mid-morning, only moments after you yourself had left for Lewisham, Watson, on that Josiah Amberley affair. Dominick was alert and full of news, but soon began to cough at the smoke from my pipe.

"My dear chap," I said, rising. "Your bronchial tubes, of course. Come, we shall take a stroll."

We headed towards the British Museum at a brisk pace, as the streets were only moderately busy. As we went, he handed me various envelopes containing slips of paper which held the results of the police activity over the last twelve or so hours. He admitted that he hadn't ventured to read them as yet.

"Promising," I said, examining one of the slips, "And as I suspected. Good."

Noticing our bearing, I remarked that we might pass by Coptic Street, if we chose.

"Very apt," said Dominick, pausing on the corner. "I must confess, Mr. Holmes, your enquiries seem to take us in a number of different directions at once."

"A fair observation, but I believe you will find all roads lead to Rome."

"The Vatican is involved?" He sounded slightly alarmed. "Are not the Patriarchs enough?"

I patted him on the arm. "Merely a turn of phrase, Inspector. It is quiet here. Let us talk. Firstly, I assume that the matter will be in tomorrow's newspapers?"

310

He looked glum.

"If not the evening editions today, sir. I imagine that '*Bloody Crime at Museum*', and "*Mystery of the Severed Hand*' will be prominent. It was all that the authorities could do to hold it this long. There will be speculation about the Urabi movement and Egyptian Nationalists, but no mention of the Coptic Patriarchs or the missing texts. That, at least, we have suppressed."

"I see. Now, let me put three possibilities to you, and see which of them takes your fancy. The first is this: Welby the night-watchman is alive but captive, his stump hastily dressed, in the hands of the Egyptian Nationalists. Perhaps his body will be left on a prominent place as a warning – or it may be that he will never be seen again."

"I follow you so far."

"The second possibility is that he is dead. His body was dumped, yet to be discovered, or was fed to the Crocodile-God Sobek, a sacrifice made necessary by Britain's folly."

He gave a tight smile. "Dead, possibly, but I shall discount that last part, sir."

"Very well. The third is that Welby is involved in the crime – that he is alive, healthy, and in hiding somewhere, whilst arrangements are made to dispose of the St. Anthony Texts."

The inspector blew out his cheeks, and held his head low for some moments.

"Then this is," he said at last, "simply a theft. Dressed up – I cannot untangle that part as yet – to cause shock and confusion, purely as misdirection. A knife, a severed hand, the writings on the wall – I wondered about the use of both Arabic and hieroglyphs, in connection with Coptic writings. Little of it fitted with what I have read of the Egyptian Nationalists."

"You show much promise, Inspector. It was cheap showmanship, at heart." I patted the pocket in my coat where lay the intelligence from the police. "I had your colleagues make urgent enquiries at the teaching hospitals. A hand went missing from the anatomy room at St. Luke's three days ago. It was thought to be a prank; it was in fact intended for the scene at Laughton House.

"Furthermore, the curved knife was far *too* bloody. I conjecture that blood was splashed over it, and the floor, probably from a pig or other slaughterhouse animal. Again, for effect. Had the regular police force alone been left to work on this puzzle, they would probably have seen no deeper.

"One of these other notes gives us further information. Mr. Maltwood informs me that, as per my request last night, he re-examined the text scrawled on the basement wall. On consideration he doubts that a true Arab wrote it. The style is too crude, like something copied – or written by one who to whom the tongue is not native. Maltwood had also provided a summary of what else he believes to be missing. A mixed bag of minor artefacts and papers, all easily portable."

"What does this leave us with, Mr. Holmes?"

"It leaves us with *two* criminals, Inspector. Two criminals who wanted the St. Anthony Texts, before they were shipped to Egypt. The other items taken are irrelevant, removed to confuse the police. There was one man inside – Welby – and at least one confederate, conceivably the one who paid Welby to betray the trust placed in him by the museum."

"Can we catch them? Can we retrieve the texts in time?"

"Possibly, Inspector, possibly.

He frowned. "If there is no threat to national security, if this is merely showmanship, Mr. Holmes, then I hardly have any further role in this matter."

His point was fair, but I had other considerations.

"It might be wise not to share that conclusion with your superiors," I said. "Time is still of the essence, and I have no patience for having to communicate with an unknown inspector from one of the Divisions. Let us assume that Mr. Gorst would prefer us to complete this task together."

"Very well, sir."

"Then I urge you to make immediate enquiries into Welby's background. I will be at Baker Street by five this evening. If you return then, I will have further news."

I left a worried Dominick to his work and strode along Coptic Street, deep in thought. I had a fancy that I might speed up the investigation and, accordingly, I called upon four addresses that afternoon, with indifferent results. My fifth venture was far more satisfactory.

Morgan's Empire Tobacco, off Russell Square, is an excellent establishment. I may engage their services in the future. Mr. Morgan himself came out of his office when I informed his assistant who I was. The proprietor was a short, genial man who rubbed his hands enthusiastically.

"So, Mr. Holmes. What an honour! This would be in relation to the police sergeant who called on us yesterday evening."

"It would." I described what I sought in more detail, bearing in mind my additional microscope work.

"I can satisfy you there, sir. 'Indian Chief' is very distinctive. Larger stems, and more of them, plus distinctive sweetening agents. Here, I'll

312

open a fresh jar especially for you. We are, as I told your sergeant, the main suppliers of such tobaccos on this side of London. I believe Merrick and Sons, of Greenwich, may stock it, but I wouldn't swear to that."

He took me into the stockroom, and was as good as his word, letting me examine and then sample the tobacco.

"Is this the brand, Mr. Holmes?"

"It is. You have been most helpful, Mr. Morgan."

"Then I shall furnish you with the customer's details." His moon-like face almost split with his smile. "Before you go, could I perhaps press you to some of our 'Special Black Turkish'. Our own blend, quite strong. I understand from Dr. Watson's stories that you do like a pipe or two."

I accepted the pouch he offered, and we parted in good spirits on both sides.

Dominick returned to our rooms looked tired and drawn. I asked him immediately about his enquiries into Welby's background.

"A common enough story, Mr. Holmes – apprenticed in the textile trade, no great advancement. A roundsman for one of the railway companies, with an average record, and then a night-watchman. He had – *has* – a room in Blackfriars, but has not been seen there these last three nights."

"And his family?"

"Deceased, except for a sister no longer in this country."

I looked up. "She lives in America, does she not? In Boston, to be more precise."

He looked astounded. "You made the same enquiries before me?"

"No, I made connections, Inspector. And I deduced a likely solution."

"Then there is definite progress?"

"There is." In deference to the inspector, Mrs. Hudson brought coffee and he sipped it, clearly eager to ask a host of questions.

"Ten minutes or so, Inspector, and then we will be rewarded."

We sat quiet, each in his thoughts, Dominick so contemplative that the eventual rap on the door startled him. Mrs. Hudson showed in a white-faced young man with his hat in his hands.

"Take a seat," I said, my face stern.

He did so.

"Sir, am I to be in trouble?" His voice quavered – he was no more than twenty-two or -three. From his voice and appearance I placed him as of decent Kentish stock, neither wealthy nor poor.

"Not if you tell all, Mr. Ailford. However, this is Inspector Dominick of the Special Branch, which will indicate to you how a serious a matter this is."

The boy nodded.

"Ailford is a medical student, Inspector. Let us hear his story."

Awkward but clear spoken, the student explained. A "gentleman", as Ailford called him, had been enquiring of the students at St. Luke's the week before, saying that he was in the theatrical business and could badly do with a human hand for a forthcoming production. "These *papier-mâché* jobs, they simply won't do for a sophisticated audience." And the man had winked. "They'll think it a prop, but be impressed by how realistic it it. I'll pay, of course, and all will be strictly between us."

Most had demurred, but Ailford had bills, and wished not to bother his father again. He assented, knowing that he was due in anatomy classes the following day. It would not have been the first time that an ear or a finger had been misappropriated to be used in a prank. A whole hand was asking a lot, but the man was offering ten guineas.

"Did you not wonder at his story?" asked Dominick.

"Not at all, sir." The boy shuffled his feet. "We had been at a show only last month where the corpse of a murdered uncle showed itself upon stage. So badly had it been crafted that half the audience burst into laughter."

The theft was simple – it had only to be recent, the hand of a grown man, neither young nor ancient.

"The easiest thing to find in London, I imagine," said Dominick. "So many accidents, to say nothing of murderous brawls."

Ailford agreed that almost all the bodies he saw were of that nature. He had wrapped the hand in many layers of brown paper, and hastened himself to The Crossed Swans, not far from where the students themselves watered. The man took the parcel and paid in full.

The student gave a creditable description, one which Dominick agreed was the spit of Charles Welby. With the inspector's assent I dismissed Ailford, who had no real harm in him, adding the admonishment that he should not speak a word to his comrades.

"You have narrowly avoided direct involvement in a serious crime," I said sternly. "Consider this a lesson to keep to yourself."

When he had gone, his face even paler than before, I turned to the inspector.

"We know our quarry."

"I shall have word around every Division within the hour. They understand manhunts." Dominick pushed aside his coffee. "I pray that we can take the fellow in time."

I permitted myself a smile.

"I believe I have the exact address where we may take the perpetrators, and possibly the St. Anthony Texts as well. However, I dare not be complacent. I urge you to wire to have the ports alerted. They are to seek an American citizen, a woman, alone or accompanied. I expect her to be taking passage to the States within the next couple of days."

"An American woman?"

"In her early fifties, strongly built, and most likely dressed simply, without frills or fancies."

The inspector looked dubious, but hurried away to contact his superiors.

A half-hour later he returned, the matter arranged.

"Are you armed, Inspector?"

"Yes, sir."

At his suggestion we gathered a sergeant and two constables from Bow Street and made our way north towards Camden Town in a growler. The carriage jerked abominably, but got us to our destination – a hotel of a reasonable class, stone-fronted and three stories high, not far from the Regent's Canal.

"The Arlington." Dominick glanced at me. "You believe Welby to be holed up in there?"

"Either Welby or his employer."

He directed the uniformed constables to attend to the back of the building, with the sergeant to await us outside the main entrance.

Inside, the Arlington was tasteful, though not grand. A man I took to be the manager, by his age, suit, and general appearance, was at the front desk.

"We seek Mrs. Harding. A matter of urgency," I said.

"I . . . it is not the Arlington's policy to – "

Dominick thrust his warrant papers at the man, whose eyes widened.

"Room 109, sir."

We took the broad stairs two at a time, swiftly locating the first floor room. Dominick had his revolver in his hand.

"Stay back, Mr. Holmes."

The inspector surprised me by kicking out at the door with one heavy boot, which action splintered the area around the handle. He shouted "Police!" and threw himself into the room. I followed more cautiously.

This time Charles Welby was unable to disappear. His body lay in the middle of the large room, his own blood soaking the carpet. The knife in his chest was not a *jambiya*, but of the type Americans call a Bowie Knife. One of the windows was wide open. I rushed to it, to see a figure in a long buff coat descending an iron ladder, riveted to the wall in case of fire.

"Dominick! She must have seen us arrive."

He joined me, and fired a warning shot in the figure's general direction, but too late. We heard the high sound of a constable's whistle, and could only hope that they were alert.

"Go after her, man!" I urged him, and went to the dying Welby. The wound was clearly fatal. This was no time for sentiment.

"The St. Anthony Texts. Does she have them? Tell me now, if you wish a doctor!"

His eyes were barely open, and there was bloody foam on his lips.

"N-no . . . in my crib . . . The Red Lion."

"You must be clear with me – The Red Lion Inn . . . ."

"On Houghton Street," he managed. "S-she would not pay . . . what I asked, the bitch!"

The manager flapped and fluttered, sending first for the doctor and then for the local police. I scribbled a hasty message to Bow Street and gave one of the hotel boys a half-crown to deliver it immediately.

Dominick and his borrowed men were nowhere to be seen. The local doctor could do nothing for Welby, who spoke no more. He died within a quarter-of-an-hour. Examining the room as I waited, I discovered sufficient to confirm my suspicions.

Dominick returned soon after, dejected.

"We did not take her, though the search continues. I assume she was the American woman of whom you warned me. My only consolation is that I am sure she had no papers of substance with her – certainly nothing as bulky as the texts we seek. Let us trust that the port authorities have more luck. Did Welby – "

"He is dead. I do not think I will disappoint you, Inspector, but ask no further questions until we reach our next destination." I gave a grim smile. "In case I have blundered."

We took a hansom to The Red Lion, Houghton Street, where according to my instruction, constables were at the door, watching for "Mrs. Harding", or anything else untoward. I had made it clear that no packages were to leave the premises.

The landlord informed us that he had a few residents on the floors above the family living quarters. One was a quiet man, Charlie Orde, who again answered to the description of Charles Welby. He had taken a room there only the week before.

316

The room on the third floor, barely a garret, was lightly furnished with a washstand, a cot by the window, and a large seaman's chest, padlocked, opposite it. The chest was partly covered with a canvas cloth, and must have served as a table. Dominick had the lock off with one blow of his revolver stock.

He looked at me.

"You believe that the missing items – "

"Go ahead, Inspector. If I am correct, yours is the right."

The seaman's chest was a treasure trove, a Laughton House writ small. Jumbled under old blankets were the damaged *ushabtis*, along with various scrolls, and underneath all, the heavy leather-bound book that should contain the St. Anthony Texts. Dominick passed it to me with care, and I opened it with equal reverence.

This was no Book of Kells, no great illuminated volume from one of the ancient monasteries, gold-blocked and lavish in its *initia*, those beautiful and exaggerated first letters. Rather, I found its simplicity strangely humbling. Inside the later binding, itself much worn, were aged sheets of vellum, the edges roughly cut. And on those sheets, crabbed writing – a faded sepia – which occasionally changed direction and became minute marginalia. A glance was enough to convince me that the contents, in two quite different scripts, represented the Greek and Coptic writings that Eldon Gorst sought.

"My God, Mr. Holmes. You have done it," said Dominick. "In less than two days. You are a miracle-worker."

"If I had taken more than two days, this might be headed out of the country, to be lost forever," I pointed out.

It was growing dark as we took our prizes directly to Gorst at the Foreign Office, having ascertained that he was working late in hope of news. When we entered his temporary office, a decanter of whisky and three glasses stood on the desk.

I passed him the St. Anthony Texts, swaddled in a borrowed policeman's cape. He unwrapped the book and laid it reverentially next to the decanter. His examination was as careful as my own.

"Genuine," he announced. "By God, genuine. All is well!"

He pressed a glass of whisky on us both.

"Gentlemen, I am in your debt. Soon I shall be on *HMS Aconite*, along with this fine book, and a message from the Archbishop of Westminster to his brother-in-faith, the new Coptic Catholic Patriarch. I shall also be returning to my true work amongst the pashas and fellaheen of Egypt. It will be a relief."

We sat down and began to answer various questions about the day. Gorst had no interest in the mechanics of the crime, once we had assured him there was no evidence of nationalist involvement. He wondered why I had dismissed that aspect so quickly, though.

I smiled. "Because I understand misdirection, Gorst, and have used it myself. Too many aspects of the case were for show – had they been more careful, the subterfuge might have held out a day or so longer. The hand was an over-melodramatic touch. The story of Welby's ring, with its tragic connection, was too obviously intended to make the police assume that it was indeed his. That was my first inkling. And even severing another's hand, however messily done, does not cover the knife so entirely with blood. In actual fact, a bone saw had been at work, but not at Laughton House – there were no fragments of bone to be found anywhere.

"I decided that everything I saw was for effect, and so considered the evidence in an entirely different light. The appearance of the hand was too good for it to be that of a tramp or beggar, and its condition showed it to be recent, hardly a grave-robbing. The anatomy classes were the obvious source, and students are easily influenced. The clumsy but earnest efforts of Bow Street frightened the culprit into confessing immediately, and agreeing to share what he knew."

"Clear enough, when you put it that way," said Gorst.

"The criminal with half-a-brain often exerts him – or herself – too far. Arabic writing might have convinced for a while. The added hieroglyphs were another excess."

Dominick accepted a top-up for his whisky.

"Once Mr. Holmes had made it clear that this was not a matter of national security, but a burglary, it was easier to see what had occurred. Welby was the inside man and the foot-soldier, promised – I imagine – a fine purse for the job. A night-watchman's pay is not extravagant."

"But what of this tobacconist nonsense?" Gorst seemed more relaxed, even amused now. I returned his smile.

"Welby could not know quite what he was looking for, and would certainly not know Arabic or ancient Egyptian. They also had to ascertain if what was sought was still at the Laughton. I had detected a woman's perfume on the air in the basement. A curator's assistant informed me that a woman identifying herself as Welby's sister had been there the night before. She said that Welby had forgotten his provisions and flask. Another subterfuge – he had no living relatives in England."

"Then the police – "

"Had not thought to ask the right questions. On the floor, I found some curious spatters, well away from the bloody scene. I thought at first that something had been spilled, but a microscope confirmed the presence of vegetable matter. Specifically, *Nicotiana tabacum*.

318

"The chewing of tobacco is a particularly American vice these days, and I knew that a woman was somehow involved. Morgan's Empire Tobacco had supplied a 'mature' American lady staying at the Arlington Hotel with her favourite chewing tobacco, 'Indian Chief'. I had found residue of the same tobacco, suitably masticated, in the basement of the annexe."

"So – " began Dominick.

"I considered the significance of the St. Anthony Texts being returned to Egypt, and the fact that the texts would soon be under naval guard, in the light of the above. This sparked in me a singular thought . . . Mrs. Clemency Jenning, of Boston."

The two men looked at me without any recognition of the name.

"Maltwood would know of her, as would some of the senior staff at the British Museum." I chuckled. "An unusual woman, the widow of an avid collector of antiquities. She herself was an acolyte of a British Egyptologist, the late Amelia Edwards, until their ways parted. Miss Edwards did not believe in separating Egyptian finds from their native land and authorities, unless absolutely necessary. Mrs. Jenning believed, as did her wealthy husband, in acquiring these items by any means, claiming that their natural guardians were no longer up to the job.

"The British Museum holds on to its finds with tenacity, and there is much public admiration of the monumental and the marvellous – the mummified forms of the pharaohs and their consorts, the spectacular architecture of classical Egypt. To true Egyptologists – and Mrs. Jenning is certainly one of those – such items as the writings of ancient priests and the St. Anthony Texts are far more important. The Coptic language is, as you know, Gorst, descended from the original language of the pharaohs."

I took out my cigarette case, offering Gorst and Dominick a smoke.

"Detection is a science, gentlemen. We combine physical evidence with knowledge of motive and opportunity. And we employ logic all the while. The limited availability of specific brands of American chewing tobacco. The likelihood of students to misbehave, especially for money, and so forth. I have no doubt that Mrs. Jenning somehow learned of Welby from his sister in Boston. That must have seemed an additional piece of luck for her, to have a direct contact she could influence."

"Good heavens!" Gorst made a few notes in a small book. "Mrs. Clemency Jenning, you say."

"We may yet take her when she tries to leave the country, sir," said the inspector. "If Mr. Holmes is correct – my apologies, I should have said 'in light of Mr. Holmes's undoubtedly correct information' – she did murder Welby in an argument over money for his part in the affair."

319

"His knuckles were bruised, and there were indications of disagreement – a broken glass under the table in the hotel room, a chair over-turned." I said. "It may have been self-defence, when he grew acquisitive for his reward. Incidentally, Dominick, there are a few other points for your eventual notes of the case. For example, Welby's keys, beneath the dried blood, showed traces of wax. He had made an impression of them."

Dominick nodded. "Which is why there were no signs of forced entry."

"Just so. The annexe locks will have to be changed. I imagine she let herself in on the night of the crime, and assisted in identifying the St. Anthony Texts, as well as fabricating evidence. Welby packed up the items and hauled them away to his temporary lodgings until Mrs. Jenning was ready to head back to the States. It would not have done to have them sitting in her hotel room. It is unfortunate for her that she still pursued the habit of chewing tobacco, even in the basement of Laughton House."

Gorst rose to his feet. "Gentlemen, you have done an exemplary job."

"I fear I did little enough, sir," said Dominick.

I waved my hand at this.

"You undertook everything I required off you, Inspector, and most efficiently, at that. I am certain you will be a great asset to the Special Branch."

"Thank you, Mr. Holmes."

When the inspector had gone, I looked to Gorst, who was staring out into the night.

"Mrs. Jenning is clever. I doubt they will take her," I said.

"What do you suggest? To be candid, she no longer interests me greatly. I will soon have two Patriarchs to please and placate, ensuring that they consider Britain's interests when they address their flocks."

"There are those in the United States who would seek to curtail Mrs. Jenning's activities," I suggested. "They will be interested in many aspects of these recent events"

"Then inform or commission them, as you see fit, though say nothing of the St. Anthony Texts, I beg you, Holmes. Otherwise, you have my full backing, and that of the Foreign Office."

And so, Watson, that is where the matter stands to this very day.

Holmes sat back with an expression of satisfaction which I could not deny him. I took a handkerchief to my nose, wondering if October had decided to infect my own sinuses.

"Have you crossed paths with this Jenning woman before then, Holmes?"

"No. She has, however, been in my files for some time – just in case. Not exactly a criminal mastermind, but what some might call 'a canny old bird', less easy to trap or flush out than most of her sex. I did flush her from the Arlington, but still she flapped her way back to cover somehow."

"And these Patriarch chaps – all is well over there?"

"The ceremony – and the handing over of the St. Anthony Texts – proceeded entirely according to plan. So now we have two Coptic Patriarchs, Watson. Both in Alexandria and both, it may amuse you to know, called Kyrillos."

For the first time that day, I smiled.

> *"You know that I am preoccupied with this case of the two Coptic Patriarchs, which should come to a head to-day."*

Sherlock Holmes – "The Adventure of the
Retired Colourman"

NOTE

1 – For more information about this tale, see "The Adventure of the Dragoman's Son" by John Linwood Grant in *Holmes Away From Home – Adventures From The Great Hiatus – Volume I: 1891-1892* (2017, Belanger Books)

The Conk-Singleton
Forgery Case
by Mark Mower

T he highly obsessive collector can be a danger both to himself and to all of those who would stand in the way of his compulsive personality. Place a rare or desirable artefact within his grasp and he will go to extraordinary lengths to own it. Tempt him with the unique or definitive piece and he may risk life or limb to satisfy his desires. That Arthur Conk-Singleton was an obsessive collector was clear to all who knew him. What was not so clear was whether his acquisitiveness had led to his death.

It was in the spring of 1900 that Holmes was first invited to assist Scotland Yard in the murder investigation. Arthur Conk-Singleton was a wealthy retired banker who appeared to be fanatical about money in all its forms. The fifty-eight year old bachelor had filled his South Kensington home with a rare and prized collection. No fewer than seven of his well-proportioned rooms had been fitted out with large display cabinets containing banknotes, coins, and promissory notes from all parts of the world. The collection contained some of the earliest and most sought-after examples of paper money, produced in China during the Tang and Song dynasties of the 7th Century. His more recent acquisitions included banknotes and coins issued by the unified territories of Italy and Germany. In fact, there was no currency that the man had overlooked in his quest to build the ultimate collection.

As a trustee of the Numismatic Society of London, Conk-Singleton was, by all accounts, a well-regarded, but inherently secretive, collector. Only a handful of his colleagues had ever been invited to the house; fewer still had been shown around the entire collection. He had only one known relative – a bedbound older brother, Francis, who lived in Eastbourne and claimed to have had little time for his sibling, and even less interest in Arthur's hobby. As a devout Anglican, Francis held to the age-old maxim that *money is the root of all evil*. And while shocked to hear of the murder, he said it came as no surprise, explaining to the police that Arthur had cultivated few real friendships in life and seemed content to make an enemy of anyone who stood between him and his next acquisition.

The sequence of events leading to the murder seemed straightforward enough. In the early evening of Sunday, 13th May, Conk-

Singleton had received a visitor. He had been alone in the house at the time, his elderly housekeeper being in the habit of attending an evening church service at nearby St. Stephens. That he had known the caller was clear from the evidence in the parlour. Conk-Singleton had poured two glasses of expensive Madeira, which had then been consumed – the empty glasses and bottle were still sitting where they had been placed on a small oval table between two comfortable armchairs. At some point thereafter, the two had made their way from the parlour into the largest of the rooms, in which the currency collection was housed. It was there that the body had been found. Conk-Singleton had been shot once through the back at close range by a small handgun. The wound had been sufficient to kill him relatively quickly. Having been absent for less than two hours, the housekeeper had returned to the house around eight-thirty to find her employer dead.

It was late in the afternoon on the day after the murder when Inspector Lestrade called in at 221b. At that time, we had become used to his social calls and the news that he often brought from Scotland Yard. Sometimes he would share the particulars of one case or another and Holmes would do his best to point the capable detective in the right direction. On this particular occasion our friend seemed most subdued, and Holmes was quick to encourage him to tell us what troubled him.

"An odd case, Mr. Holmes – one that should be straightforward, but is proving to be anything but."

My colleague leaned forward in his chair, offering Lestrade a ready-made cigarette from his silver case and passing across an ashtray. "Then you must tell us all about it!"

Lestrade outlined the key facts of the case as I have already set them before you. In the twenty-four hours since being called to South Kensington, his officers had conducted extensive enquiries, interviewing the housekeeper, nearby neighbours, officials at the Numismatic Society of London, and the brother in Eastbourne. While they now knew more about the victim and the manner of his death, the motive for the killing remained a mystery. A single bullet had been removed from the man's heart during the *post-mortem*. It had come from the barrel of a Colt Derringer .41-calibre rim-fire pistol. No one had been seen entering or leaving the house, and no shot had been heard by any of those living close to the ex-banker.

Holmes and I listened intently. When Lestrade paused, I asked, "Could the motive have been robbery?"

"No, Doctor. As far as we can determine, nothing has been taken. The housekeeper is a woman of meticulous habits. She has been with her employer for over twenty years and knows every square inch of the property. She says that she can see nothing out of place."

"Then perhaps the robbery was foiled. Could it have been the return of the housekeeper that prompted the culprit to flee?"

"Again, we do not believe that to be the case. The house has only two doors, front and rear. Both were locked when the housekeeper returned, she having her own set of keys. The key to the back door was still in the lock, so the killer could not have left that way. Mr. Conk-Singleton was as fanatical about security as he was with his collection. All of the windows have locks and each was secure when we arrived. The front door must have been the point of exit, for the locking mechanism can be sprung from the inside, but is reset as soon as the door is shut. Had the killer left when the housekeeper arrived, they would have passed on the threshold. Beyond that, I see it as no coincidence that our assailant arrived when the housekeeper was absent. I believe he planned it that way, knowing she would be out."

Holmes then spoke. "That is possible, but by no means certain. Now, tell us more about this Society to which our man belonged. Are you thinking that the killer may have been a member?"

Lestrade nodded, adding, "Since retiring from the bank two years ago, Conk-Singleton has lived as something of a recluse. The housekeeper said that he only ever left home to visit auctions and attend the bi-monthly meetings of the Numismatic Society. The infrequent visitors he received were all fellow collectors."

"Then your working hypothesis would seem to be a fair one, Lestrade. How many trustees and members are there in the Society?"

"Forty-four, of which seven are known to have previously called on Conk-Singleton."

"Then your list of suspects is not extensive."

"No, but it is problematic."

"How so?"

"Each man has a solid alibi for where he was at the time of the murder."

"I see. And you have no other leads?"

Lestrade took a final draw on his cigarette, before stubbing it out in the ashtray beside him. "No."

"So how did you leave the scene of the crime? I hope you have not allowed the *meticulous* housekeeper to destroy any evidence that might remain?"

Lestrade snickered. "Mr. Holmes, I know your methods well enough! I have a constable at the property with strict instructions to let no one in without my say so. The housekeeper has been persuaded to move out for a couple of days and is currently staying with her sister in Nuneaton. Naturally, I was hoping that you might find time to travel across to South Kensington to see if we have missed anything."

My colleague gave him the broadest of smiles. "Your faith is well placed, my friend. Watson and I would be delighted to assist. And there is no time like the present!"

It took us little time to travel by carriage to the handsome Italianate townhouse on Gloucester Road. We were greeted at the door by a young constable who looked visibly relieved when Inspector Lestrade announced that there was no further need for him to remain on guard at the property.

Holmes was eager to learn what he could, and with his magnifying glass to hand asked Lestrade to direct him immediately towards the parlour. The room he entered was spacious with a high ceiling and ornate chandelier. The décor was distinctly masculine – the curtains, wallpaper, and furnishings being dark green in colour and giving the room a sombre, almost funereal feel. To the left side of the room I could see the small oval table and armchairs where the Madeira had been poured. Close by was a large mahogany chest on which sat a Tantalus, an assortment of glasses, and a dozen or more bottles of fortified wine.

Holmes approached the table slowly, taking in all aspects of the scene before him, and scrutinising the carpet beneath the table and the seat of one of the chairs. With a small pair of tweezers, he picked at the chair a couple of times, removing some tiny fragments which he placed in an envelope that he had withdrawn from a pocket. Lestrade and I knew better than to interrupt him as he went about his work.

He then turned his attention to the tabletop itself. Having run the magnifying glass over the glasses and bottle, he announced suddenly, "You were not wrong, Lestrade. This exquisite Bual Madeira was produced by Blandy's and does not come cheap. And yet, Conk-Singleton's other wines tell me that he was certainly no connoisseur. Perhaps this had been a gift to him or a one-off purchase. Either way, I would suggest that he opened this particular bottle in order to impress his visitor. And impressed she seems to have been, for the glass is completely drained."

Lestrade's face lit up. "The visitor was a woman?"

"Without doubt. There were two long dark hairs on the seat of the chair. I would venture that these were not left by the elderly housekeeper. The visitor used a gloved hand to wipe the lipstick from her glass, but has left one tiny – but telling – smudge near the rim. The lipstick is unusual. It was manufactured by Guerlain, the French cosmetic company. I know this because I have made a particular study of popular cosmetics and hope one day to complete a monograph on the subject."

"Then our killer is indeed a bold one, Mr. Holmes."

"Yes. And I think we can take it that the timing of her visit was suggested by Mr. Conk-Singleton."

"Why do you say that?" I asked.

"Because he knew that his housekeeper would be absent at that time. I'm sure that our ex-bank manager would not want it known that he had been entertaining a lady caller in his parlour on a Sunday evening. That much is speculation on my part. It remains to be seen whether it is borne out by the facts."

With nothing further of note in the parlour, we made our way to the large room in which Conk-Singleton's body had been found. Lestrade's men had positioned a thin line of white cord to indicate where the body had been. Holmes seemed impressed by the initiative they had shown. He then focused on the murder weapon. "The Colt Derringer was an ideal pistol for our killer – lightweight, easy to operate, and small enough to be concealed within a handbag. At close range, it required no great expertise. The report from the gun would have been relatively quiet, helping to explain why none of the neighbours heard the shot. In any case, this room sits within the centre of the house, well away from the boundaries of the property."

He began to examine the cabinet closest to where the body had fallen, his magnifying glass being used to scan the area around the locks and handles of the two doors of the glass-fronted case. The ceiling in this room was significantly lower than that of the parlour, and the cabinet stood at a height of about seven feet. Inside was arranged a display of American banknotes, all clipped expertly into position, each with its own printed caption beneath, detailing dates of issue and other pertinent information.

"The cabinet is unlocked, Lestrade. There are finger marks on both the glass and the handles of the doors, which must be Conk-Singleton's. Had you not noticed?"

The man from Scotland Yard stepped closer to the case and followed Holmes's outstretched finger. "Well, I never! No, I didn't think to check, as I could see that none of the banknotes were missing. Do you think that's significant?"

"Yes. It lends weight to Watson's theory that the motive may have been robbery. It could be that our lady killer shot Conk-Singleton in order to steal one of these banknotes and replaced it with a duplicate."

"Like a forgery, you mean?"

"Possibly." Holmes opened the doors to the display case and stepped closer. Through the lens of the magnifying glass he began to examine each of the banknotes in turn and then began to chuckle. "Now it is my turn to be surprised. While I am no expert in American currency, I would say that all of these particular notes have one thing in common."

"Which is?"

"They are *all* forgeries – for this is a display of counterfeit notes. And beautifully executed they are too, with the exception of this one." His hand had extended towards a twenty-dollar bill which sat at eye level in the centre of the display, labelled "*E Ninger, 1885*". "Compared to the others, this is a crude piece of work – a banknote printed from a poor quality engraved plate. Note how indistinct the representation of the eagle is. An accomplished counterfeiter would never be content with such work."

I had to confess to being confused. "Holmes, are you saying that this woman killed Conk-Singleton in order to steal a counterfeit note, and merely replaced it with another forgery? I can see no sense in that."

"As strange as it might seem, I do believe that to be the case. We clearly have more ground to unearth. Now, let us examine the other display cabinets."

It took us a good hour to complete the tour of the entire collection housed within the seven rooms. At the conclusion of this, we had learned one further significant fact. The vast majority of Conk Singleton's collection was made up of genuine banknotes and coins from across the globe. But he had set aside one room for an unusual collection of American counterfeits – the very room in which he had been murdered.

Stood once again within the room, Lestrade asked, "Why do you think he collected only American counterfeits?"

My colleague took a short while to answer. "A very astute question. While I cannot be sure at this stage, I would say that our man collected only the most prized and valuable of banknotes and coins. Nothing we have seen today looks commonplace. The two most forged currencies in recent decades have been the U.S dollar and the British pound. Both hold a value beyond their own shores, and are therefore copied across the world. But collecting the very best counterfeits is problematic. While poorly-forged currency does not stay in circulation long – and is readily destroyed by any bank that discovers it – a well-executed counterfeit may remain undetected for some considerable time. When these are uncovered, the authorities will often retain and study them in order to identify the engraver at the heart of the criminal enterprise. Tracking down the pushers and passers of forged banknotes is not difficult. Getting to the counterfeiter often is."

327

I was still confused. "So you are saying that the supply of counterfeits is limited, for when they are detected they are either destroyed or put under lock-and-key by the banking authorities."

It was Lestrade who answered. "Yes, Doctor. And the supply is even more restricted in this country, for it is illegal to be in possession of a forged note. All counterfeit currency must be turned over to the Bank of England."

To which, Holmes added, "Precisely. Conk-Singleton faced no restrictions in collecting American forgeries, but would have been acting outside the law in accumulating British counterfeits."

My bemusement continued. "That may help to explain why he collected only American banknotes, but I still do not understand why he wanted to acquire forgeries in the first place, when they have no monetary value. Surely, of itself, a forgery is worthless."

Holmes chortled. "In most cases, yes. But you are missing the point. These well-executed counterfeits are often seen by collectors as *works of art*. And in short supply, their value can soar way beyond the face value of the currency they imitate." He pointed once more at the display case. "This collection covers what I believe is often referred to as the 'Golden Age of Counterfeiting' – the thirty-year period to 1896 when the most accomplished American forgers made their mark and operated with relative impunity in the face of attempts by the U.S Secret Service to shut them down. For example, this hundred-dollar bill is the work of Charles F. Ulrich, a Prussian by birth. Having made the passage to the U.S. in the 1850's, he produced engraved plates for some of the finest counterfeits the world has ever seen. This specimen could fetch as much as two-thousand dollars at auction. I suspect that Conk-Singleton's entire collection is literally worth a fortune."

"Then why did our thief and murderess not take the other forgeries?" said I.

"That," replied Holmes, "is our key line of enquiry. For therein lies the answer to this mystery. Why indeed?"

We spent a further half-hour searching through Conk-Singleton's personal correspondence. It was Lestrade who eventually uncovered the crucial piece of information, a ledger book detailing every item housed in the South Kensington collection. It demonstrated that Conk-Singleton had been collecting for a good thirty years, but had been accumulating items in greater numbers since retiring two years before. Every entry in the book showed what had been acquired – the date of its purchase, the name of the seller or auction house, and the price paid. We spent some time looking over the section on American counterfeits, trying to find each corresponding item in the display case before us. What it revealed did not answer our primary question, but did highlight another anomaly. The twenty-dollar *"E Ninger"* exhibit, which Holmes believed had been stolen and replaced, had been obtained from an *"Edward Marr"* on the *"16ᵗʰ August 1896"*. Unlike every other item listed in the ledger, it had no recorded purchase price. Where there should have been a written value, Conk-Singleton had merely added a dash.

"Curious," said Holmes. "Perhaps he was given the banknote or exchanged it for something else. He may even have stolen it. I am sure that all will become clearer when we have located our mystery woman."

"And how do you plan to do that, Mr. Holmes?"

"My dear Lestrade. You must leave this matter with us, for there is still some legwork to be done. It may be weeks, rather than days, before I am in possession of all the pertinent facts, but feel confident that we can eventually wrap up this little conundrum for you."

A look of joy swept across the inspector's ferret-like face. "That is extremely kind. I am very grateful to you both."

Holmes's assessment proved to be accurate, for it was indeed some weeks before we were able to bring the matter to a close. In the days following our visit to South Kensington, he made a dozen or more trips to the telegraph office, despatching telegrams to some of his contacts in America and reading through his collection of *"Counterfeit Detector"* booklets, which had been produced by John S. Dye, the U.S. Treasury expert. Every new piece of information seemed to invigorate him.

Inspector Lestrade continued to visit us, and it was during this same period that Holmes assisted him with "The Adventure of the Six Napoleons". But on the matter of the Conk-Singleton forgery case, Holmes refused to be drawn until he had completed his investigation.

The final conclusion came unexpectedly. Holmes had been reading through some papers that had arrived by post that particular morning. He turned to me and announced, "Watson, I have been a fool! Thus far, I have determined why Conk-Singleton was able to obtain the Ninger counterfeit and the reason he was so keen to own it. I also know all about the man from where he obtained it. Yet none of this placed me any closer to our killer. In fact, I had begun to fear that this illusive *femme fatale* might remain hidden. It's only now that I realise just how slow I've been to consider *how* Conk-Singleton knew her, and the reason she was invited to his home. To this point, I had imagined their coming together was the result of a sordid romantic affair, driven by the desires of the unmarried ex-banker. How wrong I was!

"I asked the Numismatic Society of London to send me details of all their members. These papers arrived earlier. I fear that I've been blinded by my own chauvinism. A perusal of the information reveals that the Society currently has two *female* members. One is an eighty-six year old widow from East Grinstead, who has taken over the membership of her late husband. The other is a *Mrs. Jean Carrington*, a thirty-eight year old American who currently resides in Southwark. Alongside an obvious fascination with currency collecting, she lists her wider interests as 'painting, sculpture, and plate engraving'!"

"Good heavens!" said I. "Sounds like the profile of a counterfeiter!"

"Exactly – it is too much of a coincidence. I suggest we arrange to meet up with Inspector Lestrade and pay a visit to this Mrs. Carrington. On the way, I will brief you both about what I have discovered to date. Let us hope that she can complete our understanding of the Conk-Singleton case!"

Having received from Lestrade a reply to our earlier telegram, we arranged for a four-wheeler to take us to Bow Street Police Station, where the doughty inspector agreed to meet us for the trip to Southwark.

The afternoon was exceptionally warm and sunny, and Lestrade's forehead glistened with perspiration as he climbed into the carriage and hastily removed his jacket. Dispensing with the pleasantries, Holmes began to tell Lestrade about Mrs. Carrington, outlining the facts of the case as the carriage headed south of the city.

"It seems you were a little economical with the background information on Arthur Conk-Singleton, Lestrade. While you mentioned that he had recently retired from a 'city bank', he had actually been in a senior position within the Bank of England itself. In fact, he was responsible for investigating the activities of counterfeiters. In this role, he was called to look into the affairs of a seventy-year-old American forger by the name of Edward Marr, who had been caught in possession of two engraved plates and a printing press used to produce some illicit five-pound notes that had gone into circulation in the early part of 1896.

"Edward Marr was extremely fearful about the position in which he found himself, having a number of previous convictions for 'shoving', or passing counterfeit money. He knew that if the bank could prove him to be the engraver of the forged plates, he was likely to spend the rest of his natural life in prison. Conk-Singleton had a reputation for being tough on those he investigated, and ruthless when it came to recommending the charges the police should bring against suspects. So imagine the surprise within the bank when he announced in the August of that year, at the end of his month-long investigation, that Marr should face only the charge of passing counterfeit money, as there was no evidence that he had actually engraved the plates. The bank had little choice but to accept his conclusions, but suspected that some conspiracy had been involved. In short, it was this episode that led to him being 'persuaded' to take early retirement from the bank."

Lestrade was quick to see the significance of what he had heard. "So it is not far-fetched to imagine that Conk-Singleton and Marr struck a deal. Perhaps the pair got to know each other during the investigation and Conk-Singleton let it slip that he collected American counterfeits. Marr then says he can lay his hands on a rare forged note, but only in return for the investigator's help in reducing his likely sentence . . . ."

Holmes beamed. "My thoughts exactly! If you remember the date in the ledger, he obtained the Ninger counterfeit on the sixteenth of August – the day *before* he concluded his investigation into Edward Marr."

"So what happened to the forger?" I asked.

"Marr was sentenced to seven years in Wandsworth Prison, where he would end his days. Eighteen months into his sentence he was stabbed to death. The authorities were unable to determine who had murdered him, but the prison governor concluded that the death had been an execution. Marr was well connected in London and New York and knew all of the principal counterfeiters operating in both cities. Shortly before his death, he had approached the governor, offering to trade information on his former associates in return for a commutation of his sentence. It seems that someone was eager to prevent that from happening."

Lestrade was perched on the edge of his seat, listening attentively to every word. "This Mrs. Carrington must have some connection to Marr. Could it be his daughter?"

"That is my working hypothesis, given her age, nationality, and interests. 'Carrington' would be her married name."

"And the murder is revenge for what Conk-Singleton had done to her father?"

"More likely revenge for what he *didn't do* for her father. He clearly helped to reduce the charges brought against the forger, but at the end of the day Marr still received a seven-year stretch. If he could not shorten his sentence, he knew he was likely to die in prison. He therefore took the risky step of approaching the prison governor with the offer of information."

I still had a nagging concern about one feature of the case. "If you are correct, that would explain why Mrs. Carrington was driven to kill Conk-Singleton. But why did she go to the trouble of replacing the Ninger counterfeit? In exacting her revenge, she could have stolen the entire collection of counterfeit notes, especially if they are as valuable as you suggested some weeks back."

"A good point, Watson, and a very telling one. The Ninger counterfeit had been her father's and is extremely valuable. It was the only banknote in Conk-Singleton's collection that could tie her to the crime. She could not leave it behind, but clearly did not want anyone to know it had been replaced. And it was a subterfuge that nearly worked, for both the housekeeper and our friend Lestrade here were unaware that anything had been taken from the display cabinet."

Lestrade smiled weakly, but added, "She must have planned it that way, for she clearly had with her another forged note to replace it."

"Precisely so, and I think it highly likely that the note she replaced it with was one that she had produced herself."

"As a counterfeiter!"

"You've got it. No doubt she was encouraged by her father to learn plate engraving from an early age."

By this stage our carriage was heading along Borough High Street close to the Marshalsea Prison. The streets and pavements were crowded with all manner of street vendors, idlers, and loiterers. It was but a short distance to our destination.

"Why is this Ninger counterfeit so sought after?" I asked.

Holmes grinned, and it was clear that he had been waiting for the moment when he could tell this part of the story. He savoured every part of the narrative that followed.

"You may remember, a year or so ago, I had occasion to assist William P. Hazen, chief of the New York bureau of the Secret Service, with the arrest of two would-be assassins. When their plot to kill President McKinley had been thwarted, the pair fled to London hoping to escape justice. I was able to track them down to their hideout in Bermondsey. They were eventually extradited to the United States. Hazen was extremely grateful for my assistance, and we have maintained a regular contact ever since.

"The Secret Service has two distinct, yet unconnected duties. Firstly, it operates to protect the presidency. But it is also the agency charged with preventing and detecting all forms of domestic currency counterfeiting. Hazen was only too pleased to respond to my various telegrams and provide information on both Edward Marr and the enigmatic Ninger. As it transpired, he is very well acquainted with the latter.

"Emanuel Ninger is a well-built, blue-eyed man with a sandy-coloured beard. He arrived in the United States with his wife, Adele, in December 1882, having travelled by steamship from the Dutch port of Rotterdam. Then aged thirty-five, Ninger was principally a sign painter, although his initial choice of profession brought in little money. The couple settled first in Hoboken, but using some money Adele had inherited from her first marriage, decided to buy a farm in Westfield,

New Jersey. It was here that Ninger began to produce the counterfeit notes for which he has become infamous.

"Unlike most forgers who engrave the copper plates from which counterfeit banknotes can be printed, Ninger is a pen and ink counterfeiter, at one time dubbed 'Jim the Penman'. He would obtain fine quality bond paper from the same mill as that used by the U.S Treasury's Bureau of Engraving and Printing to produce genuine banknotes. He then cut the paper to size and soaked the rectangles in a weak solution of coffee, giving them the appearance of age. While still wet, he placed the bond paper over the face of a genuine note and carefully aligned the two on a pane of glass. As the bond paper would be very nearly translucent, he was then able to see every feature of the legal tender, which he could trace onto the bond paper using a hard lead pencil. When the paper was completely dry, he would set about the delicate and time-consuming task of copying the detail of the original banknote using pen and ink, and adding colour with the application of a camel hair brush.

"For over ten years, Ninger produced his exquisitely hand-drawn banknotes and passed the bills himself on monthly trips to Manhattan. In that time, he may have produced as much as $40,000 worth of bogus currency. One curious feature of his work was the omission of the credit line: *'Engraved and Printed at the Bureau of Engraving and Printing'*. It was almost as if he did not want anyone else to take the credit for his artistry.

"Of course, the enterprise could not continue as it did forever and, on a fateful trip to New York in March 1896, he was arrested for trying to pass a fifty-dollar counterfeit in a saloon bar. In May of that year, he was sentenced to serve six years in the Erie County Penitentiary. Since that time, Ninger's rare counterfeits have continued to gain in value, being eagerly sought by collectors across the world. Ironically, they are highly-prized by other forgers, who recognise that they have more than just street value. Chief Hazen was not in the least surprised to learn that Edward Marr, a former resident of Manhattan, should have been in possession of one of Ninger's finest twenty-dollar bills."

"That is truly remarkable!" cried Lestrade, shaking his head in astonishment.

"I agree. Now, let us see what Mrs. Carrington has to say for herself. If I am not mistaken, we have just arrived at her address on Lant Street.

We stepped down from the carriage a few doors along from the house in question. Holmes paid the driver and asked him to wait for a short while in case we found no one at home.

333

The property sat in the middle of a block of three small but neatly-proportioned two-storey houses. Stood before the red-painted entrance, Holmes rapped on the door with his walking cane. The sound echoed down the hallway of the house. Presently, we heard a key being turned in the lock and when the door opened, there stood before us a slim, elegant woman with a mass of long dark hair. Her penetrating blue eyes flickered quickly across our faces, but she retained a confident-looking composure.

"Mrs. Jean Carrington?" asked Holmes.

"Yes. Have you come about this month's rent? I have told the landlord that I will have it for him by Friday of this week." Her New York accent was unmistakable.

"No," replied my colleague. "We are here about a more serious matter. My name is Sherlock Holmes and this is my colleague, Dr. Watson." Pointing to his right, he then added, "And this is Inspector Lestrade, of Scotland Yard."

The mention of the metropolitan force brought an unexpected smile to her countenance. "I see. Well, you had better step in then, gentlemen."

We followed her down a narrow hallway before turning right into a small sitting room. It was a tidy but sparsely furnished room containing a settee and single armchair. At Holmes's direction, Mrs. Carrington sat in the chair, while Lestrade and I took the two-seater. Holmes continued to stand and came straight to the point. "We have reason to believe that you are acquainted with a man named Arthur Conk-Singleton?"

"*Are acquainted*?" she intoned, her accent becoming noticeably more pronounced. "Don't you mean, *were acquainted*? The guy's dead, after all."

Holmes ignored the jibe. "Perhaps you could tell us when you last saw him?"

There was no deceit in her response. "That would be the Sunday when I shot him, I guess." She reached for a small box on the walnut table beside her.

Lestrade was about to rise from the settee, but Holmes gestured for him to remain seated. "That is remarkably honest of you, Mrs. Carrington."

"*Remarkably honest*?" She opened the small box and removed from it a cigarette, which she then lit with a match. "You Englishmen have such a turn of phrase. There's no real honesty to this, just the recognition that I'm done for. I had hoped my little trip to South Kensington had gone unnoticed by Scotland Yard, but I see that is not the case. There would be no other reason for you to be here, so I see little point in denying anything. Conk-Singleton had it coming."

334

". . . For what he did to your father, Edward Marr?"

"My word! You have done your research! Yeah, my father languished in a jail cell because of that man and was killed by another convict. Did you know that? Did you also know that Conk-Singleton double-crossed him?"

"We know that Conk-Singleton took the Ninger counterfeit as part of the deal he struck with your father."

For the first time she looked genuinely surprised. "Are you a Pinkerton man? You seem to know an awful lot about this."

"No, I'm a consulting detective. I'm aware of your father's long career as a forger and your own talents as plate engraver. It was you that produced the counterfeit which now sits in the Conk-Singleton collection, masquerading as the work of Emanuel Ninger, wasn't it?"

"There's no stopping you, is there? Take a walk further down that hall and you'll find all the tools of my trade. I've been engraving plates in that back room for the past three years. Little good it did me. Some months I can barely afford to pay the rent."

"It would be helpful if you could tell us how you first became acquainted with Conk-Singleton."

"Now, there's a story!" She stubbed out what remained of her cigarette and reached for another. Holmes stepped forward and held out his silver case. She took one of his hand-rolled cigarettes and lit it before continuing.

"Thank you, sir. My father moved to this country some years ago and I came with him, my mother having passed when I was ten years old. He had always been an expert forger and hoped I would pick up the trade. But while I was a decent enough engraver, I lacked his expertise and wanted a different life. I met and fell in love with an insurance salesman named Benjamin Carrington. We married and moved to a decent property north of the river. My father understood that I wanted a stable life and went his own way. For a while, Benjamin earned enough for us to be comfortable, but then he fell ill with consumption. Five years ago he died, leaving me alone with just a small inheritance. And after that my father was arrested.

"I moved around for some months, eventually renting this place. With the small amount of money I had left, I invested in some decent tools and began an engraving business. At first I undertook legitimate work, producing plates for the insurance company that Benjamin had worked for, but the money was poor. So I made contact with some friends of my father's and began to turn out plates for banknotes. They paid me well for a finished plate, but it was a slow process and took me

335

weeks to complete each one. In my spare time, I took to painting and sculpting, my real passions in life.

"To better understand currency design, I joined the Numismatic Society of London. It gave me access to lots of banknotes, some of which I would then copy. I was something of a novelty within the Society, being one of only two female members, but everyone was pleasant enough. Arthur Conk-Singleton took a particular interest in me and was always inviting me to view his collection. But I had no interest in the man or his banknotes until the day he mentioned that he had within his home a genuine Ninger counterfeit.

"I should explain that in the summer of 1889, my father spent some time in Manhattan, and while there managed to obtain a twenty-dollar counterfeit produced by Emanuel Ninger. At the time, it was something of a novelty, but being a traditional engraver, my father knew it was a thing of beauty. He treasured that banknote, watching the value of Ninger's work rise and, believing that one day when he came to sell it, it would enable him to escape his life of crime. While I never knew the details of what happened, friends of my father's told me that he had been forced to give up the Ninger when he was under investigation by the Bank of England.

"My suspicions were aroused as soon as Conk-Singleton mentioned the Ninger. I knew there had to be a connection. I made some discreet enquiries at the Society, asking another member about the man's earlier career. When I was told that he had worked for the Bank of England and had been responsible for investigating counterfeiters, I knew he had played some part in my father's downfall. Without giving him any hint as to my interest, I mentioned to him at one of the meetings that I would be interested in seeing his collection. He was thrilled and invited me to South Kensington that following weekend, suggesting that I should visit on the Sunday evening when his housekeeper was at church.

"I had already set my mind on taking back the Ninger and – as you have rightly ascertained, Mr. Holmes – decided to replace it with a queer note of my own. As for Conk-Singleton, he was a powerfully-built man, so I was taking no chances. I packed my small handgun for protection and took a cab that afternoon.

"When I got to the High Street in South Kensington, I asked the driver to set me down a couple of streets away from Gloucester Road. I had deliberately dressed in some drab clothes and did my best to keep my face covered. I was pretty certain when I arrived at his front door, that no one had seen me.

"Conk-Singleton was charming at first, and we shared a glass of Madeira wine and chatted about his collection. I asked him how he'd obtained the Ninger, acknowledging that I knew his work to be rare. What he said in response both shocked and appalled me. He said he'd been investigating a 'low-life forger who deserved the gallows', but learnt that the felon owned a genuine Ninger. He laughed as he said he'd agreed to a trade – the forgery in return for him 'putting in a good word' with the authorities, to get my father off the counterfeiting charge.

"I've been in some scrapes in my time and know just how to keep a poker face, but I'll admit, it was all I could do to keep from drawing that gun and shooting him there and then. Luckily, as I placed my glass down on his table, he suggested we go and view his collection of U.S. counterfeits. I followed him into the room and watched as he stood before the cabinet, talking endlessly about the banknotes – how much he'd paid for each one and how much they were now worth. When he finally pointed at the Ninger, I asked if I could see it close-up, to better appreciate the delicate brush work on the Treasury seal. He stepped forward and, with a key he took from his waistcoat, unlocked the double-doors of the cabinet.

"I knew this would be my best opportunity and reached into my bag to retrieve the Derringer. Placing it quickly in the centre of his back I fired. Just the one shot, but enough to floor him – there was no struggle, no words, and no remorse. As I said earlier, he had it coming. I took the Ninger, substituting it with my own forged note, and headed back to the parlour, where I wiped my lipstick from the wine glass. I then left via the front door and caught a cab back home. That's the story, all told."

I cast a glance towards Lestrade, who sat open-mouthed and dazed by the disclosure. In its own way, it was one of the most chilling accounts of murder I had ever heard – that such an act could be recounted with not so much as a hint of compunction. Holmes appeared to take a very different view. "Thank you, Mrs. Carrington. That is most enlightening."

We allowed her to attend to a few domestic affairs and then waited for her to fashion her hair and retrieve a light jacket and parasol from the hallway, before accompanying her out into the street. The four of us then walked up to Borough High Street to hail a suitable carriage for the trip to Scotland Yard.

It was not our finest case, but it was one that Inspector Lestrade was often to reflect upon as we sat together in the upstairs room of 221b. For the Conk-Singleton murder, Mrs. Jean Carrington was to face the gallows in the prison yard of Newgate on a particular cold November morning. Her final words to the chaplain were, "I wish to die, as I have lived, without regret. But I hope my place in Heaven is assured."

"Put the pearl in the safe, Watson," said he, "and get out the papers of the Conk-Singleton forgery case.

Sherlock Holmes – "The Six Napoleons"

NOTES:

As a result of time earned for good behaviour, Emanuel Ninger was eventually released from the Erie County Penitentiary in July 1900, a few months after our investigation of the Conk-Singleton case. He was told officially that he still faced two indictments, although later that year these were marked *nolle prosequi* by the U.S. Attorney, who announced that he did not intend to prosecute the case against Ninger. As far as is known, Ninger never returned to counterfeiting.

It was not until the passing of an Act on the 4th March, 1909, that American residents were required to turn over all counterfeit currency and stamps to the U.S. Treasury. Since that time, the Secret Service has been active in tracking down and destroying counterfeit U.S notes wherever they are held. The Conk-Singleton forgeries eventually met the same fate, except for one. The remarkable twenty-dollar bill produced with such care by Emanuel Ninger stills sits on display within the Black Museum of Scotland Yard. – JHW.

338

Another Case of Identity
by Jane Rubino

In endeavoring to select, from Sherlock Holmes's many cases, those which best illustrate his extraordinary powers, I have often struggled to reconcile the appetites of the reader with the tastes of my friend. Although Holmes might succumb to a touch of the dramatic in the course of an investigation, he maintained that my accounts of them should instruct, rather than excite, the reader, and often chided me for introducing touches of color and life which, though appealing to the public, were abhorrent to my friend.

There was, of course, a third party to be satisfied: The publisher. At times, a problem might offer some unique feature of interest, or analytical *tour de force,* and yet its abstruse details, or its unwieldy length, or my friend's failure to bring the problem to a decisive conclusion, did not accommodate the publisher's demand for a clear and concise narrative. If the reader supposed, from my published sketches, that all of Holmes's cases were discrete, independent, and swiftly resolved, it was due to these constraints of the publisher, and also to my facility for extracting the thread of a single narrative from what was often a very tangled and quite elongated skein.

One such skein had begun to unravel some months before the Priory School abduction, with the Abergavenny and Ferrers matters, and a reader may have assumed, from my account of the first, that the three affairs were entirely detached from one another. This was not the case.

The Abergavenny gang, you may recall. Clever, ruthless, and skilled at disguise, they were highwaymen of the first order, exploiting railways rather than roadways. These four would board a train, one disguising himself as anything from a portly banker to an elderly clergyman. Making his way to the compartment of a lone traveler, this imposter would ease his prey into one of those congenial *tête-à-têtes* that often relieve the dullness of travel. Much later, a railway cleaner, would come upon the dazed victim, who had no recollection of how he had got a lump on his head and a chloroform-soaked rag upon his face, nor where his valuables had gone.

Until the event which I am now about to relate, it was believed that these robberies were the work of one cunning scoundrel, whose course was so irregular that it left the police utterly confounded. Once, two months had elapsed between robberies, and once there had been three in

339

a week; once, as little as an emerald signet ring had been taken, and once a courier had been robbed of twenty gold bars. The oldest victim had been a lady of seventy-nine, the youngest a lad of eighteen.

It was after nine o'clock, on the solemn evening of the twenty-third of January, '01, when the clatter of hooves and the rasp of wheels against the curb drew me to the window. I looked down and saw Inspector Stanley Hopkins spring from a four-wheeler, followed by a police officer, who was directed to take his post at our doorstep. Hopkins then handed down a lady, veiled and wrapped in a black overcoat.

"Take pity on our landlady and see to the door, Watson," said Holmes. He took up the poker to prod at the dwindling blaze in the grate, as I went to admit Hopkins and his companion.

"A sad evening, Mister Holmes" said the inspector, as he walked into our sitting room. "But time and crime, they do not wait upon mourning, do they?"

"And I think you are not here to pass the time. Do step in, madam." Holmes addressed the trembling figure in the doorway. "It is a very cold night, and I see from where I stand that you are shivering. Take this chair by the fire. And Watson, we might all do with a drop of brandy."

A few more reassuring words from Holmes coaxed the lady into the room. She sank into the chair and drew back her veil with shaking hands, and I saw that she was barely out of her teens, a tall, slim, brunette, with clear-cut features and luminous dark eyes. And yet, the gaze was restless and fearful, and her features were drawn and pale as ash.

"Mister Holmes, Doctor Watson, this is Miss Nellie Archer." Hopkins raised his glass and said, "God save His Majesty and long life to him," before he continued. "Now, Miss Archer, don't be afraid – we are three stout men here, and an officer at the door. Tell these gentlemen of your experience."

"I see that it has been an alarming one," said Holmes as he took the chair opposite her. "Tell it in any way you like. I only ask that you leave nothing out."

"I am an orphan, Mr. Holmes, and quite alone in the world," she began, her hands twisting at the folds of her overcoat as she spoke. "I have always had a knack for play-acting and I sing rather well, and so, when I was discharged from the orphanage, I decided to try to make my way on the stage."

"How old were you when you left the orphanage?" Holmes asked.

"Sixteen."

"Pray, continue."

"For three years, I've managed to get by. I keep a room in town, but last year, I was engaged by Mr. Esmond's theatrical company – a touring company – and for several months, we've traveled from Scotland to Newcastle, Leeds, Manchester and, last week, Wales – six days at the town hall in Abergavenny. Four days ago – Saturday – was our final performance, and we were to return to town on Sunday. Mr. Esmond's booking agents had nothing more for us until spring."

"An interesting life for a young lady," said Holmes.

At the word "interesting", she gave something like a laugh and a sob. "When an error our arrangements delayed us by a day, a local acquaintance of Mr. Esmond, the Honorable Godfrey Morgan, offered his hospitality for the night and got us to the Bristol Station yesterday afternoon. We are a party of ten all together. Mister Coates and Miss Huddleston – the principal players – took a first-class compartment and Mr. Esmond took another for himself so that he may go over the receipts. The rest of us traveled in second class. There is a comfort stop at Swindon, and everyone made for the refreshment rooms – everyone but Mr. Esmond. He carried the cash-box, you see, and always kept it with him in his compartment until we reached our destination."

"What was in this cash-box?" asked Holmes.

"About two-hundred pounds, I think. And Miss Huddleston's jewel case."

"I see. And so, it was not unusual for him to remain behind. What was unusual?"

"I was the last to leave our car, and as I made my way along the platform, I passed Mr. Esmond's' compartment window. A gentleman was with him."

"One of your party?"

Miss Archer shook her head.

"Can you describe him?"

"I only saw his profile. He wore a wide-awake with the brim pulled low, and a loose, dark traveling cloak, and had side-whiskers and tinted spectacles, which I thought was odd, as it was evening."

"Disguise," Holmes muttered. "Pray, continue."

"I had just got to the refreshment rooms when a man came running from the telegraph office with the unhappy announcement of Her Majesty's death, and so I turned back to bring the news to Mr. Esmond. As I approached his car, his companion sprang down and knocked me to the ground. And then," the girl looked down at her lap, "he ran off."

"No, Miss Archer," Holmes said, gently. "You must tell me what happened *before* he ran off?"

"He had removed his spectacles, and he looked down at me and gave me a start – "

"Because you recognized one another?"

341

She shuddered and nodded. "He crouched down, his face inches above mine. I shall never forget the look in his eyes!"

"And that was when he did this?" Holmes leaned forward and drew back the collar of her overcoat to expose the purple marks where a strong hand had gripped her by the throat.

The girl pulled up her collar to cover the bruise. "I thought he would choke the life out of me."

"Scoundrel," I muttered.

"What next?" said Holmes.

"The passengers began to leave the refreshment rooms and return to the train, and of course they had all heard the news by then and there was a great deal of commotion. He said, 'Miss Archer of Lower Sloane Street, I know where you can be found.' And then he was gone. I got to my feet and ran to Mr. Esmond for help, and found him." She reached for the brandy that I had set beside her chair. "There was a horrible swelling upon his brow, and a rag over his face. I chafed his throat and hands and . . . ." Her voice dropped to a whisper. "His hands were cold."

"There will be a post-mortem," Hopkins interjected. "To determine if it was the blow or the chloroform that did him in. Still, it is a hanging matter."

Holmes shook his head, gravely. "The cash-box, I presume, was gone. Was anything else missing?"

"Mister Esmond's watch and chain. And his ring. An Imperial topaz set in gold, a gift from His Royal – from His Majesty."

"What did you do next?"

"I heard the whistle and the train began to move, and I ran to find a passenger guard – I daresay he took me for a madwoman . . . ."

"That fellow – Webb is his name – is sharper than many at the Yard," declared Hopkins. "He knew it for another of the railway jobs, and when Miss Archer told him how she had recognized her attacker, he wondered if these robberies might be the work of more than one. So he had her pass through the cars, pretending to look for some mislaid trinket, to see if she might spot any of her assailant's chums. She gave a nod to three of them, and the guard kept watch, and when they alighted together at Paddington, he found a police officer and got him to follow the three. The officer trailed them to a fox-hole at North Wharf Road. That's when I was sent for. I obtained a warrant, and turned up a small share of the plunder. You would have read of their arrest, if Her Majesty's death hadn't pushed news of it to the side, but it will be in every morning paper."

"But," I interjected, "even if the guard supposed that the robberies were the work of more than one, why would he think that Miss Archer might know them all, just because she recognized the one who attacked her?"

"Because," said Holmes, "she did not simply tell the guard that she *knew* her assailant, but where they had met. It was the Abergavenny engagement, correct?" Holmes regarded the girl's astonishment with a smile. "A young actress, alone in the world – who does she know, save her traveling companions, and I think we may eliminate them as suspects. Now such companies, as a matter of economy, often travel with only the primary players, and secondary roles are cast from local stock. These men were part of some theatrical club?"

"Yes! Mr. Esmond enlisted them from a local dramatic society."

"Two land agents, a wine merchant, and a newspaper reporter," spat Hopkins. "A find job they did, acting out the part of decent citizens and men of business!"

"Whose business required them to frequently travel by rail," said Holmes. "I daresay they worked out details of these robberies while traveling as businessmen, or at one of several fox-holes where they've laid aside the rest of the plunder."

"But the victims were not all business travelers," Hopkins protested. "For a few, it was their first time ever on a train, and Esmond himself was only on that train because of a delay."

Holmes shrugged his shoulders. "These were crimes of opportunity, Hopkins. This gang knew every line and route and way-station as well any railway employee, and so did not need to single out prey in advance of the crime. They could adapt the *modus operandi* to whatever prey crossed their path. Had the unhappy news of Her Majesty's demise not sent Miss Archer back to Esmond's compartment, the assailant would have shed his disguise, resumed the character of a man of business, and alighted at Paddington with his companions before poor Esmond was discovered. Well, Hopkins, my congratulations to you and to this fellow Webb."

"You may hold back my share until we have Miss Archer's assailant. When she testifies in court, and I hear the jury pronounce 'Guilty as charged!', that will be thanks enough for me."

"Who will prosecute? Avory?"

"Sir Jeremy Ferrers."

"Sir Jeremy has never lost at trial," I said. "It will be hard labor for the lot."

"For the fugitive, it will be the rope," replied Hopkins. "But I must nab him first, and the sooner the better. I know that you keep your own kennel, Mister Holmes. Perhaps you would loose your hounds."

"You've got nothing from the prisoners, I gather."

343

"I told them that their comrade will likely carry off the rest of the plunder – it's calculated to be near fifty-thousand – and leave them to lag, and their only hope of leniency is to give up the spoils and the fugitive. But they are as tight as three clams. They believe that if they say nothing, the case will break down. I have hopes that tomorrow, when every newspaper from here to Abergavenny publishes all we know of the scoundrel, that someone may come forward with information, if only for Miss Huddleston's offer of a five-hundred-pound reward."

"The newspapers will publish all they know of me, too!" cried Miss Archer, her voice trembling with emotion. "'I know where you can be found,' he said!"

"Miss Archer," said Hopkins, a bit impatiently. "Until we have this fellow in a cell, a constable will be posted in front of your lodgings, day and night."

"What is a constable against a cold-blooded thief and murderer who knows that I can identify him?" The poor girl choked back a sob. "I cannot go to court – why must I? You have the photograph – "

"What photograph?" Holmes demanded.

Hopkins drew a cabinet card from his pocket and handed it to Holmes. "It was from the Abergavenny engagement."

"When was this taken?" Holmes's keen gaze was fixed upon the card.

"Saturday evening," said Miss Archer. "Mr. Esmond gave a small supper party after the final performance and had a photograph taken of the entire cast. He meant to have cabinets made up as gifts for the dramatic society."

"A small supper party, with its wine and spirits and informal banter. The perfect occasion to loosen tongues and draw the conversation toward altered travel arrangements and cash boxes and jewels and a young actress's address in town." Holmes held the card up to Miss Archer and pointed to one of the figures. "The fellow who knocked you down – was it he?"

"Yes."

"James Osmond," said Hopkins. "The wine merchant."

"The wine merchant," Holmes echoed. He turned his gaze back to the photograph, a strange smile playing over his lips. "Well, well," he said as he rose from his chair. "I agree with Inspector Hopkins, Miss Archer. You will be quite safe at your lodgings. I will loose my hounds, and he will soon be apprehended. Hopkins, I think it would be best if you see Miss Archer home."

I confess that I was taken aback by this curt dismissal, and Miss Archer was as well. She rose from her chair, cast one last despairing glance at Holmes and then dropped the veil over her face and followed Hopkins from the room.

"You were rather cold, Holmes," I said when they had left us. "The poor girl is frightened out of her wits."

"As well she should be. Her testimony can send this Osmond to the gallows. A cornered beast is always a dangerous one."

"Unless the beast has fled England."

Holmes resumed his chair, lit his pipe, and stretched his long legs toward the fire. "His partners have been apprehended, his name and image will be in every morning paper, and there is a five-hundred-pound reward. That argues for flight. But a cache worth some fifty-thousand? Will he abandon that, or hide away until he can see his way clear to recover it? A grasping cad like our Mister James Osmond inclines me toward the latter." Holmes tossed the cabinet to me. "He is third from the left, seated at the feet of the lady I presume to be Miss Huddleston. What do you make of him?"

I studied the image of a sturdy, middle-aged man, unexceptional but for the piercing, light-colored eyes. "An average-looking fellow. I see nothing of the villain about him."

"Perhaps that is why he has been such an accomplished one. Have another look, Watson. Concentrate on the eyes, subtract a dozen or so years."

I looked at the photograph again. "Osmond!" I cried. "Why – It is James Windibank!"

"Alias 'Hosmer Angel'. After he used Miss Mary Sutherland so cruelly, did I not say that he would rise from crime to crime until he reached the gallows?"

"Why did you not tell this to Hopkins?"

"This Osmond or Windibank or whatever he now calls himself is a cunning fox. If he catches the scent of the official force, he will go to ground. No, we must lie low and allow him to slink back to his familiar den."

"Abergavenny?"

"Camberwell."

"Camberwell!" I protested. "Surely not! The gang's first robbery was nearly two years ago, so if he has been passing himself off as the Welsh wine merchant, James Osmond, long enough to fall in with this gang – "

"Or to organize it."

"Or to organize it, then he abandoned Mrs. Windibank more than two years ago – after he ran through all of her money, I daresay. If she is still living, and still resides at their Camberwell address, I cannot think

345

she bears him anything but ill will. She would certainly not give him aid and shelter."

Holmes shrugged. "I will concede your superior knowledge of the fair sex. And yet, it is also true that few men believe that they have lost all future claim on a woman's forgiveness, no matter how badly they have treated her in the past."

For the next several days, I saw nothing of Holmes. Late one afternoon, I had just rung for tea when a dirty, arthritic beggar-woman hobbled into our sitting rooms, leaning heavily upon the knob of a battered cane. Tendrils of ash-colored hair poked from the shawl covering her head, and an ear trumpet hung from a cord 'round her waist. Her "Mr. Sherlock Holmes?" was followed by a coarse, phlegmy cough.

"Madam, Mr. Holmes is away, and I have no idea when I may expect him."

"I'll wait, then," she said, and sank into the basket chair. Her head dropped upon her breast, and after a moment, she let out a great snore and fell silent. So motionless was she that I thought she had lost consciousness. I laid my hand upon her wrist to feel for her pulse and the creature began to shake with laughter and sat upright.

"Holmes!"

"Do you like the get-up?" With one motion, he threw off the shawl and wig and tossed the cane on the hearth. "They're quite taken in down at Lyon Place, where Mrs. Windibank still resides. She is in a sorry state, Watson," he said, soberly. "However she conspired with Windibank to dupe poor Miss Sutherland, she pays for it now. Laid low with rheumatism and must let rooms to make ends meet."

"Have you been lodging there in this character for the past week?"

"I am Mrs. Sherrinford, a widow, somewhat deaf and living on a small pension. Mrs. Windibank can afford only one servant, a tweeny who works for half-wages, and Mrs. Sherrinford has got into the habit of taking tea with her in the kitchen, to spare little Alice the exertion of carrying up my tray. She is a chatty little thing, and in less than a week, I have learned that Mrs. Windibank never speaks of her husband but to curse him, goes nowhere but to the grocer or the parish infirmary, has no visitors, and receives nothing in the post except bills – until this week. This week, she received a letter every day."

"From Windibank?"

"I believe so. According to Alice, Mrs. Windibank tore them to bits and tossed them into the fire, except for the one that arrived this morning. Alice happened to see her open the envelope and out dropped a signet ring with a green stone."

"An emerald signet ring was among the stolen items."

Holmes nodded. "Mrs. Windibank read the letter, put the ring on her finger, and then told Alice to prepare one of the spare rooms for her brother, who would be arriving in town next week. A week from today to be precise."

"When the attention of all of London will be on the funeral procession," I said. "But why not confront her immediately?"

"She may not know where he is, or she may know and lie and then send him warning. No, better to wait. Alice has been given the half-day, and Mrs. Sherrinford will offer to get her own tea in the kitchen so that Mrs. Windibank may entertain her brother. He is expected at five, so you must smooth Hopkins' ruffled feathers, and both of you must be at the kitchen door at a quarter-to-the-hour."

"What of Miss Archer? Will she be safe if Windibank is in town and at large for the next week?"

"Hopkins' men will keep anyone from getting into her room, and she is too frightened to leave it."

Hopkins' feathers required considerable smoothing, but eventually he was appeased by the prospect of getting his hands on Windibank, and by Holmes's assurance that the inspector would be given all credit for the arrest.

At dusk on the appointed day, Hopkins and I descended to the kitchen area of Mrs. Windibank's residence, where Holmes was waiting. "Are your arrangements in place?" he whispered.

"Two constables were installed next door last evening," the inspector replied in hushed tones. "As soon as Windibank enters, one will take to the pavement, and the other will go 'round to the alley. We will have him in a box."

"Then all that is left is to be silent and wait."

A half-hour passed before we heard the clang of the bell, and then the footfall above, followed by the scrape of chairs and the clatter of silver and china plate, as the pair sat down to tea.

Their conversation was scarcely audible from where we stood below, but gradually the exchange grew louder and more animated, and we were able to catch a few words of Windibank's wheedling entreaties and the lady's tearful replies. Holmes motioned for us to follow him, and we crept up the stair single-file and paused on the landing. Holmes put a finger to his lips and Hopkins drew out his revolver and cocked it silently.

Suddenly, we heard the gentleman shriek in pain and cry out, "For God's sake! Mary!"

"Did you think I would ever forget, James Windibank!" she screamed, wildly. "Did you think I could ever forget how you left me with nothing!"

Holmes sprang into the room, Hopkins and I at his heels. Mrs. Windibank was standing above her husband, her white fingers still gripping the handle of the knife that she had plunged just above his collarbone.

"Stop!" Hopkins trained his weapon on the pair. Holmes seized the lady's wrist and wrenched the bloody knife from her grip, while I snatched the table napkins and pressed them to the wound.

"Is it serious, Watson?" Holmes asked.

"Serious, but not grave. He will be fit to stand in the dock."

"I will see you hang, James Windibank!" the poor woman shrieked and then collapsed into a paroxysm of sobs and laughter, declaring over and over that she would see Windibank hang.

Hopkins whistled for the waiting constables, and the pair were removed, the hysterical woman to a cell and the wounded thief to St. Giles' Infirmary under police guard.

"Well, Hopkins," said Holmes as we sat over a whisky-and-soda at Baker Street. "The arrest will be a great relief to poor Miss Archer, and you will have the satisfaction of hearing the pronouncement of 'Guilty as charged!'."

"I will call on her first thing in the morning, though I daresay the early papers will reach her before me."

The next morning, I came down to find Sherlock Holmes at the breakfast table with those early papers spread out before him. "'*Railway gang ringleader captured!*' '*Dogged investigation by Inspector Stanley Hopkins!*' '*Trial of the century!*' Somewhat premature on that, I think!" he laughed, and swept the papers onto the carpet.

Suddenly, our door was thrown open and Hopkins burst into the room. "Miss Archer!" he cried. "She's gone!"

"Gone?" I echoed. "Gone where?"

"No one knows. She has completely vanished. I cannot find anyone who has seen her for – My God!" He sank into a chair and ran a shaking hand over his forehead. "For more than a fortnight!"

"It was only a fortnight ago that you brought her here," I protested.

"Tell us all," said Holmes, "and keep it in as good an order as you can manage."

"I escorted her home – she was in a wretched state – and the next morning, it was just as she had feared. The arrest of the three and the fugitive's escape, and Miss Archer's involvement in the business, were in all of the morning papers. One account even gave her Lower Sloane Street address. Sir Jeremy Ferrers went straight away to Lower Sloane Street to assure her that she would be protected until the fugitive was apprehended, and also to lay out what would be expected of her when it all came to trial. I spoke to him afterward – he said that he had never seen a witness so terrified. She declared that she could not be protected so long as Windibank was at large, and she could not bear to face him in a courtroom once he was captured. This morning, when I went to tell her of Windibank's arrest, she was gone, and no one can vouch for seeing anything of her since Sir Jeremy's visit."

"What of her landlady?" said Holmes. "Her fellow lodgers?"

"Miss Archer kept a room at one of those modern dwellings that caters to single working women. A half-dozen bed-rooms, and a bath-room and lavatory on each floor, and a common kitchen. There are maids available, but most of the ladies are of this new, independent class who tend to their own needs and go their own way – days or weeks may pass when they see little of one another, and of course, Miss Archer had been traveling a good deal. None of them recall seeing her since her return from Abergavenny. I have just come from Sir Jeremy, who is beside himself with worry – for the girl, of course, but for his case as well."

"There is no case without her testimony," muttered Holmes. "Or a weak one at best. But you say that you examined her room, Hopkins? Was there anything that was missing or out of place or suggestive of violence?"

"There was no signs of disorder at all. Everything was neat and trim. A few items of clothing in her wardrobe, books and trinkets upon a shelf. There was a trunk where she stored her linen and some costume pieces, and which she also used for a night table. No letters, no photographs or diaries or papers of any kind, save for the programs from her performances that she fixed to the walls. Of course, without knowing what *ought* to be there, I cannot tell if anything was missing, save the overcoat she was wearing when we saw her last."

"That is suggestive," said Holmes. "What do the constables tell you?"

"They swear that Miss Archer never left the house."

"And yet she is gone. Therefore, the constables are wrong."

"Where can she be, Mister Holmes?"

"Where can she be?" Holmes murmured, and he then sat for several minutes with his brows drawn down, his fingertips tapping on the arm of his chair. "No one has seen her in her room after Sir Jeremy's visit a fortnight ago," he said at last, "and no one has seen her leave it. And yet, young ladies do not vanish into thin air – certainly, if they did, their overcoats would be left behind. It would be easier to establish *where* she might be, Hopkins, if we could establish the 'how' and 'why' of her disappearance. Was she lured away by trickery, removed by force, or did

349

she leave of her own free will? The constables say that she did not leave the house. Do they say who entered it?"

"The landlady's sons occasionally visit, and the lodgers are permitted to entertain gentleman friends in the downstairs parlor. All of these gentlemen were asked to identify themselves before they were admitted, and none to Windibank's description. And yet . . . ."

"And yet, she was last seen some days before Windibank's arrest."

"'I know where you can be found,' he told her," Hopkins groaned.

"Have you questioned him?"

"No, I go to do that now."

"He's still at the infirmary?"

"Yes."

"May we accompany you?"

"I hope that you will. If he has harmed the poor girl, it will take the two of you to keep me from finishing what Mrs. Windibank started."

Windibank lay in a solitary room, with a constable at the door. The loss of blood had given him a ghastly pallor, but his gaze was sharp as that of a wary animal keen to avoid a trap. "Well, well," he greeted my friend with an infuriating smirk. "Journeys end in lovers' meetings."

"There is no love lost between you and Mrs. Windibank," said Holmes, coolly. "She would be happy to see you on the gallows."

"She will be disappointed then. What can they charge me with?"

"Conspiracy," said Hopkins.

"That will be difficult to prove."

"Fraud. You have impersonated – "

"I have *impersonated* no one. I may change my name, if I like. You would as soon charge Mr. Holmes here with impersonating – what was the lodger's name? Mrs. Sherrinford?"

"Theft of property."

"What? The ring? A trinket I bought from a street peddler. I hoped to smooth things over with my wife."

"That trinket was taken from Miss Henrietta Soames in a railway robbery last November."

"Yes, I read something of that. Surely, she does not accuse me. As I recall, the newspapers reported that the experience left her quite shaken – too shaken to say anything at all."

"The death – the murder – of Mr. Wilfred Esmond."

"Esmond? The theatrical manager? Yes, I read of that in the papers, too. I met the gentleman in Abergavenny. I was very sorry to hear of his passing."

"Miss Nellie Archer will testify that she saw you with Esmond just before she found his body, and that you made threats against her life."

Windibank pursed his lips as if trying to recall the lady. "Ah, yes, the young actress. A timid, high-strung girl, the sort who would be threatened by her own shadow. As for seeing me with Esmond, that will be her word against mine – if she does not faint dead away in the witness box or is not too shaken to say anything at all."

"What have you done with her?" Hopkins demanded. "Where is she?"

"What? Why – " Windibank's gaze darted from Hopkins to Holmes. "I believe she mentioned that she lived at Lower Sloane Street, in one of those modern ladies' dwellings. I would allow no daughter of mine to live in such a place."

Holmes laid his hand upon the inspector's sleeve. "Come, Hopkins, there is nothing more to be learned here."

"I have tried to keep you from the rope," Hopkins cried as he wrenched his arm from Holmes's grasp. "But if you are determined to swing, I wash my hands of you!

"He's done her," the inspector muttered, as we stood in the corridor. "I do not know how, but – "

"I don't think so," said Holmes. "Did you see his expression? You took him by surprise when you asked where she was. I maintain that Miss Archer was lured away, forcefully abducted, or fled. I can think of no inducement that might coax her from the protection of her room. Abduction would have been a great risk in an active lodging house, with a constable at the door. I pains me to say it, but I believe that she ran away."

"But surely, that would be for the best," I said. "If she did not leave under duress – "

"But she *did* leave under duress," interrupted Holmes. "Fear, working on the imagination of a girl such as Miss Archer, one with no friend or relation to offer her protection or advice, is the worst kind of duress. She has been gone as long as a fortnight and in my experience, the longer someone has been missing, the weaker the prospect grows of a safe and sound recovery."

For the next weeks, all of Holmes best efforts to trace the young actress ended in frustration and failure, and the few cases that came his way could not keep him from sinking into periods of solemn reflection that inevitably ended with a heavy sigh and a "Poor girl – where can she be? We all ought to have done more for her!"

It was in the middle of March, on as bleak and chilly an evening as the one that saw the commencement of the Abergavenny matter, I once again heard the clatter of a cab drawing to a halt at our door. I looked down to see Inspector Hopkins descend alone, carrying a large, wrapped bundle under one arm.

At the sound of his step upon the landing, Holmes threw open the door. Hopkins entered, and giving us a grave look and shake of his head, he dropped his bundle onto the carpet.

"A wherryman found it, dropped from Westminster Bridge and snagged upon a nail at the pier just below," he said as he drew its oilcloth wrapping away from a lady's black overcoat and a mantle. "Ten days ago."

"Ten days!" I cried.

Hopkins nodded. "He'd pulled it free and sold it to a dealer in second-hand clothes, who tossed it aside until today, when he meant to clean and mend it fit to sell. That's when he found the veil stuffed deep into one of the pockets. This was tucked beneath it." Hopkins produced a sheet of paper, that had been folded many times over. "He recalled Miss Archer's name from the newspaper accounts, and so he brought it to the Yard."

Holmes held it up to the light, and we saw, printed in bold pencil, "*I would rather die than live in fear of death. Nellie Archer.*"

"It is just by chance that it caught on the nail when she tossed it, or the Thames would have turned it all to mush."

"No, Hopkins. She did not toss it. She hung it where she knew it would be found. Look what trouble she took to preserve the note, to print it so that it was clearly legible. She would not have taken such pains and then risked having it washed away." Holmes looked down at the coat and mantle and then threw the oilcloth back over them. "Has her body been recovered?"

"Ten days or more will take a body clear down to Gravesend. I begin a round of the mortuaries tomorrow morning, but first, I must call on Sir Jeremy. I confess that I dread it. A mad business, suicide. And the loss of Miss Archer's testimony may well mean that the trial will end with an acquittal, and that is if the charges do not break down and there is no trial at all."

There was to be a trial, but a number of delays pushed it to the middle of May. Six days before its commencement, Holmes received this cryptic summons: "*Luncheon. Both. My lodgings. 1 p.m. Mycroft.*"

At the appointed hour, we were ushered into the sitting room of Mycroft Holmes's Pall Mall lodgings. Our host, who had been gazing out the window, stepped forward to greet us. "Sherlock! Doctor Watson! Our fourth – " He gestured to the table that had been laid for four. " –

352

will be here in one minute, precisely! Only this morning, he solicited my opinion on a singular problem, but it may call for some energy to see it through. I hope that I do not take you away from anything pressing."

"It is Sir Jeremy Ferrers?" said Holmes.

"Yes – ah! There is the bell."

"How did you know that it was Sir Jeremy?" I asked.

"Mycroft was looking toward the window opposite, which is the third floor of the Diogenes Club. It takes sixty seconds for a reasonably fit man to make his way from there to Mycroft's door," replied Holmes.

"But how do you know that the reasonably fit man is Sir Jeremy?"

"Because the third floor of the Diogenes Club is a private suite occupied by the club's only resident, Sir Jeremy's uncle, Sergeant-Major Ferrers."

"The Crimean War hero?" As a military man, I well knew the name Hugh O'Connor Ferrers. "He lives at the Diogenes Club?"

"Yes. He, with Mycroft, was one of its founders."

"I meant . . . I thought he was . . . ."

"Dead?" said Mycroft. "No, he is not dead. Much worse, I am afraid. He is forgotten. But here is the nephew now!"

I had been introduced to the distinguished barrister some weeks earlier, when he had called at Baker Street to discuss the status of the Abergavenny gang's trial. "I have just enough of a case to bring them to the dock, but I see them slipping through the net, and it cuts me deeply. It is not pride, Mr. Holmes – I cannot expect to go through my whole career without ever facing one defeat. If it was only gold and valuables that were lost – but Esmond was murdered. And the girl, driven to take her life. An acquittal will be hard to bear."

Yet it was not bitterness that I saw upon the barrister's pale features when he entered the room, but agitation. "Very good of you both to come!" he cried as he shook Holmes's hand and then mine. "I confided the matter to your brother this morning, who advised me to lay it all before you. I hope it may prove to be trivial."

"It does not concern the trial, then?"

"No, no, it is a family matter. It is my uncle, Sergeant-Major – that is, *Mister* – Ferrers, which is how he prefers to be addressed, when he has occasion to be addressed at all. The others at the club know to leave him to himself. As his sole relation, I am tolerated, but frankly," Sir Jeremy gave a self-deprecating smile, "he cannot even stand me for very long."

"I think even Sherlock would be called a sociable fellow by comparison," said Mycroft.

"You have heard of the Crimean episode?" Sir Jeremy continued, as

353

we took our places at the table. "Such tales, over time, are often wildly exaggerated, or they are reduced to a passage or two in history books, or worse, they are forgotten altogether. It pains me to think that, in my uncle's case, it is the latter. More than once, I have urged him to write his memoir of that period, but to no avail."

"He may find the experience painful to re-live," I said.

"Yes," the barrister nodded. "So, you can imagine how astonished I was when my uncle told me some weeks ago that he'd come over to my way of thinking. 'History will make a muddle of it!' he said to me. I suppose the old fellow knows that the time is getting shorter when he can set down his version of the experience."

"And has this project begun?" asked Holmes.

"Oh, it has more than begun, it is nearly finished – or was. Once my uncle made up his mind, he did not waver. He charged Walters – his manservant – to place advertisements for a secretary, someone who could take dictation and typewrite. You may have noticed, Mister Mycroft Holmes, some weeks ago, that a few dozen fellows were ushered up to my uncle's quarters, and sent packing not five minutes later. At last Uncle settled upon a candidate, a young Mister Noone."

"And how did your uncle come to choose him?"

"According to Walters, Mister Noone had no references, but he was well-spoken, owned a typewriter, and was the only candidate of those few dozen who knew anything of Balaclava and Sevastopol. Do they teach nothing of history in the schools these days?"

"And what were Mister Noone's duties?" Holmes asked.

"Six days a week, from nine o'clock in the morning until four thirty in the afternoon, my uncle would dictate his tale, and Mr. Noone would write it down – "

"He would not type it?"

"No. Uncle could not stand the clatter of a typewriter – he has been very sensitive to noises since his ordeal. Mister Noone would write as my uncle dictated, read back passages when requested to do so, and make note any corrections or amendments, and when they had done for the day, Mister Noone would take the handwritten papers home and produce a typewritten draft. The next day, my uncle would – according to Walters – order Noone to read back the draft, rebuke him for reading too loudly or not loudly enough, point out all of the errors he had made, call him a bungler, threaten to sack him, and then they would continue on."

"A sensitive task," said Holmes, smiling in my direction, "to satisfy a man with such an exacting and difficult temperament."

"So I imagine," said Sir Jeremy. "And yet, Walters told me that

Mister Noone suffered my uncle's abuse with the patience of a saint, and after a time, they seemed to get on quite well. And, of course, my uncle paid handsomely."

"You said that the project *was* nearly finished," said Holmes. "Has there been an interruption?"

"Yes, Mister Holmes. Two days ago – Monday – Mister Noone did not arrive, nor did he send any message to explain his absence. Uncle did nothing about it, but when the young man did not appear yesterday morning, Uncle sent Walters to his address – he lodges at Catherine Street. The landlady told Walters that the last she had seen of Mister Noone was Saturday evening. He stepped into a cab carrying a large carpet bag and his typewriter case. She supposed he meant to take a holiday, but thought no more of it – he was paid through the month."

"Had Mister Noone come to work on Saturday?"

"Yes."

"Have the police been called in?"

"No," said Sir Jeremy, grimly. "Walters pressed for it, but Uncle refused – he would not stand to have, as he expressed it, 'those bunglers nosing into my affairs.' So yesterday evening, Walters wrote to me, apologizing for troubling me only days before the trial, and imploring me to meet him this morning at the entrance to the club, where he laid out the entire matter. I assured him that it was most likely a simple misunderstanding, one that would smooth itself over in a day or two. Still, I thought it would do no harm to consult with your brother, Mister Holmes, who advised me to put the matter before you."

"Had Walters observed anything out of the ordinary on the secretary's last day of employment? Anything that might have offended the young man?"

"Not offensive, no, but Walters did say that my uncle had become agitated when he began to recount the particulars of the battle."

"Legend has it that he carried eight of the wounded to safety, one after another, and with a bullet lodged in his shoulder," I said.

Sir Jeremy nodded. "And then, took the standard from a fallen comrade and led the charge, and on the battlefield, he lost an eye and wounded his leg and suffered the burns to his face. My uncle may be a legend, Doctor Watson, but the story is absolute truth, just as it is true that he refused both the Victoria Cross and a knighthood."

"And this was the first time your uncle has ever spoken of the episode?" Holmes asked.

"Yes. Walters said Uncle became quite distraught, and that it was only Mister Noone's extraordinary patience and compassion that got the old fellow through it. And then, when Uncle asked Mister Noone to read

355

back the passage, it was the secretary who was so moved that he could scarcely find his voice. When they had finished for the day, Mister Noone laid his hand upon my uncle's shoulder and said, 'Thank you, Sergeant-Major.' Quite deliberately addressing Uncle as 'Sergeant-Major'. You know that he will only be called 'Mister'."

"And this was last Saturday?" Holmes asked.

"Yes."

"And afterward, Mister Noone returned to his lodgings, packed his belongings, stepped into a cab, and vanished."

"Yes."

"Saturday," Holmes repeated with a frown. "And today is Wednesday. The loss of four days presents me with a very serious handicap. It is imperative that I speak with your uncle."

Sir Jeremy sighed, heavily. "Of course. I would not put you off, but my uncle doesn't know that Walters spoke with me, or I with you, and it may take some coaxing to persuade him to meet with you. If tomorrow will suit . . . ."

"Tomorrow morning, then, but no later. In the meantime, I will trouble you for the secretary's address. After lunch, I will take my researches there.

"I did not want to press him with the trial so near," Holmes said, as our cab rattled toward Catherine Street. "The possibility that Windibank and his gang may walk away free men weighs heavily upon him. I confess, there are times when I wish that we had held back and allowed Mrs. Windibank to finish the scoundrel."

"Surely not. Better to allow the law – "

"The law and justice are not always the same, Watson."

"What do you make of the secretary's disappearance?"

Holmes shrugged his shoulders. "I have no data. There may, of course, be a simple explanation – some urgent family matter called him away, or he went off to interview for a new post, since this one was nearing its end. Some romantic pursuit, perhaps."

"But why not have the goodness to send a word of explanation to Ferrers, particularly since Walters told Sir Jeremy that they had been getting on quite well. Though I must confess," I added, "it is very strange to think of the old recluse on easy terms with a young employee who is so opposite him in every respect."

"Well," said Holmes, with a smile, "I daresay it would not be the first case of two very different fellows making their way to common ground. Come – here is the address."

Mister Noone's landlady spoke highly of her young tenant. "He was a quiet, polite young man, he did not smoke, and went nowhere but to his job. His room has not been touched since Saturday," she added, as she ushered us into the chamber. "He was so neat in his ways and kept it in such good order that the maid had very little to do."

"And he has lived here for two months?" Holmes asked.

"A bit more, sir. He took the room in early March."

"Can you describe him?"

"He was quite young, not so tall as you nor your friend. He had dark hair and a clipped moustache and was rather pale – not sickly, mind you. Overwork, I expect. Six days a week, he was with his employer and on Sundays, you would hear him clacking away upon his typewriter. His dress was neat, though rather odd."

"In what way?"

"His waistcoats were quite loud, but his suits were plain and not smart at all – shabby and ill-fitting." She directed our attention to the only garments left in the room, a threadbare jacket and trousers hanging in an open wardrobe, and a worn collar laid out on the dressing table. "Bought second-hand, I suppose."

"You say that the room has not been touched?" Holmes asked, as he examined the clothes. "I see no personal effects, no books or photographs, no hint of pastimes or hobbies."

"Other than his work, I know of nothing he did to pass the time but read the papers. He took in six a day – *The Telegraph*, *The Echo*, *The Daily Mail*, *The Illustrated Police News*, *The Times*, and *The Express*."

"Did he seem interested in any particular news item?"

"I cannot say. But he never marked up any of the articles or cut them out, and always kept the papers smooth and neat so that they might be passed downstairs to anyone who wished to read them."

"Very considerate of him. Did he receive any correspondence?"

"None that I saw."

"Did he ever have any callers?"

"No, never."

"And when he left on Saturday, he had just the one large carpet-bag?"

"And his typewriter case, yes, sir."

"Did you ever see what he was typing?"

"No, sir. I once thought that he might be writing a novel."

Holmes thanked the landlady, and we left.

"There was very little to see, Holmes."

"But a great deal to observe."

"What did I fail to observe?" I said. "There were no papers or photographs or letters or personal effects, not even a pen-wipe or a shaving brush. The waste-paper basket was empty. Nothing but a few shabby items of clothing better suited to the dustbin than the ragman."

"'Shabby and ill-fitting' was how the landlady describe his attire. Could garments he left behind be any worse than those he took away with him? So why not take all?"

"Perhaps he had not enough room in his carpet bag."

"Or not enough room to *spare*. Perhaps they had to give way so that he might have room for an item that was more valuable to him than a few scraps of clothing."

"Ferrers' memoir?"

"Ferrers' memoir," Holmes repeated, grimly.

"You imagine that he means to sell it?"

"What I *know*," Holmes replied, "is that only last year, every copy of *London to Ladysmith* was gone in a few weeks, and that does not take in the American market. Young Churchill is said to have earned no less than ten-thousand pounds. Only think what price a memoir like Ferrers' would command."

"The treacherous scoundrel!" I cried. "After all old Ferrers endured – to be deceived in such a fashion, and by a young fellow he had come to like and trust! Perhaps, Holmes, it would be better if he were to hear this troubling news from his nephew."

"I cannot lay that burden upon Sir Jeremy when he has the trial to think of. And can I forego the opportunity to meet a living legend? No, we will call at the Diogenes Club tomorrow."

And so we would have done, but on the following day, as Holmes and I were preparing to set out from Baker Street, Doctor Thorneycroft Huxtable of the Priory School staggered into our rooms and collapsed upon the carpet.

His insistence – once he was revived – that Holmes accompany him to Mackleton was met with an immediate refusal. "Only a very important issue could call me from London at present," said my friend, but when he understood the nature of the crisis – that one of Huxtable's pupils, the only child of the Duke of Holdernesse, had been abducted – he could not reject the plea for his help.

"What can be done, Watson? The plight of a helpless child must take precedence over the loss of Ferrers' memoir. We must go." He dashed off a note to Sir Jeremy, stating only that a matter of extreme urgency required his immediate attention, and within the hour, we were on a train to the North.

With his singular ability to put one problem out of his mind when another demanded his energies, Holmes devoted all of his powers to the recovery of the young heir and by Saturday afternoon, the motive for the abduction was revealed and the boy was safely recovered. When a few minor enquiries from the local officials detained us by a day, Holmes sent a wire to Sir Jeremy – *"Return to Baker Street Sunday p.m. Call if you can. Holmes"* – and another to our landlady to inform her that we would dine at seven on Sunday evening.

We arrived at Baker Street just before seven to find our landlady waiting for us at the door. "A young man left a parcel for you this morning, Mr. Holmes," she said. "And Sir Jeremy Ferrers called twice this afternoon. He said that he could not take the time to call again, and left you a note."

"Poor fellow," I said. "The trial begins tomorrow. He must be all nerves."

"Oh, no!" the landlady protested. "He was in high spirits, quite cheerful, indeed! After he wrote out the note, he smiled and shook my hand and said that tomorrow would be a very fine day."

Holmes and I exchanged a puzzled look and then hurried up to the sitting room. On his desk, Holmes found a note lying upon a parcel wrapped in brown paper. He snatched the note and read aloud: "*'Mister Holmes. Remarkable turn of events. You must come to court. You will not testify. Sir Jeremy Ferrers.'*"

"How strange!" I said. "Can the gang have confessed?"

"If that were the case, there would be no trial. But what is this!"

Holmes had been peeling back the parcel's brown paper wrapping as he spoke, and beneath it lay a bundle of neatly typed pages – the military exploits of Sergeant-Major Hugh O'Connor Ferrers.

Holmes stared at the object in astonishment, and then rang for the landlady. "You say a young man left this?"

"Quite early this morning," she replied. "He put it into my hands and said I was to give it to Mister Sherlock Holmes, and then rushed off before I could ask for his name or card."

"A young man, slender and poorly dressed, with dark hair and a moustache?"

"Yes, that was he."

"Mister Noone's conscience got the better of him," I said when our landlady had left us.

"So it would seem," Holmes muttered, as he examined the document, or rather its brown paper wrapping. The ends had been folded, and secured with glue, and Holmes ran his thumb over the edges, then held one corner to his naked eye, then to his nose, and finally examined it with his glass. His gaze clouded over with a faraway look, and then cleared and he let out a great laugh and wrung my hand. "This is it, Watson! The key to it all!"

359

He tossed the object onto his desk, "I must go out," he said. "You will do better to dine alone rather than in the company of one of the dullest brains in all of Europe."

"You're not taking the document to Ferrers?" I said, as he made for the door.

"No, no. Tomorrow will suffice."

I dined alone, and then took up the Ferrers document. The secretary's landlady had wondered if her lodger had been writing a novel and indeed, the account was so astonishing that it seemed almost a work of fiction, and one quite filled with the sort of color and life that even Holmes would not disdain.

Holmes returned within an hour, placed a sheaf of handbills in his desk drawer, and sat down to his belated dinner. "The curtain falls on a singular drama Watson – and yet, I do not deserve an ovation. Throughout, I have failed to balance information with imagination, and imagination is as essential to my art as reason. But Sir Jeremy must be allowed to take his bow, and so tomorrow we shall be there to applaud him."

I had never been counted among those who peruse the sessions papers or queue up for admission to watch the sensational trials. But that morning, Holmes and I arrived early for the Abergavenny gang's trial to find that Hopkins had arrived before us. "What is the meaning of it?" he demanded. "Sir Jeremy says that my testimony may not be needed. Is the case to be dismissed?"

"My dear Hopkins, there is the law and then there is justice – we must trust that on this rare occasion, the two of them will align."

There was a hush as the officials took their places and then the accused were brought to the dock. "Scoundrels!' Hopkins muttered. "And Windibank the coolest of the lot! Ah – here is Sir Jeremy. He puts on a good face."

Sir Jeremy's opening remarks were brief. He concluded them by submitting the cabinet photograph to the jury, and declaring that he would call only two witnesses.

The first was Webb, the railway guard. His account laid out the incident in a straightforward fashion, which the defending counsel attempted to offset by compelling Webb to admit that he had personally witnessed no criminal act, nor seen any of the defendants in Esmond's company. When asked if he wished to redirect any questions to the witness, Sir Jeremy seemed on the point of declining, and then, almost as an afterthought, asked, "Mr. Webb, I have not asked how long you had been employed by the railway."

360

"Twenty-two years, sir."

"You have worked on a number of routes in that time?"

"Yes, sir."

"And you were well aware of these series of railway robberies?"

"Yes, sir."

"And, to your knowledge, how many such crimes had been reported prior to Mister Esmond's death?"

"Fifty-three, sir. Going back about two years."

"And how many of them occurred *since* Mr. Esmond's death?"

The guard seemed puzzled for a moment, and then a broad grin spread over his face. "None, sir. Not one."

"Excellent," Holmes muttered. "Excellent."

I had expected Sir Jeremy's second witness to be another railway employee, or one of the constables who had attended Windibank's arrest. When the name "Miss Nellie Archer!" was called out, I confess my mouth dropped open and Hopkins gasped aloud, as a young girl in a fashionable walking dress and velvet turban strode up to the witness box, pausing only to cast a look of cool contempt upon Windibank, before she turned her attention to Sir Jeremy.

"It cannot be Miss Archer!" Hopkins gasped.

I, too, could not believe that this poised young lady was the same terrified girl who had come to our sitting room only months ago.

And yet it was, for she recounted, under Sir Jeremy's examination, the same experience that she had she had described to us at Baker Street, and yet this time, she spoke with calm assurance, and her narrative was both persuasive and precise. When it was the defending counsel's turn to question her, he employed every strategy in his power to rattle her composure and drive her to contradictions and tears. Yet not once, in testimony that went on for well over an hour, did she hesitate. Her voice remained firm and her responses remained clear and consistent, and when his interrogation was done, it was the defending counsel who came away looking crushed and defeated.

As the girl stepped down, she turned back once to cast one final scathing glance at Windibank, and then walked out of the court-room.

I shall never forget the look of disbelief upon the faces of the gang when the jurors brought in a verdict of "Guilty as charged!" Custom allowed them to make a statement before sentence was passed, and Windibank's three confederates, hoping to mitigate their sentence, gave up the whereabouts of the stolen property. As for Windibank, he had nothing that would mitigate a sentence of death.

Holmes excused himself as we left the courtroom, and went to exchange a few words, and leave a note, with the undersheriff. "I think a celebration is in order," he said, when he rejoined us. "I expect a few guests for luncheon at Baker Street. Will you join us, Hopkins?"

"No, I must get back to the Yard. The verdict was all the celebration I need."

When he left us, Holmes handed me a note. "Be a good fellow and give this to our landlady. I have a number of errands, but I will return before one."

I returned to Baker Street and was once more reading the Ferrers document when the landlady and the page entered, working a small table into the room, which they set against ours, vanished and then carried in a pair of white table cloths, napkins, and silver and laid for six. They vanished once more, and a half-hour later, three fellows from one of the better restaurants carried a number of covered trays down to the kitchen, while a wine merchant and then a confectioner laid a half-dozen bottles and a tower of hothouse fruit and bonbons upon our sideboard.

Holmes arrived at a quarter-to-the-hour and looked over the arrangements with satisfaction. "There is the bell – and I know Mycroft's step!"

The slow, heavy tread of Mycroft Holmes was accompanied by a second step that was equally labored, and the sound of a cane striking upon the stair. The door opened and Mycroft entered, followed by a tall and fearsome stranger. His broad shoulders were bowed with infirmity and gloom, one side of the deeply-lined face had been burned to a slick, red scar, and the eye above it was filmy and sightless, the eyebrow singed away. The hand that gripped his cane was large and powerful, but the other, tucked into Mycroft's elbow, was withered and useless.

This ogre scanned the room with his one good eye. "So!" he barked. "You are Mycroft's brother – the detective!"

"I am, sir. I have the honor of addressing Sergeant-Major Ferrers of Crimean fame."

"Fame be damned!" he bellowed. "And you, I suppose," he continued, turning his eye upon me, "are Watson, the scribbler! Walters reads your tales to me."

"Yes, sir."

"Mycroft said that it was imperative that I come – life or death!"

"A bit of exaggeration," said Holmes. "But I think that I will be forgiven for it presently. Will you take a place at the table, sir? This is the most comfortable chair. And Mycroft will sit beside you. The bell again!'

A moment later, Sir Jeremy entered. He had scarcely opened his lips to greet us when he saw the elder Ferrers. "Uncle! Why – I am surprised to see you!"

"Why should you be surprised?" thundered the old soldier. "May I not go out if I like? Or perhaps you are surprised because you imagine me to be in my grave – you and all of England!"

"Do not stand on ceremony, Sir Jeremy. Please take a place at the table. We are expecting only one more, but I think we will be forgiven for indulging in a toast to Sir Jeremy's victory this morning." He examined the bottles on the sideboard and selected a Spanish sherry.

"You must thank Miss Archer for that," said the barrister. "When she called on me yesterday – you can imagine my astonishment. We had all taken her for dead! And when she said that she had made up her mind to testify, I was overjoyed. I was of course," he added, "obligated to inform my worthy opponent of Miss Archer's intention, and fully expected him to object to it. He insisted upon consulting first with that scoundrel Windibank, and to my surprise, Windibank agreed to it. Encouraged it, in fact."

"A fatal miscalculation," said Holmes. "Windibank expected to see the terrified girl he'd left on railway platform in Swindon. But perhaps," said Holmes as he filled our glasses, "I may suggest another cause for celebration." He took the manuscript from his desk and laid it at the side of old Ferrers' plate.

"What! Is it here, all of it? I thought it was – " Ferrers voice choked, and he fell silent for a few moments. "Thank you, sir," he muttered at last.

"You must not thank me. It was left at my door yesterday by the same person who took it."

"Noone came to his senses, did he? Never doubted for a moment," the old fellow blustered. "I have forgotten a good deal, but I still how to recognize a good man when I meet one."

"But why did he bring the document to you?" asked Sir Jeremy.

"I have some small reputation as a liaison in delicate transactions. There is the bell again – I think our last guest may give us a more thorough explanation. This document, after all – or, more particularly, its recovery – represents more than your uncle's history. It is the final link in a chain of events, set off, I suppose, when the villain Windibank descended from the merely contemptible to the criminal. Long before he crossed paths with – Ah! Miss Archer! Do step in."

It was indeed the young actress who paused in the doorway, looking 'round at our party. Upon seeing a lady, old Ferrers lurched to his feet, and the poor girl took a step back and for a moment, I thought she would turn and bolt down the stairs. The confident young lady of the courtroom had vanished and she was once again the pale, trembling girl who had first come to our rooms in January.

363

"Who is this?" he demanded. "Why does she hang back? I am no beauty, girl, but neither am I a beast!"

Holmes stepped forward and took her elbow, guiding her to the old soldier. "Mycroft, Sergeant-Major Hugh O'Connor Ferrers, allow me to present Miss Nellie Archer. Miss Archer is an actress. Will you sit?" He held out the chair opposite Ferrers and she sank into it, her gaze turning to the manuscript.

Holmes filled the girl's glass. "I had just been telling my friends that the document you look upon is the final item in a rather prolonged sequence of events which began with you, Miss Archer, on the evening before our first meeting in January."

"What has she to do with my papers?" demanded Ferrers. "Why is she so pale? Am I so hard to look upon?"

Holmes had remained standing behind Miss Archer's chair. He laid a hand upon her shoulder. "Shall I tell it, Miss Archer, or will you?"

The girl raised her chin, and I saw something of the resolution she had shown in the witness box as she looked 'round the table. "I would not blame any of you if you cannot forgive me. I was so frightened – it is no excuse for my conduct, I know that now, but I have never been so frightened of anything in my life as I was when I saw James Osmond standing over me, saying, 'I know where you can be found.' And I ran to Mister Esmond for help and he was . . . . And that fiend was at large and knew where to find me, and nothing Inspector Hopkins or anyone said could reassure me. I was afraid, and I ran away. I was a coward. I am truly sorry, Sir Jeremy."

"My dear girl," said he, kindly, "whatever possessed you to feign a suicide?"

"It was in one of Mrs. Alexander's novels, *A Second Life*. Miss Huddleston was always buying books and magazines to read on the train, and when she was done with them, she would pass them down to me. The heroine escapes a cruel husband by tricking everyone into believing she has killed herself. Even what I wrote in the note was taken from a magazine story – *Weighed and Wanting*."

"You left your coat where you knew it would be found," said Holmes.

She nodded. "When you have little money and no friends, your only diversions are reading or walking about. The area around Westminster Bridge is so full of life – so many people, day and night. I knew someone would see it."

"I do not understand how you got out of your lodgings without being seen by the constable," said Sir Jeremy.

"An excellent question," said Holmes. "But let us come back to this

364

document, which was left at my door yesterday morning. It was wrapped in that – " he pointed toward the sheet of brown paper on his desk, " – and sealed with an adhesive. I recognized the particular scent of alcohol and resin: Spirit gum, which every actor has at hand. It is used for fastening on facial hair – side-whiskers, false eyebrows, moustaches. That scent touched off a theory – an improbable one, I admit – which took me to your Lower Sloane Street address, Miss Archer. You left behind a few possessions, and your kind landlady, not knowing what to do with them, put them away in your trunk and has stored the trunk in her cellar. The good woman allowed me to examine its contents. You left your copy of *A Second Life* behind, Miss Archer. The heroine does not just flee from a cruel husband, she takes on another identity. You also left these."

Holmes removed several theatrical programs from his desk drawer and laid them in front of the girl. "The one on top – it was the performance you gave at Abergavenny. The role of the Moustique, the cabin boy, was played by Miss Nellie Archer. And this one, the operetta, *Maritana* – Lazarillo, the page, is played by Miss Nellie Archer. It is not uncommon for a slender young girl who can sing in the mezzo to soprano range to take on the role of a boy. You've played several such roles. Of course, the costumes of a traveling theatrical company are not of the best fabric, and indifferently tailored since they must make do for a variety of forms and figures."

As he spoke, he gently lifted the turban from her head. To my astonishment, her dark hair had been cropped short.

"What is the matter with the girl?" demanded old Ferrers. "Has she been ill, or is this a new fashion?"

"Sir Jeremy asked why the constable did not see Miss Archer when she left her lodgings, and I say that he *did* see her. Or rather, he saw a shabbily dressed young man wearing the rather loud waistcoats and second-hand tweeds that one might find in the wardrobe of a small theatrical troupe. Now we know that the resident ladies at Lower Sloane Street are permitted to receive gentlemen callers. Miss Archer had only to cut her hair, don one of the male costumes, and then wait until just after the evening constable came on duty. He would have supposed that his colleague had permitted this young man to enter the house, and so he had no reason to question his departure."

"I even wished him a good evening," Miss Archer said, with a sheepish smile.

"And took on a '*second life*' – disguising yourself as a young man," I said.

"Miss Archer escaped and persuaded everyone that she was a

suicide, but there was then the problem of where to go. She has neither friends nor family, but in town there are any number of quiet lodging houses where a young person may hide away. The daily newspapers kept you abreast of the Abergavenny gang, Windibank's arrest, the upcoming trial, and one day, you happened to see an advertisement in one that a reclusive Crimean war hero was looking for someone to transcribe his memoirs. There were a number of applicants, but few of them could typewrite. You can typewrite, can't you, Miss Archer?"

The beginnings of astonished comprehension upon Sir Jeremy's face must have mirrored my own.

"Mister Esmond gave me a typewriter so that I could assist him with the company's correspondence," Miss Archer said in a low voice. "At the orphanage, the older girls were taught typewriting. They believed that it might help us to find employment."

"Only one young man applying for the post knew anything of Sergeant-Major Ferrers and his experience in Crimea. Did you not say, Miss Archer, that the company had stopped the night with a friend of Mister Esmond's – the Honorable Godfrey Morgan?"

"Morgan!" barked the old soldier. "I knew the fellow! Cavalry! Nerves of iron! He and his mount both came out of it – what was the damned animal's name –"

"Mister Briggs," said Miss Archer, softly.

"Mister Holmes!" cried Sir Jeremy, his gaze fixed on Miss Archer. "What are you saying?"

"I am saying that a frightened young girl disguised herself as a young man, and with her typewriting ability and knowledge of Crimean War history, took the post of secretary to a military hero."

"'*Noone*'," said Mycroft, with a chuckle. "'*No one*'."

There was a moment of stunned silence, and then the explosion of old Ferrers: "What! What!" He slammed his palm onto the table, rattling china and silver. "What – you do not say that this – this – *girl* – " He half rose, and reaching across the table, gripped Miss Archer's chin in his hand and turned her head to study her with his good eye.

"Uncle, please." Sir Jeremy eased the old soldier back into his chair.

"I deceived you, sir," said Miss Archer. "And I wish I could say that I am sorry, but I'm not. My money was running low and I needed to find some work – and even if you didn't take me on, I couldn't pass up the chance to see you for myself."

"To see a sideshow monstrosity!"

"I might see a sideshow monstrosity anywhere, and it would only cost a penny," she retorted, with some of the boldness she had shown in the witness box. "But I might go my whole life without seeing a real

366

hero."

"Who says I am a hero?" bellowed the old soldier.

"I do," she said, firmly. "When I left you last Saturday, I only meant to give myself a little time to think – I knew you would look for me at Catherine Street, so I packed my things and took a room in a small hotel and I spent the next week typing up your story, and reading it over – how you saved all of those men, and what you sacrificed, and at what cost, and when you were not much older than I am now. How could I be such a coward? I went out and bought this dress – you were very generous, sir – and on Sunday morning, I wrapped the document and brought it here. I was afraid if I gave it to Sir Jeremy, he would be angry at how I had tricked his uncle, and I knew that Mister Holmes would know how to get it back to you. And then, I went back to the hotel and changed clothes and called on Sir Jeremy to apologize for abandoning him, and tell him that if he still needed my testimony, I would go to court."

"What a shock you gave me! After we talked, I called here at Baker Street. I daresay the note I left was was scarcely legible."

"This is an outrage!" cried Ferrers. "Do you mean to say that there was no Mister Noone! That for six weeks, this – this *girl* – had been playing the part of my secretary?"

"I hope you will forgive me, sir."

"You are a charlatan! A cheat! A fraud! For six weeks! Six days a week for six weeks!"

"Uncle, please." Sir Jeremy's eyes were alight with mischief, and he could scarcely hold back his laughter as he said, "After all, you have always been able to recognize a good man when you meet one."

Old Ferrers cast a baleful eye upon his nephew, and then he gasped, and went quite red in the face, and there was a long pause, and he cried, "Six weeks! Six weeks!" and burst into peal after peal of laughter. "Six weeks! What do you say to that, Mycroft! No women at the Diogenes Club! It is there, in the charter! Six weeks! Come here, girl! Mycroft, move aside and give the girl your place."

Miss Archer went 'round, and bent over the old gentleman and placed a kiss on his scarred cheek.

"Six weeks," he said again. "Well, why do we not have that toast that you spoke of, Mr. Holmes. We shall have it now, and I will propose it. To a new age!" he said.

And we raised our glassed and echoed, "To a new age!"

"My colleague, Dr. Watson, could tell you that we are very busy at present. I am retained in this case of the Ferrers Documents, and the Abergavenny murder is coming up for trial.

367

Only a very important issue could call me from London at present."

Sherlock Holmes – "The Adventure of the Priory School"

NOTE

Wilfred Esmond, actor and entrepreneur, actually lived until 1913 and died while traveling to an engagement, though not as a result of foul play. Jessie Huddleston, a popular operetta star, did perform briefly in Esmond's company. She died at age eighty-six in 1969. Godfrey Morgan, and his mount, Mister Briggs, did return from the Crimean War to settle on Morgan's estate in Wales.

The Adventure of the
Exalted Victim
by Arthur Hall

As I sit here in our rooms in Baker Street, recording some of my extraordinary experiences as the friend and colleague of Mr. Sherlock Holmes, it occurs to me that many of our adventures began within these walls. But this was not always so. One exception that comes to mind is the curious affair of Mr. Wallace Abrahams and his unfortunate brother, which I will attempt to relate here from my notes and the vestiges of my recollection.

We had visited Lestrade at Scotland Yard, on Holmes's insistence. For once it was my friend who congratulated the inspector, on his successful handling of the case that sent Kirkby to the gallows.

"You did well, Lestrade. He was a particularly brutal murderer."

"The difficult part of it all was proving that Kirkby was in London at the time," the little detective said. "He had half-a-dozen witnesses who swore that he drank with them in a pub in Brighton that same night."

"The witnesses were so adamant that I doubted that their testimony was bought," Holmes recollected. "When you requested my assistance, my first act was to examine the official records to ensure that Kirkby had no twin or close relative of similar appearance. Finding none, I journeyed to Brighton and eventually discovered a local stage actor of small parts who looked enough like our man to have needed no more than a little make-up to complete the deception."

Lestrade nodded. "Your help saved me from much embarrassment, Mr. Holmes, as well as preventing a guilty man from cheating the law. One thing has puzzled me, though."

Holmes brought his gaze back from a study of the inspector's office ceiling. "Pray tell me. I will enlighten you if I can."

"When the actor was brought to London to be charged as an accessory, we saw how close the resemblance was. Yet you had no difficulty in telling the two men apart, at any time. How were you able to do this?"

"This mystified me also." I remarked.

"There really is no mystery about it," Holmes gave one of his quick, patient smiles. "Did either of you notice a peculiarity in Kirkby's mode of dress?"

Lestrade and I glanced at each other, and then it came to me. "Kirkby never wore a cravat. He tried a scarf around his neck."

"Excellent, Watson. You will recall that the actor, Murton, dressed similarly to aid the prosecution's case in demonstrating that one man could be substituted for the other. He had been promised leniency, for doing so."

"I remember," said Lestrade.

"Then the difference becomes clear, does it not, when we remember also that Murton was formerly a naval man. He tied his scarf in another fashion – a seaman's knot."

"It seems to me that it should be *me* congratulating *you*," Lestrade said. "All that was left for me was the arrest."

"Thus adding one more to your considerable record." Holmes picked up his hat and got to his feet.

At that moment the desk sergeant appeared in the doorway.

"This gentleman insists on seeing you, Inspector Lestrade."

A small man, I estimated him to be in his mid-sixties, was ushered in as we took our leave. He removed his bowler and I saw that he was completely bald, save for his thick side-whiskers and magnificent handlebar moustache. Holmes and I wished him good morning as we passed, and Lestrade invited him to be seated.

The following morning, I sat reading one of the early editions as Holmes stared wistfully from the window. Mrs. Hudson had cleared away our breakfast things before he finally spoke.

"Have the brandy decanter ready, Watson."

"It is a little early for me, Holmes."

"Of that I have no doubt, but the poor fellow who is about to visit us may benefit from a glass. He is in a highly excitable state, and we have already made his acquaintance, briefly."

I poured the drink and kept it in readiness, and a few minutes later a quick exchange at the door was followed by a noisy ascent before our good lady showed in the gentleman whom we had left with Lestrade yesterday.

"Mr. Wallace Abrahams, to see Mr. Holmes," she announced before withdrawing.

"My dear fellow," Holmes began. "I see that you are in some distress. Sit with us here and take a glass of brandy to calm your nerves before telling us how we can assist you."

Our visitor obeyed gladly and gulped the spirit down. As he replaced the glass on the tray, a puzzled look came into his eyes.

Holmes realised his difficulty at once. "Forgive me for not introducing ourselves, Mr. Abrahams. I am Sherlock Holmes, and this is my friend and colleague, Doctor John Watson, to whom you may speak with the same confidence as you would to myself."

Mr. Abrahams recovered himself slightly, and looked from Holmes to me and back again. "Thank you, gentlemen. You may recall that we met briefly in Inspector Lestrade's office, yesterday."

"Indeed we did. Is it the same matter that brings you here today?"

"It is, Mr. Holmes, and I am desperate."

"Was Lestrade unwilling or unable to assist you, then?" my friend enquired.

"He tried, sir. He said I was probably mistaken, that grief can do that to a man, and he sent constables to the house, but they found it empty."

"I think," said Holmes, "that we are approaching this from the wrong direction. Pray take a moment to reflect, and then tell us all from the beginning. A little more brandy, perhaps?"

The little man shook his head, and then realised that he still wore his hat and removed it. "My apologies, and no more to drink, thank you, sirs. What I am about to tell you is a story hard to believe, but I need a clear head to tell it all the same."

"Then if you are ready, pray proceed."

"You know already that my name is Wallace Abrahams. I am fortunate that I am retired from work."

"I had gathered as much."

The puzzled expression returned to our visitor's face. "How did you know that, sir?"

"The condition of your hands tells me that you did manual labour for some years, but the surface of the skin now appears smooth, revealing that the work has ceased. You are obviously no longer a young man, so retirement was a natural conclusion."

"Why, that is extraordinary, that you should see that." Mr. Abrahams smiled for the first time. "I worked on the railways, laying track and dragging those wooden sleepers. I saved every penny that I could. I never married – never met the right woman. When his wife died, five years ago, Garland came to live with me in the house I bought."

"Garland is your brother? I enquired.

"He is – or *was*." His face fell, presumably as he was reminded of his troubles. "Now, after all this – I cannot be sure."

Holmes looked at him thoughtfully. "Please enlighten us as to this most curious situation."

371

"One month ago," Mr. Abrahams put his head in his hands and spoke in a trembling voice, "I returned home to Clapham in the late afternoon. The road in which I live is usually quiet, being in the Old Town and not far from the Common, but that day it was clogged with fire brigade carts and people wanting to see what was going on. I turned a corner and saw to my horror that it was *my* house that was ablaze, and as I watched, a fireman carried out the charred remains of Garland. Then came a shower of sparks as the roof fell in."

"So you were left without shelter," I observed.

"No, I was fortunate in having another house nearby, a small place that I often let out. At that time, it was vacant, and so I moved there, to be alone with my grief. Then, yesterday, I walked through Clapham. I have taken to wandering aimlessly for hours, and I passed a house with turrets like a castle. As I walked by, the great double doors opened and four men came out. With them, to my astonishment, was Garland, as alive and well as we are sitting here now. I could not believe my eyes. I made to approach him to ensure that I was not mistaken or going mad, but one of his companions, a huge bearded brute, pushed me roughly aside and said in a harsh foreign accent, "If you interfere, we will kill you. Make no mistake.""

Holmes looked up thoughtfully. "Did you recognise any of the men accompanying your brother?"

"I am certain that I had never seen any of them before."

"Did your brother appear to recognise you?"

"He had a look of terror and, I thought, of abject hopelessness. A coach swept them away then, and I could do nothing."

"Did you notice anything else unusual about him?"

Our client considered. "A small thing. I suppose it has no significance."

"It is my experience that small things often have much significance."

"Well, it was just that Garland was unshaven. For him that is unheard of, for he has always been most particular about all aspects of his appearance."

"That is highly significant. From there you went to Scotland Yard?"

"I did, and the outcome was as I have mentioned. When nothing was found at the house, I asked Inspector Lestrade if anything more could be done. At first, he asked me to seriously consider whether I could have been mistaken, and when I replied that I was quite certain that my brother was alive, although I had seen his burnt body, he said that if I believed there was any mystery here, I should consult you. He then gave me your address."

"That was most kind of the good inspector."

There was a moment of silence, except for the sound of a trotting horse outside, as Mr. Abrahams sat very still, seemingly full of nervous anticipation. It was impossible to read Holmes's expression, but I knew that his mind would be racing.

"I have only a few more questions, Mr. Abrahams, then I will bid you good day," he said at last. "I will most certainly look into this and let you know the results. Firstly, at your brother's funeral, did you notice anything out of the ordinary?"

Our visitor's relief at gaining Holmes's help was evident as he said, after some little thought: "Only that the minister, the Reverend Potter, with whom I am acquainted, was replaced by a priest I had never seen before. The reason was never explained, nor has Reverend Potter been seen since. There is another priest there now."

"Did this replacement priest, by any chance, have a foreign accent?"

"He had a strange accent, certainly, but I couldn't tell if it was foreign."

"Was it, for example, anything like that of the man who prevented you from speaking to your brother?"

He hesitated, then shook his head again. "I could not be certain."

"Very well. At what church was the funeral held?"

"It was St. Thaddeus, in Clapham."

Holmes gave me a quick glance to ensure that I was making notes.

"And finally, please describe your brother to us."

Mr. Abrahams said nothing, but reached inside his coat to produce a photograph which he handed to Holmes, and I saw a strange look in my friend's eyes. In an instant it was gone, and I leaned over to see a portrait of an elderly, rather stout gentleman. He was clean-shaven, and his hair had thinned considerably above his brow. I could see no reason for Holmes's astonishment.

"May I keep this?" he asked.

"You could keep every penny that I own, if that would bring Garland back to me, Mr. Holmes. He is, or was, my only remaining relative."

"Fortunately, that will not be necessary," my friend smiled. "You will hear from me soon."

Mr. Abrahams made to rise, but stopped. "Forgive me, I have quite forgotten to tell you the other side of this."

"There is something more?"

"There is, and I should have told you at the beginning. Since my encounter with the men who were with Garland in Clapham, I have been followed by one or other of them. I thought I was imagining this at first, but now I am sure."

"This changes the picture considerably," Holmes said as he got to his feet. "We will accompany you to your home, and see what move they make."

I was able to summon a passing hansom, and we were soon on our way. Holmes looked in every direction, as did I, but we saw nothing as we joined the heavy traffic.

"A-ha!" he exclaimed as we progressed along Baker Street, and I peered back to see a man in a long black coat frantically attempting to attract the attention of a coach driver who was setting down a fare on the opposite side of the road.

"We shall see if we can make things a little more difficult for him." Holmes rapped the roof with his stick, telling the driver to take the next turn and directing him through a maze of side-streets.

By the time we reached Mr. Abraham's house, a three-storey red brick building in a quiet tree-lined street on the outskirts of Clapham, we were certain that our pursuer had not reappeared.

"It will be best if we enter with you to inspect the premises," Holmes advised.

"But what do you expect to find?"

"I wish to be certain that our adversaries have not been here before us, or are concealed within. Be in no doubt that your life is in danger, Mr. Abrahams. We must test every step in our investigation before we commit ourselves."

"I am not sure that I understand you,"

The hansom rattled away, taking a different return route on Holmes's instruction, before he answered.

"Firstly, I am not at all convinced that you were not being followed, long before you were aware of it."

"I suppose that is possible."

"Indeed, it is *likely*. I suspect that those holding your brother prisoner are threatening to kill you in order to be sure of his co-operation, although you were not meant to know this. Also, remember what was said to you when you encountered them."

"But to what end?"

"I am unsure, as of now. My theory has yet to be proven."

We entered the house and I remained in the hall with Mr. Abrahams, while Holmes checked every room. When this was over, he called to us to join him on the first floor, and we climbed the steep stairs cautiously.

"This window," he indicated, "gives an excellent view of the area immediately outside your front door. I recommend that you use it to view any callers, and do not admit anyone, even a uniformed constable, other than Inspector Lestrade, Doctor Watson, or myself. I will ask Lestrade if he can spare a man to watch the house, but not approach."

"Thank you, Mr. Holmes," he glanced at me. "No, thank you both."

"I need hardly remind you," Holmes said, "to ensure that all outer doors and windows are locked at all times, until this affair is over. Good day, Mr. Abrahams. You will hear from me soon."

With that we left him. A brisk walk took us to the centre of Clapham, where Holmes despatched a telegram.

"That was to Lestrade?" I ventured as he rejoined me outside the Post Office.

"No, to Mycroft."

"Your brother is somehow connected to this case?"

Holmes raised his hand as a hansom came towards us, after leaving a fare further along the street. "Only as a source of confirmation. I believe that certain information from him could reveal to us our adversary's purpose."

I knew better than to press him further. Experience has long taught me that Holmes will rarely confide his thoughts prematurely.

We boarded a hansom and set off for Baker Street. I turned from the window to see him with his eyes half-closed.

"Holmes, we have just passed the house that Mr. Abrahams described. It must be that, for there is none other like it anywhere here. Do you not wish to examine the rooms?"

He shook his head and gave a long sigh. "I fear that little purpose would be served, after Lestrade's men have trampled through the place like a herd of cattle. Also, you will have observed the downstairs windows being adorned with new curtains, telling us that the owner has already re-let the house and that any clues will almost certainly have been obscured."

We said nothing more, Holmes sitting with his head on his chest as was his custom when he was unravelling a case, until we reached our lodgings. Mrs. Hudson had prepared a sumptuous lunch of roast lamb with mint sauce, which he ate with unusual appetite. He refused the dessert of apple pie and clotted cream, however, and as soon as I had finished mine, he leapt from his chair.

"Come, Watson. If you are free this afternoon, you may care to accompany me back to Clapham. I have revised the direction which this investigation is to take."

"I am free until the end of the week, as you know, and with you of course. Are we to visit Mr. Abrahams again, so soon?"

"Not at all. There are things I must know before we proceed further, of which I can learn only at St. Thaddeus."

"The church where Mr. Abrahams' brother's funeral was held?"

"Precisely."

Except for two elderly ladies placing flowers on the graves of departed loved ones, the churchyard was deserted as we arrived. Holmes led the way past the lych gate and along the gravel path to the ancient iron-studded door. It squealed like a tormented spirit as he pushed it open, admitting us to a cavernous, echoing interior.

There were two people here, one moving about in the far shadows and the other standing stiffly at the lectern, bathed in the pattern of coloured light from the stained-glass windows. I could see that this figure wore priest's robes, which flowed around him as he became aware of us and approached. He looked at us curiously, as if about to remind us that there was no service until later in the day.

"Can I assist you gentlemen?"

"Good afternoon, Reverend. My name is Sherlock Holmes," my friend replied. "I would be grateful for some information."

Recognition dawned immediately on the priest's young and studious face. "The consulting detective? Yes, I have read of you, sir." He switched his gaze to me. "And this must be Doctor Watson, who so ably chronicles your exploits. I am pleased to meet you both, gentlemen, but how can I help?"

"I am enquiring about a funeral service that was conducted here, about a month ago."

"Just before I commenced my work here, in fact." The Reverend indicated that we should follow him into an alcove near the organ, where he selected a thick volume from a pile of dusty books. "Do you have the name of the deceased?"

Holmes nodded. "I understand that it was Mr. Garland Abrahams."

The priest whipped through the pages.

"Here it is," he cried at last. "The whole thing was very odd indeed, actually. I was told about it when I was sent to take over here." He turned to us, slightly embarrassed. "Forgive me. I should have introduced myself. I am Reverend Brookes, and I was given this parish because my predecessor, Reverend Potter, apparently abandoned his post."

"Unusual, wouldn't you think, for a man of the cloth?"

"It is indeed," Reverend Brookes continued, "but there is something here more unusual still. Strange, even."

376

"And what is that, pray?" Holmes enquired.

"Well, and I must tell you gentlemen that I am still puzzled by this now, as are the church authorities. It seems that Reverend Potter left on the very day of Mr. Abrahams's funeral, leaving no one to take the service. It came to be administered by another priest, a Reverend Smith."

"But why is that strange?" I asked.

Reverend Brookes spread out his hands, as if emphasising his confusion. "Because, dear sirs, the church authorities know nothing of this man. He observed the funeral rites, though rather abruptly, and left. Some of the mourners have asked me about him because he was unfamiliar to them, but I can tell them nothing."

This came as no surprise to me since I had already deduced, as Holmes must have done before me, that Reverend Brookes was not the priest described by Mr. Wallace Abrahams: His accent was neither strange nor foreign.

"Curious indeed," Holmes observed. "So you, yourself, never actually met this man?"

"No, but there I can help you." He turned and called into the shadows behind us. "Mrs. Clement! Come here for a moment, please."

A tiny elderly lady wearing a pinafore over her dress emerged from the shadows near the altar, where it was just possible to see that she had been arranging flowers.

After introducing us and explaining our purpose, Reverend Brookes went back to his work at the lectern and Mrs. Clement spoke in a low voice.

"I was here on the day of Mr. Garland Abraham's funeral," she began, "as I have been every day, these many years. I confess to not approving of this priest who appeared unannounced, nor of his manner. Sirs, do you blame me for that, when he rushes through a sacred ritual with such disrespect?"

"Not at all," said Holmes. "But apart from the way he conducted himself, was there anything in particular that struck you as unusual?"

There was no hesitation. "Two things stand out to me. You understand, gentlemen, that I am not normally what you might call an inquisitive person, but out of concern for the deceased and those grieving, I was anxious that all should proceed properly."

"Of course," my friend assured her with a trace of impatience.

"Well, the first thing was his accent. I don't like foreigners in our churches and, although he tried to disguise it, that voice did not stem from this country."

"I see. Tell me, pray, about the other thing that you so astutely noticed."

Her eyes glowed suddenly, in the way of someone about to disclose a secret. "It was the coffin. That Reverend Smith hardly moved away from it. He watched it as if he were expecting Mr. Abrahams to rise up out of it and come back to life! But what really puzzled me was something I overheard, accidentally you understand, in a conversation between Reverend Smith and one of the undertaker's men. Someone wanted the coffin opened so they could put something in with him, I don't know why, unless it was a relative or friend wanting to leave something for sentimental reasons. His brother, the other Mr. Abrahams, approved, even though it was at such a late stage, but when this was put to Reverend Smith, he was appalled! He shrank back against the casket as if he was protecting it, and would not continue with the burial until the idea was abandoned. He even quoted a scripture to support his actions which I swear he made up, because in all my years here, I've never heard of it. What do you think of that, sirs?"

"Extraordinary!" I exclaimed.

"Most peculiar," Holmes answered. "However, we will take up no more of your time. You and the good Reverend Brookes have been most helpful. Good afternoon to you both."

With that, he swept us quickly away. A hansom answered his call and, on our way back to Baker Street, he settled into one of his long silences. I, however, could not contain my confusion any longer and risked an interruption.

"Holmes, I am puzzled by this turn of events. That the unusual accent of this mysterious priest aroused suspicion I can understand, but what of his concern for a sealed coffin?"

He raised his head from his chest. "All his words and actions obviously reveal his anxiety that the casket should not be opened at any cost," he said thoughtfully. "We know that the contents cannot, if Mr. Abrahams is to believed, be the remains of his brother, and must therefore have been those of someone else."

I felt a flash of inspiration. "Could the body of Reverend Potter have been hidden there?"

"I have considered that, and will give it my attention later. There are other possibilities, however. For example, it could be that the remains that the gang holding Mr. Abraham's brother have caused to be placed there are female, possibly because no others were available quickly enough to be placed in the burning house. In that case, the deception would of course have been discovered at once, if the coffin lid were removed. It seems to be essential to their plans that he is believed to have died."

378

"Do you believe that the unfamiliar accent of the man who threatened Mr. Abrahams in the presence of his brother, and that of this unknown priest, are the same, thereby connecting these two events?"

"I have thought so since the circumstances were first explained to us."

With that he lapsed back into his thoughts and I disturbed him no more.

After dinner, I settled into an armchair with the evening edition of *The Standard,* while Holmes busied himself searching his index.

"It does not seem to have been reported," he mused to himself. "I must see Lestrade."

"What are you looking for?" I asked.

He looked at me as if he had suddenly become aware of my presence. "Sorry, old fellow, I was lost in my thoughts. In the morning, I must go to Scotland Yard, and then to see Mycroft, whose reply to my telegram has summoned me to the Diogenes Club. You are welcome to accompany me, if you would care to."

"I regret, Holmes, that I must return to my practice unexpectedly. You will recall that I also received a telegram. It was from the *locum* currently running my practice, and who seems to be having some sort of difficulty. I said I would call in to see him, to put matters right."

"Of course," he said a little disappointedly. "If you must, you must. I hope you settle things quickly."

"I expect to be back by mid-afternoon."

"Capital!"

He said no more, but spent the evening conducting experiments at his laboratory bench. When I had finished reading, I decided to repair early to my bed, and he acknowledged my leaving with a distracted grunt. But I could not sleep, and heard him still working far into the night.

The remains of Holmes's breakfast were on the table when Mrs. Hudson served mine the next morning. I arrived at my practice early and returned to Baker Street as I had predicted, by mid-afternoon. I had not yet had time to call to Mrs. Hudson for tea before the front door slammed and I heard him bound quickly up the stairs.

The door burst open and he strode in with a spring in his step.

"The day went well," I observed.

"Indeed, and my demeanour evidently demonstrates as much." He hung his coat and hat on the stand and at once sat down in the empty armchair, facing me across the low table.

379

"Shall I ring for tea?"

He took up his cherry-wood pipe. "A little later. First I must tell you what I have learned."

I saw that this was to be one of the rare occasions when my friend would be forthcoming about his activities, and I was keen to listen.

"I am all ears, Holmes."

"When I left here this morning, I went directly to Scotland Yard," he began as he blew a smoke ring at the ceiling. "I was convinced that a priest of Reverend Potter's experience would not abandon his calling in such a way, and it occurred to me that the most likely reasons for his disappearance would be if he were held prisoner or murdered."

"Was Lestrade able to throw any light on this?"

"Sadly, he was. On the day that Mr. Garland Abraham's funeral took place, a body was recovered from the Thames. Its head and limbs had been removed, and the rats had found it first, but it has been identified as that of Reverend Potter from a tattoo on its shoulder."

"That is ghastly," I said, reacting to the body's condition. "But is it not strange that a priest should be tattooed?"

Holmes shook his head. "Not in this case. Before he became a man of the cloth, Potter was a naval man like Murton, the actor. He served for years in the tropics, where tattoos are common as a protection against malaria. Apparently they act as a barrier against the disease, in some way."

"I have heard of this, before now."

The silence of the room was interrupted briefly by cries from the street below, and by the neighing of a passing horse. Holmes knocked out his pipe and continued.

"After telling the good inspector about our discoveries, I caught a hansom to Pall Mall. I knew that Mycroft would be at the Diogenes Club at that time of day, and I was left in the Stranger's Room while he was summoned."

I learned forward eagerly. "And what did you learn? Could he help?"

"Oh, yes. I now know who we are up against, and why. I do not exaggerate, Watson, when I tell you that the outcome of this will have a considerable effect on the future of the British Empire."

I was profoundly shocked. "Good heavens! How can this be?" Before my friend could answer, it came to me. "Of course – the foreign accents. There is an international conspiracy involved here!"

"Indeed. You are not wrong, even if a little late forming the correct conclusion. Our adversary is none other than Imperial Germany, and our country is under a threat that is as yet largely unrecognised. Were it not for Mycroft, I would still have been unaware of it."

"Then what is the next step?" I enquired. "There must be something that we can do against them."

"Not yet. According to my brother, they cannot move for at least a month. Their actions depend on the first of a series of forthcoming events that begin then. We must wait, however much of a trial that is."

A week went by, without incident. It was then that Holmes was presented with the problem that I have chronicled elsewhere as "The Disappearance of Lady Frances Carfax", but because of the persistent danger to Mr. Wallace Abrahams, concerning which he would tell me no more, he was unable to leave the capital. It was therefore I who journeyed to Lausanne as his representative, only to be unexpectedly joined by him quite soon. My first question to him was of course concerning the situation that he had left behind, and his answer was that he could no longer bear to stagnate.

"But what of Abrahams?" I asked with concern. "Is the danger past?"

"By no means," he inhaled from his briar and blew out a swirling cloud of smoke. "I decided that I could leave if I increased his protection adequately. Barker, the private enquiry agent whom I have used before, is watching Abraham's house independently of Lestrade's men who, thanks to Mycroft's influence, continue their duty. Barker is under orders to contact me by wire at the slightest change. Also, so that Abrahams can have some freedom and is no longer a prisoner in his own house, I have hired two prize-fighters, including McMurdo, whom we know of old. That, I think, should suffice until we return."

This new case progressed, and was brought to a satisfactory conclusion when the lady was saved, although Holmes's disappointment at the escape of our adversaries was written on his face. The subject soon dropped from our conversation, however, once we were back in London and seated again in our familiar sitting room. Two days passed before he received a telegram from Mycroft consisting of only two words: *It begins.*

He passed it across the breakfast table for me to read, after which I saw on his face a deep frown of concern.

"Holmes," I said quietly, "is it not time that you revealed to me the true nature of this affair involving the Abrahams brothers? What is the enemy's purpose? What is it that begins soon?"

His eyes were as hard as flint when his gaze fell upon me, so that I felt that I had intruded, but they were soon to soften as his expression cleared and he replied in his most reasonable tone.

"You are quite right of course, Watson. I probably should have confided in you earlier. If there is any excuse for me, old friend, it is that I was overwhelmed by the gravity and enormity of the situation. The seed that Abrahams planted with us has grown into a mighty tree."

"Very well, Holmes, but tell me now. Who are these German agents? What is their purpose?"

"According to Mycroft, they are four of their best operators, from the same stable as Oberstein. Their leader, if I am not much mistaken, is the man who threatened Mr. Wallace Abrahams, the same who has ensured that he is constantly in fear of death to ensure the co-operation of his kidnapped brother. His name, or least the one he currently uses, is Kurt Bekker."

"Scoundrels!" I exclaimed. "But still, I see no purpose in all this."

Holmes nodded. "That is easily corrected. Pray hand me the photograph of Abraham's brother, which stands on the shelf near your right arm."

I complied, and he placed his hands so that they shielded part of the likeness. "Now, imagine him with a full beard. Has he not now become familiar to you?"

I peered at the picture, over his shoulder. At first I saw nothing but what I had seen before, then all at once I realised the truth of it all.

"Great heavens, Holmes! He looks like . . . ."

"Almost a twin, wouldn't you say?"

"I would swear," I had to pause, for it was suddenly difficult to breathe, "that this is a likeness of . . . ."

"Of The Most Honourable Robert Gascoyne-Cecil, Third Marquess of Salisbury, KG. PC. FRS. DZ." Holmes finished. "You could be forgiven for believing so," a quick smile flittered across his face and was gone, "but it is, as was represented to us, of Mr. Garland Abrahams. I saw the hidden resemblance at once, at first sight of the photograph. That is why I consulted Mycroft, because the implications were immediately apparent."

"But this is awful. Bekker and his men clearly intend to substitute this man for the Prime Minister. But why would they do this?"

"I could find no reason, despite considerable research. But again, it was Mycroft who supplied the answer. Once we were alone in the Stranger's Room, he told me all. During the next few months, members of the Spanish, Italian, and French governments will visit our capital at different times. During the course of these visits, each will meet the Prime Minister, prior to a decision being reached on a vital and far-reaching matter. If the kidnapped Mr. Abrahams were substituted, not only would Bekker and his men learn of the proceedings, but they could instruct him, on pain of his brother's death, to sabotage any or all of the meetings."

"This is monstrous. Did Mycroft confide in you the substance of the discussions?"

"Only in general terms, as far as his position would allow. Each of these foreign dignitaries is party to a plan, a treaty, that if implemented would benefit our country considerably, but would work against the interests of Imperial Germany. Clearly, Bekker and his friends have been sent to disrupt this agreement, to our detriment."

I considered for a moment. "Holmes, what do you suppose they intend to do to the Prime Minister, once he is in their hands?"

"I regret, this is not known."

"If harm came to him, it would mean war."

"Precisely. Hence my rather dramatic warning about the Empire's future."

A bewilderment such as I have never known settled upon me, and it seemed like a long time before I was able to raise my head from my hands. My friend had not moved.

"Holmes, what must we do?"

"Some things have been done already. I have arranged with Lestrade to be present at the meeting place before the Spanish Minister for Foreign Affairs arrives tomorrow. I trust you will accompany me?"

"As ever."

A rare softness came into his eyes. "My Watson never changes."

I tried to assume his cold approach towards the task ahead, not very successfully. "Tell me then Holmes, how things are to be."

I took my watch from my waistcoat pocket and peered at it by the light of the moon. It was now four in the morning, and the first glimmer of dawn was a streak in the eastern sky. We had been here, in this closed police wagon, for more than an hour.

"You are sure, Mr. Holmes, that they will come today?" In the darkness, Lestrade moved in his seat to relieve the cramp that was setting in.

From his position opposite me, I heard my friend reply. "They will come. It would be a paramount act of foolishness to continue the risk they are running, when the substitution could be made today."

"Thank God," I said, "that this plot was discovered, and that the Prime Minister will be far from here."

"But, thanks to Mycroft, all indications are that he is already here to meet the Spanish Minister, when in fact the meeting has been reappointed and will take place elsewhere later today. My brother's influence has ensured that the newspapers were misleading on that point."

"I have had their man who was watching Mr. Abrahams arrested," Lestrade said without taking his eyes from the gates. "My men did not notice anyone else loitering nearby."

"Barker is very proficient," Holmes acknowledged. "So, we are now dealing with the remaining three, led by Bekker."

We fell silent and I looked ahead in the gathering light. The straight gravel path led from the guarded gates to the house, perhaps half-a-mile distant. Berrymount Manor was a two-storey structure in the Georgian style, wide with a round tower surmounted by a weather vane protruding from its midst. Holmes had mentioned that a red carpet and other temporary additions had been installed in advance to give the appearance of an impending foreign dignitary's visit.

"I think we should take up our positions now, Lestrade." he said as he adjusted his ear-flapped cap.

At the inspector's order, the driver shook the reins and the horse moved slowly along the path, followed by the second wagon containing six armed constables. We had gone less than halfway to the house when we passed a group of trees on our left, while the ground fell away in a steep bank to our right.

"This will do," Holmes decided.

We all got out and the wagons returned in the direction they had come. We left the path eventually for concealment among four mighty oaks nearer the gates. The constables hid themselves among the trees, while Holmes, Lestrade, and I lay on our stomachs on the slope opposite with the remaining two.

It was a cold morning. On arrival, I had noticed a faint mist around the base of the trees and a heavy dew upon the grass. We were in the heart of the Surrey countryside, and our party was made up of two additional constables that Lestrade had requisitioned from the Dorking force to supplement the four from Scotland Yard.

Almost two hours passed.

"Look!" Lestrade said urgently, and we all turned to watch the gates.

A four-wheeler had arrived, and the guards at the gates conversed with the driver. After a few moments entry was allowed, and the gated closed heavily.

"At last," Holmes whispered.

"How did they get past the sentries so easily?" I wondered aloud.

"This was all planned carefully in advance, Watson," my friend replied. "They would not have let such a small difficulty deter them, although I confess I do not yet know how it was overcome."

The coach advanced at a slow trot until it had drawn near. From the trees across the path a constable emerged, waving his arms. The coach obediently came to a halt.

"Who goes there?" he demanded.

"We are a special auxiliary bodyguard for the Spanish Minister for Foreign Affairs," came the reply tinged with foreign accent. "Here to prepare for the arrival of His Excellency."

The constable advanced, and I felt myself grow tense. He circled the coach and I was able to see four dark silhouettes within. Finally, he approached and asked for documentary proof, and was given papers which he examined and returned. He stepped back then, and peered into the coach.

"And who is the man accompanying you?"

"He is the chief assistant to His Excellency."

"I think not, Herr Bekker." Holmes said as we stood up beside Lestrade. "I think not, indeed."

From that moment, chaos reigned. The coach doors on both sides burst open and several shots were fired. A shotgun flared and the constable who had hailed the coach went down. The remaining constables, Holmes, Lestrade, and myself returned their fire, and the man with the shotgun sank to the ground. The huge figure of Bekker, dragging his prisoner with him in a clumsy stagger, ran for the trees, firing as he fled.

Two constables fell to the remaining occupant, who fired from inside the coach. I emptied my service revolver into it and heard an agonised cry. A bullet whipped past Lestrade's face and he fired twice at Bekker in response.

"Careful, Lestrade! We must not hit the other man!" Holmes warned.

The little detective lowered his pistol as the fugitives disappeared into the trees.

I stumbled across the path with Holmes and Lestrade at my side. One of the fallen constables moaned in pain as we ran past, calling Lestrade's name.

"See to him. Lestrade!" Holmes shouted. "They cannot escape now!"

Lestrade hesitated, and then stopped to attend his comrade. Holmes and I increased our efforts across the lawn, steadily gaining on Bekker. Garland Abrahams cried out as he was pulled mercilessly on. Bekker must have realised that we could not fail to overtake them, for he turned abruptly and they vanished behind a tall leafy hedge.

"It is a maze," Holmes observed. "If they have taken refuge there, they are finished, since the only entrance is also the exit."

"One moment, Holmes." I paused to reload my pistol, and he did the same.

We approached the hedge cautiously, to find that it was indeed the beginning of a maze. Around the first corner we stopped, guns at the ready, but all that faced us was empty space. The only sound was a faint rustling from a breeze that had sprung up, and I was about to proceed when my friend gripped my coat sleeve.

"Not that way, Watson. That pile of dead leaves over there is undisturbed, so they cannot have passed." He glanced around us. "On the other hand, I see that there is a fresh footprint in the mud at the end of this aisle. If this puzzle follows the traditional pattern, I expect to find Herr Bekker and his unfortunate captive awaiting us at the end of the next row, for it will certainly be a dead end."

Holmes was quickly proven correct. We rounded the corner with our backs pressed against the hedge to come face-to-face with Bekker, who held a pistol to his captive's head.

"Get back!" he growled in his beard, and I noticed that his accent was thickened by fear. "Leave this place, and take all the police with you, or I will shoot this man."

To my astonishment, Holmes lowered his revolver.

"I am most surprised," he said in a mocking tone, "to find an agent of Imperial Germany hiding behind a helpless man. Have you no honour, sir?"

Bekker said nothing, but looked from Holmes to me and then back.

"Has it occurred to you, Herr Bekker," Holmes continued, "that the moment you kill your prisoner, you deprive yourself of your only protection against us?"

Bekker's expression remained unaltered, but I could sense that he was frantically searching his mind for a way out. Mr. Abrahams was trembling uncontrollably, and was shaken in an attempt to make him still. "I will do it, if you do not desist!"

"But what will you gain?" Holmes asked. "If you destroy your shield, we will cut you down, and you know this. If you surrender and let him live, you will at least be alive until you face the hangman. You must see that this is the only choice you have. Come now, a man of your experience in your line of work should be able to tell when he is finished."

I recall hearing my friend's voice fade away among the leafy walls surrounding us. Then there was a moment of absolute silence, I suppose while Bekker considered what had been said. I had the impression that Holmes knew something of this man, or of this type of man, that was lost to me, and a glance at his flint-like expression confirmed this.

Fear left Bekker's face, leaving it with a corpse-like blankness. Slowly, but very deliberately, he moved his pistol from his prisoner's head and placed it next to his own. With his eyes open, he blew his brains out, and fell as his blood-spattered captive stumbled towards me.

"At least this way, he can be said to have died for his country," Holmes said as we escorted Mr. Abrahams, whose terror had turned to relief, away from the ghastly scene. "I have no doubt that his death will be recorded like that."

The constable that Lestrade had stayed behind to tend had died in his arms.

"It should have been I who stayed while Lestrade accompanied you," I said as we left through the gates. "I could perhaps have saved his life."

"No," Holmes replied, "I saw the man's wounds. They were mortal, and your attention would have made little difference."

"I was able to ease the pain of the injured constables, at least."

On our return to the scene, Lestrade had summoned the drivers of the police wagons who had been kept on hand as possible reinforcements, and dispatched one of them to bring medical help. I refused to leave until it arrived, and then the inspector had sent us back to Baker Street in the remaining wagon, after having secured our promise that we would make a statement at Scotland Yard the following day.

As the grounds of Berrymount Manor receded, Holmes gave a long sigh.

"Do not distress yourself, Watson. As always, you did all that you could."

I earnestly hoped that he was right, and it gratified me that he thought so, but as our journey continued, I found myself doubting and entering a melancholy state of mind. In effort to dispel this, I turned my thoughts back to the events of this morning.

"You have explained much of this case, Holmes," I said at length, "but one thing still puzzles me."

The wagon rattled over a cobbled street and he raised his head from his chest. "Just one?"

"I mean about the intended substitution of Mr. Garland Abrahams for the Prime Minister. How did they propose to effect this?"

"Sometimes I could believe that you are able to read my mind." He gave a short laugh. "I was in fact thinking of that very question. As I have already said, everything from beginning to end was meticulously planned, so we can be sure that their intentions were tried and tested. Perhaps Mycroft knows more, since he is much more acquainted with such people and their connections than you or I. Until I can speak to him, we will have to be patient, but afterwards I will tell you what I can so that you can record this little affair as one of your over-dramatized stories."

"They must have had some sort of help with their preparations, which means that there are more of their agents, or at least sympathisers, near at hand."

"Undoubtedly."

"So they are here, among us. Is there nothing we can do?"

"Nothing as yet, I am afraid to say, but when such ones show their hand, we must be ready. For now, having left Mr. Abrahams in Lestrade's charge, and having ensured that his brother will shortly receive the good news, I can think of nothing but the breakfast that Mrs. Hudson will shortly serve us."

"You know that I cannot possibly leave London while old Abrahams is in such mortal terror of his life."

Sherlock Holmes – "The Disappearance of
Lady Frances Carfax"

388

Appendix:
The Untold Cases

The following has been assembled from several sources, including lists compiled by Phil Jones and Randall Stock, as well as some internet resources and my own research. I cannot promise that it's complete – some Untold Cases may be missing – after all, there's a great deal of Sherlockian Scholarship that involves interpretation and rationalizing – and there are some listed here that certain readers may believe shouldn't be listed at all.

As a fanatical supporter and collector of pastiches since I was a ten-year-old boy in 1975, reading Nicholas Meyer's *The Seven-Per-Cent Solution* and *The West End Horror* before I'd even read all of The Canon, I can attest that serious and legitimate versions of all of these Untold Cases exist out there – some of them occurring with much greater frequency than others – and I hope to collect, read, and chronologicize them all.

There's so much more to The Adventures of Sherlock Holmes than the pitifully few sixty stories that were fixed up by the First Literary Agent. I highly recommend that you find and read all of the rest of them as well, including those relating these Untold Cases. You won't regret it.

David Marcum

A Study in Scarlet

- Mr. Lestrade . . . got himself in a fog recently over a forgery case
- A young girl called, fashionably dressed
- A gray-headed, seedy visitor, looking like a Jew pedlar who appeared to be very much excited
- A slipshod elderly woman
- An old, white-haired gentleman had an interview
- A railway porter in his velveteen uniform

The Sign of Four

- The consultation last week by Francois le Villard

- The most winning woman Holmes ever knew was hanged for poisoning three little children for their insurance money
- The most repellent man of Holmes's acquaintance was a philanthropist who has spent nearly a quarter of a million upon the London poor
- Holmes once enabled Mrs. Cecil Forrester to unravel a little domestic complication. She was much impressed by his kindness and skill
- Holmes lectured the police on causes and inferences and effects in the Bishopgate jewel case

The Adventures of Sherlock Holmes

"A Scandal in Bohemia"
- The summons to Odessa in the case of the Trepoff murder
- The singular tragedy of the Atkinson brothers at Trincomalee
- The mission which Holmes had accomplished so delicately and successfully for the reigning family of Holland. (He also received a remarkably brilliant ring)
- The Darlington substitution scandal, and . . .
- The Arnsworth castle business. (When a woman thinks that her house is on fire, her instinct is at once to rush to the thing which she values most. It is a perfectly overpowering impulse, and Holmes has more than once taken advantage of it

"The Red-Headed League"
- The previous skirmishes with John Clay

"A Case of Identity"
- The Dundas separation case, where Holmes was engaged in clearing up some small points in connection with it. The husband was a teetotaler, there was no other woman, and the conduct complained of was that he had drifted into the habit of winding up every meal by taking out his false teeth and hurling them at his wife, which is not an action likely to occur to the imagination of the average story-teller.
- The rather intricate matter from Marseilles
- Mrs. Etherege, whose husband Holmes found so easy when the police and everyone had given him up for dead

"The Boscombe Valley Mystery"
NONE LISTED

"The Five Orange Pips"
- The adventure of the Paradol Chamber
- The Amateur Mendicant Society, who held a luxurious club in the lower vault of a furniture warehouse
- The facts connected with the disappearance of the British barque *Sophy Anderson*
- The singular adventures of the Grice-Patersons in the island of Uffa
- The Camberwell poisoning case, in which, as may be remembered, Holmes was able, by winding up the dead man's watch, to prove that it had been wound up two hours before, and that therefore the deceased had gone to bed within that time – a deduction which was of the greatest importance in clearing up the case
- Holmes saved Major Prendergast in the Tankerville Club scandal. He was wrongfully accused of cheating at cards
- Holmes has been beaten four times – three times by men and once by a woman

"The Man with the Twisted Lip"
- The rascally Lascar who runs The Bar of Gold in Upper Swandam Lane has sworn to have vengeance upon Holmes

"The Adventure of the Blue Carbuncle"
NONE LISTED

"The Adventure of the Speckled Band"
- Mrs. Farintosh and an opal tiara. (It was before Watson's time)

"The Adventure of the Engineer's Thumb"
- Colonel Warburton's madness

"The Adventure of the Noble Bachelor"
- The letter from a fishmonger
- The letter a tide-waiter
- The service for Lord Backwater

- The little problem of the Grosvenor Square furniture van
- The service for the King of Scandinavia

"The Adventure of the Beryl Coronet"
NONE LISTED

"The Adventure of the Copper Beeches"
NONE LISTED

The Memoirs of Sherlock Holmes

"Silver Blaze"
NONE LISTED

"The Cardboard Box"
- Aldridge, who helped in the bogus laundry affair

"The Yellow Face"
- The (First) Adventure of the Second Stain was a failure which present[s] the strongest features of interest

'The Stockbroker's Clerk"
NONE LISTED

"The "Gloria Scott"
NONE LISTED

"The Musgrave Ritual"
- The Tarleton murders
- The case of Vamberry, the wine merchant
- The adventure of the old Russian woman
- The singular affair of the aluminum crutch
- A full account of Ricoletti of the club foot and his abominable wife
- The two cases before the Musgrave Ritual from Holmes's fellow students

"The Reigate Squires"
- The whole question of the Netherland-Sumatra Company and of the colossal schemes of Baron Maupertuis

The Crooked Man"
NONE LISTED

The Resident Patient"
- [Catalepsy] is a very easy complaint to imitate. Holmes has done it himself.

"The Greek Interpreter"
- Mycroft expected to see Holmes round last week to consult me over that Manor House case. It was Adams, of course
- Some of Holmes's most interesting cases have come to him through Mycroft

"The Naval Treaty"
- The (Second) adventure of the Second Stain, which dealt with interest of such importance and implicated so many of the first families in the kingdom that for many years it would be impossible to make it public. No case, however, in which Holmes was engaged had ever illustrated the value of his analytical methods so clearly or had impressed those who were associated with him so deeply. Watson still retained an almost verbatim report of the interview in which Holmes demonstrated the true facts of the case to Monsieur Dubugue of the Paris police, and Fritz von Waldbaum, the well-known specialist of Dantzig, both of whom had wasted their energies upon what proved to be side-issues. The new century will have come, however, before the story could be safely told.
- The Adventure of the Tired Captain
- A very commonplace little murder. If it [this paper] turns red, it means a man's life . . . .

"The Final Problem"
- The engagement for the French Government upon a matter of supreme importance
- The assistance to the Royal Family of Scandinavia

The Return of Sherlock Holmes

"The Adventure of the Empty House"

- Holmes traveled for two years in Tibet (as) a Norwegian named Sigerson, amusing himself by visiting Lhassa [*sic*] and spending some days with the head Llama [*sic*]
- Holmes traveled in Persia
- . . . looked in at Mecca . . .
- . . . and paid a short but interesting visit to the Khalifa at Khartoum
- Returning to France, Holmes spent some months in a research into the coal-tar derivatives, which he conducted in a laboratory at Montpelier [*sic*], in the South of France
- Mathews, who knocked out Holmes's left canine in the waiting room at Charing Cross
- The death of Mrs. Stewart, of Lauder, in 1887
- Morgan the poisoner
- Merridew of abominable memory
- The Molesey Mystery (Inspector Lestrade's Case. He handled it fairly well.)

"The Adventure of the Norwood Builder"
- The case of the papers of ex-President Murillo
- The shocking affair of the Dutch steamship, *Friesland*, which so nearly cost both Holmes and Watson their lives
- That terrible murderer, Bert Stevens, who wanted Holmes and Watson to get him off in '87

"The Adventure of the Dancing Men"
NONE LISTED

"The Adventure of the Solitary Cyclist"
- The peculiar persecution of John Vincent Harden, the well-known tobacco millionaire
- It was near Farnham that Holmes and Watson took Archie Stamford, the forger

"The Adventure of the Priory School"
- Holmes was retained in the case of the Ferrers Documents
- The Abergavenny murder, which is coming up for trial

"The Adventure of Black Peter"

- The sudden death of Cardinal Tosca – an inquiry which was carried out by him at the express desire of His Holiness the Pope
- The arrest of Wilson, the notorious canary-trainer, which removed a plague-spot from the East-End of London.

"The Adventure of Charles Augustus Milverton"
NONE LISTED

"The Adventure of the Six Napoleons"
- The dreadful business of the Abernetty family, which was first brought to Holmes's attention by the depth which the parsley had sunk into the butter upon a hot day
- The Conk-Singleton forgery case
- Holmes was consulted upon the case of the disappearance of the black pearl of the Borgias, but was unable to throw any light upon it

"The Adventure of the Three Students"
- Some laborious researches in Early English charters

"The Adventure of the Golden Pince-Nez"
- The repulsive story of the red leech
- . . . and the terrible death of Crosby, the banker
- The Addleton tragedy
- . . . and the singular contents of the ancient British barrow
- The famous Smith-Mortimer succession case
- The tracking and arrest of Huret, the boulevard assassin

"The Adventure of the Missing Three-Quarter"
- Henry Staunton, whom Holmes helped to hang
- Arthur H. Staunton, the rising young forger

"The Adventure of the Abbey Grange"
- Hopkins called Holmes in seven times, and on each occasion his summons was entirely justified

"The Adventure of the Second Stain"
- The woman at Margate. No powder on her nose – that proved to be the correct solution. How can one build on such

397

a quicksand? A woman's most trivial action may mean volumes, or their most extraordinary conduct may depend upon a hairpin or a curling-tong

The Hound of the Baskervilles

- That little affair of the Vatican cameos, in which Holmes obliged the Pope
- The little case in which Holmes had the good fortune to help Messenger Manager Wilson
- One of the most revered names in England is being besmirched by a blackmailer, and only Holmes can stop a disastrous scandal
- The atrocious conduct of Colonel Upwood in connection with the famous card scandal at the Nonpareil Club
- Holmes defended the unfortunate Mme. Montpensier from the charge of murder that hung over her in connection with the death of her stepdaughter Mlle. Carere, the young lady who, as it will be remembered, was found six months later alive and married in New York

The Valley of Fear

- Twice already Holmes had helped Inspector Macdonald

His Last Bow

"The Adventure of Wisteria Lodge"
- The locking-up Colonel Carruthers

"The Adventure of the Red Circle"
- The affair last year for Mr. Fairdale Hobbs
- The Long Island cave mystery

"The Adventure of the Bruce-Partington Plans"
- Brooks . . .
- . . . or Woodhouse, or any of the fifty men who have good reason for taking Holmes's life

"The Adventure of the Dying Detective"

"The Disappearance of Lady Frances Carfax"
- Holmes cannot possibly leave London while old Abrahams is in such mortal terror of his life

"The Adventure of the Devil's Foot"
- Holmes's dramatic introduction to Dr. Moore Agar, of Harley Street

"His Last Bow"
- Holmes started his pilgrimage at Chicago . . .
- . . . graduated in an Irish secret society at Buffalo
- . . . gave serious trouble to the constabulary at Skibbareen
- Holmes saves Count Von und Zu Grafenstein from murder by the Nihilist Klopman

The Case-Book of Sherlock Holmes

"The Adventure of the Illustrious Client"
- Negotiations with Sir George Lewis over the Hammerford Will case

"The Adventure of the Blanched Soldier"
- The Abbey School in which the Duke of Greyminster was so deeply involved
- The commission from the Sultan of Turkey which required immediate action
- The professional service for Sir James Saunders

"The Adventure of the Mazarin Stone"
- Old Baron Dowson said the night before he was hanged that in Holmes's case what the law had gained the stage had lost
- The death of old Mrs. Harold, who left Count Sylvius the Blymer estate
- The compete life history of Miss Minnie Warrender
- The robbery in the train de-luxe to the Riviera on February 13, 1892

"The Adventure of the Three Gables"

399

- The killing of young Perkins outside the Holborn Bar
- Mortimer Maberly, was one of Holmes's early clients

"The Adventure of the Sussex Vampire"
- *Matilda Briggs*, a ship which is associated with the giant rat of Sumatra, a story for which the world is not yet prepared
- Victor Lynch, the forger
- Venomous lizard, or Gila. Remarkable case, that!
- Vittoria the circus belle
- Vanderbilt and the Yeggman
- Vigor, the Hammersmith wonder

"The Adventure of the Three Garridebs"
- Holmes refused a knighthood for services which may, someday, be described

"The Problem of Thor Bridge"
- Mr. James Phillimore who, stepping back into his own house to get his umbrella, was never more seen in this world
- The cutter *Alicia*, which sailed one spring morning into a patch of mist from where she never again emerged, nor was anything further ever heard of herself and her crew.
- Isadora Persano, the well-known journalist and duelist who was found stark staring mad with a match box in front of him which contained a remarkable worm said to be unknown to science

"The Adventure of the Creeping Man"
NONE LISTED

"The Adventure of the Lion's Mane"
NONE LISTED

"The Adventure of the Veiled Lodger"
- The whole story concerning the politician, the lighthouse, and the trained cormorant

"The Adventure of Shoscombe Old Place"
- Holmes ran down that coiner by the zinc and copper filings in the seam of his cuff

- The St. Pancras case, where a cap was found beside the dead policeman. Merivale of the Yard, asked Holmes to look into it

"The Adventure of the Retired Colourman"
- The case of the two Coptic Patriarchs

About the Contributors

The following contributions appear in this volume:
The MX Book of New Sherlock Holmes Stories
Part XII – Some Untold Cases (1894-1902)

"**Anon**." is a devoted Sherlockian and player of The Game.

Brian Belanger is a publisher and editor, but is best known for his freelance illustration and cover design work. His distinctive style can be seen on several MX Publishing covers, including *Silent Meridian* by Elizabeth Crowen, *Sherlock Holmes and the Menacing Melbournian* by Allan Mitchell, *Sherlock Holmes and A Quantity of Debt* by David Marcum, *Welcome to Undershaw* by Luke Benjamen Kuhns, and many more. Brian is the co-founder of Belanger Books LLC, where he illustrates the popular *MacDougall Twins with Sherlock Holmes* young reader series (#1 bestsellers on Amazon.com UK). A prolific creator, he also designs t-shirts, mugs, stickers, and other merchandise on his personal art site at *www.redbubble.com/people/zhahadun*.

Derrick Belanger (who also has a story in Volume III) is an educator and also the author of the #1 bestselling book in its category, *Sherlock Holmes: The Adventure of the Peculiar Provenance*, which was in the top 200 bestselling books on Amazon. He also is the author of *The MacDougall Twins with Sherlock Holmes* books, and he edited the Sir Arthur Conan Doyle horror anthology *A Study in Terror: Sir Arthur Conan Doyle's Revolutionary Stories of Fear and the Supernatural*. Mr. Belanger co-owns the publishing company Belanger Books, which released the Sherlock Holmes anthologies *Beyond Watson*, *Holmes Away From Home: Adventures from the Great Hiatus* Volumes 1 and 2, *Sherlock Holmes: Before Baker Street*, and *Sherlock Holmes: Adventures in the Realms of H.G. Wells* Volumes I and 2. Derrick resides in Colorado and continues compiling unpublished works by Dr. John H. Watson.

Nick Cardillo has loved Sherlock Holmes ever since he was first introduced to the detective in *The Great Illustrated Classics* edition of *The Adventures of Sherlock Holmes* at the age of six. His devotion to the Baker Street detective duo has only increased over the years, and Nick is thrilled to be taking these proper steps into the Sherlock Holmes Community. His first published story, "The Adventure of the Traveling Corpse", appeared in *The MX Book of New Sherlock Holmes Stories – Part VI: 2017 Annual*, and his "The Haunting of Hamilton Gardens" was published in *PART VIII – Eliminate the Impossible: 1892-1905*. A devout fan of The Golden Age of Detective Fiction, Hammer Horror, and *Doctor Who*, Nick co-writes the Sherlockian blog, *Back on Baker Street*, which analyses over seventy years of Sherlock Holmes film and culture. He is a student at Susquehanna University.

Sir Arthur Conan Doyle (1859-1930) *Holmes Chronicler Emeritus*. If not for him, this anthology would not exist. Author, physician, patriot, sportsman, spiritualist, husband and father, and advocate for the oppressed. He is remembered and honored for the purposes of this collection by being the man who introduced Sherlock Holmes to the world. Through fifty-six Holmes short stories, four novels, and additional Apocryphal entries, Doyle revolutionized mystery stories and also greatly influenced and improved police forensic methods and techniques for the betterment of all. *Steel True Blade Straight.*

C.H. Dye first discovered Sherlock Holmes when she was eleven, in a collection that ended at the Reichenbach Falls. It was another six months before she discovered *The Hound of the Baskervilles*, and two weeks after that before a librarian handed her *The Return.* She has loved the stories ever since. She has written fan-fiction, and her first published pastiche, "The Tale of the Forty Thieves", was included in *The MX Book of New Sherlock Holmes Stories – Part I: 1881-1889.* Her story "A Christmas Goose" was in *The MX Book of New Sherlock Holmes Stories – Part V: Christmas Adventures*, and "The Mysterious Mourner" in *The MX Book of New Sherlock Holmes Stories – Part VIII – Eliminate the Impossible: 1892-1905*

Steve Emecz's main field is technology, in which he has been working for about twenty years. Following multiple senior roles at Xerox, where he grew their European eCommerce from $6m to $200m, Steve joined platform provider Venda, and moved across to Powa in 2010. Today, Steve is CCO at collectAI in Hamburg, a German fintech company using Artificial Intelligence to help companies with their debt collection. Steve is a regular trade show speaker on the subject of eCommerce, and his tech career has taken him to more than fifty countries – so he's no stranger to planes and airports. He wrote two novels (one a bestseller) in the 1990's, and a screenplay in 2001. Shortly after, he set up MX Publishing, specialising in NLP books. In 2008, MX published its first Sherlock Holmes book, and MX has gone on to become the largest specialist Holmes publisher in the world. MX is a social enterprise and supports two main causes. The first is Happy Life, a children's rescue project in Nairobi, Kenya, where he and his wife, Sharon, spend every Christmas at the rescue centre in Kasarani. In 2014, they wrote a short book about the project, *The Happy Life Story.* The second is the Stepping Stones School, of which Steve is a patron. Stepping Stones is located at Undershaw, Sir Arthur Conan Doyle's former home.

Lyndsay Faye BSI, ASH is the author of a number of critically acclaimed books, including the Sherlockian volumes *Dust and Shadow*, about Sherlock Holmes's attempt to hunt down Jack the Ripper, and *The Whole Art of Detection*, containing fifteen Holmes adventures. Additionally, she has written *The Gods of Gotham*, which was nominated for the Edgar Award for Best Novel, *Seven for a Secret, The Fatal Flame, Jane Steele*, and the forthcoming *The Paragon Hotel.* Faye, a true New Yorker in the sense that she was born elsewhere, lives in New York city with her husband, Gabriel.

Thomas Fortenberry is an American author, editor, and reviewer. Founder of Mind Fire Press and a Pushcart Prize-nominated writer, he has also judged many literary contests, including the Georgia Author of the Year Awards and the Robert Penn Warren Prize for Fiction. His Sherlock Holmes stories have appeared in *An Improbable Truth, The MX Book of New Sherlock Holmes Stories – Part VIII: Eliminate the Impossible (1892-1905)*, and the forthcoming MX collection *Some Untold Cases.*

James R. "Jim" French became a morning Disc Jockey on KIRO (AM) in Seattle in 1959. He later founded *Imagination Theatre*, a syndicated program that broadcast to over one-hundred-and-twenty stations in the U.S. and Canada, and also on the XM Satellite Radio system all over North America. Actors in French's dramas included John Patrick Lowrie, Larry Albert, Patty Duke, Russell Johnson, Tom Smothers, Keenan Wynn, Roddy MacDowall, Ruta Lee, John Astin, Cynthia Lauren Tewes, and Richard Sanders.

Mr. French stated, "To me, the characters of Sherlock Holmes and Doctor Watson always seemed to be figures Doyle created as a challenge to lesser writers. He gave us two interesting characters – different from each other in their histories, talents, and experience, but complimentary as a team – who have been applied to a variety of situations and plots far beyond the times and places in The Canon. In the hands of different writers, Holmes and Watson have lent their identities to different times, ages, and even genders. But I wanted to break no new ground. I feel Sir Arthur provided us with enough references to locations, landmarks, and the social conditions of his time, to give a pretty large canvas on which to paint our own images and actions to animate Holmes and Watson." Mr. French passed away at the age of eight-nine on December 20th, 2017, the day that his contribution to this book was being edited. He shall be missed.

Mark A. Gagen BSI is co-founder of Wessex Press, sponsor of the popular *From Gillette to Brett* conferences, and publisher of *The Sherlock Holmes Reference Library* and many other fine Sherlockian titles. A life-long Holmes enthusiast, he is a member of *The Baker Street Irregulars* and *The Illustrious Clients of Indianapolis*. A graphic artist by profession, his work is often seen on the covers of *The Baker Street Journal* and various BSI books.

Paul D. Gilbert was born in 1954 and has lived in and around Lindon all of his life. He has been married to Jackie for thirty-nine years, and she is a Holmes expert who keeps him on the straight and narrow! He has two sons, one of whom now lives in Spain. His interests include literature, ancient history, all religions, most sports, and movies. He is currently employed full-time as a funeral director. His books so far include *The Lost Files of Sherlock Holmes* (2007), *The Chronicles of Sherlock Holmes* (2008), *Sherlock Holmes and the Giant Rat of Sumatra* (2010), *The Annals of Sherlock Holmes* (2012), and *Sherlock Holmes and the Unholy Trinity* (2015). He has finished *Sherlock Holmes: The Four Handed Game*, to be published 2017, and is now working on his next novel.

Melissa Granger, Executive Head Teacher of Stepping Stones School, is driven by a passion to open the doors to learners with complex and layered special needs that just make society feel two steps too far away. Based on the Surrey/Hampshire border in England, her time is spent between relocating a great school into the prestigious home of Conan Doyle, and her two children, dogs, and horses, so there never a dull moment.

John Linwood Grant is a writer and editor who lives in Yorkshire with a pack of lurchers and a beard. He may also have a family. He focuses particularly on dark Victorian and Edwardian fiction, such as his recent novella *A Study in Grey*, which also features Holmes. Current projects include his *Tales of the Last Edwardian* series, about psychic and psychiatric mysteries, and curating a collection of new stories based on the darker side of the British Empire. He has been published in a number of anthologies and magazines, with stories range from madness in early Virginia to questions about the monsters we ourselves might be. He is also co-editor of *Occult Detective Quarterly*. His website *greydogtales.com* explores weird fiction, especially period ones, weird art, and even weirder lurchers.

John Atkinson Grimshaw (1836-1893) was born in Leeds, England. His amazing paintings, usually featuring twilight or night scenes illuminated by gas-lamps or moonlight, are easily recognizable, and are often used on the covers of books about The Great Detective to set the mood, as shadowy figures move in the distance through misty mysterious settings and over rain-slicked streets.

Arthur Hall was born in Aston, Birmingham, UK, in 1944. He discovered his interest in writing during his schooldays, along with a love of fictional adventure and suspense. His first novel, *Sole Contact,* was an espionage story about an ultra-secret government department known as "Sector Three", and was followed, to date, by three sequels. Other works include four Sherlock Holmes novels, *The Demon of the Dusk, The One Hundred Percent Society, The Secret Assassin,* and *The Phantom Killer,* as well as a collection of short stories, and a modern detective novel. He lives in the West Midlands, United Kingdom.

Mike Hogan (with a story in Part XI as well!) writes mostly historical novels and short stories, many set in Victorian London and featuring Sherlock Holmes and Doctor Watson. He read the Conan Doyle stories at school with great enjoyment, but hadn't thought much about Sherlock Holmes until, having missed the Granada/Jeremy Brett TV series when it was originally shown in the eighties, he came across a box set of videos in a street market and was hooked on Holmes again. He started writing Sherlock Holmes pastiches several years ago, having great fun re-imagining situations for the Conan Doyle characters to act in. The relationship between Holmes and Watson fascinates him as one of the great literary friendships. (He's also a huge admirer of Patrick O'Brian's Aubrey-Maturin novels). Like Captain Aubrey and Doctor Maturin, Holmes and Watson are an odd couple, differing in almost every facet of their characters, but sharing a common sense of decency and a common humanity. Living with Sherlock Holmes can't have been easy, and Mike enjoys adding a stronger vein of "pawky humour" into the Conan Doyle mix, even letting Watson have the second-to-last word on occasions. His books include *Sherlock Holmes and the Scottish Question,* the forthcoming *The Gory Season – Sherlock Holmes, Jack the Ripper and the Thames Torso Murders* and the Sherlock Holmes & Young Winston 1887 Trilogy (*The Deadwood Stage; The Jubilee Plot; and The Giant Moles*), He has also written the following short story collections: *Sherlock Holmes: Murder at the Savoy and Other Stories, Sherlock Holmes: The Skull of Kohada Koheiji and Other Stories,* and *Sherlock Holmes: Murder on the Brighton Line and Other Stories.* www.mikehoganbooks.com

In the year 1998 **Craig Janacek** took his degree of Doctor of Medicine at Vanderbilt University, and proceeded to Stanford to go through the training prescribed for pediatricians in practice. Having completed his studies there, he was duly attached to the University of California, San Francisco as Associate Professor. The author of over seventy medical monographs upon a variety of obscure lesions, his travel-worn and battered tin dispatch-box is crammed with papers, nearly all of which are records of his fictional works. To date, these have been published solely in electronic format, including two non-Holmes novels (*The Oxford Deception* and *The Anger of Achilles Peterson*), the trio of holiday adventures collected as *The Midwinter Mysteries of Sherlock Holmes,* the Holmes story collections *The First of* Criminals, *The Assassination of Sherlock Holmes,The Treasury of Sherlock Holmes,* and the Watsonian novels *The Isle of Devils* and *The Gate of Gold.* Craig Janacek is a *nom de plume.*

Roger Johnson BSI, ASH is a retired librarian, now working as a volunteer assistant at the Essex Police Museum. In his spare time, he is commissioning editor of *The Sherlock Holmes Journal,* an occasional lecturer, and a frequent contributor to The Writings About the Writings. His sole work of Holmesian pastiche was published in 1997 in Mike Ashley's anthology *The Mammoth Book of New Sherlock Holmes Adventures,* and he has the greatest respect for the many authors who have contributed new tales to the present mighty trilogy. Like his wife, Jean Upton, he is a member of both *The Baker Street Irregulars* and *The Adventuresses of Sherlock Holmes*. .

David Marcum (who also has a story in Volume II) plays The Game with deadly seriousness. He first discovered Sherlock Holmes in 1975, at the age of ten, when he received an abridged version of *The Adventures* during a trade. Since that time, David has collected literally thousands of traditional Holmes pastiches in the form of novels, short stories, radio and television episodes, movies and scripts, comics, fan-fiction, and unpublished manuscripts. He is the author of *The Papers of Sherlock Holmes Vol.'s I* and *II* (2011, 2013), *Sherlock Holmes and A Quantity of Debt* (2013, 2016), *Sherlock Holmes – Tangled Skeins* (2015, 2017), and *The Papers of Solar Pons* (2017). Additionally, he is the editor of the three-volume set *Sherlock Holmes in Montague Street* (2014, recasting Arthur Morrison's Martin Hewitt stories as early Holmes adventures,), the two-volume collection of Great Hiatus stories, *Holmes Away From Home* (2016), *Sherlock Holmes: Before Baker Street* (2017), *Imagination Theatre's Sherlock Holmes* (2017), the authorized eight-volume reissues of the Solar Pons stories, the three-volume set of Canonical Sequels *Sherlock Holmes: Adventures Beyond the Canon*, and a number of forthcoming volumes including a Solar Anthology and the complete Dr. Thorndyke adventures. Additionally, he is the creator and editor of the ongoing collection, *The MX Book of New Sherlock Holmes Stories* (2015-   ), now at twelve volumes, with another in preparation as of this writing. He has contributed stories, essays, and scripts to *The Baker Street Journal, The Strand Magazine, The Watsonian, Beyond Watson, Sherlock Holmes Mystery Magazine, About Sixty, About Being a Sherlockian, The Solar Pons Gazette,* Imagination Theater, *The Proceedings of the Pondicherry Lodge*, and *The Gazette*, the journal of the Nero Wolfe *Wolfe Pack*. He began his adult work life as a Federal Investigator for an obscure U.S. Government agency, before the organization was eliminated. He returned to school for a second degree, and is now a licensed Civil Engineer, living in Tennessee with his wife and son. He is a member of *The Sherlock Holmes Society of London, The Nashville Scholars of the Three Pipe Problem* (The Engineer's Thumb"), *The Occupants of the Full House, The Diogenes Club of Washington, D.C., The Tankerville Club* (all Scions of *The Baker Street Irregulars*), *The Sherlock Holmes Society of India* (as a Patron), *The John H. Watson Society* ("Marker"), *The Praed Street Irregulars* ("The Obrisset Snuff Box"), *The Solar Pons Society of London*, and *The Diogenes Club West (East Tennessee Annex)*, a curious and unofficial Scion of one. Since the age of nineteen, he has worn a deerstalker as his regular-and-only hat from autumn to spring. In 2013, he and his deerstalker were finally able make his first trip-of-a-lifetime Holmes Pilgrimage to England, with return Pilgrimages in 2015 and 2016, where you may have spotted him. If you ever run into him and his deerstalker out and about, feel free to say hello!

Nik Morton hails from the northeast of England and has lived in Spain with his linguist-musician wife Jennifer for the last fifteen years. He served in the Royal Navy for twenty-three years and has been writing for fifty-three years. He sold his first story in 1971 and has had 120 short stories published – some winning awards – in several genres such as action, adventure, romance, ghost, horror, sci-fi, western and crime. To date, six collections of his short stories have been collected and published, the latest being Leon Cazador, P.I. His Sherlock Holmes pastiche 'The Very First Detective: The Killing Stone' is published in the October 2018 issue of Mystery Weekly Magazine. He has edited periodicals and contributed hundreds of articles, book and film reviews to magazines. He has chaired several writers' circles and run writing and screenplay workshops, and judged competitions. He has edited many books, and for the period 2003-

409

2007 he was sub-editor of the monthly colour magazine, Portsmouth Post, and for 2011-2013 he was Editor-in-Chief of a U.S. publisher but stepped down to spend more time on his various writing projects. Since 2007, he's had thirty books published, among them the psychic spy series: Mission: Prague, Mission: Tehran, and Mission: Khyber, a modern vampire thriller set in Malta, Chill of the Shadow, a Sister Rose thriller, The Bread of Tears, and a romantic thriller set in Tenerife, An Evil Trade. His latest books are a sci-fi time-travel adventure, Continuity Girl, a noir western/homage to Edgar Allan Poe, Coffin for Cash, and the third in a fantasy series (co-written under the pen-name Morton Faulkner), Floreskand: Madurava. His guide Write a Western in 30 Days – with Plenty of Bullet Points is a best-seller and has reviewers recommending it for writers of all genres, not just westerns. To learn more about Nik follow him on twitter https://twitter.com/nik_morton or read his regular blog posts, http://nik-writealot.blogspot.com.

Mark Mower is a member of the *Crime Writers' Association, The Sherlock Holmes Society of London* and *The Solar Pons Society of London*. He writes true crime stories and fictional mysteries. His first two volumes of Holmes pastiches were entitled *A Farewell to Baker Street* and *Sherlock Holmes: The Baker Street Case-Files* (both with MX Publishing) and, to date, he has contributed chapters to six parts of the ongoing *The MX Book of New Sherlock Holmes Stories*. He has also had stories in two anthologies by Belanger Books: *Holmes Away From Home: Adventures from the Great Hiatus – Volume II – 1893-1894* (2016) and *Sherlock Holmes: Before Baker Street* (2017). More are bound to follow. Mark's non-fiction works include *Bloody British History: Norwich* (The History Press, 2014), *Suffolk Murders* (The History Press, 2011) and *Zeppelin Over Suffolk* (Pen & Sword Books, 2008).

Sidney Paget (1860-1908), a few of whose illustrations are used within this anthology, was born in London, and like his two older brothers, became a famed illustrator and painter. He completed over three-hundred-and-fifty drawings for the Sherlock Holmes stories that were first published in *The Strand* magazine, defining Holmes's image forever after in the public mind.

Jane Rubino is the author of A Jersey Shore mystery series, featuring a Jane Austen-loving amateur sleuth and a Sherlock Holmes-quoting detective; *Knight Errant, Lady Vernon and Her Daughter*, (a novel-length adaptation of Jane Austen's novella *Lady Susan*, co-authored with her daughter Caitlen Rubino-Bradway, *What Would Austen Do?*, also co-authored with her daughter, a short story in the anthology *Jane Austen Made Me Do It, The Rucastles' Pawn, The Copper Beeches from Violet Turner's POV*, and, of course, there's the Sherlockian novel in the drawer – who doesn't have one? Jane lives on a barrier island at the New Jersey shore.

Robert V. Stapleton was born and brought up in Leeds, Yorkshire, England, and studied at Durham University. After working in various parts of the country as an Anglican parish priest, he is now retired and lives with his wife in North Yorkshire. As a member of his local writing group, he now has time to develop his other life as a writer of adventure stories. He has recently had a number of short stories published, and he is hoping to have a couple of completed novels published at some time in the future.

S. Subramanian is a retired professor of Economics from Chennai, India. Apart from a small book titled *Economic Offences: A Compendium of Crimes in Prose and Verse* (Oxford University Press Delhi, 2012), his Holmes pastiches are the only serious things he has written. His other work runs largely to whimsical stuff on fuzzy logic and social measurement, on which he writes with much precision and little understanding, being an economist. He is otherwise mainly harmless, as his wife and daughter might concede with a little persuasion.

Daniel D. Victor, a Ph.D. in American literature, is a retired high school English teacher who taught in the Los Angeles Unified School District for forty-six years. His doctoral dissertation on little-known American author, David Graham Phillips, led to the creation of Victor's first Sherlock Holmes pastiche, *The Seventh Bullet*, in which Holmes investigates Phillips' actual murder. Victor's second novel, *A Study in Synchronicity,* is a two-stranded murder mystery, which features a Sherlock Holmes-like private eye. He currently writes the ongoing series *Sherlock Holmes and the American Literati*. Each novel introduces Holmes to a different American author who actually passed through London at the turn of the century. In *The Final Page of Baker Street*, Holmes meets Raymond Chandler; in *The Baron of Brede Place,* Stephen Crane; in *Seventeen Minutes to Baker Street*, Mark Twain; and in *The Outrage at the Diogenes Club*, Jack London. His most recent novel is *Sherlock Holmes and the Shadows of St. Petersburg*. Victor, who is also writing a novel about his early years as a teacher, lives with his wife in Los Angeles, California. They have two adult sons.

The following contributions appear
in the companion volume:
The MX Book of New Sherlock Holmes Stories
Part XI – Some Untold Cases (1880-1891)

Hugh Ashton was born in the U.K., and moved to Japan in 1988, where he remained until 2016, living with his wife Yoshiko in the historic city of Kamakura, a little to the south of Yokohama. He and Yoshiko have now moved to Lichfield, a small cathedral city in the Midlands of the U.K., the birthplace of Samuel Johnson, and one-time home of Erasmus Darwin. In the past, he has worked in the technology and financial services industries, which have provided him with material for some of his books set in the 21st century. He currently works as a writer: Novelist, freelance editor, and copywriter, (his work for large Japanese corporations has appeared in international business journals), and journalist, as well as producing industry reports on various aspects of the financial services industry. Recently, however, his lifelong interest in Sherlock Holmes has developed into an acclaimed series of adventures featuring the world's most famous detective, written in the style of the originals, and published by Inknbeans Press. In addition to these, he has also published historical and alternate historical novels, short stories, and thrillers. Together with artist Andy Boerger, he has produced the *Sherlock Ferret* series of stories for children, featuring the world's cutest detective.

Deanna Baran lives in a remote part of Texas where cowboys may still be seen in their natural habitat. A librarian and former museum curator, she writes in between cups of tea, playing *Go*, and trading postcards with people around the world. This is her latest venture into the foggy streets of gaslit London.

Leslie Charteris was born in Singapore on May 12th, 1907. With his mother and brother, he moved to England in 1919 and attended Rossall School in Lancashire before moving on to Cambridge University to study law. His studies there came to a halt when a publisher accepted his first novel. His third one, entitled *Meet the Tiger*, was written when he was twenty years old and published in September 1928. It introduced the world to Simon Templar, *aka* The Saint. He continued to write about The Saint until 1983 when the last book, *Salvage for The Saint*, was published. The books, which have been translated into over thirty languages, number nearly a hundred and have sold over forty-million copies around the world. They've inspired, to date, fifteen feature films, three television series, ten radio series, and a comic strip that was written by Charteris and syndicated around the world for over a decade. He enjoyed travelling, but settled for long periods in Hollywood, Florida, and finally in Surrey, England. He was awarded the Cartier Diamond Dagger by the *Crime Writers' Association* in 1992, in recognition of a lifetime of achievement. He died the following year.

Ian Dickerson was just nine years old when he discovered The Saint. Shortly after that, he discovered Sherlock Holmes. The Saint won, for a while anyway. He struck up a friendship with The Saint's creator, Leslie Charteris and his family. With their permission, he spent six weeks studying the Leslie Charteris collection at Boston University and went on to write, direct, and produce documentaries on the making of *The Saint* and *Return of The Saint,* which have been released on DVD. He oversaw the recent reprints of almost fifty of the original Saint books in both the US and UK, and was a co-producer on the 2017 TV movie of *The Saint*. When he discovered that Charteris had written Sherlock Holmes stories as well – well, there was the excuse he needed to revisit The Canon. He's consequently written and edited three books on Holmes' radio adventures. For the sake of what little sanity he has, Ian has also written about a wide range of subjects, none of which come with a halo, including talking mashed potatoes, Lord Grade, and satellite links. Ian lives in Hampshire with his wife and two children. And an awful lot of books by Leslie Charteris. Not quite so many by Conan Doyle, though.

Craig Stephen Copland confesses that he discovered Sherlock Holmes when, sometime in the muddled early 1960's, he pinched his older brother's copy of the immortal stories and was forever afterward thoroughly hooked. He is very grateful to his high school English teachers in Toronto who inculcated in him a love of literature and writing, and even inspired him to be an English major at the University of Toronto. There he was blessed to sit at the feet of both Northrup Frye and Marshall McLuhan, and other great literary professors, who led him to believe that he was called to be a high school English teacher. It was his good fortune to come to his pecuniary senses, abandon that goal, and pursue a varied professional career that took him to over one-hundred countries and endless adventures. He considers himself to have been and to continue to be one of the luckiest men on God's good earth. A few years back he took a step in the direction of Sherlockian studies and joined the *Sherlock Holmes Society of Canada* – also known as *The Toronto Bootmakers*. In May of 2014, this esteemed group of scholars announced a contest for the writing of a new Sherlock Holmes mystery. Although he had never tried his hand at fiction before, Craig entered and was pleasantly surprised to be selected as one of the winners. Having enjoyed the experience, he decided to write more of the same, and is now on a mission to write a new Sherlock Holmes mystery that is related to and inspired by each of the sixty stories in the original Canon. He currently lives and writes in Toronto, Buenos Aires, New York, and the Okanagan Valley and looks forward to finally settling down when he turns ninety.

Jayantika Ganguly BSI is the General Secretary and Editor of the *Sherlock Holmes Society of India*, a member of the *Sherlock Holmes Society of London*, and the *Czech*

Sherlock Holmes Society. She is the author of *The Holmes Sutra* (MX 2014). She is a corporate lawyer working with one of the Big Six law firms.

Denis Green was born in London, England in April 1905. He grew up mostly in London's Savoy Theatre where his father, Richard Green, was a principal in many Gilbert and Sullivan productions, A Flying Officer with RAF until 1924, he then spent four years managing a tea estate in North India before making his stage debut in *Hamlet* with Leslie Howard in 1928. He made his first visit to America in 1931 and established a respectable stage career before appearing in films – including minor roles in the first two Rathbone and Bruce Holmes films – and developing a career in front of and behind the microphone during the golden age of radio. Green and Leslie Charteris met in 1938 and struck up a lifelong friendship. Always busy, be it on stage, radio, film or television, Green passed away at the age of fifty in New York.

Stephen Herczeg is an IT Geek, writer, actor, and film-maker based in Canberra Australia. He has been writing for over twenty years and has completed a couple of dodgy novels, sixteen feature length screenplays, and numerous short stories and scripts. Stephen was very successful in 2017's International Horror Hotel screenplay competition, with his scripts *TITAN* winning the Sci-Fi category and *Dark are the Woods* placing second in the horror category. His work has featured in *Sproutlings – A Compendium of Little Fictions* from Hunter Anthologies, the *Hells Bells* Christmas horror anthology published by the Australasian Horror Writers Association, and the *Below the Stairs, Trickster's Treats, Shades of Santa, Behind the Mask,* and *Beyond the Infinite* anthologies from *OzHorror.Con, The Body Horror Book, Anemone Enemy,* and *Petrified Punks* from Oscillate Wildly Press, and *Sherlock Holmes In the Realms of H.G. Wells* and *Sherlock Holmes: Adventures Beyond the Canon* from Belanger Books.

Will Murray is the author of over seventy novels, including forty *Destroyer* novels and seven posthumous *Doc Savage* collaborations with Lester Dent, under the name Kenneth Robeson, for Bantam Books in the 1990's. Since 2011, he has written fourteen additional Doc Savage adventures for Altus Press, two of which co-starred The Shadow, as well as a solo Pat Savage novel. His 2015 Tarzan novel, *Return to Pal-Ul-Don,* was followed by *King Kong vs. Tarzan* in 2016. Murray has written short stories featuring such classic characters as Batman, Superman, Wonder Woman, Spider-Man, Ant-Man, the Hulk, Honey West, the Spider, the Avenger, the Green Hornet, the Phantom, and Cthulhu. A previous Murray Sherlock Holmes story appeared in Moonstone's *Sherlock Holmes: The Crossovers Casebook,* and another is forthcoming in *Sherlock Holmes and Doctor Was Not,* involving H. P. Lovecraft's Dr. Herbert West. Additionally, his "The Adventure of the Glassy Ghost" appeared in *The MX Book of New Sherlock Holmes Stories Part VIII – Eliminate the Impossible: 1892-1905.*

Paul W. Nash is a librarian, bibliographer, and printing historian. He has worked at the Royal Institute of British Architect's Library in London and the Bodleian Library in Oxford, and is currently editor of *The Journal of the Printing Historical Society.* He writes fiction and composes music as a relaxation.

Robert Perret is a writer, librarian, and devout Sherlockian living on the Palouse. His Sherlockian publications include "The Canaries of Clee Hills Mine" in *An Improbable Truth: The Paranormal Adventures of Sherlock Holmes,* "For King and Country" in *The Science of Deduction,* and "How Hope Learned the Trick" in *NonBinary Review.* He considers himself to be a pan-Sherlockian and a one-man Scion out on the lonely moors of Idaho. Robert has recently authored a yet-unpublished scholarly article tentatively entitled "A Study in Scholarship: The Case of the *Baker Street Journal*'. More information is available at *www.robertperret.com*

Gayle Lange Puhl has been a Sherlockian since Christmas of 1965. She has had articles published in *The Devon County Chronicle*, *The Baker Street Journal*, and *The Serpentine Muse*, plus her local newspaper. She has created Sherlockian jewelry, a 2006 calendar entitled "If Watson Wrote For TV", and has painted a limited series of Holmes-related nesting dolls. She co-founded the scion *Friends of the Great Grimpen Mire* and the Janesville, Wisconsin-based *The Original Tree Worshipers*. In January 2016, she was awarded the "Outstanding Creative Writer" award by the Janesville Art Alliance for her first book *Sherlock Holmes and the Folk Tale Mysteries*. She is semi-retired and lives in Evansville, Wisconsin. Ms. Puhl has one daughter, Gayla, and four grandchildren.

Tracy J. Revels, a Sherlockian from the age of eleven, is a professor of history at Wofford College in Spartanburg, South Carolina. She is a member of *The Survivors of the Gloria Scott* and *The Studious Scarlets Society*, and is a past recipient of the Beacon Society Award. Almost every semester, she teaches a class that covers The Canon, either to college students or to senior citizens. She is also the author of three supernatural Sherlockian pastiches with MX (*Shadowfall*, *Shadowblood*, and *Shadowwraith*), and a regular contributor to her scion's newsletter. She also has some notoriety as an author of very silly skits: For proof, see "The Adventure of the Adversarial Adventuress" and "Occupy Baker Street" on YouTube. When not studying Sherlock, she can be found researching the history of her native state, and has written books on Florida in the Civil War and on the development of Florida's tourism industry.

Roger Riccard of Los Angeles, California, U.S.A., is a descendant of the Roses of Kilravock in Highland Scotland. He is the author of two previous Sherlock Holmes novels, *The Case of the Poisoned Lilly* and *The Case of the Twain Papers*, a series of short stories in two volumes, *Sherlock Holmes: Adventures for the Twelve Days of Christmas* and *Further Adventures for the Twelve Days of Christmas*, and the new series *A Sherlock Holmes Alphabet of Cases*, all of which are published by Baker Street Studios. He has another novel and a non-fiction Holmes reference work in various stages of completion. He became a Sherlock Holmes enthusiast as a teenager (many, many years ago), and, like all fans of The Great Detective, yearned for more stories after reading The Canon over and over. It was the Granada Television performances of Jeremy Brett and Edward Hardwicke, and the encouragement of his wife, Rosilyn, that at last inspired him to write his own Holmes adventures, using the Granada actor portrayals as his guide. He has been called "The best pastiche writer since Val Andrews" by the *Sherlockian E-Times*.

David Ruffle was born in Northamptonshire in England a long, long time ago. He has lived in the beautiful town of Lyme Regis on the Dorset coast for the last twelve years. His first foray into writing was the 2009 self-published, *Sherlock Holmes and the Lyme Regis Horror*. This was swiftly followed by two more Holmes novellas set in Lyme, and a Holmes children's book, *Sherlock Holmes and the Missing Snowman*. Since then, there has been four further Holmes novellas, including the critically acclaimed *End Peace*, three contemporary comedies, and a slim volume detailing the life of Jack the Ripper. When not writing, he can be found working in a local shop, 'acting' in local productions, and occasionally performing poetry locally. To come next year is *Sherlock Holmes and* *the Scarborough Affair*, a collaboration with Gill Stammers, in which David is very much the junior partner.

Hailing from Bedford, in the South East of England, **Matthew Simmonds** has been a confirmed devotee of Sir Arthur Conan Doyle's most famous creation since first watching Jeremy Brett's incomparable portrayal of the world's first consulting detective, on a Tuesday evening in April, 1984, while curled up on the sofa with his father. He has written numerous short stories, and his first novel, *Sherlock Holmes: The Adventure of The Pigtail Twist*, was published in 2018. A sequel is nearly complete, which he hopes to publish in the near future. Matthew currently co-owns Harrison & Simmonds, the fifth-generation family business, a renowned County tobacconist, pipe and gift shop on Bedford High Street.

Richard Dean Starr has written or edited more than two-hundred articles, columns, stories, books, comics, screenplays, and graphic novels since the age of seventeen. His original fiction and non-fiction has appeared in magazines and newspapers as varied as *Cemetery Dance, Science Fiction Chronicle, The Southeast Georgian, The Camden County Tribune, Suspense Magazine*, and *Starlog*. His licensed media tie-in stories have appeared in anthologies including *Hellboy: Odder Jobs, Kolchak: The Night Stalker Casebook, Tales of Zorro, The Lone Ranger Chronicles*, and *The Green Hornet Casebook*, just to name a few. In addition, Starr co-authored *Unnaturally Normal*, the first *Kolchak: The Night Stalker/Dan Shamble: Zombie P.I.* team up comic book with *New York Times* bestselling author Kevin J. Anderson, and co-edited the *Captain Action* comics line with Matthew Baugh. As a recognized film industry script consultant, Starr has contributed to feature motion pictures starring acclaimed actors including Malcolm McDowell, Tom Sizemore, Amber Tamblyn, Haley Joel Osment, Costas Mandylor, Robert Culp, Richmond Arquette, and Zach Galifianakis, among others.

Kevin P. Thornton has experienced a Taliban rocket attack in Kabul and a terrorist bombing in Johannesburg. He lives in Fort McMurray, Alberta, the town that burnt down in 2016. He has been shortlisted for the *Crime Writers of Canada* Unhanged writing award six times. He's never won. He was also a finalist for best short story in 2014 – the year Margaret Atwood entered. We're not saying he has luck issues, but don't bet on his stock tips. Born in Kenya, Kevin was a child in New Zealand, a student and soldier in Africa, a military contractor in Afghanistan, a forklift driver in Ontario, and an oilfield worker in North Western Canada. He writes poems that start out just fine, but turn ruder and cruder over time. From limerick to doggerel, they earn less than bugger-all, even though they all manage to rhyme. He also likes writing about Sherlock Holmes and dislikes writing about himself in the third person.

Marcia Wilson is a freelance researcher and illustrator who likes to work in a style compatible for the color blind and visually impaired. She is Canon-centric, and her first MX offering, *You Buy Bones*, uses the point-of-view of Scotland Yard to show the unique talents of Dr. Watson. This continued with the publication of *Test of the Professionals: The Adventure of the Flying Blue Pidgeon* and *The Peaceful Night Poisonings*. She can be contacted at: *gravelgirty.deviantart.com*

The MX Book of New Sherlock Holmes Stories

"This is the finest volume of Sherlockian fiction I have
ever read, and I have read, literally, thousands."
– Philip K. Jones

"Beyond Impressive . . . This is a splendid venture for a great cause!
– Roger Johnson, Editor, *The Sherlock Holmes Journal,*
The Sherlock Holmes Society of London

Part I: 1881-1889
Part II: 1890-1895
Part III: 1896-1929
Part IV: 2016 Annual
Part V: Christmas Adventures
Part VI: 2017 Annual
Part VII: Eliminate the Impossible
Part VIII – 2018 Annual
Part IX – 2018 Annual (1879-1895)
Part X – 2018 Annual (1896-1916)
Part XI – Some Untold Cases (1880-1891)
Part XII – Some Untold Cases (1894-1902)

In Preparation

Part XIII – 2019 Annual

. . . and more to come!

Publishers Weekly says:

Part VI: *The traditional pastiche is alive and well . . . .*

Part VII: *Sherlockians eager for faithful-to-the-canon plots and characters will be
delighted.*

Part VIII: *The imagination of the contributors in coming up with variations on the
volume's theme is matched by their ingenious resolutions.*

Part IX: *The 18 stories . . . will satisfy fans of Conan Doyle's originals. Sherlockians will
rejoice that more volumes are on the way.*

The MX Book of New Sherlock Holmes Stories
Edited by David Marcum
(MX Publishing, 2015-   )

MX Publishing

MX Publishing is the world's largest specialist Sherlock Holmes publisher, with several hundred titles and over a hundred authors creating the latest in Sherlock Holmes fiction and non-fiction.

From traditional short stories and novels to travel guides and quiz books, MX Publishing caters to all Holmes fans.

The collection includes leading titles such as *Benedict Cumberbatch In Transition* and *The Norwood Author*, which won the 2011 *Tony Howlett Award* (Sherlock Holmes Book of the Year).

MX Publishing also has one of the largest communities of Holmes fans on *Facebook*, with regular contributions from dozens of authors.

www.mxpublishing.co.uk (UK) and *www.mxpublishing.com* (USA)

Lightning Source UK Ltd.
Milton Keynes UK
UKHW042053301118
333214UK00001B/20/P